I0757505

UNBOUND

Book Two of The Blacksea Odyssey

J.A. Vodvarka

Copyright © 2024 by J.A. Vodvarka

All rights reserved.

No part of this publication may be reproduced, distributed, or transmitted in any form or by any means, including photocopying, recording, or other electronic or mechanical methods, without the prior written permission of the publisher, except as permitted by U.S. copyright law. For permission requests, contact J.A. Vodvarka at www.javodvarka.com.

The story, all names, characters, and incidents portrayed in this production are fictitious. No identification with actual persons (living or deceased), places, buildings, and products is intended or should be inferred.

Book cover illustration and interior art by Chris Yarbrough.

Line and copy editing by The Editor & the Quill.

Proof reading by Markham Correct.

No generative AI was used in the creation of this book. Every bit of this book — the writing, cover art, and interior graphics — is the result of human creativity and effort.

First edition 2024.

Be fierce . . . and be a *fucking* god.

By J.A. Vodvarka

The Blacksea Odyssey

Unworthy
Unbound
Unyielding

Whiskey & Wagers – A Blacksea Odyssey short story

Author's note

Unbound is an epic fantasy book that is intended for mature audiences (18+). For a list of content warnings, please see the last page.

Unworthy Synopsis

The story up until now...

NYSSA BLACKSEA is the only adept at her guild who is not able to use magick, compensating for her perceived weakness by becoming a formidable fighter. She's now twenty-five and has been waiting some time to receive her post in service of the Empire. Doubt festers in the back of Nyssa's mind—will she ever be seen as anything other than an anomaly?

When an adept, QUINN, runs away from another guild, Nyssa is tasked by the master of that guild, CERIL ANELOS, with bringing his fugitive back. She travels to the city of Ocean's Rest with her protective best friend and fellow adept, ATHEN FENNICK. Here they meet up with a tracker who will help them find Quinn, ARYIS DEVITT, an eager but naive adept and member of royalty. Aryis is keen to prove herself, and looks up to Nyssa. While in Ocean's Rest, Nyssa gets into a scuffle with a brother and sister from a guild of assassins and spies.

With a line on their fugitive thanks to Aryis, Nyssa and her comrades venture out to find Quinn on the first night of a winter festival. Their mission goes horribly awry when they are attacked by wraiths—a mindless undead threat not seen in the Empire for thirty years. Nyssa is almost killed staving off the attack, narrowly surviving. But she comes out bearing the poison mark of a blood wraith—a more sentient creature that seemed to mysteriously recognize her.

Nyssa continues her quest to find Quinn, which takes her, Athen, and Aryis across the ocean to the island of Jejin. They capture Quinn, finding not a dangerous adept, but a scared and walled-off woman. Quinn tries to escape several times, finding that while her magick doesn't affect Nyssa, challenging Nyssa's sense of duty and honor is the way to get a rise out of her. Quinn reveals how she was mistreated by Ceril, planting seeds of doubt in Nyssa's mind, and accuses her of being a blindly loyal lap-dog. Is the system that raised her as noble and uncorrupt as Nyssa thought?

On their way back to return Quinn to Ceril, their ship is attacked by the pirate ELIAS, and the four adepts are taken for ransom. While being kept prisoner, Nyssa grows closer to Quinn, and continues to doubt whether she's doing the right thing by bringing her back. The delay in returning to the Empire and achieving her goal angers Nyssa, but she and the crew are forced to work together when the blood wraith from the winter celebration attacks the ship. Knowing that the powerful creature will tear the ship apart, Nyssa drags it overboard into the icy Black Sea, drowning in the process.

Quinn risks her life to save Nyssa from the sea and Elias revives her. As Nyssa recovers, Quinn reveals more dark secrets about Ceril, and Nyssa begins to wonder if the undead things attacking her and her friends could have been sent by him--a dangerous accusation to make without proof. Nyssa and Quinn settle into a begrudging peace with one another, with Nyssa trying to ignore the budding spark of attraction she feels towards Quinn.

Once back in Ocean's Rest, Nyssa is awarded her post and Quinn is to be returned to her guild and Ceril. Nyssa can't help but feel she's failing her responsibility to protect a fellow adept, and seeks counsel from her guild master and adoptive father, ERON. Shortly after, Eron is assassinated by a woman wearing Nyssa's face.

Grieving Eron's death and scared for Quinn's safety, Nyssa makes the decision to go after Quinn and her escort before they arrive back at the guild, choosing her own code of honor over her duty. Finding that Quinn has escaped into the woods, Nyssa convinces Quinn that she's not a threat and is there to help. They are attacked by the assassin siblings Nyssa encountered back in Ocean's Rest. They admit to killing her mentor, Eron, and reveal that it was Ceril who created the wraiths, confirming Nyssa's suspicions.

Nyssa and the siblings fight to the death. She kills the brother, but the sister manages to escape. Quinn and Nyssa head back to Ocean's Rest, where they plan to escape by ship. They are found and captured by Ceril and Imperial Justiciars, who carry out the Empress's justice.

Nyssa is found guilty of treason and presented with a horrific decision - will she sacrifice her own life to stop Quinn's execution? She decides to adhere to her code of honor and sacrifice herself. The Justiciars are disappointed in her decision, and instead of killing her, mark her Unworthy, making her a cursed pariah.

At the moment of Quinn's execution, Nyssa has a magickal awakening, and is consumed by a great power that she can scarcely control, feeling Quinn awaken as well. Together, they kill the Justiciars in self-defense, escaping from Ceril, knowing the Empire will now hunt them down for their crimes. Nyssa is forced to leave her friends and her life behind, headed towards an uncertain future. She has decided to betray her guild and to cast her own shadow.

Two souls, forever entwined, chaos dancing in eyes and blood, born
between realms and belonging to the stars.

Two souls, forever entwined, clash with fists and blade, dragging the tips
of their swords across the world.

Two souls, forever entwined, dance and howl, as ancient magick unfurls
and envelopes the light.

Two souls, forever entwined, bend and break, hurling to earth to die and
be forever reborn.

STORM'S RAGE

Quinn pushed her way through the crowded streets of Ocean's Rest, desperate to get to the docks. She pulled a limping Nyssa along with her and hoped that Elias's pirates were still waiting to help them escape.

If they're not...we're dead.

Nyssa and Quinn had left death and destruction back in Ocean's Keep. Six Justiciars—the living symbol of Imperial justice—lay dead by their hand.

As the light dwindled, so did Quinn's hope, but she had to keep moving.

Nyssa's auburn curls tumbled around her face as her head listed forward.

"How's your leg?" Quinn asked, hurrying her along.

"It would be a lot better if you hadn't stabbed it," Nyssa mumbled.

"One day we'll look back at that and laugh."

"I'll punch you in the face if you laugh, I swear on my life," Nyssa hissed through her teeth, her deep-blue eyes flashing in warning.

At least she has some humor left in her.

Nyssa didn't deserve what the Justiciars had done to her, forcing her onto her knees and cutting her from lip to chin to mark her as a traitor. Restless anger simmered in Quinn's chest. *All because she helped me.*

The only thing keeping Quinn moving was fear. Nyssa slowed, and Quinn looped an arm around her for support, checking to make sure the scarlet scarf was still pulled up over Nyssa's chin, covering the black Mark of the Unworthy.

"I'm fine," Nyssa objected.

"Shut up and let me help you. Using magick expends energy, and you're not used to it."

In a day of frightening twists and turns, Nyssa suddenly exploding with dangerous magick made the least sense of all. And Quinn's own magick had changed beyond her recognition—she could now completely destroy magick itself instead of merely suppressing it for a few minutes. She had killed a Justiciar by snuffing out his magickal core. His very soul.

The thought made her stomach reel.

What did I do?

The closer they got to the docks, the louder the din of the sea became—the familiar creaks and dings of the ships a welcome sound. Once at the wharf, she asked a dockworker where the small boat slips were located and followed his instructions, her heart thumping in her chest. Dusk had come and gone, and she was worried that Jerrin had given up on waiting. They were hours late.

"Come on," she said, weaving a path through the throng of people and cargo, doing her best to guide Nyssa, whose tall, muscular frame was becoming harder to support. Nyssa was breathing heavy, likely dead on her feet from exhaustion. Lamps lit the way, allowing the dockworkers to continue their tasks into the night. They came to a stop at the dock with the small boat slips.

"We're almost there, Nyssa," Quinn panted, pulse racing, covered in a sheen of sweat despite the winter chill.

"Can you see them?"

The pier stretched out over the water, dimly lit by smaller lanterns that left large gaps of night between illuminated spots. "It's too dark to tell."

Quinn grunted under Nyssa's weight but got them moving again.

"I'm so sorry about this," Nyssa said.

"You saved my life today. I'm more than happy to drag your ass these last few feet to freedom."

Farther down the dock, she spotted a group of people.

"Oh gods, please be Jerrin," Quinn whispered under her breath.

As she drew closer, her heart pounding wildly, the figures started moving toward them.

"Fuck," Quinn cursed under her breath. She couldn't tell if it was Jerrin and his crewmates or pickpockets looking for easy coin—or worse.

A voice cut through the dark. "Quinn? Nyssa? That you?"

"Jerrin!" Quinn breathed, her heart leaping. She'd never been happier to see that shock of red hair and scraggly beard. "I can't believe you waited."

"Of course we waited. Elias would have my hide if I didn't. What's wrong with Nyssa?"

Quinn looked over at Nyssa, whose head hung. "Long, weird story. She's exhausted, and I'm not doing much better. Help me with her."

He moved to the other side of Nyssa and pulled her arm around his shoulder. She picked up her head and smiled at him. "Jerrin, you beautiful ginger bastard."

He beamed at her, but his smile fell as his eyes slid to her exposed chin, a mix of concern and something else swirling in their light-green depths. "Oh, Nyssa, what did they do to you?"

"Nothing compared to what I did to them," she mumbled.

A familiar deckhand with cropped blonde hair stepped forward. "Hey, boss, we have company," Yuha said, her hand moving to her sword as her eyes trailed beyond Quinn and Nyssa.

Quinn looked over her shoulder. "Shit."

Six dark figures walked toward them, cutting them off from the main wharf.

"Who is it?" Nyssa asked.

"Obsidian Rule, if I had to guess."

"Get to the boat, ladies. My men will take you back to Elias. Yuha and I will keep them busy for as long as we can," Jerrin said, stepping past them and drawing his sword.

Nyssa straightened her spine, letting go of Quinn to put her hand on Jerrin's shoulder. "They'll cut you down in seconds. Get Quinn to the boat and shove off."

The woman was maddening. Making another self-sacrifice for Quinn was out of the question. "You're not doing this to me again," Quinn said, stepping up next to her. "I'm staying right here to fight."

The six assassins had stopped fifty feet from them. Quinn braced for an attack, but the Obsidian Rule just stood, waiting.

"What are they doing?" she asked.

Nyssa shook her head, her eyes fixed forward.

Something is wrong.

Quinn squinted in the dark. One of the adepts was gone, leaving five behind. The hackles on the back of her neck rose. Nyssa threw her arm across Quinn's chest and pushed her back as a shadow shimmered in front of them and lunged.

A sharp, searing pain sliced into Quinn's side. She cried out and she fell to one knee.

Nyssa yelled, her magick bursting forth, shards of blue light raging along her skin. She was a beacon in the darkness, the crackle of energy making Quinn's hairs stand on end.

Quinn fell over, gingerly touching her stomach. Her hand came back slick and warm with blood. She tried to call her own magick forth, but she couldn't concentrate through the pain. *Focus...c'mon...f—focus.*

Nyssa let loose a bolt of blue, reeling back from the force of it. The magick crashed harmlessly into the dock. Their attacker had disappeared. She dropped to a knee and grabbed Quinn's hand.

Nyssa's mere touch vibrated with power, resonating deep within her.

"Quinn..." Nyssa winced at the blood, her glowing blue eyes filling with fear.

Jerrin and Yuha stared down at Nyssa, their mouths open.

"Guys, help me, please," Nyssa panted.

Jerrin scrambled next to Quinn and pulled his scarf off, pressing it against her belly. Down the dock, the Rule adepts started to move. She clutched at Nyssa, trembling. She was going to die on a cold, dark pier.

"Nyssa, they're coming," she breathed.

Bright blue energy twisted around Nyssa. She balled up her fists, extended her hands at their attackers and released a shock wave of lightning, filling the air with an electric energy that vibrated through Quinn's body.

Nyssa let out a wordless cry. The roar of thunder filled Quinn's ears, growing louder and louder, drowning everything out until she couldn't tell if the sound came from the sky or Nyssa.

She turned her eyes down the dock as lightning leapt from Nyssa's hands and crashed into the wood, splintering it. Jagged bolts arced from adept to adept, their bodies dropping to the dock. The electricity kept traveling, reaching the main wharf, hitting four dockworkers. They fell, unmoving.

Innocent people.

Quinn shouted Nyssa's name, but the woman didn't stop. Didn't even blink. Nyssa was lost in rage, her eyes on fire, her mouth agape in a howl of fury.

Quinn grabbed Nyssa's wrist, gasping at the torrent of power flowing through them both. She gritted her teeth against her pain and focused. Shadow wound around Quinn's and Nyssa's hands. Though scared of hurting Nyssa, Quinn had to stop her before countless bystanders were killed. She pushed through the pain and zeroed in on suppressing Nyssa's magick bit by bit, trying to pull her back from the edge.

The blue fire disappeared from Nyssa's eyes and she slumped over in a heap on the dock.

Quinn gasped. *No! I pushed too hard!*

Jerrin shouted at his men. "Get back to the tender. Yuha, get Nyssa. Quinn, you think you can walk?"

She nodded through her pain as Yuha picked Nyssa up, her body limp in the big woman's arms. A dark shard of worry caught in Quinn's throat. If Nyssa was hurt because of her....

"You got gut stabbed," Jerrin said. "If we stop the bleeding and get you back to Buck, you'll be gold." His voice held a high note of tension that made her doubt she would live to see the Whisper again.

She didn't want to die—she had tasted a few weeks of freedom, and though it was a strange, exhausting, and confusing experience, it had been the best few weeks of her life. She desperately wanted *more*.

Jerrin helped her to her feet, and she moaned, intense pain radiating from her stomach. He hurried her to the boat and eased her to its floor. Yuha laid Nyssa next to her.

"Get back to the Whisper!" Jerrin ordered, kneeling next to Quinn and pressing down on her wound. "I'm not going to move from your side, okay? You keep talking to me, you hear? Maybe fill me in on why Nyssa lights up like a lightning storm now? Can you do that for me?"

Quinn nodded weakly and strung sentences together that she hoped made sense, answering his questions to stay awake as they rowed out to meet Hannah's Whisper.

She looked over at Nyssa, who hadn't moved since she touched her.

Voices from above startled Quinn. The tender was no longer bobbing on the waves, but rather rising up. Gentle hands moved Quinn from the tender to the deck where they laid her down. Elias's concerned face appeared above her, soon pushed out of the way by Buck, the ship's cranky cook and medic. He squinted down at her through his goggles, and a deep moan escaped Quinn's lips as he pulled her shirt up with shaky hands.

She found herself having a bizarre urge to apologize for her sad state.

"Oh, girl, what did you and—mmm—Nyssa get yourselves into?" Buck mumbled before yelling for clean towels and his medicine bag. She closed her eyes and began to drift.

A loud, angry voice startled her back to consciousness. Elias. "Nyssa has been marked. Fucking Justiciar bastards!"

The clucking of a chicken matched his fervor. Fontaine, his odd Old Folk quartermaster.

His face appeared again above Quinn. "Don't you go dying on my deck now, love. Nyssa already tried that once, and I didn't much appreciate it." He yelled over his shoulder to set a course for Unbound Waters and to get underway immediately. "Veil up! I don't want anyone following us!"

Elias looked back down at her. "We saw your light show all the way out here. Fuck's sake, woman, what was that?"

Quinn tried to speak, her voice weak and distant. She sounded broken. "That was Nyssa, not me. Don't...don't let me die. She'll kill me if I die..."

Buck appeared again, pouring something on his hands. The sting of rum hit her nostrils. "Boys!" he called out. "Hold her down. Get more light over here!"

Quinn's head lolled to the side, and she focused on Buck. "What are you doing?" Hands pinned her arms and legs to the deck.

Buck peered down at her. "I'm sorry for this, girl, but I have to see if you're hurt—mmm—on the inside."

Quinn blinked at him. "What does that—"

A white-hot pain forced a cry of agony out of her as Buck probed around her wound. Her mind flooded with panic.

I'm going to die...

"Gonna have to burn a healing disk on her, Cap. Her guts need—mmm—mendin'. She'll die without it," the old man said. Quinn shook her head at him. She saw the pain Nyssa endured from healing disks and wanted nothing of the sort. If Nyssa had a difficult time bearing the—

"Do it," Elias ordered.

The familiar *crack* of a healing disk filled her with dread. "Hold her down!" Buck yelled at the crew surrounding them. He hovered over her. "This is gonna—mmm—burn, girl."

"Please don't—"

An unbearable searing pain overloaded Quinn's senses as Buck pressed the disk into her side. Magick exploded through her abdomen, twisting around her organs. An oppressive, squeezing sensation raged through her. The roar of blood in her ears almost drowned everything out. She could barely hear Buck swearing as she struggled and howled.

Just as she was about to beg him to stop, darkness overtook her.

STORM'S WAKE

Justiciar Medias kept her face still as the Arch Master of the Areshi Empire grew progressively redder while he yelled at anyone within earshot.

"Where are Nyssa and Quinn?" Ceril shouted at Medias, a massive stone titan lurking behind him. "I want them dead for what they've done!"

Justiciar Medias growled under her breath but maintained her calm exterior. If she faltered now and Ceril sniffed out her lies, everything she had promised Nyssa would be for naught. Beside her, Reece's breathing quickened. Hopefully the woman could keep her mouth shut. That damned titan hadn't stopped Nyssa and Quinn, but it could crush them.

"Gone, Arch Master," Medias replied, averting her eyes away from the bodies and blood of the Justiciars still littering the floor. Bile rose in her throat.

"How? How did they escape you?"

"This place is rife with hidden passages. The tunnels under the Keep are a maze. I didn't—"

Footsteps behind her caught their attention. Lilliana, Athen, and Aryis entered the Great Room, the latter going pale, her eyes fixated on the dead.

Ceril gestured at them. "Why didn't you stop them? I ordered you to stop them!"

Athen opened his mouth to speak, but Medias interceded. "Did you really expect them to succeed where your construct failed?" she asked, waving her hand at the stone titan assembled from the gray marble of the Keep's floor.

"So my Justiciars and adepts failed," Ceril said.

"We are not *your* Justiciars," Medias replied, her voice low. *The gall of this man.*

"We do not—and will never—answer to you."

Ceril sneered at Medias before turning to Lilliana. "Your guards, why did they do nothing?"

Lilliana's face remained calm, though the tension was evident along her jawline.

"My guards do not make a habit of assaulting my guests. What happened was a disaster of your making, Ceril."

"No, it was a matter of Imperial business," Ceril replied.

"This is my city. My home." Lilliana stepped forward and glared at Ceril. "You spilled blood in *my* home."

He shook his head at the woman. "To be very clear, Nyssa and Quinn spilled this blood. Look around you, woman. They are murderers!"

"Your petty vendetta against Nyssa caused all of this!" Lilliana hissed. She pushed past him and reared back a fist, letting it fly at the massive stone construct. It reeled back, its chest cratered, before it shuddered, then slouched forward and burst apart, chunks of stone raining onto the floor.

Lilliana whirled back around, her face a mask of anger. "And now I hear you have Obsidian Rule scouring my city? I want them out immediately. You are to leave first thing tomorrow. If you have issue with that, take it up with the Empress."

Goddamn it. Medias ground her teeth. Rule assassins after Nyssa and Quinn? The rumors were true: Ceril did have an uncommon influence over that guild and its adepts.

"I am the Arch Master. Watch how you speak to me."

Lilliana seemed unfazed. "This is Ocean's Rest. *My* city. And I want you gone."

Ceril looked around the room, dark anger settling on his face. "Your city, indeed. I will leave tomorrow morning to see the Empress. She will know what happened here."

Medias spoke up. "The Empress will receive my firsthand account when I return to Cardin. Keep that in mind. Any inconsistencies on your part would likely be viewed negatively, regardless of your status."

He glared at Medias and turned to leave, his footsteps receding as he exited the Great Room. All she wanted to do was hang her head and try to process the events of the day. To rest. To give in to the exhaustion and soreness in her body, but she had to maintain her composure.

She turned back to the others. "I need to speak to the four of you privately. Now."

"You don't order me around anymore than Anelos does," Lilliana snipped.

Reece spoke up. "Please do as Medias asks."

Lilliana's brows furrowed, glancing at Reece before glaring at Medias. "My goddamn office. Now."

Medias narrowed her eyes at the command. Few people intimidated Medias: her own mother; the Empress; and perhaps now Lilliana.

The Lioness of Ocean's Rest still has teeth.

AN UNLIKELY ALLY

Athen paced back and forth, his eyes trained on Medias. She and the other Justiciars had descended on Ocean's Keep days earlier, hunting for Nyssa and Quinn, forcing Reece to help them. Hurting her in the process.

Now six of them lay dead by Nyssa's hand.

She had magick. How is that possible? He ground his teeth, holding his tongue.

Aryis dropped down into a chair, her face blank. Athen went and crouched down beside her. "You okay?"

"No. Not in the least."

He gave her arm a gentle squeeze before taking the seat next to hers, sitting forward, ready to move against the Justiciar if need be. Protecting his family—including Nyssa—was his only care now.

Lilliana rounded her desk and sat down, frowning up at Medias.

Why did Reece vouch for the Justiciar? After everything that's happened?

Medias stood rigid next to Reece, pulling at the bottom of her dark-red leather jacket, the white mask of the Justiciar covering the top half of her face, making her expression damn near impossible to read.

                    J.A. VODVARKA

"What do you want from us, Justiciar?" Athen asked, his mind reeling. What if Nyssa didn't make it to safety? She would be killed on sight if caught.

The very thought knotted his stomach.

The Justiciar's red eyes bored into him. "We need to—"

His mother held her hand up and opened a desk drawer, pulling out four small orbs. She tossed them in the air, and they hung there, waiting for direction.

"Four corners," she instructed, and each of the orbs rushed to a corner of the room, shimmering with pale-green light. "We're safe to talk now—we're encased in a silencing ward." His mother had likely paid a hefty price for the enchantment, but it was invaluable at times like this, when they couldn't be sure if the Keep was clear of spies or eavesdropping enchantments. Obsidian Rule presence in the city didn't bode well. The guild's spies and assassins would certainly move against their family if they were suspected traitors to the Empire.

And letting Nyssa and Quinn escape was tantamount to treason.

Medias stepped toward the window, glancing down at the city. Every inch of the woman was buttoned up tight. The sides of her head were shaved—much like Aryis's—the rest up in a topknot so neat that Athen believed she must have ordered it to behave. Just as controlled as the parts of her face left uncovered. No upturn of her lips or narrowing of her eyes. Just stillness.

She turned to address them. "What I am about to say must be kept between those of us in this room. My life depends on it."

Athen was intrigued, despite his distrust for the Justiciar.

"I found Nyssa and Quinn before they escaped. In exchange for Nyssa sparing my life, I made her a promise—I would protect the four of you, making sure fault from her actions didn't fall upon you."

Athen scowled. "Why would you do that? You're a Justiciar, your only duty is to the Empire."

"I foresaw today's events. My actions were—and are—carefully orchestrated to ensure the survival of your two friends."

Athen barked out a rueful laugh. "That's utter bullshit. You marked Nyssa!"

"Foresaw?" Aryis asked, and Athen turned to her, watching her blank expression shift to a strange mixture of confusion and excitement. "What exactly do you mean?"

"I'm a seer."

The room fell silent.

A seer? Such magick was extremely rare.

Medias glanced around. "Telling you that puts my life in your hands. It's a secret I've kept to myself my whole life. I'm trusting you with this information so you will trust me in return."

"A seer...." Aryis mused. "Like the Whitepeak Mystics?"

That's a guild I haven't heard mentioned in forever.

Whitepeak had been disbanded over a century ago out of fear of their power, though the seers were still around up in the Northern Wilds. The Empire had been too scared to hunt them all down and kill them.

"I'm nothing like them. The Mystics may have one or two visions in a lifetime. I have twenty or more a year."

Aryis's mouth fell open. "Twenty a *year*?"

Anger stirred in Athen's chest. "If you foresaw what happened today, then why didn't you stop it? You fucking marked Nyssa!"

"I can't explain why, but my visions of Nyssa and Quinn change. But one of the few constants was Nyssa's mark. In every scenario where they survived and escaped Arch Master Anelos, Nyssa was marked. Always. I had to ensure that happened," Medias said.

"Why?" Athen asked. "Why would you risk your life for them?"

The Justiciar hesitated before answering. "I'm honoring a promise I made to someone dear to me. That is all I will tell you."

He turned to Reece, who had been silent the whole time, and she was rarely without opinion. "Is this true?"

Reece stared at Medias, a look of pure ire coating her features. Rarely had Athen seen Reece wear her anger and hate so plainly, but the Justiciars had used her to hurt Nyssa. "I can't read her emotions. At all. So any tremors that I'd usually read as lies are just—not there. Something is done to the Justiciars at Ambershine to change them, make emotions impossible to detect. But I was there when she let Nyssa and Quinn go free and she did make a promise to them. But is she lying? Is this some fucking game? I have no idea."

The Justiciar returned Reece's glare. "When I took the Amberis and donned this mask, I became impossible for empaths to read," Medias said.

Athen scowled and watched Medias. If she did anything to threaten them, he'd be quick to act. His mind turned back to his best friend. "I don't understand what happened today. Nyssa doesn't have magick—what did she do to those Justiciars?" He looked around the room for an answer.

His mother leaned forward and tapped her fingers on her desk, addressing Medias again. "Nyssa and Quinn—do you know what they are?"

"Of course," Medias replied. "Their eyes give them away."

Athen turned his palms up. "Want to give us a hint?"

"Nyssa and Quinn are Cursed Gods."

Cursed Gods?

They were myths. Legend. Murderous assholes.

Shit.

"How is that possible?"

"That is something I can't answer," Medias replied. "But let's hope that Nyssa and Quinn aren't corrupted by their power like the Cursed Gods of the past. What I saw today gives me confidence that they will forge a new legacy. You know Nyssa's heart, Athen. Is my optimism misplaced?" Her red eyes waited for his answer, but it seemed the Justiciar already knew.

"Her heart is true...as is her sense of honor. We all saw that today. I should have trusted her." Athen looked down at his hands, a helplessness settling over him. *Cursed Gods.* His heart hurt for Nyssa. She would be hunted now.

Lilliana cleared her throat, redirecting everyone's attention. "What is our next move?"

"Do you trust me now?" Medias asked.

"I trust Reece without fail. And if she vouches for you, Justiciar—"

"I've simply told you what I witnessed," Reece interrupted. "She could be lying about being a seer, hoping we'll help her find Nyssa."

Medias moved closer to Reece, and Athen tightened his grip on the arms of his chair, ready to move.

"How do you think Master Justiciar Elken knew of your special connection to Nyssa? I told him I heard a rumor about the two of you, but that's not true. I saw you together in a vision, talking in a dark courtyard the night of First Master Eron's death. You comforted Nyssa and told her that Quinn was different, just like her. What were the words you used? Her emotions 'shine bright like the sun.' Isn't that how you—"

Reece lunged at Medias, catching her with a fist that glanced across her jaw. Athen sprang from his chair and caught his sister around the waist as Medias took a step back, barely fazed.

Reece struggled against him. "Let me go!"

His mother was quick to her feet, rounding the desk. "Reece! Calm down. I understand you're distraught—"

"I'm not distraught, I'm pissed," Reece hissed. "This bitch helped Elken use me. They made me hunt down Nyssa. He was in my head, hurting me—" Her voice broke and she shook in Athen's arms. His heart ached for her.

Straightening her jacket, Medias reset her haughty posture. "Everything happened as it had to, otherwise there would be more than six Justiciars lying dead in your Great Room. You are alive because of me, empath. Show some gratitude."

A rush of air left Reece.

"I am going to return to Cardin to give Empress Kalla a recounting of what happened, or at least the version of events that I choose. And I will tell her that the best chance of finding Nyssa is staying here, at the Keep, as the city's in-residence Justiciar. The pretense is I'll be her eyes and ears here. With Eron dead, you four are her only friends in the world, and it will be easy to convince Ceril and the Empress that she'll try to contact you again."

Reece shook her head. "So you're going to move in? No. No, that's not happening."

Medias narrowed her gaze at Reece. "I made a promise to Blacksea. And I will honor that promise. You cannot deter me from protecting the lot of you—and her in the process. You've seen Ceril's hatred. Felt it. He will simply not let her live."

Athen relaxed his grip on Reece but remained by her side should she find Medias worthy of another punch. If Medias was telling the truth, she could be the help they'd need to keep Ceril at bay.

"Reece," Athen said softly, "you saw her pledge her loyalty to Nyssa. We have to...fuck, we have to consider this."

"I'm considering slitting her throat and dumping her body in the sea," Reece hissed.

Athen considered the Justiciar. Nyssa put her faith in Medias. It might have been in the spur of the moment, but Nyssa was rarely wrong about people. "Reece, if Nyssa trusts Medias, then we need to respect that. She's a smart woman. She trusted her gut about Quinn and Anelos, and we didn't listen to her. Eron is dead and she's running for her life because I didn't listen to her. We need to do this for Nyssa."

Reece's expression wavered, her anger melting slightly. "For Nyssa," she mumbled, crossing her arms and glowering at the Justiciar.

Medias turned to his mother. "I cannot do any of this without your permission, Lady Fennick."

"A Justiciar, in my home," Lilliana mused. She glanced to Reece and Athen before saying, "Fine. Stay in the city. Stay here in the Keep. Run naked through the streets if you like. Just stay the fuck out of my way."

Medias nodded, bowing her head slightly to his mother. A small show of respect.

"Ceril's responsible for the wraiths and Eron, isn't he?" Athen asked Medias.

"I have no proof, nor have my visions given me the information you crave, but I'd stake my life on it. He's a very dangerous man."

Athen sat back down next to Aryis, his stomach in knots. "I argued with Nyssa. Turned her away when she needed me."

"We both did," Aryis added. "We should have asked more questions, cared more about why Quinn ran in the first place, but we just did as we were told."

Aryis buried her face in her hands, and a cold lump formed in the back of Athen's throat. He had never before failed Nyssa when she needed him. The thought of her on the run and him not being able to help twisted him up inside. He reached over and put his hand on Aryis's knee.

"After everything that's happened, will you still stay in Ocean's Rest?" he asked her, swallowing as he waited for her answer. Every second he spent with Aryis made him yearn to know her more, and he found himself wanting to lean on her in moments like this—and be her support when she needed him. The burgeoning affection startled him, but he welcomed its warmth as it nuzzled into his heart.

Aryis took a breath. "If you'll still have me, Lady Fennick?"

After a moment, Lilliana gave Aryis a tight smile. "Of course you're still welcome to stay. And you'll be safe here. I'd rather that than you off in Cardin, close to Ceril."

"Good, that will keep you all close," Medias added.

For the first time that awful day, Athen felt a small sense of relief. Aryis had come to mean a great deal to him in a short time. The thought of her staying pushed the pain and sadness back a few inches, if only for a moment.

"Now, as to how we all should proceed," his mother said, sitting back down in her chair and steepling her fingers in front of her lips. "We bury Eron. We have to mourn our friend and mentor, pay him our respects. Athen, I want you to take over the job Eron had intended for Nyssa. With that wraith attack still on everyone's minds, we need to build up better defenses for the city. I want a fighting force. Tap into every single faction of this city to recruit members. Reece will smooth the way with the faction heads. We need their buy-in or it won't work. Aryis, your first task is working with Athen to create a budget for this defense force. Weapons, uniforms, provisions."

Aryis nodded enthusiastically, stealing a quick glance at Athen.

His mother turned to Reece. "I also need you to get more involved with my whisper network. Learn all the players. I've held them in my confidence for a long time, but we need to expand our eyes and ears. Try to shield Nyssa and Quinn, if we can, and protect ourselves."

"Understood," Reece said, her face emotionless.

"Justiciar Medias, could you give us all a moment in private?" Lilliana asked.

Medias nodded and left the office. The four of them sat in silence for a moment. Dusk fell upon the city outside of his mother's massive office window. Athen looked out past the city to the sea, hoping that Nyssa had found safety wherever she was.

Lilliana spoke, her voice low. "Reece, I want you to keep an eye on our Justiciar when she takes up residence here."

"Hell no. I don't want anything to do with her. I don't trust—"

"Precisely why I need you to do as I ask," Lilliana insisted, drawing a deep frown out of Reece.

"I'll do as you wish, but sometimes you expect too much," Reece said, standing. "If the Justiciars had hurt Athen, would you ask the same?"

When Lilliana failed to answer, Reece stalked out of the office, leaving them alone in the waning light of day.

A CURIOUS AMUSEMENT

The next morning, Medias stood under one of the Keep's gigantic oak trees dotting the main courtyard, waiting on Lilliana's attendants to bring a jitney around for the short ride to the train station a mile outside the city. She picked at the bark on the tree, thinking about how to approach the Empress. Movement out of the corner of her eye caught her attention.

Reece strode across the courtyard, her silvery hair flowing behind her as she marched with purpose toward Medias, stopping five feet away. She crossed her arms over her chest.

"Empath."

"My name is Reece Ae'Shen," the woman replied, her dark eyes admonishing Medias silently.

"Are you here to punch me again?"

"I assume you heard about what happened at the docks last night?"

Medias nodded. "It's unfortunate that bystanders got hurt."

"It wouldn't have happened if the Obsidian Rule didn't try to stop Nyssa and Quinn."

"I know."

Reece paused and narrowed her eyes. "If I suspect, at any time, you're playing both sides or doing anything to break your promise to Nyssa, do not for one second think I was lying about killing you."

The audacity of the woman to not only threaten Medias once, but to reiterate that threat…it angered her. But it was somewhat intriguing. No one stood up to a Justiciar.

"I honor my promises, empath."

Empaths could sense emotions and some were even said to have the ability to detect lies, but Justiciars were altered to obfuscate their thoughts and feelings. Medias would never forget the bitter tonic she was made to drink the day she was marked and masked. The searing burn of the liquid lasted in her blood for hours, the pain nearly unbearable.

Medias watched for Reece's reaction, but her face remained hard. She would have to watch herself—even though Reece's magick didn't work on her, she didn't doubt the woman could read people far better because of what her empathic abilities taught her about body language, tone of voice, and facial expressions.

Medias pushed off the tree, taking a couple steps toward Reece, using her six-inch height advantage to tower over her.

Surprisingly, Reece didn't back down. Most people would, out of deference.

"It must be so confounding for you to not be able to sense if I'm telling you a lie," Medias mused, an uncharacteristic smile tugging at her lips. The empath was a curious amusement.

"You have your tricks, Justiciar. And I have mine," Reece replied, offering a smirk in return. "Now if you'll excuse me, I have to tend to my duties. I look forward to holding you to your word when you return."

Medias ground her teeth as she watched Reece leave. Justiciars commanded equal parts fear and respect, and Medias was used to downcast eyes and capitulation. Nyssa was the first person willing to meet her gaze and dared to push back.

And now this Reece woman followed suit.

Aggravating.

A whistle from a Keep attendant pulled Medias out of her thoughts as he brought the jitney around. She turned and took one last look at the Keep before walking to the jitney and climbing inside its small cab. She would count the days until she could get back to Ocean's Rest and remove that smug grin from the empath's face.

THE NIGHTMARE

Quinn sat up with a jolt. Stinging pain lanced her side, making her cry out, her hand flying to her side. She pulled up her shirt. Memories of the previous night flooded her mind as she gingerly touched the bandage over her stitches. Blue light caught the corner of her eye, and she turned to Nyssa's bed across the room.

Something is wrong.

Really wrong.

Nyssa struggled in her sleep. Blue lightning sparked off her skin, a low rumble vibrating in their room.

"Shit-shit-shit!" Quinn swung her legs off her bed, stifling another cry. She eased herself to her feet and stumbled a few steps, but the pain of her stitches straining and the vibration of the ship beneath her drove her to her knees. She clutched her side, her trembling hand coming away wet with blood.

The door to their stateroom flew open, and Elias staggered in, ricocheting off the doorframe. He flung himself toward Nyssa and grabbed her shoulders, shaking her. Nyssa moaned a whispered "No!"

"Wake up, Nyssa! Wake up!" he screamed. Lightning skittered across his hands and arms, causing him to let go as he hissed in pain.

Nyssa sat upright and shouted something impossible to hear and her eyes flew open, pupils flashing with bright-blue fire, the scar down her face glowing with the same cobalt intensity, as did the poison scar that radiated out from her left shoulder and down her arm. Brilliant azure lightning arced off of her body into the bed, wall, and floor. Elias fell back, avoiding getting struck again.

Not thinking, Quinn reached out, sending tendrils of shadow around Elias and yanking him away from Nyssa. He landed on his ass next to Quinn and stared at her, mouth agape.

She crawled closer to an unconscious Nyssa, drew up to her knees, and grabbed Nyssa's arm. The raw power flowing under her grip made her gasp, like sticking her hand in a torrential river of lightning. Darkness swirled around her hand, inching up Nyssa's arm.

"Calm down; calm down; calm down; calm down," Quinn whispered, her magick twisting around Nyssa. A brilliant blue ball of energy lit up inside Nyssa, as though shining through her skin. Quinn gasped. It could only be one thing—Nyssa's soul and the core of her new-found magick. Quinn dove tendrils of shadow into Nyssa's body, winding it around that pulsing sphere of life and power. She concentrated, careful to slowly suppress the magick coursing from the soul through Nyssa's body. Bit by bit, she calmed the wildly fluctuating magick. Its lightning thinned and dimmed, before disappearing.

The ship's shaking abated as Nyssa's magick receded. Quinn exhaled and pulled her own magick back, willing the shadow away.

Elias returned to the bed, carefully touching her. "Wake up, Nyssa. C'mon."

Jerrin ran into the room, his eyes wide. After a moment, he knelt beside Quinn. "You're bleeding. Probably popped a stitch."

Trembling and sweaty, she tried to stand but couldn't find the strength.

Jerrin put his arm around her. "I've got you."

"Elias?" a weak voice asked. Nyssa was awake. "What happened?" She swung her legs off the bed and saw Quinn and Jerrin on the floor. Her face fell. "What did I do?"

"You just had a nightmare and it got a little out of control," Elias explained. He stood and sat down next to her on the bed, catching Quinn's eye and mouthing a 'thank you.'

"Quinn, you're bleeding!" Nyssa said, concern etched on her face.

"I'm okay," Quinn replied. A lie. Her wound was on fire, but she didn't want to cause Nyssa any more distress. She swallowed down a lump in her throat.

Nyssa leaned forward and put her head in her hands, her deep-auburn curls falling around her face. Her shoulders trembled.

Elias took her hand in both of his. "You're safe now," he said, his voice soft and comforting. "We all are. Don't fret, love. Quinn calmed your power."

"I don't know exactly how I did it." She had just instinctively reached out and pulled Nyssa back from the brink. The experience was similar to how she had used the small modicum of magick she once possessed, but this new power was...astonishing.

Nyssa looked up at Elias. "What if this happens again?"

Elias and Jerrin shared a look, one that Nyssa noticed. "What?" she asked, her voice hollow.

"There...there was an accident on the docks," Jerrin started. "The Obsidian Rule—"

"You stopped the assassins," Quinn interrupted, needing to somehow soften the blow for Nyssa. "You were exhausted and trying to save us with everything you had. Your magick got out of control. A few dockworkers got caught up in the shock wave and...I'm sorry Nyssa..."

Nyssa's face fell. "How many...how many did I kill?"

Quinn swallowed. "Four."

The look on Nyssa's face sent a spike of regret through Quinn. Nyssa was raised with an honor code and a fierce protective streak. This information had to break her heart.

"People died on the docks because I can't control this power. I..." Her voice hitched. She exhaled a shuddered breath. "Elias, I'm a danger to you and the crew."

"You were having a nightmare, and that must have caused you to flare up like a storm. Let Buck mix you a tonic that'll give you dreamless sleep, yeah?" Elias asked.

"But—"

"No arguments out of you, girl," he replied. "We're here to help."

Though a pained sadness clung to her, Nyssa nodded. She rubbed absentmindedly at her left shoulder, at the scar where the blood wraith plunged a dagger into her.

Quinn exhaled sharply, realizing how the dark-gray scar looked like lightning. The strange irony of it now.

"Let me go get Buck for the both of you," Elias said, standing. He stood over Quinn and gently pushed the hair out of her face, offering a soft smile. "Good job tonight, love, but let's get you back in bed."

Nyssa watched as Jerrin helped Quinn back to her bed, holding a towel to Quinn's side, drawing a hiss of pain out of her. She nervously spun the lone ring on her left hand, her fingertips skimming over the engraving of a Kraken. A gift from Athen—it was one of Nyssa's most prized possessions. Not that she had much to claim as her own. But she needed to hang on to him and fight against a darkness that made her heart ache.

Her whole life had flipped upside down in one strange, inexplicable instant.

She got up, crossed the room, and knelt by Quinn's bed. "Jerrin, can you go get us some water?"

He nodded and left the room.

Quinn grimaced as she settled back in her bed, wisps of her long, dark-brown hair stuck to the sweat on her forehead.

"Let me help." Nyssa put her hand over the towel on Quinn's wound, keeping it tight to her side.

"At least I found I can suppress the effect of your magick without making you pass out, though I don't know how I did it. If I were Aryis, I'd see that as great progress and write it down in my journal."

Nyssa snorted softly. "And quietly talk to yourself while doing it."

"I thought I was the only one that noticed that!" Quinn laughed, then groaned. "Don't make me laugh...."

Quinn laid her hand on top of Nyssa's, pressing gently. The contact was electric.

She smiled. "You know, you don't have to compete with me. You got me good in the leg but going and getting yourself stabbed in the gut was really above and beyond."

Quinn gritted her teeth and gave her a reproachful look.

"There she is. That green-eyed spirit that knocked me on my ass in Jejin."

Quinn squeezed her hand, and the small gesture made the back of Nyssa's neck grow hot. When Quinn was injured, Nyssa's rage exploded and took over. She had been ready to lash out and kill their enemies to protect them both.

To protect Quinn.

"I'm glad I'm still alive. Though I have to say, Buck poking around my intestines was decidedly the least fun thing I think I've ever experienced," Quinn said with a frown.

Nyssa narrowed her eyes at her. "You were almost killed back in Ocean's Rest, yet a little poke in the belly is what you disliked most?"

Quinn hissed out a laugh, her grip tightening on Nyssa's hand. Its warmth calmed Nyssa, like a warm breeze washing away the chill of night. "I told you to not make me laugh, asshole."

"I can't help that you find me entertaining." Nyssa winced at Quinn's pain. Probably not the best time to lay on the charm, but hopefully it took Quinn's mind off her popped stitches.

Quinn's face settled into a serious expression. "I'm sorry about what happened in Ocean's Rest. I wish the Justiciars had listened to us."

She and Quinn had to flee Ocean's Rest, death nipping at their heels. Her life had changed irrevocably when she chose to save Quinn from Elken's blade.

No, that wasn't right, was it? Meeting Quinn for the first time set Nyssa on a different course. And something deep inside her understood that Ceril wanted to punish Quinn for her disobedience and force her back into solitude to do his bidding. He was a cruel, petty man, as proved by the scars on Quinn's back.

"I don't regret helping you," Nyssa said.

"But it cost you your friends. Your future."

Nyssa shook her head and met Quinn's bright-green gaze. "It cost me neither of those things, Quinn. Not really."

Quinn didn't seem convinced. "I know Athen is like a brother to you, and Aryis seemed to be a fast friend. I thought you and Reece were…"

She didn't finish her thought, whatever it might be. Truth was, whatever Nyssa had started with Reece—something she had desperately tried to keep casual—left her with a hollow ache. She couldn't deny that feelings had begun to develop, and if she had stayed in Ocean's Rest, there was no telling where their relationship would have gone.

Now, Reece's safety—along with Athen's and Aryis's—was entrusted to Justiciar Medias, a woman she barely knew.

Nyssa cleared her throat and pulled herself out of her thoughts. She couldn't dwell on what had happened, what she had left behind. If she did, she might spin apart, her heart shattered.

"No regrets, I promise. My future is now my own."

Pain weighed Quinn's expression down, her eyes flicking to Nyssa's chin. "Why did you save me? You could have been free. Marked, but free."

Nyssa shook her head, resting a hand on Quinn's knee. "Free? No. If I would have let them kill you, I would have lost myself."

Quinn's eyes didn't leave her face. "You were going to sacrifice your life for a stranger?"

"A stranger?" Nyssa chuckled. "You stabbed me in the leg. That makes us at least acquaintances."

To her credit, Quinn didn't laugh, though she bit her bottom lip, nearly driving Nyssa to distraction.

Nyssa paused for a moment, trying to collect her thoughts and better explain herself. Letting Quinn die would have gone against the code of honor that Eron had instilled in her growing up. She smiled, his memory bittersweet; his loss a sharp dagger in her heart.

"I once asked Eron why he adopted me. He said that when you save others, you save yourself. I didn't completely understand what he meant, but maybe I do now…because of you."

Quinn's eyes dipped away from Nyssa's face. It was impossible to miss the color rising on her cheeks, making her light freckles stand out.

"Nyssa...what's happening to us? Why do you now have magick? Why is my magick so different?"

"I don't know." Her thoughts turned back to their escape and what had happened on the docks. Whatever was inside of her surged out of control and she had killed people. *Innocent* people. Snuffed out the lives of strangers who were just in the wrong place, caught in her rage. They had families, friends....

How many people were left mourning in her wake?

Her magick was dangerous. *She* was dangerous.

A hand fell on Nyssa's shoulder. "Out of the way, Stitches. I gotta—mmm—fix up the girl here," Buck said from behind her. "I'll get you your tonic in a—mmm—sec. Help ya sleep without killin' the rest of us, eh?"

Nyssa flinched from the sting of guilt of the danger she posed and reluctantly pulled away from Quinn, moving aside for Buck. She lay down on her bed, folding her hands behind her head, her thoughts flying in all directions. Across the room, Quinn didn't make so much as a whimper while Buck stitched her back up.

Brave woman.

"The healing disk got your insides sorted but didn't have enough juice to get this cut healed. You can't be jumpin' outta—mmm—bed like that," Buck admonished Quinn. "Gotta get better disks if you two gonna be gettin' hurt so damn much."

He approached Nyssa with a small black bottle in his hand. "A swallow of this before bed will quiet your—mmm—dreams."

Nyssa grabbed the bottle, took a swig, and grimaced. It tasted like uncooked potatoes.

Could be worse.

She screwed the cap back on and tucked it next to her as a wave of drowsiness hit her.

What if the tonic didn't work? What if she had another nightmare and put everyone in danger again?

Nyssa looked over and found Quinn's eyes on her. She tried to say something, but her mind folded in on itself and sleep overtook her in mere moments.

THE CHICKEN AND THE CURSED GODS

Nyssa and Quinn rested for a few days before they were summoned by Elias to his stateroom. The air was hazy with sweet tobacco smoke and Nyssa took a deep breath, enjoying the fragrance for the moment.

Elias sat at his drafting table, his sleeves rolled up and enough buttons of his shirt undone to display a tuft of blue chest hair against his blue skin, traits of his Koja heritage. Fontaine perched atop the dark, polished wood, clucking with fervor.

They were in a heated discussion, man and chicken, and Nyssa smiled at the absurdity of the scene.

"If you knew the second they stepped foot on this ship, why didn't you tell—"

Fontaine clucked louder and pecked at the table. Whatever she was saying seemed to anger Elias.

"I have a feeling you're arguing about us," Nyssa murmured to Quinn.

Elias ignored Nyssa and pointed a finger at the chicken. "Look, I'm trying to—"

Fontaine clucked at him again before she flapped her wings and flew a few feet away from the table, landing in a flurry of white feathers. Suddenly, the room flooded with blinding golden light.

Nyssa rubbed her eyes and blinked, while Quinn cursed under her breath.

"Fuck, a little warning next time!" Elias groused.

"I…" a woman's voice croaked, cleared, then continued, "I forget how delicate your eyes are. And how odd speaking with a real voice is after twenty years."

As Nyssa's eyesight returned, she blinked in disbelief. A naked woman stood in the middle of Elias's quarters. Stunningly beautiful, with pale skin and long white hair that shimmered like gossamer wings, her golden eyes lit upon Elias. A sly smile brightened her face.

"Goddamn it, Fontaine!" Elias stood up, rooted around a chest of drawers, and pulled out a purple blanket.

"I thought this was your favorite part?" the woman said, her voice low and silky. Elias tossed the blanket at her. She pulled it around her with a sigh and laughed at Nyssa and Quinn. "The look on your faces right now—it never grows old."

Nyssa tried to speak and failed. Quinn offered no better.

"You have questions. Come sit down."

Nyssa and Quinn joined Elias at the drafting table. Nyssa asked, "Is this what you really look like?"

Fontaine shrugged. "I forget. I've taken so many forms over the years that I don't remember my truest self. But this is what I look like now."

"Why do you choose the form of a chicken instead of this one?" Quinn asked.

Fontaine smiled at her and shrugged, offering no answer. She spun around on her heels and giggled.

"Will you please sit down?" Elias asked. "You turn into a child when you get proper legs."

Fontaine bent over him to pat his cheek before taking a seat. "You're so grumpy when you're serious."

Nyssa raised an eyebrow, enjoying every moment of Elias's frustration. "I really like this version of you, Fontaine."

"So, this form is pleasing, then?" Fontaine asked.

"Very," Nyssa replied with a smirk. "But besides being nice to look at, it's great to actually *talk* to you. I won't lie, I did sometimes wonder if Elias was a little crazy and just talked to a pet chicken."

Fontaine threw her head back and laughed, her hand flying to her chest. "Oh! It feels weird to do that again after so many years. My, how I've missed having proper legs and fingers and lips, and eyes on the same side of my head. Perhaps I'll stay like this for a while."

Elias cleared his throat. "Oh, now you want to be yourself again? After all these years?"

"What are years to me? And I was always myself, the packaging just changed," Fontaine said, drawing a bit of a pout out of Elias. She flipped the blanket off her shoulders and tied it around her waist before sitting back down at the table, completely unconcerned about her naked breasts.

Quinn turned bright red, trying to look at anything but Fontaine.

Nyssa suppressed a chuckle. *Priceless.*

"Why did you change?" Nyssa asked. "After so many years as a chicken?"

Fontaine smiled. "I've spent the last twenty years trying to...come to terms with something difficult. Then you two come into my life. A rebirth of extraordinary circumstance, and ancient magick once again flowing into the world. You are a pool of great power I would love to dip my toes into."

"A rebirth of what?" Quinn asked, finally finding her voice.

Laughing, Fontaine cocked her head at them. "You don't know what you are?"

"Confused, that's what we are," Nyssa replied.

"I sensed something different about you both as soon as you came aboard the Whisper. I didn't understand it then, but now I know for certain. You are two very brave but scared Cursed Gods."

Nyssa opened her mouth, but no words came. Her brain tripped over itself trying to understand what Fontaine meant, halfway wondering if she was being toyed with or if she was still in her bunk dreaming.

Elias stood and gathered mugs and a bottle from a cabinet behind him, pouring wine into them. "These will have to do." He shoved them toward Nyssa and Quinn.

"Cursed Gods...that's not possible. We're not..." Quinn stammered, her voice hollow.

A scowl, almost comical, settled on Fontaine's face. "You doubt me?"

"No, I..." Quinn fumbled over her words. "Cursed Gods are myths."

"Their stories are a thousand years old, but hardly myths. Cursed Gods were the last mortals who wielded pure ancient magick. They died out as the world changed and ancient magick receded. The trees stopped singing. The seas no longer bellowed their song. Any creatures with a hint of ancient magick in them retreated to the edges of the world, driven away by fear."

From what Nyssa recalled about her history studies, Cursed Gods had a rather dubious past. "Weren't the Cursed Gods dangerous?"

Fontaine curled her bottom lip out. "True. The last of the Cursed Gods were murderers, drunks, and sibling-fuckers. Power-hungry assholes clashing against each other, leaving the skies burning and large swaths of land hollowed out, killing everything in their wake."

Great. Nyssa rubbed her forehead. *Just fucking great.*

"But the first of the Cursed Gods were a wonder to behold," Fontaine continued. "Powerful. Graceful. Great protectors and warriors. Just like you could both be. Only their stories aren't as salacious as those who left a path of destruction in their wake, so the heroes are lost to history. Unfortunately, an ugly legacy is something you will have to combat."

Quinn sat silent for a moment before breaking into laughter. "This is a fever dream. It has to be. I got stabbed, developed an infection, and now I'm hallucinating."

Nyssa sighed and flicked Quinn's ear, making her flinch. "Does that feel like a hallucination?"

Quinn glared at her.

Fontaine tapped her fingers impatiently on the tabletop. "Ladies, please."

Nyssa shook her head. "Quinn's right, though, this is crazy. We're...gods?"

"Don't get hung up on the word. There are plenty of middling 'gods', both real and fake, running around. Fortune tellers call themselves gods when they're merely hucksters. I'm Old Folk and some consider us gods because we have a bit of the ancient stuff infused in our magick. Cursed Gods are powerful mages who have nothing *but* ancient magick." Fontaine sipped at her wine. "Oh, this is so much better with a proper tongue!"

Elias rapped his knuckles on the table. "You two have already displayed the telltale markers of a Cursed God: glowing eyes and your magick covering every inch of your skin. Quinn, you seem to have some control over your power, bring it forth."

She swallowed, the color draining from her face, but she nodded and closed her eyes. After a second, threads of thick darkness curled around her skin, billowing off of her like smoke. It was stunning, the shadows of the night winding around her body.

"Open your eyes, Quinn," Elias said.

Quinn obeyed, lifting her lids. Her irises glowed bright green, as if lit from within, the whites of her eyes almost iridescent from the contrast. She was stunning.

Nyssa almost forgot to breathe.

"Nyssa your eyes glow like hers, but brilliant blue," Elias said.

Quinn closed her eyes and the dark energy disappeared.

"I-I know. I saw them in a mirror. I hardly recognized myself," Nyssa murmured, remembering the image: eyes blazing blue, the scars on her face and arm pulsing with energy, lightning sparking and arcing on her skin. She didn't look like herself. Not one bit.

Fontaine laughed and guzzled her wine, pushing the mug toward Elias. "My dear girl, you are more yourself now than you have ever been. I know it feels strange right now, but—"

"Feels strange?" Nyssa asked, bolting to her feet. "This is impossible. I don't want this! I've never had magick, you said as much when you two captured me."

"I didn't sense regular magick in you, the kind your guild wished you had. But ancient magick was there, just...dormant. But it woke up, didn't it?" Fontaine asked.

"I was tested several times when I was young, and they said I was mundane. How is this possible?" A lump rose in Nyssa's throat.

Years of taunts and fights—all those times she had been bullied for being different, finding herself at the losing end of a fight—was the pain just meaningless?

"They hurt me because I wasn't like them," Nyssa seethed, "and now you're telling me my magick was just *dormant*? Somehow locked inside of me? How?"

"Nyssa, please calm down," Elias said, his voice carrying an edge of alarm.

Nyssa held up her hands, and arcs of blue lightning jumped between her fingers. The poison scar that snaked from her left shoulder down her arm pulsed with blue energy. Her breathing grew ragged as her heart sped up.

Anger had pulled her magick forth.

Nyssa stepped away from the table, lightheaded. "I don't know how to control it!"

"Calm yourself," Fontaine said, reaching for her, but Nyssa instinctively recoiled.

"I don't want to hurt you," she whispered.

People had died precisely because she couldn't control her magick. They didn't deserve what happened to them.

"Hey," Quinn said, her voice quiet and steady, drawing Nyssa's attention. "You know how to control it. Remember what Medias and Reece said. Just center yourself."

Quinn smiled, her face open and trusting. Nyssa took a deep breath and closed her eyes. She had studied Ithais-Toru, the martial art of the Emerald Order, for over fifteen years. It had provided her a center, a calm stillness where she found peace. But now everything churned and raged inside of her in a way that felt very much out of her control. Her mind simply wouldn't settle.

A hand enveloped her own, and an intense, vibrating energy buzzed through her body. Her eyes flew open. Quinn stood in front of her, darkness swirling around her.

"Holy shit, you feel that?"

Quinn swallowed and nodded. "I'll suppress your magick, but I'd rather you figure this out yourself. You have to."

Nyssa's eyes darted to Elias and Fontaine before returning to Quinn, who didn't break eye contact.

How could she be so calm?

"Nyssa, just try," she whispered.

Nyssa ignored the beads of sweat that ran down her back. She closed her eyes again and narrowed her focus, forcing her mind to calm itself, cajoling it into behaving.

I'm stronger than this. Her mind locked in on her mentor...her father. *What would Eron have her do?*

Falling back on his meditation training, she pictured flat, round river rocks in her mind's eye. As a child, she'd collected them, and she drew them back to her now, layering one on top of the next, imagining each stone was a thread of magick she put in its place. The tower of blue and green and red rocks became her only focus, everything else slowing and stilling.

She inhaled and drew her magick back, folding it into the center of her body.

When she finally opened her eyes, Quinn was smiling at her, the glow gone from her irises. Quinn gave her hand a gentle squeeze before letting go, and Nyssa immediately missed the contact.

Its vibrancy. Its warmth.

"Good girl," Quinn said with a quiet laugh of relief. Nyssa exhaled.

She nodded at Fontaine and Elias. "Tell us more about the Cursed Gods."

"Come sit down," Fontaine said. She went to Elias's bookshelf, pulled a book down, and flipped through its pages until she found what she was looking for.

"Two souls, forever entwined,
chaos dancing in eyes and blood,
born between realms and belonging to the stars.
"Two souls, forever entwined,
clash with fists and blade,

dragging the tips of their swords across the world.
"Two souls, forever entwined,
dance and howl,
as ancient magick unfurls and envelopes the light.
"Two souls, forever entwined,
bend and break,
hurling to earth to die and be forever reborn."

The foursome sat there for a few moments, Fontaine watching Nyssa and Quinn.

"What is that book?" Quinn asked.

"The poems of Jang En-Shah. He was alive during the era of the last Cursed Gods. This is the lore of what you are," Fontaine said, pointing to the page. "'Two souls'—Cursed Gods come in pairs, to balance each other out. 'Forever entwined'—you were both bound to each other from birth. And the rest—the 'chaos dancing in the eyes,' no other magick manifests itself like that. The eyes give it away."

Nyssa frowned. She had read some Jang En-Shah, but nothing about Cursed Gods. "What about the other parts of the poem? The parts that are destructive and violent?"

"Oh, those? Yes, well, Cursed Gods have a bit of a reputation, but you don't have to be assholes, right?" Fontaine asked.

"Are you serious?" Quinn sighed and narrowed her eyes at Fontaine. "That's your advice? 'Don't be assholes'?"

"Isn't it always that simple? Be an asshole. Or don't. Let the power corrupt you or control it. It's *your* choice, Quinn."

Nyssa put her forehead in her hand and groaned. "I'm going to get a headache from all of this."

Reaching across the table, Fontaine grabbed her hand and squeezed. "Do you know how exciting this is? Your very existence means a long cycle of ancient magick missing from the world has ended. Soon, it will be full of song again."

"I still don't understand...I didn't have magick, but somehow I really did, but I just couldn't use it?"

Fontaine smiled. "Your essence—call it a soul, a life force, spark, whatever—is magick itself. Not being able to use its power made you like most other people: a non-magick user. Calling you magickless was the mistake. I felt your power. Just as your empath did."

Quinn slammed her hand down on the table, startling the rest of them. Her face lit up. "I saw it, Nyssa! Underwater, when you were drowning, I saw your magick. I thought it was my mind playing tricks on me, but I felt it too. It pulsed through me when I grabbed you. It hurt like hell."

"Is this what you tried telling me after Nyssa drowned?" Elias asked.

"Yes! We thought it was my mind playing tricks from being under the water for so long."

"Perhaps Nyssa had to die to awaken as a Cursed God," Fontaine said, "and you had to be with her to become one too. It's too much of a coincidence for your little adventure under the waves to not have done something to spark your powers, so to speak."

"I could have done without the dying part," Nyssa murmured.

"Amazing," Fontaine mused. "Born on the same day, bound to find one another by fate, and born again in the sea. Forever entwined."

Forever entwined. Nyssa glanced at Quinn. At least she knew how to control her darkness powers and her ability to negate magick...

Negate magick.

Nyssa brightened. "If this is magic, Quinn can remove it." She pointed to the Mark of the Unworthy.

"Of course! Why didn't I think of that?" Quinn reached forward, darkness swirling around her hand, the magick's coldness penetrating Nyssa's skin. "I did this with the poison, so it should—"

"Quinn, no!" Fontaine said, rushing off her chair to pull Quinn's hand back, breaking her contact. "Shit, too late."

"What? Look, the mark is gone," Quinn protested.

The look on Fontaine's face fell. "Oh, my dear girl, no. It's bone magick, bonded to Nyssa. You temporarily negated the mark." She moved from Quinn's side to take one of Nyssa's arms. "Elias."

"On it."

"What the fuck is going on?" Nyssa asked.

Elias gripped Nyssa's upper arm. She tried to pull free, annoyed, but pain exploded from her chin, radiating through her whole body. Just like when Medias cut her. She started shaking uncontrollably, her blood like molten steel, legs giving out.

"No! What did I do?" Quinn asked, sounding so far away.

Fontaine's voice rumbled next to her ear. "Breathe through it, Nyssa."

Nyssa threw her head back, gulping in air, desperate for relief. Elias and Fontaine held her up as she trembled, hot pain slicing through every fiber of her being.

The agony subsided after had to be the longest minute of Nyssa's life, and Elias and Fontaine helped her to a chair at the table.

"I'm so sorry, Nyssa. I didn't mean to hurt you," Quinn said.

"Bone magick doesn't obey the rules," Fontaine said. "It's one of the few that rivals ancient magick in its power. The problem is, it buries itself deep, infusing into the bone. You can't get rid of it." Fontaine turned to Nyssa. "I'm sorry, sweet girl. The mark is back...and permanent."

Nyssa bowed her head, and Elias poured her another cup of wine. At least she had stopped shaking. She gingerly touched her chin.

She caught Quinn's eye and smiled. "It's okay, Freckles, you were just trying to help. The pain is gone."

"Are you sure?" The soft and vulnerable look on Quinn's face was quite a change from the sharp fury of the woman she chased back in Jejin. The one who caught Nyssa with a surprising punch, knocking her squarely on her ass.

That seemed so long ago.

"Ah, Blacksea's fine," Elias said, squeezing her shoulder before retaking his seat across from her. "Tough woman."

Quinn asked, "Bone magick? That's a forbidden discipline."

Fontaine sighed into her wine mug. "Bone, blood, flesh, soul, death—all categories of magick forbidden by the Empire and throughout the larger world, yet somehow there are certain spells that those in power will overlook when they're useful. Like blood bonding items to owners. Or infusing Justiciar ceremonial knives with bone magick to mark those they wish to punish. Where is the line between 'good' magick and forbidden magick? Funny thing that, the hypocrisy of it all."

Of course forbidden magick was still used when it benefited the Empire. It made Nyssa simmer with anger. Running her fingers around the lip of her mug of wine, Nyssa asked, "What do we do now?"

"That we will figure out. But we'll protect you," Fontaine said. "I somewhat like you both now."

Nyssa shook her head. "Our being here puts you all in danger. We can't ask for your help." She didn't know what she'd do if anyone on the Whisper got hurt because of her.

Elias reached across the table and took her hand. "Let me make this clear. You and Quinn saved all twenty souls aboard this ship when you took on that blood wraith. That creature would have torn through my crew and put this boat at the bottom of the Black Sea. That's a debt I can't properly repay. So let me fucking help you, okay?"

Nyssa sighed and gave him a nod. Having Elias and Fontaine on their side gave her hope.

He clapped her on the back. "Good. I'll say one thing—you're never boring, Blacksea."

Fontaine stood up and stretched. "I suppose I should properly introduce myself to the crew. They expect a chicken, not this lovely beast." She ran her hands over her breasts and down her torso.

Elias groaned and slid off his stool. "I better come with you. And can you put some clothes on? We'll find something for you in the storeroom."

With a frown, Fontaine threw up her hands. "Fine."

"And you say *we're* never boring?" Nyssa quipped.

"Come on, then," Fontaine said, shrugging off her blanket as she walked out the door. "Let's go get me some clothes."

"Shit," Elias hissed, taking off after her.

THE EMPRESS

Justiciar Medias kept her eyes downcast while Empress Kalla Simac-Areshi chastised her for her failures. Kalla stood with her back to a massive window, the light casting a glow around her modest figure. Arch Master Anelos sat across from Medias, his eyes glued to her. Everything she said would be picked apart, scrutinized by him. Caution and cunning were all she had in the moment.

The Empress approached the table, placing a hand atop its worn, gray wood. Medias had come to hate this room, with its stark-white stone walls, soaring ceilings, and tall, skinny windows. Its unobstructed sunlight streamed into the room to infiltrate every corner. There was nowhere to hide.

"Six Justiciars are dead at the hand of two adepts, one of which you met with just months ago. I want to know how this happened," Empress Kalla said.

Medias cleared her throat. Every response now had to be measured, exact. "As you know, Nyssa Blacksea had no magick until the incident at Ocean's Rest. Her sudden display of power was a surprise to everyone, most of all to Blacksea herself, I suspect."

"And Quinn? The one I spared after she abandoned her guild? What of her?"

Medias eyed Ceril. "Perhaps the Arch Master has some insights?"

His lips curled up slightly. "At Arcton, her abilities were a mere fraction of what I saw of her in Ocean's Rest. Somehow her magick changed. Those glowing eyes—"

"Cursed Gods. How the hell did this happen? What an utter disaster," Kalla spat. "We lost a Master Justiciar."

Medias raised her gaze up to the Empress's face. There was a tension around Kalla's light-blue eyes, though she still looked impeccable in her simple black suit and fur-lined coat. Her close-cropped hair, said to have turned white by the end of the Mire War when she was only twenty-three years old, was topped with a small, thin silver crown. It was unadorned, twisted into the shape of stag horns, their points meeting at the front of the crown.

How much did Anelos hate sitting at the table as Arch Master instead of Emperor, as he was once promised? Rumor was he gave up a fiancée for the throne, foregoing marriage for the crown. He had to simmer with resentment, the throne snatched away from him by the Great Houses and given to an eighteen-year-old girl instead. With the Empire on the cusp of war, no less. But Kalla was a far better choice, having studied military arts at Wayland. Ceril only seemed adept at navigating bureaucracy, a politician to his core.

His hatred of Nyssa made sense in such a context. A magickless girl flew in the face of all guild rules, an anomaly that Ceril had to resent. He was, if nothing else, an elitist when it came to the guilds and Imperial rule. First Master Greye allowing Nyssa to be an adept in one of the Empire's most prestigious guilds must have smacked of favoritism to Ceril. And his misplaced resentment caused him to strike out at her, setting all the current events in motion. So much had been taken from him while she was handed an unearned exemption from sacred guild law.

If Ceril was willing to use forbidden magick to hunt Nyssa, how long would it take before he picked Kalla apart? His eyes were always cast upon the throne.

Empress Kalla rapped her fist lightly on the table. "What are we to do about Blacksea and Quinn? They slaughtered my Justiciars. Ambershine is up in arms. Arch Justiciar Decia is demanding swift and violent action."

"Understandable," Medias replied. "I imagine Decia wants their heads."

"Yes, and I'm putting a bounty on both of them. Five hundred thousand gold marks to bring them to me."

Medias swallowed hard. A bounty that large was unheard of. The amount would have every bounty hunter and mercenary in the world on the hunt for Nyssa and Quinn.

"Five hundred thousand *each*. No one must doubt my dedication to seeking justice. Or stopping the threat they pose." The Empress started pacing. "We had two Cursed Gods in our grasp, in our damn guilds, and couldn't capitalize on either one. After all the effort to procure Quinn..."

Medias frowned. *What...what does that mean?*

"Empress, let me assume the burden of finding them," Ceril offered. "I will put the Obsidian Rule on their trail."

Of course Ceril would so *graciously* volunteer to hunt them down. His ego wouldn't have it any other way. What an unmitigated asshole.

Kalla continued pacing. "Fine. But I want them alive, do you understand? I want to see them executed here in Cardin."

"Empress," he replied, bowing his head.

Medias jumped in. "Empress Kalla, Arch Master Anelos, I would like to assist. They killed my brethren before my eyes and I..." Dramatically pausing, hoping to sell her conviction that Nyssa and Quinn had wronged them all, she cleared her throat. "It is my duty to protect this Empire. I failed. I will not fail again."

A beat passed. Ceril spoke. "What do you suggest, Justiciar?"

It was the opening she was looking for. She needed the Empress to agree if she was going to protect Nyssa's friends as she promised. "It's been decades since a Justiciar held a post in Ocean's Rest, and I understand the Empire's hand's-off policy when it comes to that city, but circumstances have changed. Assign me to Ocean's Rest as its Justiciar. I can investigate First Master Greye's death and the wraith attack while keeping my eyes and ears open. Nyssa's only friends are there. At some point, she will try to contact them."

Ceril scoffed. "I highly doubt they'll slip up in front of a Justiciar."

"I'll watch Fennick, Ae'Shen, and Devitt. They'll make a mistake at some point, Arch Master. Their emotional ties to Nyssa make them weak," Medias said before directing her gaze back to Kalla. "Let me find Nyssa Blacksea and Quinn for you, Empress."

Kalla fixed her eyes on her, but Medias didn't flinch. Not now; not when she needed permission to return to Ocean's Rest. She had to be ready to serve at the Empress's whim but not seem too eager. It was a delicate balance.

"And what of the empath in House Fennick?" Kalla asked. "Can we leverage her?"

Medias smirked. "She's Blacksea's lover, Empress, and has some special tie to the woman. She will lead me to Nyssa, I guarantee."

"Your thoughts, Arch Master?"

Ceril's unnerving pale-blue eyes and dyed black hair, combined with an ill-fitting youth enchantment, made his face unnaturally taut for a man his age—the sheer vanity galling in and of itself. Stack his disdain and arrogance on top of it and it was all Medias could do to resist drawing her dagger across his traitorous throat.

"This one is right. Nyssa's friends are her weakness and she is theirs. Athen views Blacksea as a sister. Medias will root them out."

"We will have justice for my fallen brothers and sisters. Blacksea and Quinn will be executed for their crimes, and anyone aiding them will fall. I swear to you, Majesty."

Kalla regarded Medias for a moment, making her heart flutter as she waited for an answer.

"Very well. Return to Ocean's Rest. Be my eyes and ears. I want Blacksea and Quinn on their knees."

Medias stood and clutched her hands behind her back. "Their lives are yours, Empress."

"You may not get to them first," Ceril said with a smirk. "I'm sending out the Sea Viper after a pirate ship the two are rumored to be on."

Medias's stomach twisted. The Sea Viper was faster than any other vessel in the Imperial fleet, and it ran invisible and silent when cloaked.

She made a show of being pleased, even though she began to sweat under her mask. "Most excellent news," she lied.

She bowed and quickly turned and left the room, her heart beating in her ears, worried for Nyssa and Quinn.

COLDLIGHT

Quinn stilled on the deck of Hannah's Whisper and closed her eyes, letting the winter sun warm her. After searching in the ship's storage room, she scrounged up some new clothes—a pair of dark denim pants, a few warm cotton shirts, and a cream-colored sweater that smelled like the sweet tobacco Elias favored. Fontaine had approached her with a black wool coat, the same worn by the crew, and insisted she take it.

"It's far too nice, I can't accept it," Quinn had said, but before she could protest further, Fontaine made her try it on. It fit perfectly. And that was that.

Spring would be upon them soon, ushering in an all-too-short four months of warm weather before autumn descended again. It had been days since Fontaine shared what she knew of the Cursed Gods, and Quinn was still trying to wrap her head around her new, strange reality.

Questions swirled within her mind, consuming her thoughts. Did Ceril suspect she was a Cursed God? Was that why he constantly tested her power? How exactly had she come to be at the Citadel? Who were her parents?

Quinn wanted to beat the truth out of Ceril and leave him for dead after what he had done to her. How small he had made her feel, the evidence of his hate and disdain crisscrossed on her back.

The chill in the sea air, the brine nipping at her nose, evened out her anger and kept it at a dull roar at the base of her spine. She would tap into it when needed—whenever she came face-to-face with Ceril again.

A warm, comforting buzz crept into Quinn's chest, blooming slow like a flower in the sun. She turned to find Nyssa approaching, the loose curls in her auburn hair gently waving around her face in the wind.

It was odd how they could sense each other when close, though also strangely comforting. Nyssa was the first to mention it days prior.

"Do you—this is going to sound weird—but do you feel me when I'm near?" she had asked.

Quinn had laughed with relief and nodded. "I thought I was going insane, letting this Cursed God stuff go to my head."

The women later told Fontaine about the sensation, who giggled. "Your magicks call to one another, godlings. Forever entwined!" she said before strolling away, frustratingly close-lipped at times.

Nyssa still wore her guild leathers, her white cotton shirt half-tucked lazily into her leather pants, her black leather jacket—the one possession aside from her sword and boots that seemed to mean anything to her—unzipped despite the chill on deck. Her black leather boots were buckled part-way up, the tops open and unruly.

Typical Nyssa.

Quinn smiled to herself. If only she could look a fraction as good with as little effort. Nyssa gave her a little wave, unexpectedly brightening Quinn's day. Another strange feeling.

Raising her hand to return the wave, she paused. The air around Nyssa began to shimmer and shift, and Quinn's stomach sank.

A man appeared in the air behind Nyssa, dropping to the deck before straightening and drawing his sword. Quinn recognized his attire immediately.

Obsidian Rule.

"Nyssa, behind you!" Quinn yelled.

Nyssa whirled around.

Another man appeared out of thin air, landing on the deck, a blade at the ready. Then came another. And another. Nyssa was quickly surrounded by Rule adepts.

And she was without Winter's Bite.

Quinn tensed as Nyssa sprang into action, dropping the first attacker with a fist. The others surrounded her, and she stood her ground, but she didn't summon her magick.

"We're under attack!" Quinn yelled.

More men and women landed on the deck of Hannah's Whisper, and bright pops of light exploded in the air. Quinn stumbled backward and threw her forearm over her eyes, trying to blink away the white stars. Men and women yelled, the clanging of steel against steel filling Quinn's ears as the crew came to the defense of the ship.

Tears streamed down her face as her eyesight returned. She gasped when she saw Nyssa lying on the deck, clawing at the wood. Blue lightning flickered over her bare skin but died out as she struggled to get to her feet.

An assassin's fist put her back down.

Another Rule adept snapped something around Nyssa's neck—something Quinn knew all too well.

A void collar.

No! Quinn curled her hands into fists, ready to fight—

A small orb landed at her feet, releasing a blinding blast of bright light. She stumbled backward, disoriented, her eyes useless and her ears ringing. Smoke filled her lungs, and she coughed violently. Cries from all over the deck assaulted her ears as she fumbled around with her hands and found the mast, pulling herself toward it to get her bearings.

Elias shouted, and Fontaine cried out in pain, sending a cold shiver of fear through Quinn. She reached into herself to draw her magick forth.

Nothing happened.

Panic slammed into her gut. She tried again. Tendrils of shadow wisped around her fingers, then died out.

Something was wrong.

She rolled her back against the mast and peered down toward the bow while her eyes cleared. The Whisper's crew fought against the invaders, out-powered, the attackers weaving spells that pushed them back. Elias battled, sword in hand, but he was close to being overwhelmed by two adepts.

Smoke curled through the air, covering the deck in a light-gray smog. The invaders wore metal masks over their mouths. Quinn realized the masks weren't to obscure their identities, but to protect them from the smoke bombs.

In the middle of the deck lay Nyssa, unconscious, with her hands bound behind her. And that *fucking* collar around her neck.

Quinn gritted her teeth as rage thrummed under her skin.

A black orb rolled across the wood toward Elias's feet, exploding into a cloud of black smoke. Elias tried to move away, his flames licking at his fingers before disappearing. His magick was rendered useless.

Quinn peeled off her heavy coat and wrapped her crimson scarf around her nose and mouth several times, pulling it tight. She scrambled up to her feet and crouched down, quickly running along the starboard side of the ship as the fighting continued on the portside. Her stitches strained, and she stifled a yelp of pain from the sharp sting. Buck could fix her up later. She needed to fight back.

Her pulse thundered in her ears. *I hope I don't get myself killed.*

As Quinn drew closer, a Rule adept spotted her. The man started moving his fingers like the legs of a spider. Quinn shot forward and tackled him, knocking the wind out of him and interrupting his spell. She landed on top of him and cried out, pain radiating from her wound. She groaned and pushed herself up on her hands. The adept snatched at the dagger affixed to his belt.

Without thinking, Quinn beat him to the weapon, pulling his dagger out of its sheath and driving it into the assassin's chest. His eyes widened, a wet gurgle bubbling behind his mask. He struggled underneath her, and she fought the urge to vomit as blood coated her hands. She had killed before, but not like this. Not by driving a blade into the heart of another person.

She held fast to the dagger, not letting go until the adept stopped moving. She raised her head and winced, gasping as Elias fell to the deck, his sword kicked away from him. Fontaine lay next to him, still. Behind her, Jerrin tried to pull the mask off one of the Rule adepts but was dispatched with a sword hilt to his temple. He collapsed to the deck, blood dripping down his face. The crew of the Whisper was losing. Some, she quickly realized, were dead.

Cold fear rippled through Quinn's body, followed by white-hot rage.

With a snarl, she pushed herself off the adept's body, taking his dagger with her. She stood up and breathed deep, trying to clear her lungs of the black smoke that suppressed her magick. Quinn held her stolen dagger tight in her fist.

"That's Quinn!" a familiar voice yelled. "Collar her!"

Black orbs sailed toward her through the air, and she sucked in a breath, closing her eyes to avoid the blinding flash that accompanied the smoke. She fell forward onto the dead adept and fumbled at his head, finding his mask and removing it, pulling it over her face. The breath she sucked in was cold and fresh, devoid of smoke.

Quinn opened her eyes and found herself surrounded by black haze. She reached inward for her magick again, and it was there, dull and muted, like a frozen star. Standing up, she curled her hands into fists.

Fingers dug into Quinn's shoulder, and she pulled away instinctively but tripped over something at her feet and tumbled across the deck. She turned over on her side and found herself facing Nyssa, who lay a few feet away. She was conscious again, struggling against her restraints, a snarl of anger on her face.

A sharp blow to Quinn's back forced a cry from her throat, blinding pain radiating around her ribs. Nyssa yelled and fought against her bindings as hands encircled Quinn's arms and violently yanked her onto her feet.

Another adept moved toward Quinn, a cold, dark metal band in his hand. Just like the one around Nyssa's neck. Just like the one Ceril made Quinn wear after she touched him and briefly took his magick away.

Bile rose in her throat. She struggled in the grip of her captors, roaring with rage.

The adept with the void collar got close to Quinn. She desperately kicked a foot up at him, catching him by surprise, connecting with his chest and forcing him back.

She wasn't going to be collared without a fight. Ever again.

She doubled over and screamed, willing herself to break free of her captors. Her magick burst forth and rippled across her skin. Shadow coiled around her and she turned the edges of it sharp, driving barbs of darkness into the adept's neck.

Blood exploding out of his mouth. The void collar slipped from his hand and clanged against the deck.

Barely in control of her power or her anger, Quinn had one thought—retribution. She stood straight and raised her hand, sending a spike of darkness toward another assassin. It ripped through his chest, and he toppled over dead.

"Retreat!" the woman cried out. Quinn recognized the voice again and the dark eyes filled with hate.

Efla.

The woman who had assassinated Eron and tried to kill Nyssa. Efla and her Rule adepts vaulted over the starboard handrail, landing on a ship as it shimmered into view, sleek and black and far smaller than the Whisper.

The ship peeled away from Hannah's Whisper, the air around it whirling with golden light before it disappeared.

Quinn wavered for a moment before dropping to her knees, panting. She looked around her, trying to clear her head. When she spotted Nyssa, she scrambled over to help her sit up. She untied Nyssa's wrists, fumbling at the rope as her hands trembled.

Quinn braced Nyssa's face in her hands. "Are you okay?" she asked, breathless.

Nyssa tugged at Quinn's shirt. "You're bloody! Are you hurt?"

"What?" Quinn looked down. Her white shirt and hands were covered with crimson. She pulled it up to check on her stitches. They had held through the fight, though her wound ached. She let out a relieved sigh. "I'm fine. It's not my blood."

"You did good, Freckles," Nyssa rasped.

Quinn inspected the metal band around Nyssa's neck. It was secured by a normal lock that needed a key and not a magick bond she could nullify.

"Find the key to this thing so we can get it off Nyssa," Quinn said to no one in particular.

Elias quickly started barking orders and the crew sprang into action. Yuha rummaged in the pockets of a dead adept, pulling out a key. She bent over Nyssa and opened the void collar's lock, gently removing the metal band from her neck.

Nyssa shuddered and fell forward with a gasp. Quinn caught her, more than familiar with the surge of nausea that accompanied the sudden rush of magick returning. It could be quite jarring.

"Easy. Void collars aren't fun," she said, thankful that Nyssa was free. Nyssa straightened and gave her a soft smile, putting a hand on her shoulder to steady herself.

"Please don't throw up on me," Quinn requested.

"I'll try not to," Nyssa replied with a groan, reaching for Quinn to pull her into a hug. The gesture came as a surprise and Quinn found herself temporarily stunned into inaction. After a second, she returned the embrace, her heart hammering in her chest.

"I'm so glad you're safe," Nyssa murmured.

CURSED

Nyssa's heart filled with sorrow as she covered the face of a woman who died defending their ship. Three dead crew members. Dead because the Empire was after her and Quinn.

More bodies to add to her ledger.

Elias set a course for the Black Sea, to retreat deeper into Unbound waters, where no nation had jurisdiction over them. Fontaine hissed as Buck pressed a cloth to a small cut on her head and shooed him away, insisting she was fine. She bent over and riffled through the pockets of a dead Rule assassin and pulled out a black orb.

Fontaine frowned. "Coldlight bombs. Nasty things."

"The same metal that's in void collars?" Quinn asked.

Fontaine nodded. "Ground into a dust and dispersed as smoke in flash bombs."

"Coldlight is extremely rare. And weapons like these are illegal. Only Justiciars are allowed to possess void collars. How do Rule assassins have Coldlight?"

"Do you expect them to play by Imperial rules? Little fucking bastard assholes," Fontaine groused, spitting on the body of the dead assassin. She looked at the crew. "Go through all their possessions. Take their weapons, void collars, Coldlight bombs, masks—anything we can scavenge. Then toss the bodies overboard."

The crew scrambled to follow her orders.

"Tools of cowards! I haven't been cut off from my magick for…centuries," Fontaine spat. She leveled her gaze at Nyssa and Quinn. "Now you know that not even gods are immune to Coldlight."

The void collar had such a strange effect on Nyssa, unlike anything she had ever felt before. The power that pulsed inside of her, like another heartbeat, had receded as soon as the collar was around her neck. When she tried to pull it forth, it was like trying to grab hold of mist.

Elias rejoined Nyssa, Quinn, and Fontaine. "An Imperial navy vessel attacking an unaffiliated ship in Unbound waters violates maritime law. And not just the Laws of the Unbound Sea. These are Imperial and Eastern Continental Alliance laws they break," he said.

Quinn gestured starboard. "They were on us before we knew it."

"That was the Sea Viper, if I'm not mistaken. Fast as the wind with a stealth enchantment built in. We got lucky. Extremely lucky. They tried to take you both alive, otherwise I think we'd be mourning at least one of you."

"Nyssa, I recognized Efla," Quinn said.

A chill ran down Nyssa's spine. The assassin who killed her father had almost captured her. She had been unprepared, her sword left behind in her stateroom, and instead of trying to strike out with her magick, she'd hesitated. The Obsidian Rule got the best of her because she didn't trust herself.

Shouting disrupted Nyssa's thoughts. A small group of crewmen were arguing, pushing each other about. Nyssa heard her name mentioned.

"Hey!" Elias yelled. "What's going on?"

One of the men stepped forward and spoke up. "The marked one is cursed. She brought death with her to this ship."

Nyssa's stomach dropped.

Elias's face darkened. "How many of you are superstitious fools like Soslan? Speak up."

The rest of the crew had gathered on deck. Three others put their hands up half-heartedly, avoiding eye contact with Nyssa. Quinn stepped up next to her.

"Rells wore that mark," Soslan said, pointing. "It brings evil down on us."

An angry murmur rippled through the rest of the crew.

"That's nonsense," Fontaine said. "The mark is a punishment, not a curse. And do you four forget what Nyssa did for this ship when she saved us from that blood wraith?"

Soslan spoke again. "Elias, you put us in danger when you let the Unworthy on this ship."

Unworthy.

Nyssa bristled at the word.

Elias stalked back and forth, his hands tightly clenched into fists. "Any others feel this way?" he asked, his voice low.

The rest of the crew shook their heads, and Nyssa let out a breath, somewhat relieved. A mutiny was the last thing she wanted.

Elias stepped up to the four that had separated themselves from the rest of the crew.

"You four are confined to quarters and you'll be leaving my employ once we pull into the next port. Anyone else that has a problem with Nyssa or Quinn being on this ship can leave with them," Elias shouted before growing still. "And let me make this *very* fucking clear: You don't question my decisions. Ever. You don't fuck with this ship or its crew. And you *never* share the secrets we keep."

Quinn sucked in a breath next to Nyssa. They had not seen this side of the charming pirate—angry and dangerous, threatening death.

A murmur of agreement rose from the crew. Soslan and the three others looked at one another, sullen.

"Go on, to your quarters!" Elias yelled. "The rest of you, back to work." He gestured at Yuha. "Post guards outside their rooms. Keep a close watch on those assholes." She nodded to him, her face stern.

Elias turned to Nyssa and Quinn.

"I'm so sorry this happened, Elias. I..." Tears sprang to Nyssa's eyes, and she fought them back, dropping her head.

Why is this happening?

Elias placed a finger under her chin and lifted her head, gently touching the Mark of the Unworthy with his thumb. "This isn't who you are. We all know it. They did this to shame you."

"But he's right, Soslan is," Fontaine said. "The first to wear that mark was a Rell—and a Justiciar to boot. The Empire marked her as a traitor for her loyalty and love for her family. The first and only Justiciar to betray the Empire."

Until Medias. Nyssa chewed the inside of her cheek, worried for the woman she barely knew...or trusted.

Fontaine continued, "Nyssa, you wear that mark because they feared what you represented: A magickless woman who dared succeed as an adept, who then became an Ashcloak and challenged their rules in order to do the right thing."

Nyssa lost her fight against the tears brimming in her eyes. "I can't ask you to help us with the Empire chasing us."

Elias put his hand on Nyssa's shoulder and gave it a reassuring squeeze. "My ship, my call. What did I say about questioning my decisions? We are going to help you, so quit your protests."

Elias and Fontaine walked back to the quarterdeck, their heads bowed together, talking as they left.

"Nyssa, we need their help, so let them help," Quinn said. She looked a mess, blood on the front of her white shirt, her hands stained red. Nyssa wondered how often they would have to spill blood to protect themselves from their pursuers.

She swallowed and looked down, trying to blink back her tears. "I don't want more people dying because of me."

"You think I do? But I think we're as good as dead without Elias and Fontaine. And I...I've lived more in the last few weeks as your captive than I have my whole entire life at Arcton Citadel. I don't want to give this freedom up, Nyssa."

There was a tremble in Quinn's voice, which she quickly tried to compensate for by straightening up and clearing her throat. But she held Nyssa fast in her gaze.

"Alright," Nyssa breathed. "We stay. And we fight."

RISK AND REWARD

"Take a seat," Elias requested, his face serious.

Nyssa tamped down her nerves, scanned his stateroom, and chose the bed, plopping down and leaning back on the soft, velvety blanket. He was a man who did enjoy the finer things in life, and surrounded himself with comforts. How many of those comforts were purloined via piracy? Likely all of them.

"The bed? Really?" he asked.

She smirked. "It looked comfy. Turns out, it is."

Quinn hummed out a chuckle and took a seat next to Fontaine at the drafting table. A spicy, woodsy scent hung in the air, the remnants of the pipe tobacco the pirate favored.

"There's news." Elias ran his hands through his messy dark-blue hair. He was usually fairly put together, but his shirt was untucked and wrinkled. An air of weariness clung to him.

Nyssa eyed him. "What's happened?"

Fontaine picked up a piece of paper. "We intercepted a message from the Empire. Empress Kalla has put a bounty on your heads."

Swallowing, Nyssa closed her eyes. "How much?"

"Five hundred thousand gold marks. For each of you."

Her eyes flew open. "*Each*?" It was if an elephant suddenly sat on her chest.

Quinn's expression wavered a moment before firming up, putting on a brave face. She was good at that, raising up her walls to tightly control her emotions. Especially when on the defensive.

"Yes, each," Fontaine replied.

The four of them fell into silence. Nyssa sat back on Elias's bed, pulling Winter's Bite an inch out of its scabbard before clicking it back in place, over and over again, her thoughts dark after the previous day's attack and now this news. Her mind churned, trying to fathom just how fucked they were.

Five hundred thousand gold marks. *Each*. It was an obscene amount of money for their capture. But what chilled Nyssa's blood was they were wanted alive so the Empress could execute them herself.

Winter's Bite clicked into its sheath again, and Nyssa finally broke the silence. "Every bounty hunter, mercenary, and fortune hunter will be searching for us, not just Imperial forces."

Quinn tapped her finger on the table she sat at with Elias and Fontaine. "Can't we hide? Go to the Eastern Continent and just disappear?"

"No," Elias stated plainly. "Bounty hunters don't recognize borders. And the Empire has reach, even deep into the East. Any nation that captures you will get a generous reward and Kalla's favor."

Nyssa had never backed down and never would. "Then we fight back."

"You can fight, but you can't fight forever. And you don't want to live that type of life. Trust me, I tried that once."

Whiskey. I need whiskey.

Nyssa grabbed an empty mug and scanned Elias's booze shelf for a dark liquor to match her mood. Spotting a bottle of Froslandian whiskey, she pulled the cork and tipped the bottle into the mug.

"So, we can't hide or fight indefinitely. What the fuck do we do?" Nyssa took a swig of the whiskey and nearly coughed it out. It was thick and smoky, stronger than she expected. Aryis had mentioned drinking the stuff like it was water.

A heavy sigh escaped Nyssa. She missed the Little Hawk. Her friend. Quinn tapped the mug in front of her.

"You sure? This is strong stuff."

Her response was a pointed eyebrow.

Nyssa poured a generous amount of whiskey into Quinn's mug and watched the woman toss it back instead of sipping it. The expression on her face didn't change save for a slight flinch.

Impressive.

Nyssa sighed. "A million gold marks. The whole damn world will want a piece of us."

"I would turn you in myself if I hadn't taken a slight liking to you both," Elias quipped.

Quinn circled her finger on the table as if she were drawing, concentration etched on her face. She raised her head. "High stakes. But what if we raised them?"

The chair creaked under Nyssa as she inched closer to the table. "What are you thinking?"

"Our lives are worth a lot of money. What if we offered something of greater value? Something all the gold marks in the world can't buy?"

"What would that be?" Nyssa asked.

"Suvi Rell."

Nyssa blinked, not sure she had heard correctly. "*Queen* Suvi Rell? You serious?"

Quinn's face didn't change. "Think about it. Kalla won't turn away a chance to secure the Empire's greatest ancestral enemy. That would single-handedly end centuries of war with Thu'Dain. Our freedom for Suvi."

Nyssa couldn't believe what she was hearing. "It's...it's crazy, right?"

With a shrug, Quinn replied, "What do we do when the whole world is after us? We take our fates into our own hands and change the world."

Nyssa glanced at Elias and Fontaine to gauge their thoughts. Elias reached for the whiskey bottle and refilled everyone's cups. "It's...an *interesting* idea," he mumbled. Fontaine closed her eyes and pressed her hands to her lips.

"Fontaine?" Quinn asked.

"Shush, I need a moment to think," she replied, waving Quinn off.

Nyssa, Quinn, and Elias quietly sipped their drinks as they waited for Fontaine's thoughts.

The prospect of kidnapping a queen—a Rell no less—was insane. But their plight called for a little insanity...

Fontaine opened up her eyes. "I have no love for Suvi Rell, but let's be very clear about this. What you're talking about is trading her life for your own. You have to be comfortable with the likely outcome that she will be executed by Empress Kalla in a very public and spectacular fashion."

Nyssa set her jaw, trying to hold her emotions at bay. "It would be justice. Suvi Rell killed my parents."

Quinn's gaze shot to Nyssa, her face changing, growing soft. "You didn't tell me that."

Nyssa had to look away, scared she might break apart again, the sorrow of never having her parents in her life a dull, constant ache that threatened to resurface.

"I thought it best to leave it in the past. Taking revenge seemed out of the question, but maybe now she can serve a different purpose—our freedom."

A cold, determined look settled on Quinn's face as she glanced at the three of them. "The Rells perfected forms of forbidden magick, using it to grab for power centuries ago. That magick creates horrors like wraiths." She held up her hands, marred by small scars. "Their trapped and warded spell books did this to me. Let's end their legacy."

"This is dangerous," Fontaine said, running her finger along the rim of her mug. "But...plausible, if you find a way to get to her. She's a queen. You don't merely put an appointment on her schedule."

Nyssa swallowed. "But what about the other end of the plan? Would Kalla grant us our freedom in exchange for Suvi?"

"It would be the greatest victory for the Areshi Empire in centuries," Fontaine replied. "Revenge for past ills and the end of future wars with Thu'Dain. I'm certain Kalla would forget your supposed crimes against the Empire real quick."

"But...Ceril could put a stop to it all," Quinn said, her face serious.

"If you march Suvi Rell into Cardin, Ceril won't be able to drown out the Sun Council urging Kalla to make the deal. The Areshi Empire is tired of endless war. It would be a victory for the Empress. And it's been a long while since she's had one."

Quinn perked up, her face hopeful. "So, I'm not crazy? But how would we do this?"

Fontaine narrowed her eyes for a moment, then broke into a wide smile. "The Whitefield Vintner's Festival in the south of Thu'Dain! Suvi will be at her winery to celebrate. She goes every year like clockwork."

Interesting. "How do you know this?" Nyssa asked.

"It's a Rell family tradition," Fontaine replied. "I...might have gone to their winery once or twice to sample their wines during the Festival."

Nyssa sat straighter. "You went to their winery?"

"Nalo Rell was an extremely charming man, and I can't resist drinking rare, expensive wines for free."

"Fontaine!" Quinn admonished.

With a shrug, Fontaine swirled the liquor in her mug and downed it in one gulp. "Their family gets such a bad reputation, but some of them were perfectly lovely. And their wines are...exquisite. Besides, it was a lifetime ago—quite literally for most mortals."

Nyssa laughed. "I imagine you have some stories to tell."

"Oh, you have no idea, my love," Fontaine replied, a sly smile hinting to far more than she would likely share in the moment. "But my point being, Suvi Rell will be removed from the secure walls of her capital city. Capturing her won't exactly be easy, but it will be a sight easier at her winery. And we will help you."

"We'll have to figure out a way in," Elias said, "but you two will have our help, I promise." He and Fontaine shared a glance, his face darkening for a moment. Nyssa didn't question him, just thankful for the help.

"Autumn is only a few months away," Nyssa said.

Quinn brightened. "We could capture her, and—"

Fontaine held her hand up and shook her head. "No. It's dangerous and reckless to let you two flit about without one clue how to control your magick. You need time to learn what you are and what you can do.

A few months' time is not enough. I won't have you stumbling into your deaths."

Waiting didn't make sense, not if they could get Suvi in a few months. "But—"

Fontaine began speaking in an unfamiliar language. Bands of purple-colored magick sprang from her palms, wound around Nyssa, and tightened. Nyssa tried to resist, gulping in air as the magick constricted her chest.

"Break out of those bonds," Fontaine said.

Quinn pushed away from the table and darkness flowed out of her hands as she called her magick forth. A quick three words from Fontaine and the same purple magick coiled around Quinn. She fell to the cabin floor, her eyes dimming and returning to normal as she fought against the magick.

Grunting, Nyssa struggled against the magickal restraints, but the more she tried, the tighter the enchantment got, until breathing was almost impossible.

"Stop," she choked out.

Fontaine stepped around the table and glanced down at Quinn, who was turning red, before approaching Nyssa.

"Break yourselves free," she commanded.

"Fontaine, ease up!" Elias said.

Tears filled Nyssa's eyes as she fought for air. A heartbeat later, the magick fell away from her, and she stumbled from the sudden release of the bonds. Quinn sucked in a sharp breath and scrambled to her feet.

"What were you thinking?" Nyssa demanded, ready to throw fists. Quinn grabbed her arm.

Fontaine rounded the table and surprised Nyssa by cupping her cheek. "My dear girl, neither of you could break out of a simple trap using your magicks. You lack knowledge and control of your powers."

Nyssa dropped her head, ashamed. Eron had trained her to fight without magick, to use tricks to combat those that did, but now, even with new power, she felt useless.

"Both of you are struggling because you don't know what you can do or how to control it. You two want to change the world? Well, with Suvi

Rell, you can't rush in and arse it up. You'll get yourselves killed. That's the last thing any of us want."

"We have a few months. We can learn," Nyssa said.

"Even if you were normal mages, that would be a tall order. But you're not like anyone else. You can insist on going after Suvi before you're ready, but I will not help you. It would be suicide."

Quinn stepped forward, her hand still around Nyssa's arm. "The Empire will hunt us down. We can't run forever."

"There's an island north of the Basai Islands in the Black Sea. It's a sanctuary of sorts. Unmapped. We can go there. Stay for a while, safe from those hunting you. I will stay with you and help you understand how to control your magick," Fontaine said. "I will require your patience and a willingness to learn. Then, next year's Vintner's Festival, Suvi is ours."

Nyssa exhaled, her shoulders tense. Suvi would be within reach in just a few months. Waiting longer might drive her crazy...but...how easily Fontaine had rendered both of them useless. They couldn't afford to make any mistakes, especially if Elias and Fontaine were involved. Nyssa wouldn't sacrifice their safety due to her impatience. And if Fontaine was willing to help, the offer was too good to pass up.

But Nyssa couldn't make this decision alone. They were in this impossible mess together. *Forever entwined*, as the lore stated. "Quinn, I'm willing to wait and prepare. Are you?"

Quinn took a moment, then nodded. "Fontaine's right, we have to be smart."

"Good choice. I will teach you what you need to know. But only if you are okay with this, my old friend," Fontaine said, taking Elias's hand. He didn't look pleased.

Leaning forward, he pointed his finger at Nyssa, then Quinn. "I'm not happy about losing my quartermaster and best friend for who knows how long, but Fontaine wants to do this for you. You'd be idiots—and frankly assholes—if you declined this offer. Old Folk don't fuck around with bullshit. This is important to her."

"Then we won't decline the offer." Quinn looked at Nyssa. "This is our best option. Our only option."

"But what about the rest of you, Elias? The crew? The Empire knows we're aboard."

"Please, this isn't our first time hiding secrets from the Empire," he scoffed. "After we drop you off, we'll pull into port and make a big stink about how we dumped your asses at some Eastern city and said good riddance. We'll let Imperial agents come aboard, inspect us, and they'll find nothing. We'll be okay, I promise."

One thing didn't sit right with Nyssa. "I can't go without letting Athen know I'm alive and safe."

"We can't risk messaging Ocean's Rest," he replied.

"Elias, it's the only thing I ask."

He sucked on his teeth and sighed. "Okay. I'll send Yuha to Ocean's Rest and have her talk to him in person."

Nyssa's shoulders relaxed, and she sat back in her chair, closing her eyes for a moment. "Thank you."

THE QUEEN

A small group of men and women argued as Suvi Rell watched from her seat on the Thu'Dainian throne. Her brother lounged on the steps leading up to the ornate, overwrought chair. A rather ostentatious construct of her late father, a throne atop a platform, just so he could lord over everyone. As if being the king wasn't a high enough position.

Suvi picked a piece of lint off her deep-emerald dress and let her hand rest on her family's prized dagger, the only weapon she rescued off her father before his body was stolen by Lilliana Fennick and the Areshi fighters defending Ocean's Rest thirty years past.

The memory of it didn't burn as much as it used to, nor did the shame. The war was long over, and Suvi's father dead in an unmarked grave somewhere in the Empire to the north.

So much for the glory of battle.

With draining patience, Suvi raised her voice above the din. "You have had three months to come to me with treaty proposals and now you choose to use this time squabbling?"

The men and women—her advisors—quieted, and her head advisor, Austol, stepped forward.

"We agree that Gacheau and the Andol Republic are very good alliance candidates, we just do not agree on the third."

Suvi simmered with frustration. She had suggested the third nation, though it was not exactly independent. Not yet. "Frosland would be a major alliance for us. I understand your reticence, but I want you prepared with trade proposals should their situation as a member of the Areshi Empire shift."

When she first suggested turning her nation away from endless war with the Areshi Empire and into an international power—essentially ending the isolationism her family had installed—she tasked her advisors with finding nations amenable to being their first allies. The whole nation had bowed under the weight of centuries of Rell vendettas against the Empire, and the high families stirred restlessly under that weight. Whispers reached Suvi—talk of sedition, of finding someone other than a Rell to sit on the throne.

Rather than be another perennial loser in war, she set her sights on becoming a nation builder. She just needed advisors that shared her vision. The high families had been easy enough to sway. Promises of financial windfall—buyers for their ships, lumber, wine, cattle, fine art, and other goods—brought them in line.

Her advisors, however, lacked imagination. They had been so focused on war and nipping at the border of the Empire that they found themselves slow to tack into new winds.

"Work on Gacheau and Andol. Pull in representatives from all regions to ensure their interests are accounted for. We row in one direction as a nation now. We have resources; we have goods. And we can enrich our nation by doing what all the other prosperous nations do."

A low rumble of caution among her advisors made her groan under her breath. Austol spoke up again. It seemed he was their chosen sacrificial lamb.

"Our military leaders are not pleased with this drastic new course."

"Then perhaps they should have won a *fucking* war," Suvi growled. The faces on her advisors drained of color. She made a note to speak to the military leaders and see which ones could be brought to heel and which ones to cull. "We don't beat the Areshi Empire through war, we rival it. We surpass it and create a nation that becomes a beacon to the world in arts, magick, science, and culture. And should our vaunted military leaders have an issue with ceasing to march our countrymen and women into the Empire to have them die, then I will deal with them."

Austol cleared his throat but nodded. "Majesty."

"Oh, and regarding Frosland: draw up an alliance proposal as if they are independent. Focus on our food stores and lumber and their ships, both naval and merchant." The men and women nodded, their eyes trained on her, waiting on her every word. "Dismissed."

The advisors bowed and hurried out of the room.

Suvi heaved a loud sigh.

"They are excruciatingly dull sometimes," Matthys remarked.

"I am not asking them to raise the dead, merely draw up trade proposals, identify needs on both sides, nominate ambassadors, maybe suggest a yearly state dinner... what is so *fucking* difficult in considering a different, more prosperous future for this country?"

Matthys smiled up at her. "They like to watch your commanders move their little soldier pieces around the board. They get to share an opinion that carries no weight, then go back to drinking your wine. Advisors are the very worst of the intellectual class—expert in no one thing and adept enough at talking in circles so that they seem smart."

"And that is why you are my most prized advisor, dear brother," Suvi smirked.

He stuck his tongue out at her, childish for a man of forty-nine, though he looked in his mid-twenties, thanks to the gift of longevity magick in their bloodline. She often marveled how the magick slowed their physical aging, keeping them both looking like mirror images of one another despite the three-year age gap, Matthys's blond hair and pale green eyes matching her own.

"Why are you eyeing Frosland, dear sister? You would poke the Imperial bear in its ass?"

Suvi shifted in her throne. "Rumblings of discontent on both sides. Frosland has been kept at arm's length. Not given any true power. That will have to change soon, or they may pull out of the Empire. Ker Devitt lacks the patience of his forebearers. Good for him."

"They would be an impressive ally. Their shipbuilding alone would help turn us into a seafaring nation with the ports to draw trade."

Smiling, Suvi nodded. "You are far smarter than you look. I'm tempted to drown every last advisor and install you as my one and only."

"My first bit of advice would be to do no such thing. The paperwork alone would drive me to my death. *Blech*."

Typical of Matthys. Smart but lazy. If she didn't love him, and only him, she would have kicked him out of the palace decades ago.

He went on, "You know, I wonder what our father would say about your nation-building desires. He'd view this as a betrayal, turning your back on our family grudge against the Areshi Empire."

"Our father was a fool," Suvi said, bitterness nipping at her heart. "He's nothing now but a pale collection of bones lying in an unceremonious grave in a land this family spent centuries obsessing over. You and I will die one day, though hopefully not for a couple hundred years, and I want our family to have a new legacy. Our ancestors wasted the gift of longevity, suffering brutal deaths at the edge of a blade. I want to die of old age in my bed having built an empire without spilling a drop of blood."

The dubious look on Matthys's face gave Suvi pause. She stroked the hilt of her family's dagger with a smirk. "Well, not our own blood."

The doors to the throne room swung open, and a man hurried in, a small gray piece of paper in his hand. He bowed before hopping up the steps to the throne to hand it to her.

"Interesting news out of Ocean's Rest, Majesty," the man said before hurrying back down the steps and out of the room.

Suvi unfolded the paper and scanned it, the breath leaving her. *Impossible*.

"Dear brother, you will never imagine what our spies have learned."

Matthys turned his eyes to her.

"Come, let's retire to the dining room for some coffee, and I will tell you about a most extraordinary thing—Cursed Gods have returned."

HIDEAWAY

Nyssa scanned the ocean horizon, frowning. Were they even in the right place? "What am I looking for?"

"We're almost there," Elias said as Nyssa, Quinn, and Fontaine waited with him on the quarterdeck.

"Where? There's nothing but water as far as I can see." The sea stretched out before them, sunlight dancing on its surface, the day about as perfect and calm as one could ask for.

"Just wait, godling," Fontaine replied with a tinge of pride in her voice.

A moment later, all the hair on Nyssa's arms pricked up, a large and powerful presence bearing down on her. She took a step back, alarmed.

Quinn gasped. "What is that?"

Fontaine laughed. "That's the veil. I suspect you two can sense magick passively if it's powerful enough. That's *my* magick you feel."

"It's amazing," Quinn said, smiling.

"Yes it is."

Nyssa's skin buzzed, the sensation of the veil vibrating deep in her body, as if it sang to her. "This'll take some getting used to."

A wall of shimmering air, sparkling with gold and white flecks, rushed towards them as the Whisper pierced the veil. Its energy slipped over Nyssa, filling her with an intense, warm buzz.

Suddenly, an island twinkled into view out of nowhere, covered in lush green firs and bamboo trees. A deep cove was scooped out of the middle of the land mass that was at least big enough to hold the Whisper and five more ships with plenty of room to spare. In the back of the cove, a long dock stretched out into the water, extending from a one-story wooden house. A small rowboat was moored to it, bobbing gently on the water.

Nyssa's jaw dropped. "Shit, you hid a whole island?"

Fontaine beamed. "Yes. Took me months to weave the invisibility enchantment. This is Monk's Cove."

"Consider me completely fuckin' impressed. And here I thought changing from a chicken to woman was a feat."

"I'm rather talented," mused Fontaine with a shrug.

A welcome, elusive sense of peace fell upon Nyssa. Here, they could be safe. For a time, anyway.

"Welcome to my home," Fontaine said. "I hope you like to fish."

Nyssa hefted heavy burlap bags, one on each shoulder, thankful for the muscles her Ithais-Toru training had developed. Elias barked orders while the crew hauled bag after bag of rice, beans, flour, sugar, and other dry goods into Fontaine's house by her and the crew. They also raided Buck's galley, finding enough fresh food imbued with preservative enchantments to give them plenty of culinary choices when rice and fish grew tiresome.

Yuha made a show of carrying the heaviest items, smirking at Nyssa as if they were in some unspoken contest of strength—one Nyssa could never win. Yuha was a rare specimen of a woman and not one lick of magick augmented her strength.

Fontaine had gathered far more supplies than they could use in six months' time, but the security of having enough of everything made the isolation worth it. Footlockers of clothes had been packed for the three of them, along with soaps, linens, a crate of chickens, and other sundry items to last them six months until Elias returned to resupply them. They couldn't risk more visits than that.

Fontaine had insisted on more tins of tea and coffee than Elias felt necessary, but she crossed her arms and stood her ground. "You stockpile supplies like a squirrel and we have far more than we could ever need on this ship." Elias groused, but acquiesced. It didn't seem he had much of a mind to deny her anything she asked for, but he loved to make a show of sparring with his quartermaster.

Fontaine put everyone to work cleaning up the house, opening the doors and windows to let in light and fresh air. Nyssa fell in love with Fontaine's home instantly—it reminded her of the Emerald Order and its many sprawling buildings constructed out of wood, bamboo, and stone, with light-gray slate tiles adorning the roof. Its wrap-around porch with its view of the water would be a lovely place to rest with a cup of tea and a book.

The inside of the house was as simple as the outside—the interior walls made of thick, opaque paper that light seemed to suffuse through. The main area of the house was one big room and Nyssa wandered about eyeing the decor, circling from kitchen, dining room, and its spacious living area. There were no chairs, only cushions to sit on, which seemed to fit Fontaine's casual nature. The large, square dining table sat low to the floor, dark whorls mixing with the lighter oak grain, roughly hewn and beautiful.

Bookshelves lined the walls next to a fireplace, stuffed full with enough texts to keep Nyssa busy for years.

The bedrooms, tucked in the back of the house behind painted bamboo doors, were simple and adjoined by modest bathrooms with soaking tubs. Low platform beds sat atop bamboo mats, with wooden chests and shelves lining two walls. Nyssa took in a deep breath and dropped her rucksack on her bed, happy to finally sleep on something larger than the Whisper's narrow bunks.

She reached inside her jacket, unzipped its waterproof pocket, and pulled out a small notebook. Flipping through it, she passed poems—some complete, some woefully needing work, and others scratched through—and came to the chromoimage of her and Eron, taken on the night he promoted her to Ashcloak. An occasion equal parts sweet and bitter. She propped the chromoimage on a shelf, Eron's beaming smile warming her before she slipped the book back in her jacket.

Nyssa helped Quinn make up the beds and stock their bathrooms with towels, soaps, and bath oils. Fontaine had insisted on raiding all the luxury items on the Whisper, knowing that Elias and crew could easily restock in port, and Nyssa didn't mind one bit. Living in solitude didn't need to mean living without a little extravagance. When the two women finished and rejoined Fontaine and the others in the living room, Fontaine put her hands on her hips, eyeing Nyssa and Quinn.

"Now, house rules," she said. "We are not at your guilds. You do not have cooks or servants to do your laundry or pick up after you. Clean up after yourselves. We will be up at a reasonable hour every day for your instruction. I will not, as a rule, be delicate with either of you. Especially you, Nyssa. A lifetime of no magick leaves you without a compass. You have a lot of time to make up for." She gestured toward the kitchen. "Now, do either of you even know how to cook rice?"

Nyssa and Quinn shook their heads in unison. Fontaine sighed, drawing a chuckle out of Elias. She turned and glared at him.

"Hey, you volunteered to instruct these two," he said. "Little did you know it also meant showing them how to cook rice and boil eggs."

"Speaking of which, we have a coop for the chickens we brought. Jerrin is cleaning it out. You two will be in charge of feeding the chickens every day, gathering eggs, cleaning the coop out, and when it comes to it, slaughtering a chicken for dinner," Fontaine said.

"Easy enough." Nyssa smiled, cautiously hopeful. The last couple of weeks had been a whirlwind, and Nyssa tried to hide it, but she was exhausted. Life on Monk's Cove would be a good respite for her and Quinn. And a chance to understand who—and what—they were.

Dusk settled on the island by the time Elias, Jerrin, and the others gathered at the tender to return to Hannah's Whisper and sail to Jejin. The chill in the air made Nyssa shiver.

"You three ladies have a good time!" Jerrin said cheerfully. Nyssa wondered if he had any idea what they were in for.

Fontaine gave Elias a long hug and kissed him on the cheek. "We will see each other again in no time, old friend."

"Nevertheless, I will miss you," he murmured into the top of her head. "You have a messenger bowl, so tell me about your chicks and sign your communications with *Chicken* and I'll know it's you."

Elias let Fontaine go and hugged Quinn, who seemed dubious but tentatively hugged him back. "You're warming up to me, I see." He chuckled, turning to Nyssa, and embracing her. "You two have been on quite an adventure, Blacksea. You'll be in good hands with Fontaine. I will see you in the fall," Elias said as he let go of Nyssa. She gave him a light kiss on the cheek, and he pulled away, putting his hand over his chest, his golden eyes twinkling.

"That will sustain me until I see you again, love. Look after one another," he called out as he got into the tender and shoved off from the dock.

They waved and watched them sail off to the Whisper. Fontaine sighed and clapped her hands once. "Well, it's just the three of us now. Since you two are utterly useless in the kitchen, I will go get dinner started. Coming?"

Quinn looked at the two of them. "Can I lie down on the dock and watch the stars come out?"

Fontaine laughed. "Sweet thing, you're free to do whatever you want."

"Then that's what I'm going to do," Quinn replied, a small smile creeping onto her face.

Fontaine took her leave to return to the house. Quinn sat down on the dock and lay back, lacing her fingers behind her head and smiling up at the sky, humming lightly under her breath.

"Are you going to hover over me or sit down?" she asked.

Nyssa cleared her throat and sat next to her. During their time on the Whisper, traveling to Monk's Cove, she hadn't made much progress with figuring Quinn out. Even after everything they had been through, the woman kept a carefully constructed wall around herself, offering very little insight into her deeper thoughts.

There were times she did open up a bit, but then quickly retreated behind a smile and silence. She was good for a sarcastic barb but closed down when things got more personal, or when Nyssa asked about her past at the Citadel. She must have learned very early on to keep to herself and to form a protective shell.

That reclusive part of Quinn reminded Nyssa of herself growing up at the Emerald Order. Her peers were relentless, always seeking her out to poke and prod at her simply because she had no magick. Reaching out for friendship only got her hand slapped—or worse—and she had closed herself off until Athen arrived. Even then it took months for him to break down her walls.

Nyssa hoped that Quinn would eventually trust her and open up, perhaps share more of her time growing up. *Forever entwined* didn't seem like a mere suggestion from the lore of the Cursed Gods. They were inextricably connected now, for good or ill.

Quinn cleared her throat. "Nyssa, are we friends?"

Nyssa perked up an eyebrow, curious. "That's a strange question."

"Do you realize I have no idea what a friendship looks like?"

"It looks and feels a little something like this—or the beginnings of it, at least," Nyssa replied, waving a finger between the two of them.

Quinn sat up and looked away. "People taking any interest in me for reasons other than my magick is...uncharted territory."

Nyssa grimaced. "Is that a nautical pun?"

Laughter burst from Quinn, startling Nyssa, but the woman's unguarded smile was a welcome sight. "Oh gods, I didn't mean it to be."

Nyssa sighed, happy to see Quinn more comfortable with sharing her thoughts. She stretched and popped her back. "You know, I could use a friend. It seems I'm a little low on those."

Quinn chuckled and picked at a splinter on the dock. "Isn't this an odd conversation? After everything we've been through, we're finally trying to establish a friendship?"

Nyssa shrugged. Whatever she felt for Quinn was starting to creep beyond friendship. The spark of attraction she experienced back at Ocean's Rest was simmering into something rather distracting, no matter how hard she tried to will it away.

And it was *concerning*. She needed to hold that part of herself back. The last thing Nyssa wanted was to inject her confused feelings into whatever tentative friendship was blooming. Worse yet, run into unreciprocated feelings.

"I don't think anything about this is conventional. We're both far off our paths. I should be in Ocean's Rest leading its Emerald Order division, doing my best to protect the city," she remarked.

"And I should be dead," Quinn reminded her with a frown.

"Yeah, well, I'm glad you're not."

"I concur."

Quinn regarded Nyssa for a moment.

A ripple of nervousness ran through Nyssa, weird and unexpected. She *wanted* Quinn to like her.

"I would be amenable to exploring a friendship," Quinn finally said. "It occurs to me that we're both...not great with people."

Nyssa furrowed her brow. "I don't know where you get the impression I'm not great with people."

Quinn started to tick off on her hand the confrontations they had in the short time they knew each other. "You tried capturing me twice, succeeding once. You stopped me from escaping twice, rather rudely, I may add. Oh, wait, then there was your capturing me—at the mill—if we can call it that."

The damn self-satisfied smirk that settled on Quinn's face...the woman was maddening.

"You introduced yourself to me with a punch, Quinn! And you called me an 'ignorant brute,' as I recall. Oh, hey, you also stabbed me in the leg!"

"You were chasing me, and I didn't know if you meant to kill me!" Quinn retorted, amusement in her voice. "Did you want an engraved invitation to afternoon tea instead? Next time, don't sneak up on me in the middle of the night!"

Nyssa huffed. "You want to talk about questionable people skills? You were penniless and tried to bribe a pirate!"

Quinn smiled sheepishly and scratched the back of her head. "Yeah, not my smartest moment."

"At the time, it was funny as fuck."

"I was so mad at you for laughing at me, but just thankful—" Quinn cleared her throat.

Not about to let it go, Nyssa prodded. "Thankful for what?"

"That your ignorant brute ass wasn't dead."

Quinn flashed Nyssa a smile, a genuine smile, and it made her heart flutter. She willed herself to not blush. It didn't work. Heat crept up the back of her neck. *Dammit*. She swallowed and turned her eyes to the sky.

"The stars are starting to come out," she said.

Quinn lay back down. "It's beautiful."

The sky stretched above them, an endless growing darkness punctuated by small, dazzling points of light. There, in that moment, Nyssa felt worlds away from the danger they faced. Worlds away from her old life and everything she cherished. A chill wind kicked up, carrying the scent of winter orchids and juniper from Quinn's hair.

"Yeah, beautiful," Nyssa sighed as the stars began to twinkle overhead.

THE JUSTICIAR AND THE EMPATH

Medias focused on the open door of the empath's office. Was it meant to be an invitation? She tugged on the bottom of her jacket and lifted her chin, wanting her posture to reflect her position. It had only been five days since she took up residence in Ocean's Keep, and at every turn, Reece Ae'Shen had her eyes cast in the Justiciar's direction. Watching.

It was *highly* annoying.

Yet something about her intrigued Medias. Her stare never wavered when Medias met her gaze, a fearlessness present at every distanced encounter. Unfortunately, Medias needed the damn empath. Keeping Aryis, Athen, Reece, and Lilliana safe meant sharing information, and the empath seemed the proper path to do that. And pretending to look for Quinn and Nyssa by spying on Ocean's Rest would take skill. Failure to find them would draw suspicion.

Plausible failure, however, if experienced by a number of different Imperial agents, may not only keep Quinn and Nyssa safe, but her own ruse a secret from Anelos. Working with Reece and utilizing Lilliana's notorious network of spies could plant believable lies and send Imperial forces down promising-looking dead ends.

Pitching the idea to Reece, however, proved a daunting task.

No. Not daunting. Medias refused to be intimidated by the slight woman or her dark, watchful eyes.

One more tug at her jacket, and she moved forward, crossing the wide hall and stepping into Reece's office doorway. She waited for the empath to take notice. Reece was head down, pencil on paper, mumbling to herself.

Odd.

"Talking to yourself, empath?"

Reece flinched, her eyes flying up to Medias. "Goddammit," she grumbled. "No, I was talking to my plants."

The empath gestured to a small succulent on her desk before she dropped her pencil and shoved the papers aside. Medias smirked at the dramatic display. Lining the windowsill behind Reece was a collection of plants, their green, blueish purple, and dark orange leaves adding vibrancy to an already...interesting office.

"You talk to your plants?" she asked, taking a step inside the office, not waiting for an invitation. Reece's jawline tensed.

"They actually listen and rarely talk back. Now, what do you want?"

Medias wandered over to Reece's bookshelves, admiring the small sculptures, paintings, and knickknacks dotting the empty spaces between massive lines of books—some stacked on top of others, haphazard and crooked. She let out a low, annoyed hum at the disarray. Reece stood and closed her office door.

"Your library is a disorganized mess." Medias turned to face Reece, who approached her, getting far too close.

"My books are not disorganized, you simply don't know how I choose to order them," Reece said. "Again, what do you want? Do you have news of Nyssa and Quinn?"

After the failure of the Sea Viper, the Rule adepts on board had limped back to the capital, Nyssa and Quinn and their pirate friends proving far more difficult to capture or kill than any had expected. When Medias heard of the Rule's failure, a small spark of pride flared for the fledgling gods, proving her faith in them well-placed.

For now.

"I came to propose a working arrangement. A way of keeping you and your friends safe while hopefully keeping Nyssa and Quinn out of harm's way as well," Medias said.

Reece crossed her arms. "I don't work with Justiciars. Not of my own free will, anyway. Why are you even doing any of this? Nyssa and Quinn mean nothing to you."

Medias chewed the inside of her bottom lip before catching herself—an old nervous habit from when she was a girl. She had no desire to explain how her father believed she and Nyssa and Quinn were tied together by fate. Her private life, especially her family, was off-limits.

"I don't wish to have an adversarial relationship. Working together makes sense."

Reece frowned and stepped closer, the subtle scent of lavender gently wrapping itself around Medias. "You Justiciars tortured me. Forced me to find Nyssa and Quinn like I was a hunting dog. Do you know what that felt like? Days of being under Elken's control, feeling every emotion, not being able to quiet the world...you watched as he..." Reece shook her head, "...hurt me. And it was *you* who told him about my connection to Nyssa. You used me to find her."

Reece's alabaster skin flushed red, her eyes piercing. Medias met her gaze.

"And now Elken lies dead, rotting in a grave. Does that give you comfort?" she asked, not the least bit sad at his demise.

Reece stepped back and turned away. "It doesn't erase the pain he put me through."

Medias scowled and leaned back on the bookcase. This conversation was not going well. "I can't change the past, but I'm here as an ally."

Reece turned back. "As long as you wear that mask, you are like the rest of them, Medias. Cold. Ruthless."

The implication that she was like Elken was galling. "You don't know me, empath."

"I don't need to know you. You're a Justiciar. Imperial law and order incarnate. A puppet on a string, serving only the Empress, indifferent to those of us beneath you," Reece replied, setting her jaw and raising her head, her dark eyes full of disdain. "I don't trust you. I'll put up with you while you're here in the Keep, but we're not allies. If you step one inch out of line, I'll spill your little seer secret. I have no problem watching a Justiciar twist in the wind."

Hot anger stirred in Medias's chest. Reece's threat was explicit. Bold. The consequences of Medias's choices suddenly collided with her reality. Not only had she turned her back on the Empire and would have to keep up a daring lie, but she had no allies among those she pledged herself to protect.

Not only did they distrust her, they would gladly watch her die.

Medias pushed past Reece and left her office, fighting the urge to slam the door behind her.

THE SHADOW GOD

Quinn poked at the red web of magick that hung in the air—a simple ward woven in a few seconds by Fontaine. A buzz of magick tingled under her fingers, alive and thrilling, drawing a soft gasp through her lips.

Fontaine chuckled at Quinn's reaction. Their instruction had officially begun.

Fontaine had given them a day to relax before their instruction began in earnest, and Quinn and Nyssa had used the time to explore the narrow trails that veined through the lush forest, dotted here and there by squat stone sculptures of lions with the heads of snakes or pudgy six-armed forest gods, carved long ago and worn by time. The trails crossed a small stream with snapping turtles and bright orange-and-yellow fish swimming beneath its pristine waters.

A ruined temple lay in the middle of the island, once a place of meditation and study for long-dead monks, its crumbling green-gray walls now overrun with ivy. The roof was completely missing, and the clouds drifted lazily overhead. Despite the decay, there was an eerie serenity to the temple, its dust motes catching the rays of light and making the air dance.

More stone sculptures graced the interior of the temple, and many of them were as tall as Nyssa. They had fared no better than the building itself, many completely wrapped in foliage.

Quinn had spent some time removing the vines—the deities and spirits of the past deserved a little attention and dignity. They may be long forgotten, but they possessed a haunting beauty that she found needed to be revealed once more, even if just to her.

Now, Quinn and Nyssa sat cross-legged in a clearing near Fontaine's house, rimmed on each side by tall, swaying bamboo. The space, paved with flat gray stones, was quiet and tranquil. A chill wind brushed Quinn's hair to the side, but it carried a scent of greenery, of renewal. The island was on the cusp of spring.

"We're going to start by exploring the nature of your magick," Fontaine said, sitting opposite the two women. "You two are corporeal mages—your magick is fixed." She eyed Nyssa. "You can call forth lightning and manipulate it as your imagination allows, but your magick is fixed. You wouldn't be able to suddenly toss fireballs around like Elias. Nor do you have ethereal magick, so no spellweaving for you."

Nyssa sighed. "I may have skipped the practical magick instruction at the Emerald Order, but I know at least the difference between corporeal and ethereal magick."

"You had about as much use for magick classes as a snake needing a ladder, but I'm glad you know the basics. So, unlike the two of you, I can weave enchantments as an ethereal mage."

"Like Ceril," Quinn said, her stomach churning as his name departed from her lips. Was Fontaine more powerful than him? She had to be, as an Old Folk who had lived for centuries or more.

"Yes, like Ceril. But unlike him, I have access to Ancient Magick. As do you two." Fontaine replied. "Neither of you were likely taught much about it at all at your guilds. Ancient magick exists close to the very essence of life, the river of existence. It's powerful, but chaotic and dangerous. And rare. It runs deep throughout our world and the others."

"Our world and...the others?" Nyssa asked. "You mean the realms?"

"Yes. Those are a manifestation of ancient magick, as are the Ancient Gods within them."

Quinn ran her hands along her thighs, her palms damp despite the chilly breeze. "Whatever I was taught about the realms and ancient magick was cursory at best. How do we have this ancient magick inside of us? And why us?"

"Well, that's the big, vexing question, isn't it? Ancient magick waxes and wanes in our world. Ever since the last of the Cursed Gods died off, ancient magick has receded, but it's sprouting again in this realm. Faster than I've seen in previous cycles."

Previous cycles? Just how old is Fontaine?

"Your existence is the sign of its resurgence, but I've felt it for a few years now. But I've never felt magick like what's inside the two of you. How or why you are now Cursed Gods is a mystery to me." Fontaine poked the floating ward in front of her. "What you two can do...is unrivaled. This ward I created is simple, everyday magick. Quinn, your ability to destroy the fabric of magick itself is a spectacular gift."

"Is it?" she asked.

Fontaine cocked an eyebrow. "I've lived a very long time, and I've never heard of anyone possessing the power to affect magick. Before you manifested this power, your previous ability was merely a suppressant, like throwing a blanket over a light orb. You can extinguish the light itself now. You're extraordinary."

Quinn cleared her throat, heat rising in her cheeks. Compliments knocked her off-kilter.

"And from what I've seen of your abilities, Nyssa, you can manipulate magick. Again, unheard of as far as I know. And I've been around awhile."

"What about the Old Folk?" Nyssa asked.

"We possess some ancient magick and can use it in different forms or fashion. The Old Folk's ability to change forms is part of it, and it's taxing as hell. I make it look good," Fontaine said with a chuckle, running her hands through her hair. "And I can weave spells that utilize that ancient power."

Quinn prodded a bit more. "If you have the same type of magick as we do, then why aren't you considered gods?"

"We're merely touched by it. You two are nothing but *pure* ancient magick."

Quinn rubbed the back of her neck. Her guild had been woefully lax in covering ancient magick—likely because it was largely gone from the world.

Fontaine poked her ward again. It bowed slightly before snapping back taut. "Destroy my ward without touching it," she instructed.

Exhaling, Quinn licked her lips and held her hand up. When she brought her magick forth, dark, wispy tendrils weaved around her fingers, like the blackest smoke she had ever seen, and shadows wafted off of her skin. She sent the tendrils out, forcing them into the ward. Energy coursed through the enchantment, pulsing through Quinn's hand and arm.

Licking her lips, she stared at the ward and imagined extinguishing its magick like dousing a flame. The web's red threads dimmed.

"Concentrate. You're weakening the ward, but I want to see if you can negate it completely."

Quinn focused on quelling the ward's magick with her own. The red web flickered once before it dissipated, a small crackle of dying magick the only record of its existence.

Fontaine clapped her hands. "Amazing! Let's do that again, but with a stronger ward."

For close to an hour, Fontaine wove bigger, stronger, more powerful wards, some taking over five minutes to weave, and Quinn destroyed each one, though the effort became more and more difficult, until she couldn't completely destroy the last one, its magick pulsing bright and purple. It held fast under the force of her magick, though it did give way a little.

"Touch it, then. See if that does the trick," Fontaine requested.

Tentatively, Quinn reached out and pushed her hand against the barrier, her shadow flowing like water out of her hand. Touching the ward was a completely different experience. Its power resonated throughout her body and it was as if she *understood* its structure and composition and how to deconstruct it—not bit by bit, but with one fell swoop, like if throwing a bucket of water on a candle.

She dissolved the ward. It was so easy. Too easy. She pulled her magick back and relaxed.

"Not to sound immodest, but I am quite a talented ethereal mage. I can weave very complex, powerful spells. I can't weave a ward more powerful than the one you just negated." Fontaine seemed pleased, giving Quinn a nod. "Your physical touch will always be more powerful than your ranged magick. Be aware of that and adjust."

Quinn hesitated. "Is that why I was able to extinguish a Justiciar's life when I lay my hand on him?"

"Yes. There is no more complex magick in the world than that which lives inside our souls."

She swallowed hard at the awful memory. "I didn't mean to, though...it just happened."

"You saved my life," Nyssa said. "Don't punish yourself for it."

The way Nyssa looked at her, her gaze earnest and unwavering, made Quinn hold her breath. All her life, Quinn had to build herself into someone strong and resilient, a woman that could withstand the blows inflicted on her. And with a single look, Nyssa could wobble her.

How? *Why*?

Thankfully, Nyssa turned her attention back to Fontaine and Quinn could breathe again.

"Aryis once explained to me that truly talented ethereal mages are few and far between," Nyssa said. "She likened it to the ability to sing—everyone can sing, but only a few people have truly transcendent voices."

Fontaine smiled. "Ah yes. I have heard your singing voice, so I know you're well versed in the concept of ability without talent."

Quinn couldn't help but chuckle. But it was true. Nyssa's singing voice was atrocious. Though tempting, Quinn made no mention of it.

"Weaving spells takes a mix of factors—inherent power, talent, and the difficulty of spell. I am a powerful spellweaver, but there are still spells even I cannot touch."

"The ability to create wraiths...what type of power does that take?" Nyssa asked.

"A fairly powerful mage can do it, though you both know that sort of magick has been banned. Blood, bone, flesh, and death magicks all fall within what the world has categorized as forbidden magick. A nice, simple semantic trick to make it all seem destructive and evil, but the 'good' parts of forbidden magick are still in wide use, though everyone just glosses over that fact. How do you think healing disks work? With blood and flesh magick. Now, it's just called *healing magick* to make it more palatable."

Quinn stared down at her hands, marred by small scars—remnants of the cuts and burns from the wards on the most dangerous spell books in the Citadel that Ceril made her access for him. All full of forbidden enchantments.

"Now, Quinn, your shadow seems to be a conduit for your ability to destroy magick, but you've used it alone as a weapon. I want to explore that," Fontaine said. "Pull your shadow forth and wrap it around my hand."

Dark wisps cascaded off of Quinn's hands as she activated her magick once again. She concentrated, giving form and function to the smoky substance, pulling it forth from her body and twisting it around Fontaine's hand.

Fontaine laughed. "I can feel it, like hands around my wrist. It's cold. I didn't expect that."

"It is?" Nyssa asked, not hesitating to put her hand into the darkness. "Ah! That's amazing."

"*Amazing*? This power is *destructive*," Quinn objected.

Fontaine clucked her tongue. "It's what you make of it, Quinn. Don't assign negative traits to a magick we don't even understand yet. Concentrate and think about moving my arm with the strands of darkness."

Doing so was surprisingly easy, the tendrils like an extension of her body. Fontaine's face lit up as Quinn moved her arm back and forth.

"Now, move it *through* my hand. I want to see what it feels like."

"I don't know if that's a good idea."

"You killed a Rule adept with it. I want to understand how you did it."

Quinn frowned. "I...I just did it."

"Well, do it without hurting me."

Quinn carefully pushed the shadow through Fontaine's hand.

"I can feel it moving through me, not just the cold, but the darkness itself," Fontaine said.

"Are you okay?" Nyssa asked.

"Yes. An odd sensation, but not unpleasant. Now pull it back, Quinn."

Quinn did as she was told.

Fontaine hissed and clenched her fist. She opened her hand to reveal a bloody palm.

"Oh no." Quinn's heart dropped.

"Extraordinary!" Fontaine said, staring at the blood.

"I hurt you."

"My dear girl, that was an accident because you lost focus when you retracted the shadow, but I felt your magick, like shards of glass that cut my hand."

Quinn's shoulders bowed and she felt like a massive asshole. "I'm sorry...I..."

Holding her hand up, Fontaine said, "The wound is shallow, and we have bandages. You are being far too hard on yourself. If I gave you a cello and asked you to play a master solo, could you do it the first few times you drew a bow across a string?"

Nyssa gave Quinn a light punch on the arm. "You did good, Freckles." Her sincerity and bright smile somehow made Quinn feel better.

"Nyssa is right. You did *very* well. Your darkness seems to have different properties, depending on what you put your mind to. Harmless if you wish it to be, dangerous if you need it to be," Fontaine said. "We will continue to explore and hone your control."

Fontaine was too gracious, but her kindness was a comforting balm that Quinn needed desperately in her life. Conceding a smile, she said, "Thank you."

A fly buzzed around Fontaine, and she caught it mid-flight, popped it into her mouth, and swallowed.

Quinn gasped.

"Yuck," Fontaine said, her face contorting as she stuck her tongue out. "Old chicken habits."

Laughter exploded out of Nyssa. She flopped onto her back and shook, tears springing to her eyes, and wrapped her arms around her stomach. Quinn couldn't help but exhale a chuckle at seeing Nyssa so unbridled.

Fontaine cleared her throat. "Do not think you can distract me from exploring your magick now, Nyssa."

The laughing ceased, and Nyssa mumbled, "Fuck."

THE STORM GOD

Nyssa swallowed as a simple ward sprang to life.

Fontaine turned on a smile. "Now, let's see what you can do."

Nyssa tapped her finger on her thigh. She'd rather practice the hardest form of Ithais-Toru until she dropped from exhaustion.

"Close your eyes and feel your magick inside of you. Pulling it forward and using it is a matter of will."

Quinn spoke up. "Remember, Reece told you to use what you learned at the Emerald Order about concentrating and centering yourself. She was right."

Nyssa rubbed the back of her neck and sighed harder than she would have liked, but she couldn't ignore her melancholy at the mention of Reece, a lingering affection that still stung even as Nyssa's heart had moved on.

"I'm sorry," Quinn said, "I didn't mean to bring her up. That—that was inconsiderate of me."

"No, it's okay. I'm fine. She and I..." Nyssa's shoulders dropped, her heart heavy. How she missed those she left behind in Ocean's Rest—they were all the family she had, especially Athen. "We're not...together. Not anymore. But Reece was right. My training is an excellent place to start."

She closed her eyes and concentrated, turning inward. Meditating, calming her body and mind, was something she had done countless times. Never had Nyssa imagined she'd use the discipline she learned through Ithais-Toru to control magick, but she intended to try. She owed it to Fontaine. And Quinn.

Nyssa exhaled and pushed the world away, listening only to her breathing, and dove into herself. Before where there was nothing, now a ball of blue light pulsed in the middle of her chest. In her mind's eye, she imagined letting it expand, freeing it from its tight core.

Magick exploded across Nyssa's skin, and Quinn yelped beside her as lightning sparked in the air between them.

"Did I hurt you?" she asked.

Quinn shook her head. "No. It feels...like a million bees vibrating under my hand," she said, holding her palm over Nyssa's arm, lightning arcing back and forth between them.

"It seems neither of you can use one aspect of your magick without the rather dramatic and showy aspect manifesting physically as well. Quinn, your darkness accompanies your nullifying magick and Nyssa's lightning comes with...well, whatever Nyssa can do."

Whatever I can do.

Fontaine continued, "Nyssa, the ward, see if you can move it, like you did when you pushed those Justiciars back without touching them in Ocean's Rest."

Nyssa narrowed her eyes and focused on the ward, its red tendrils pulsing rhythmically. With the Justiciars in Ocean's Rest, she had seen the nexus of their magick glowing as if she could see inside of their chests. And she remembered wanting to get them away from Quinn as they stood over her, threatening to kill her.

Nyssa held her hand out and imagined pushing the ward with her power. She felt stupid trying to do something that—

A wave of crackling blue energy shot from her hand, and the ward bowed outward toward Fontaine and snapped back into place. Nyssa gasped.

"Marvelous! Your lightning is a conduit for your magick, just like Quinn's shadow," Fontaine said. "Hmm...if you can push the magick, so to speak, you might be able to do more. Try something different."

Nyssa scowled. "Like what?"

"Anything!"

"That's so vague. I thought you were supposed to be good at this."

Fontaine scoffed. "What gave you that idea?"

"You volunteered to teach us!"

Fontaine leaned back and braced her hands behind her, shrugging. "Who else was going to do it? We're in new territory here, so a little experimentation is necessary. Now, do as I say and try something different, Nyssa!"

Fucking Fontaine...

Nyssa gritted her teeth and stared at the ward, imagining twisting it up until it's nothing but a tangled mess.

And that's exactly what happened.

Blue lightning surrounded the ward, and it bunched into a little ball, the ends of the web fraying and shuddering until the ward spasmed and imploded with a hiss. The three women stared at the empty space where the ward had been.

"Oh my," Fontaine whispered. She quickly sat up and spoke in a language Nyssa didn't recognize, her fingers moving like she was plucking at the strings of a harp. Another ward shimmered into view, this one a dark green.

"Again," Fontaine instructed. "But move the pieces of it around if you can. Focus on precision."

Nyssa nodded and concentrated, lightning floating across her skin like gossamer threads.

One by one, Nyssa pulled at the web-like structure of the ward, tugging gently until each strand fizzled out like the wick of a candle. Eventually, the ward became unstable, quivering in the air before imploding with inert pops of light.

"You can manipulate magick. Push and pull at it, alter and unravel it until you destroy the magick if you warp it too far." Fontaine beamed a smile at them and rubbed her hands together. "Both of you can affect the very fabric of magick itself. That's...unprecedented."

Nyssa had gone from magickless to a Cursed God in the span of a heartbeat back in Ocean's Rest. Now, she had power that she couldn't even fathom. She felt like a poor vessel for such a gift.

"Now, for just your lightning power—like Quinn's shadow, it's the conduit for you to manipulate magick, but let's see what else it can do. Try this: hold out your hand and create...create a little ball of lightning in your palm."

Nyssa didn't move. The lightning force inside of her made her shudder, remembering how easily she had used it to kill.

"Nyssa, I know this part scares you, but if you can't do as I ask, then we'll be wasting our time."

"If I punched you in the shoulder, would that help?" Quinn asked.

"Don't be a smart ass."

"Then do as Fontaine says."

"Oh, you're going to boss me around now?" Nyssa asked.

Quinn narrowed her eyes. "Fontaine volunteered to help us, so let her help. We need your power against Suvi. And against whatever the Empire throws at us."

"Okay, okay." Nyssa held up her hand. Lightning danced across her skin effortlessly. All she needed to do was think of gathering it in her palm, right?

As she stared at her hand and imagined creating a little ball of energy, her magick responded, a small sparking ball of lightning forming in her palm. It was easier than she expected it to be.

"Now, toss it at me," Fontaine said, holding her hand out.

"Are you insane?"

"Focus. *Will* it to be harmless. Imagine it's just a little zap."

"I don't want to hurt you."

A cocked eyebrow was Fontaine's only response.

Nyssa closed her fingers around the ball of light, and it buzzed in her hand before she released it at Fontaine. It veered off the mark and hit Fontaine in the shoulder, who grimaced.

"Oh shit!"

Fontaine waved away Nyssa's concern. "It didn't hurt other than a little shock. Because you didn't want it to. Intention and will, Nyssa, that's the key to control! Though your aim could use a bit of work," she said with a wink. Popping up to her feet, she began pacing. "Each of you have two aspects of magick in you. Lightning and darkness, magick manipulation and negation. This is...amazing." Fontaine stopped and stared down at the two women, shaking her head and beaming a massive, brilliant smile.

Nyssa took it as a good sign and concentrated for a moment, willing her magick to calm. To her surprise, it worked. Small steps, but she would take each little victory. She rolled her shoulders, her body beginning to ache for rest. "We barely did anything and I'm already exhausted."

"Your magickal stamina will increase with time and practice. But today, that was enough." Fontaine swept around behind the women and kissed them on the tops of their heads. "You are extraordinary. Whatever twist of fate brought you into my orbit, I am truly thankful."

Fontaine marched off to the trail that led into the forest, stripping off pieces of clothing as she went.

"What the hell is she doing?" Nyssa breathed.

"I heard that, godling!" Fontaine called out, pausing to look back at them. "The trees are singing, and I'm going to dance. You two, make rice and catch some fish for lunch."

With that, Fontaine took off her bra and underwear, tossed them to the ground, and strode off into the bamboo and fir.

THE SHIMMER

Nyssa sat cross-legged on the dock facing Quinn. The last couple of weeks had been dedicated to testing and practicing their magick, Fontaine teasing it out of them. One of their warm-up exercises was sensing magick in the world, both in people—easy with only Quinn and Fontaine to concentrate on—and the ambient magick that floated around in the world.

That bit, the magick all around her, was a whole new, astounding experience.

When Nyssa first tried closing her eyes and opening up her senses, her surroundings came alive in ways she had never imagined before. The world was full of magick, beautiful and resonant, flowing all around her. The wind buzzed past her, the trees glowed with a calm presence, and the sea practically sang with magick, tugging at her, oftentimes drowning everything else out.

Except for Quinn's presence. Nothing ever drowned her out when she was near, her essence bright and breathtaking, a warm, glowing buzz that lived in the center of Nyssa's chest, like another soul nestled next to her own.

Nyssa was also learning how to discern the difference between common magick and ancient magick. Ancient magick was richer, more vibrant, and it resonated with a deep tone that reminded her of the calm expanse of the sea. When she concentrated, Nyssa could see the dark, sparkling purple in the center of Quinn's chest, electric like her own power, whirling around a core of golden light.

The colors of the world and within Quinn were breathtaking. Her whole life, Nyssa had lived in the dark, and now her vision was filled with a brilliance that made her pulse race.

Most mornings after breakfast, Fontaine had them work on sensing magick until it became easier and easier. She likened it to the forms of Ithais-Toru, creating a foundational discipline that would hone their control and concentration.

Fontaine sat nearby, watching over them as they sat quietly and let their magick flow, studying a spell book in a language Nyssa didn't recognize. It was a perfect morning for the exercise, warm and calm, and Nyssa eased into her meditative state, using techniques Eron had taught her to relax both her mind and body. She stretched her senses out and let the world's magick wash over her, becoming aware that she and Quinn were breathing in rhythm. The humming of the sea washed over her, its magick deep and all-encompassing.

It felt right. It felt like *home*.

Expanding her senses, Nyssa found Winter's Bite next to her, glowing faintly blue. When she first sensed her magick in her blade, she asked Quinn if she could sense it too. Fontaine had laughed and said, "Ancient magick leaches out of you. You've left your signature on your weapon."

Beyond Winter's Bite, beyond the dock and Quinn and Fontaine, Nyssa felt the forest, its trees glowing with magick and the flow of the breeze gently moving the bamboo and firs.

As Nyssa relaxed further, she became aware of another presence. Something she had never felt before—strange and exotic and massively powerful. It vibrated with pure ancient magick. The harder she tried to pin the sensation down, the stronger it pulsed, buzzing through her like an enveloping swarm of bees. Nyssa centered herself and pushed toward the magick.

It pushed back.

"Fuck!" Her eyes flew open.

Quinn gasped. "What was that?"

Fontaine snapped her spell book closed. "What? What did you encounter?"

"There's something...powerful, just beyond my reach. Definitely ancient magick. It felt like it was everywhere and nowhere all at once until I tried to pin it down," Nyssa said. "You sensed it too?"

Quinn nodded. "I felt you...moving. Though, not really moving but, shifting, maybe? I moved with you and whatever you found, I sensed it. It...pushed us back."

Looking to Fontaine, Nyssa held up her hands. "What the fuck was that?"

"If you sensed a great deal of ancient magick, I can only guess that you found the Shimmer—the boundary between the realms separating our world and the others that lie on top of our reality. Remember, ancient magick is rising again, and the are realms drawing closer. That you can find the boundary is...incredible."

Fontaine picked up her book and ran her fingers over the edge of the pages. "The realms are like these pages, one on top of the next."

"Have you ever been to another realm?" Quinn asked.

The crestfallen look on Fontaine's face bore the answer. "No. The Ancient Gods keep us out unless invited."

"Can we...get in?" Nyssa asked. The idea of it seemed crazy, but what if they found the boundary again and...pushed harder?

Fontaine leaned back on her hands and squinted in the morning sun. "Theoretically, I suppose it's possible? The Shimmer itself is magick, and both of you can affect magick, so...you could rip a little hole and pop into the Realms of Night or the Sky or the Deep...."

"Oh, just pop in?" Quinn asked, amused. "What would an Ancient God do if we stumbled into their world?"

"Truthfully? A number of possibilities. Kill you. Have a chat. Fuck you."

"W-what?" Nyssa asked.

"Libris, the two-faced god of the Realm of the Sky, is rumored to be extremely horny."

Nyssa huffed. "Interesting that you assume I was asking about the fucking instead of the killing."

Fontaine snorted. Fucking *snorted*.

"Oh, did I misjudge you, or are you not the one reading your way through my collection of erotic literature?"

Nyssa opened her mouth to deny it, but the blush on Quinn's face stopped her. *Well.* She'd leave it alone for now. "Would the Ancient Gods really hurt us?"

A seriousness fell over Fontaine that sent a chill through Nyssa. "I wish I knew. Generally, they don't interfere with our world, content to merely observe, I suppose. But I don't know for certain. I would avoid poking at the Shimmer. You could draw unwanted attention."

Unwanted attention? Shit.

"Noted," Quinn breathed.

Fontaine nudged them. "C'mon. Enough magick sensing. Today, we practice precision! Let's go see how many floating orbs you can shoot out of the air."

A RUSE

Athen cursed under his breath as Medias stepped inside Crae's Alehouse and scanned the room. He tensed, knowing he had to play his part perfectly to make sure Reece's plan worked. The patrons turned deadly silent in the Justiciar's presence. He put his beer down and eyed Yuha. She steeled her jaw. Medias moved toward their table, taking her time.

"What's this?" Medias asked, her eyes raking from Athen to Yuha, red gaze narrowing. "You're from the Whisper, aren't you? Tell me, you here to pass Athen information about Nyssa Blacksea and Quinn?"

Yuha kept her mouth shut.

He started, "We're just having a friendly—"

"You will be dealt with later, Fennick. If you weren't Lilliana's son, you would already be in a collar," Medias hissed. She looked back at Yuha. "Where are Nyssa and Quinn?"

Yuha remained silent as Medias moved closer.

"Stand up, woman." The order was delivered with an undercurrent of a threat—stand up *or else*.

Yuha rose to her feet, towering over Medias. Only a few inches shorter than Athen, the guard cut an impressive figure—tall, muscular, and imposing.

"I'm not an Imperial citizen. You can't push me around, Justiciar," Yuha said, her voice loud and steady. She took a step toward Medias.

"Shit," Athen whispered.

The flash of light came quick, and Yuha cried out, stumbling back into their table, sloshing their beers. Medias moved fast, wrapping her hand around Yuha's throat and forcing her head down onto the table. She held the big woman in place.

"I will ask you only one more time. Where are Nyssa and Quinn?"

Yuha grunted and grabbed Medias's wrist, trying to release the Justiciar's grip on her throat. A burst of light emanated from Medias's other hand, and Yuha screamed. Athen popped to his feet, earning a warning glare from Medias and a shake of her head. She turned her attention back to Yuha, who had tears streaming out of her eyes.

"Where are Nyssa and Quinn?"

Yuha grunted, her lips curled in a sneer. "They were on the Whisper. But after we got attacked, Elias dumped their asses in Port Golcana. He wants nothing to do with them."

Medias shook her head. "Then why have our Imperial agents been told differently by Elias himself when we caught up to him? He claims he left them off in Lishan."

"Because he wants you cunts wasting your time. Payback for attacking our ship in Unbound waters."

The Justiciar leaned back, easing up on Yuha's throat. Reaching into a jacket pocket, she pulled out a gold mark and tossed it on the pirate's chest. "Have a drink on the Empire for your cooperation."

Athen growled, "Show some goddamn respect."

If it were possible for the room to get any quieter, it did. No one spoke to a Justiciar like that. Athen braced for retribution.

Medias stepped away from Yuha and glared at him. She then turned to the rest of the bar. "Nyssa Blacksea and Quinn are enemies of the Areshi Empire. You would all do well to remember that I am the only one you need to come to with information pertaining to their whereabouts. Anyone found withholding information will answer to me. And it will be...unpleasant."

No one moved. Taking one last look around the alehouse, Medias slowly crossed to the door and left. The whole room let out one collective exhale, the tension finally easing. Athen helped Yuha sit back down, holding his hand up to Crae behind the bar to get a couple more beers.

"You okay?" he asked.

"Yeah, nothing another beer can't cure," she replied.

"I'm sorry about that, but he had to make sure it was convincing."

"Think that was good enough?"

Athen downed the rest of whatever beer Medias didn't spill and eyed the bar's patron's leaning into one another and whispering. "Oh, I think it was perfect."

MISDIRECTION

Medias perched herself on the wooden table next to piles of books, watching Aryis and Reece. A note was left under her door, instructing her to meet in the large library on the family wing of Ocean's Keep. It was quiet and isolated, its high walls lined with bookshelves with small spiral staircases stretching to long balconies lined with couches. The perfect hideaways to enjoy a pot of tea and settle in with a book. If only she had the luxury of being that casual in public.

A door in the back of the room opened, and Athen stepped through, headed toward Medias. The other women joined them at the table.

"Nyssa's alive," Athen said, his face breaking into a smile. He hugged Aryis and Reece. "They're no longer on the Whisper, but they're safe for now. Yuha smartly didn't tell me where."

The relief on all of their faces spoke to how devoted they were to Nyssa. *Good.* They would need to be if they were to keep the Cursed Gods safe.

Athen turned to Medias, his face growing serious. "Did you have to hurt Yuha?"

"This ruse needs to be believable. No half measures, Athen," she replied.

When Athen received word that someone from the Whisper wanted to meet, Reece had suggested using the meeting to plant a lie about

Nyssa's whereabouts. The lie that they were all in on, including Medias and Yuha, was now out in the world. The news of Nyssa and Quinn's supposed location was likely being whispered in the ears of every bounty hunter in Ocean's Rest. And the rumor would further spread as the days wore on. Soon everyone, including Ceril, would be looking in the wrong direction.

"I sent word to Cardin as soon as I returned to the Keep that Nyssa and Quinn were in Port Golcana," Medias said. She directed her gaze at Reece. "Your idea to plant a lie was brilliant. Port Golcana is large enough for Ceril to be searching for a while."

The empath didn't offer a response, her face inscrutable.

A compliment didn't rouse one ounce of warmth? Medias frowned.

"It was a rather good idea," Aryis enthused. "I wish I had thought of it."

Medias continued, "We need to start working on how we keep these lies and diversions up. If Lilliana has contacts on the Eastern continent, we'll need to—"

"I can take care of that from here," Reece interrupted.

Medias ground her teeth and stared at the empath. "There are aspects of the Empress's intelligence network you're unaware of. I can help you navigate those—"

"You have played your part. That's all we need for now," Reece said, the insistence in her voice drawing glances from Athen and Aryis.

Was Reece seriously going to let her grudge against Justiciars get in the way? If they worked together, they could create a believable false narrative and plant lies in all the correct places to keep Ceril chasing ghosts. And to make it appear that Medias was chasing ghosts as well—it was the only way to keep the ruse going and keep Nyssa and Quinn safe.

"I'm here to help and to protect you all for as long as I can," she said.

Reece frowned. "We can protect ourselves." And with that, she turned on her heel and left through the secret door at the back of the room. Athen and Aryis followed suit, leaving Medias to replay the conversation to see where she could have changed the empath's mind.

"Obstinate woman," Medias whispered.

A PLAUSIBLE LIE

Medias sat in the corner of the Great Room—the same room Nyssa and Quinn had spilled Justiciar blood in two scant months prior. The space had been cleaned up well. Nothing a rug or two couldn't fix.

The Great Room was a gathering place among the Keep's residents and workers that a Justiciar wasn't welcome to invade. She could have stayed secluded in the small office Lilliana had granted her, but she kept to herself and stayed busy with research and paperwork. After a while, no one seemed to care anymore that she was there.

This day, as Medias read a history book focusing on the Schism, the name given to the Rell family's split from the Empire, she surreptitiously watched Reece, who sat a few tables away with Athen, enjoying a pot of tea and a book. A rather comely woman crossed the room and sat on the edge of Reece's table, flirting shamelessly with her. The woman ran her hands through her hair and gently brushed her fingers against Reece's hand as they conversed, smiling and laughing a little too enthusiastically.

The empath's face didn't change as the woman tried to lay on the charm. Reece wasn't cold, but she wasn't reciprocating with any enthusiasm and, eventually, the woman took the hint and left, promising to see Reece later. Reece sighed and put her book down, frowning at the back of the woman as she left.

"She could have stripped naked and you would barely have cared," Athen said, his voice carrying over to Medias.

"I'm not looking to take anyone to bed right now," Reece replied.

Athen leaned forward, and Medias looked back down at her book while eavesdropping.

"You miss Nyssa, don't you?" he asked.

Medias stole a glance at Reece, who smiled for a moment before turning somber.

"I do, but our time together has come to an end. I'm not turning away women because of her. I just...I thought I was ready to trust someone again after Shay. Perhaps I'm not," Reece replied.

Hmm...who is Shay?

Athen nodded. "I understand."

Medias exhaled, disappointed, and tapped her fingers on the pages of her book, finding herself curious about Reece's past.

A commotion at the front of the room gave Medias pause, not sure her eyes were to be trusted. A man strode toward her with a retinue of six Imperial Guards—Ceril Anelos.

Here, in Ocean's Rest? Why now?

She stood up and nodded her head to him as he came to a stop at her table. "Arch Master."

"Justiciar Medias," he said without offer of even a polite smile. He looked past her and his eyes lit upon Athen, whose face went dark.

"Would you not give me a proper greeting, Lord Fennick?" Ceril asked.

Please, Athen, fake it. For your sake, fucking fake it.

The frown on Athen's face was replaced with a thin smile as he stood. "Arch Master, I didn't receive word you were going to be in Ocean's Rest." He shot a quick glance at Medias.

"I'm in the midst of visiting several guilds, including the Emerald Order, but I thought I would visit Ocean's Rest while I had a chance," Ceril said. "Justiciar Medias informed me of your meeting with a member of that pirate ship Blacksea and Quinn escaped on."

Athen stiffened. "What I do and who I meet in my city isn't the Empire's concern."

Ceril stepped forward. "You are still an Emerald Order adept and as such, an Imperial agent. With your First Master dead, you answer to me."

Athen stood silent, but his jawline flexed.

The Arch Master continued. "Best if you stop thinking of Blacksea as your friend and consider her a dangerous fugitive. She wouldn't hesitate to hurt you if she had to. Keep information from us again and you will be dealt with, regardless of your mother's status."

Ceril's voice carried, ensuring that everyone in the Great Room heard his warning. His eyes drifted from Athen down to Reece where she sat.

"And you, Miss Ae'Shen, what do you know of Nyssa's whereabouts?"

"Who?" Reece replied.

Fuck. The damn woman should be too smart to engage in games with the Arch Master. What was she doing?

"Perhaps your memory could be jostled by a Justiciar's questioning."

Reece blinked and her eyes flickered to Medias. Threatening the empath could dangerously escalate the situation—Athen was a very protective brother. Medias had to cut this chat short and divert Ceril's attention.

She rose to her full height, tugged at the sleeves of her leather jacket, and tried to appear as dismissive as possible, planting a smirk on her lips. "Master Anelos, the woman is less than useless, save for keeping track of her whores at The Feather. Questioning her would be a waste of my talent," she said, hoping he would buy the lie.

She didn't dare take her eyes off Ceril to see Reece's reaction. Convincing him that Reece knew nothing was her only goal. After a few moments, Ceril looked back to Reece with a soft huff of breath.

"You are all warned to report any communication you may have with Blacksea and Quinn or their cohorts," Ceril said. "This is an order from the Empress."

He spun back to Medias. "Justiciar, a word outside."

He turned and made for the exit. Medias glanced at Reece and bowed her head ever so slightly, hoping the empath understood it as an apology for insulting her, and followed Ceril out to the hallway.

Before she could find out what he wanted, Lilliana Fennick strode towards them with purpose, looking sharp and crisp in a dark-gray suit, displeasure written all over her face. She was trailed by her right-hand man, Pol. Tall and slim, his dark eyes were glued to Ceril.

"Arch Master Anelos, you dishonor me by not informing us of your visit," she said.

"Lilliana, if only I cared about your honor," he replied. "Need I remind you of your duty as Regent of Ocean's Rest to the Empire and your Empress? Your cavalier attitude has been humored because of the income your city generates, but don't mistake the Empress's indulgence as permission to flout her trust in you."

Lilliana's eyes narrowed. "What is this in regard to?" she asked.

Medias wondered how far the woman could throw Ceril if she wanted. Athen's strength was impressive, but Lilliana's was legendary.

"Any information about Blacksea or Quinn must be shared with Justiciar Medias and myself," Ceril replied.

"I have spoken to Athen. He will comply."

"I suggest you keep a tight rein on him, for his own benefit." Ceril sighed. "You and I used to be friends, Lilliana, and I always admired your ruthlessness. If only you had done the smart thing and left Nyssa back when she was a baby, we wouldn't be facing this problem."

A ripple of tension ran along Lilliana's jaw. The statement spiked Medias's curiosity—*what did he mean?*

"You've grown soft and sentimental, Lilliana. You are not well served by such traits, with wraiths attacking your city and two very dangerous women running from the Empire. If they ever—"

"You and I were once of like minds, Ceril, but we've traveled in different directions since the war. I became a mother, and that changed me for the better, I'd like to think," Lilliana said. There was a darkness to her eyes that made Medias uncomfortable, and Ceril shifted under her gaze. "Please do give my warmest regard to Empress Kalla." She turned and left. Pol lingered a moment, eyeing the Arch Master before following.

Ceril waited for Lilliana to disappear around a corner before addressing Medias. "I thought you were here to find Nyssa and Quinn."

"I am," Medias replied, waiting for the recrimination she knew was coming. Men like him never kept their thoughts to themselves.

"Yet you refuse to question Ae'Shen. As Nyssa's lover, she has to know something."

"The empath is a flighty, shallow thing who merely bedded Nyssa and seems to have moved on rather quickly. Before you arrived, she was flirting shamelessly with another woman." How skilled she had become at lying.

Ceril inhaled deeply and looked past her. His contempt was galling.

Medias continued. "I am mindful to tread carefully with the members of House Fennick and House Devitt."

"Neither of them are Houses with much clout."

Medias scowled. Houses Devitt and Fennick weren't one of the twelve Great Houses, true, but they still held more sway than perhaps Ceril liked. And it only took one mistake for a Great House to fall out of favor, get exiled from the Sun Council, and have another house—like Devitt or Fennick—take that revered spot.

"I'm treading carefully because the less they fear me and the less they think about me, the less they notice me. And *that* is when they will make a mistake."

Ceril sniffed. "Perhaps your approach will garner results. We shall see."

Ignoring his dismissiveness, Medias asked, "Have you heard anything from Port Golcana?"

"Yes, there have been more sightings of Nyssa and Quinn. They may be moving south along the coast. We're awaiting more information."

Medias fought back a smile. Someone had been planting rumors. *Reece.* It had to be her using Lilliana's whisper network.

"Good, so the intelligence I provided has given us what we want. I'll continue to entrench here and let you know what I find. We will have Nyssa and Quinn in no time."

Ceril nodded. "I agree. Now, I have an airship to catch."

Medias watched him leave before returning to the Great Room. She slipped into the room but stood beside the door, leaning back against the wall.

Breathe.

She had marked Nyssa as Unworthy in this room, setting their fates teetering along their current path. And by choosing to help Nyssa and Quinn, she would eventually pay for her own betrayal.

Medias shot up in bed, waking with a start. A book tumbled off of her chest. Another knock at her door let her know she hadn't been dreaming. She reached for her mask on the bedside table and moved toward the door, checking the daggers she wore strapped to her thighs. No one came to a Justiciar this late with good intentions.

She opened the door to discover Reece waiting, arms crossed over her chest. Poking her head out to check to see if anyone was around, Medias found the hallway deserted. Lilliana had stuck her in a little-used wing far from the main guest quarters. She didn't mind, the solitude suited her.

Reece strolled past Medias into the room without invite. Her loose tan pants, dark boots, and a large, cream-colored sweater were far more casual than her usual suits or dresses, and her silver hair was tied back in a messy ponytail. *Working late, perhaps?*

"Do you have business with me that could not wait until morning?" Medias asked with a frown but closed the door.

Reece surveyed the room before turning to Medias. "Your proposal to work together—I would like to revisit it."

Rather unexpected. Ceril's visit must have put a bit of a scare into her. "I am pleased to hear it."

Reece paced back and forth. "We have planted a lie, and now we must water it in order for the seedling to grow. I can do this with Lilliana's contacts and network, but I don't know all the Imperial agents in play or how Kalla's spies operate. We can leverage each other's knowledge to create a string of additional lies to cause further misdirection. Sightings of Nyssa and Quinn in one place, a rumor of a run-in with locals somewhere else nearby, and the like. We can effectively move our phantom

Cursed Gods around the world without ever truly putting them in harm's way. Thoughts?"

Reece shut her mouth and waited, her dark eyes examining Medias, which was oddly unnerving. Even though the empath couldn't sense Medias's emotions, there was something in her gaze that suggested an ability to see far beyond the surface.

Medias crossed her arms and put her fist to her mouth, thinking. Reece's idea was very much in line with her own, but she didn't want to answer immediately and seem too eager.

Let the empath stew for a bit.

After enough time had passed, Medias nodded. "A solid plan. When shall we meet? You can't continue to sneak into my room like this, it's improper."

"We'll use the pretense of working together to investigate Eron's death and the wraith attacks. It makes meeting with me easier for you without raising suspicions. Come to my office tomorrow afternoon."

Medias nodded. "Until tomorrow, then."

Reece headed to the door.

"Empath," Medias called after her.

Reece turned back, waiting.

"Today, I disparaged you to the Arch Master. Lies designed to protect you from him, nothing more." At best, it was a weak apology, but it was all Medias could muster at the moment.

Reece narrowed her eyes for a moment before slipped out the door and closing it behind her.

Medias frowned and put her fingers to her mask, lifting it off her face with a sigh. Protecting Nyssa's friends would be far easier now that she would have frequent access to Reece, though the woman would likely prove a challenge.

PUSHING BOUNDARIES

Quinn shook her head, Nyssa's fate already sealed. The woman didn't seem to learn, but at least she made for an entertaining morning.

Nyssa yelped. "Why does this bitch hate me so much?" she bellowed at the sky before sticking a finger in her mouth.

Nope. Doesn't learn.

Quinn laughed as Nyssa battled with the largest hen in the coop. Every morning Nyssa got nipped at as she gathered eggs, and every morning she grumbled. Two months into their stay on Monk's Cove and she had not made headway towards peaceful coexistence with the dominant hen.

Humming, Quinn bent over the notebook in her lap. She'd been drawing more than ever, using her mornings to work on her sketches. She smudged her finger on the charcoal, trying to perfect the likeness of Nyssa's hair, its auburn locks a challenge to get just right. They could be at any stage of unruly given the time of day or Nyssa's mood.

"Leave the chickens be and come to the clearing. Time for lessons," Fontaine ordered as she walked past the coop.

"Fine by me," Nyssa grumbled.

Quinn smiled up at her. "Have you been writing epic poems about your battle with that hen?"

Nyssa frowned. It was a small thing, a slip of information back when Quinn was a captive aboard the Whisper. Nyssa, drunk and trying her best to prove she wasn't an ignorant brute, had admitted to writing poetry. It was a delightful secret.

"I-I don't write poetry." The color on Nyssa's cheeks spoke to the contrary, but Quinn didn't push, chuckling instead.

Nyssa came and hovered over her, squinting down at the drawing in her lap—a mighty warrior locked in mortal combat with her chicken nemesis. "Are you serious?"

"Isn't it great how I capture your finest moments? My first sketch of one such moment features me punching you in the face. This is—"

Nyssa flicked a little spark of lightning at Quinn's nose. Quinn yelped with laughter and jumped off the tree stump she used as a stool. "You are a child!" she admonished, though she was happy that Nyssa was getting more comfortable using her magick. It seemed she never missed an opportunity to tease and Quinn didn't quite mind, though at times she was at a loss for how to respond. Nyssa's playful half smile was an invitation to trouble.

Nyssa laughed and made for the clearing. Quinn closed her notebook and tucked it away in the brown canvas rucksack Nyssa had found for her in the Whisper's hold. She bounced to her feet, eager to start the day's lessons. Using her magick, at Ceril's behest, filled her with dread, but now with Fontaine and Nyssa, she was learning and growing. Gaining power. And it felt freeing.

She fell in beside Nyssa, who flashed a smile at her as they made their way from the coop on the side of the house to their practice grounds down a small trail towards the interior of the island.

"You know, I tease you, but your drawings are really quite good. You have a talent," Nyssa remarked.

Quinn's brain failed to generate a response, the compliment grinding her thoughts to a halt. Heat rose in her cheeks. Thankfully, Fontaine provided a distraction, waving at them as they approached.

"What are we doing today?" Nyssa asked, sitting down on the felled tree at the side of the clearing that served as an impromptu bench.

Fontaine turned to Quinn and pointed to the edge of the forest. "I'd like you to cut down that tree."

"I don't understand."

"We've already experimented with your darkness. We know you can make it as incorporeal as mist or as hard as onyx. I would like you to create a thin, sharp blade and slice through that tree."

"I don't want to destroy a tree just to try something new with my magick. It's a living thing."

Fontaine moved closer to her and waved at Nyssa to join them. "I've taught you both how to sense magick, to find it in all living things, not just the bright cores within people. Look further."

Quinn called her magick forth, her gaze intent on the tree. A glow in its core came into focus, a long, tall vertical line of magick that started from the ground and went up as high as the treetop. Its roots glowed, too, but the tree's essence wasn't...right. What should have been contiguous flowing lines were fractured, the edges dark like rot.

"It's sick," Quinn murmured.

"You aren't killing it. You're hastening its inevitable death."

She hesitated. "What if I can't stop the darkness and it destroys other trees?"

"Why are you so reticent with your magick? Do you think your enemies will show you any measure of mercy?" Fontaine's voice was flat. Not unkind, but stern.

She felt Nyssa's eyes on her.

Because all my magick does is destroy, she wanted to say, but stayed silent. The darkness and the nullifying magick—how was her power any different from forbidden magick? Deep down, she feared she was nothing more than another example of ugliness in the world, her abilities only good for tearing things apart.

Fontaine stared at her. "The last few weeks, I've been pushing you more and more, but you both hold back. You fear your power."

Quinn could admit to being cautious—to not wandering too far outside of her comfort zone—but she didn't want to hurt anyone, including herself. Fontaine began weaving a spell, and Quinn felt a tug of magick. She opened herself up, seeing the bright and wild energy Fontaine was expending. They had learned enough from her to know whatever spell she was weaving was laced with ancient magick, its shimmer and the way it resonated far different from regular magick.

When she was done weaving her spell, its golden magick rotated around her hands and buzzed so strong Quinn could feel it in her chest. Little threads of energy broke away and floated towards Quinn, who took a step back.

"What are you doing?" she asked.

Fontaine's face remained serious. "You both need to meet me halfway or you're wasting my time."

Her magick wound around Quinn, creeping up her arms and spreading across her body, before it sank inside of her. A sudden, frightening pressure built up behind Quinn's eyes, but she fought the impulse to negate the magick.

"Face the darkness, Quinn." Fontaine stepped back and cupped her hands in front of her mouth, whispering a spell. When she uttered the last word, she pushed her hands toward the women, a column of red smoke sparking with white bursts of light.

The discomfort behind Quinn's eyes relented and the threads of Fontaine's golden magick flowed back out of Quinn, twisting around the pillar of smoke rotating between the three of them. It shuddered and began taking form, revealing the shape of a body.

First Master Ceril Anelos of Arcton Citadel stood before them.

Red smoke curled around him, his form shifting, blurring as if not entirely in focus. Quinn stumbled backward as the man who had locked her away turned his black eyes towards her. He towered over her, as he had so many times. He peered down at her, the corners of his mouth turned up in a cruel smirk. As he moved, his body seemed ethereal, darting towards her with preternatural speed.

Her eyes filled with tears. *He's not real.*

The form of Ceril advanced on her, and her legs gave out, heart pounding. A rasp of surprise escaped her dry throat, driven out by the panic that seized every part of her body.

Logic crumbled.

Nyssa shouted and rushed towards him, striking out at his chest. Her fist moved through him.

"He's not real. He's not real. He's not real," Quinn whispered, trying to call forth her magick to do something—anything—but it slipped through her fingers, her will and concentration broken. She scrabbled back along the stones. The needed to run, to escape.

Nyssa rushed to Quinn and dropped down, putting an arm around her shoulders. She reached out toward the form of Ceril, arcs of blue lightning sinking into him, and she tightened her fist. His form shifted and distorted, though his black eyes remained affixed to Quinn.

Nyssa grunted, her magick flaring up. The illusion twisted back in on itself and collapsed into a waft of red smoke that drifted away with afternoon breeze.

"You alright?" Nyssa asked, turning to Quinn, her voice gentle. "You're bleeding."

Quinn lifted her hands. She cursed under her breath, unable to stop them from trembling. A long cut on her palm stung—she must have sliced her hand on a stone when she collapsed.

She scrambled to her feet and shrugged Nyssa off of her. "I don't need your help," she said, the strain in her voice making her curse herself. She wasn't some helpless, perpetual victim that needed to be coddled. How could she allow an illusion to bring her to her knees out of fear?

Nyssa advanced on Fontaine. "Why did you do that?" A shock wave of blue crackling magick burst out of Nyssa, forcing Fontaine backward.

Fontaine steadied herself and grinned, clapping her hands once. The crack of it startled Quinn, making her shudder. "There you are! Finally, I see the warrior."

"Explain yourself!" Nyssa snarled.

"You two are holding back. You want to capture Suvi Rell? At this pace, you won't be ready. The Empress will likely have your heads rolling at her feet before then. Each of you is afraid to truly embrace your power."

"I've seen what my power can do!" Nyssa snarled. "You weren't there on the dock. You don't have a fucking awful legacy of destruction hanging over your head like we do. Cursed Gods are feared, and with good reason."

Fontaine didn't waver. "I have to get you ready to face not only Suvi, but whatever else the world throws at you. Not doing so would be a disservice to you both. Understand that."

Nyssa shook her head. "Don't ever do that to Quinn again."

Quinn shot forward, grabbed Nyssa's arm, and yanked her around. "I don't need you to protect me!"

"But—"

"You treat me like some weak little thing that needs a brave warrior to defend me. It's insulting." Her heart was pounding, anger making her shake.

Nyssa shook her head. "That's not how I think of you—"

Quinn pushed past Nyssa and confronted Fontaine. "What did you do to me?"

"I reached inside of you with my magick and pulled at your memories to see your fears and how you would confront them," Fontaine replied.

"How dare you? You have no right to use me like that!" Did Fontaine go far enough back to see Ceril whip her? Quinn's heart jumped into her throat. No one should see that...

Fontaine spread her hands wide. "What would you have me do? Coddle you both—"

"Fuck you!" Quinn yelled. She turned on her heels and stalked back to the house, her face burning with shame.

RAISING WALLS

Nyssa followed Quinn as she stormed off. "What did I do wrong?" she mumbled.

When she got inside, Quinn was standing in the kitchen, staring down at her bloody cut. Nyssa grabbed a clean towel from a drawer and cupped Quinn's hand in her own.

"Let me see that," she said.

Quinn snatched her hand away and held it to her chest, blood seeping out of her clenched fist.

"I said I don't need your help," she snapped.

"You're hurt."

Quinn shook her head. "I'm fine."

The coldness in her voice struck Nyssa like an arrow and ignited anger. "Oh, really? Because out there, you didn't seem fine."

Quinn's face didn't change. She gave Nyssa nothing—her walls were up, and it was apparent that Nyssa wasn't invited behind them.

"Then stay in here and be fucking fine." Nyssa retreated from Quinn and went to take her anger out on Fontaine, who waited in the middle of the clearing, as if expecting a confrontation. Nyssa would give her one.

"Don't ever do that again," she warned, stopping herself from revealing that Ceril had once whipped Quinn. It wasn't her secret to tell, and she wouldn't betray Quinn's confidence. The thought of what that man did made Nyssa wish she could pummel him until he begged for death.

"You two needed a kick in the ass," Fontaine said, laying her hands on Nyssa's shoulders and squeezing gently. "You're a great warrior with an unflinching sense of honor, but you have to be strong. I worry for you and Quinn if you keep holding back. Your enemies will be ruthless. I didn't know how deep Quinn's fear of Ceril is, and for that I'm sorry. But my intentions were not to hurt her so deeply."

"Hurt me, then. I deserve it. Not her."

Fontaine scowled at her. "Why?"

"This is all my fault. If I had let Quinn go instead of returning her to Ocean's Rest, she would be safe. *I* brought her back to the Empire. *I* caused this fucking mess." Shame burned deep in Nyssa. Admitting it to someone else tied her stomach in knots.

"Nyssa, you're not to blame. In the end, you chose to protect her. That's what matters."

Nyssa wanted to believe Fontaine, but she felt like a fraud.

Fontaine smiled. "Why did you give up everything to save Quinn?"

Nyssa paused, avoiding Fontaine's gaze. "She saved my life. I owe her."

Fontaine laughed and twirled around once. "Wrong," she exclaimed in a sing-song voice. "Your affection isn't transactional. It runs deep and that scares you, doesn't it?"

"Stop," Nyssa whispered.

"You only let a few people in. I reckon that's Athen, Aryis, and your empath. Oh, and Elias. Granted, he's hard to dislike. Maybe me, a little. And now, Quinn," Fontaine said.

Nyssa's growing feelings for Quinn were becoming more complex and confusing, not that she could admit that to Fontaine. What she wouldn't give to have Athen to talk to. Certainly he would have some tragically bad advice, but at least he knew her better than anyone. Knew her heart.

"Love is a confounding thing," Fontaine went on. "For someone like me, it's so fleeting, the years passing in the blink of an eye, but I can't help falling in love with everything."

Nyssa gestured toward the house. "You need to talk to Quinn. And apologize."

Fontaine sighed. "I sometimes forget how to be gentle. I spent such a long time not having to do anything of importance as a chicken. And teaching you and Quinn...it feels like the most important thing I'll do in my life."

The sentiment surprised Nyssa, who fumbled for something to say, but Fontaine left her to return to the house before she could form any words.

Nyssa walked to the giant log at the edge of the clearing and sat down, rubbing the back of her neck. Fontaine was right. No one hunting them would give them quarter. Empress Kalla would gladly have them both bow to her before Justiciars took their heads.

The thought of what could be done to them made Nyssa simmer with anger. They would need to be warriors.

Both of them.

AN OFFER

Quinn curled her hands into fists and ground them into the top of the kitchen counter, smearing blood on the rough wood surface. She wanted to hit something. Her helplessness and panic upon seeing Ceril again, even as an illusion, filled her with shame. Only that man could reduce her to nothing.

Less than nothing.

She grabbed the towel Nyssa left behind and wrapped it around her hand.

The memories of Arcton Citadel had receded for months, and she was finally starting to figure out what life looked like outside of the guild. Outside of Ceril's reach. But those memories all came crashing back with one conjuration of the man that stripped her back bare and whipped her until her world went dark.

Quinn squeezed her eyes shut, refusing to cry. But the tears came. As did the shaking. She slid down to the ground, crying in Fontaine's kitchen over a man who still held sway over her no matter the distance between them.

Minutes passed before Fontaine found her on the floor and sat down next to her.

"I'm sorry for my actions. For hurting you," Fontaine said. She reached out her hand. "May I?"

Before she could think, Quinn nodded. Fontaine moved closer and wrapped an arm around her shoulders and stroked her hair. "I'm sorry."

Quinn fought back tears. Fontaine's presence, her touch, was comforting in a way Quinn had ached for her entire life.

"Your memories were very raw and...I know what Ceril did to you," Fontaine said, her voice soft.

"I didn't want you to see that. I'm ashamed." Quinn propped her elbows on her knees and buried her head in her hands.

"Quinn, I never meant to hurt or shame you. I thought I could jostle you and Nyssa out of playing it safe with your magick," Fontaine said. She continued to smooth out Quinn's hair. "I meant it to be a lesson about pushing through fear and maintaining your concentration, controlling your magick. I went about it the wrong way."

Through her tears, Quinn asked the question she dreaded. "What if I'm no better than him?"

"Oh, Quinn, why would you ever think that?"

"My magick is dark...destructive."

Fontaine shook her head and placed her hand, palm down, on the floor between them.

"Stop me," she said.

"W-what?"

Fontaine reached down into her boot, produced a knife, and drove it toward her hand.

Quinn gasped, and her magick burst forth, creating a barrier of shadow around Fontaine's vulnerable hand. The knife pierced the darkness, its tip stuck in the solid shadow.

"Your magick is many things," Fontaine remarked. "Destructive at times, yes. But protective as well. You shielded my hand without a thought, acting on instinct alone."

"Another lesson?" Quinn grumbled.

"One you sorely need. Even forbidden magick, as maligned as it is, has its uses, some of them beneficial. Don't judge the magick by its wielder," Fontaine said, twirling the knife and returning it to her boot. "You know, Nyssa had some choice words for me. She'd much rather I hurt her than you, which tells you all you need to know about that woman's heart. She carries the guilt of returning you to the Empire."

Quinn glanced at Fontaine, who offered her a kind smile. "I don't blame Nyssa." Quinn bit her lip. It wasn't entirely the truth. Nyssa did bring her back to the Empire, even after everything Quinn revealed to her. But at the same time, the thought of Nyssa blaming herself made something inside of Quinn ache.

"Regardless, she blames herself, and that's all it takes for guilt to eat a hole in someone. Trust me," Fontaine said, a pensive look crossing her face for a moment before it was gone.

"Did she really want you to hurt her instead of me?" Quinn asked.

Fontaine nodded.

A pang of regret swept through Quinn. "I shouldn't have yelled at her. I just detest feeling weak. I don't want to be this fragile thing she has to look after."

"Thing is, you need to be looking after each *other*. And you're not helpless. Far from it, woman! You're a goddamn force of nature, I just need you to realize it." Fontaine stood, both of her knees popping. A groan rumbled out of her. "Oh, that's new. I don't like the way this body carries its age. I'm giving you the rest of the day off to rest and recover. When you're feeling up to it, go out and pick more grapes. You eat your weight in them, sweet girl."

Fontaine left Quinn alone in the kitchen with her thoughts tumbling through her head. Lashing out at Nyssa had accomplished nothing and made her stomach ache. This friendship thing was turning out to be more confounding than expected.

Quinn watched Nyssa read out of the corner of her eye, catching furtive glances her way. The chill between them hadn't abated, lasting well into the afternoon.

Sighing, she continued cleaning the winter grapes she had gathered at Fontaine's request, occasionally popping one in her mouth and humming to herself. She smiled, remembering the first grape she had every eaten, practically giggling with delight when the tiny fruit burst in her mouth, sweet and cool. The food at Arcton Citadel didn't include a lot of variation, and certainly offered nothing as delightful as a grape.

She popped one into her mouth let out a loud hum of satisfaction. A sneaky smile flickered across Nyssa's face—one Quinn pretended not to notice, concentrating instead on the nervous flutter in her stomach every time Nyssa chanced a glance over. Perhaps Nyssa thought she was being sly, her soft curls tumbled around her face as she pretended to read, but the slow page turns gave her away.

Finally, Nyssa tossed her book aside, strolled into the kitchen, and leaned against the counter, the scent of her bath oils drifting Quinn's way—white musk and a hint of verbena. "Quinn, can we talk?"

Quinn took a deep breath and cleared her throat. "If I may say something first...I'm sorry for how I reacted earlier. You didn't deserve that. I...I was an asshole."

"More of an arrogant ass, I'd say," Nyssa replied, her shoulders relaxing. "You were right earlier. You're not some weakling that needs to be protected. But I want you to know *how* to protect yourself. I would like to teach you Ithais-Toru. If...if you're amenable."

A quiver of excitement ran from the top of Quinn's head down to her toes, but she kept her face steady, popping a grape into her mouth. "I would like that. I already know how to throw a pretty good punch."

Nyssa shook her head, flashing that maddeningly endearing smile of hers. "Yeah, I remember, Freckles."

STUDENT AND TEACHER

"Fuck!" Quinn yelled, limping away from Nyssa. "FUCK!"

Nyssa twirled her wooden practice sword and stalked back and forth, trying to suppress a smirk. The summer heat finally had washed over Monk's Cove and Quinn became its victim— she was covered in a sheen of sweat, her breaths ragged. Nyssa, while not a fan of the hotter weather, had the benefit of a lifetime of training, barely perspiring.

After training for a few weeks, Nyssa decided to put a practice sword in Quinn's hand. They didn't have the luxury of years to train like she did at the Emerald Order. A shortcut or two was necessary, as long as Quinn kept up. And it turned out Quinn was a rather good student.

"Were that a real sword you'd have lost your leg at the knee," Nyssa remarked.

"That hurt!" Quinn growled.

"I had to make my point."

"Did you have to make it so hard?"

Nyssa shrugged. "Your knee will be fine. You were getting a bit full of yourself. Carelessness will get you injured. Or worse." Nyssa pointed at the scar on the left side of her face that ran from forehead down through mid-cheek. "This was earned because I got cocky."

Quinn rubbed her leg and walked in a circle to shake off the pain. "Do you mind telling me what happened?"

Nyssa walked over to the fallen log and picked up a canteen. She took a drink and tossed it to Quinn, who joined her as a cool breeze kicked up, blowing her hair away from her face.

"At the Emerald Order, Athen and I were sparring with real swords. I was being a cocky asshole, thinking no one could come close to my skill with a blade. Mind you, I was thirteen and a little idiot. I got careless, and he caught me, slicing right through my face," Nyssa explained before sitting down. "Athen thought he'd blinded me. He was so scared. I've never felt as helpless as I did that day, watching him cry. I never had the scar healed over completely because I wanted the reminder of how I hurt one of the few people in the world that gave a damn about me. My arrogance caused *him* pain."

A realization struck her. *I've never told anyone why I didn't get the scar healed properly. Not even Eron.*

Quinn sat down beside Nyssa with a soft groan and handed the canteen back. "I remember accusing you of using that scar to intimidate people when we first met."

"I remember that night. You were an asshole." Nyssa chuckled. "I was ready to knock you on your ass."

"Sorry for being an arrogant prick." Quinn gave her a warm, genuine smile. "You know, now I can't imagine your face without that scar."

"Really? You like the scar, do you?" Nyssa teased.

Color rose in Quinn's cheeks but she didn't answer. Nyssa's smile grew bigger as the other woman averted her eyes and made a show of asking for more water. She enjoyed watching Quinn get flustered over little things. Though she was a hard woman to read at times, blushing always gave her away. Even when she retreated behind her emotional walls.

"Moving like a fighter is new to me, but I think my body is slowly getting used to it," Quinn remarked, changing the subject.

"Sakei designed Ithais-Toru to be a flexible martial art. He believed it needed to fit the strengths of each individual. For you, that's your speed and wits. You're fast and elusive." Nyssa glanced at Quinn, who smiled to herself. "You're rather good at this, I will admit."

Quinn's blush deepened. She must have been starved for any words of praise at Arcton Citadel, ostracized and isolated because of her magick. Even though Nyssa had no magick, the Masters at the Emerald Order couldn't ignore her fighting ability. She was praised often. Quinn likely yearned for one kind word. Just one.

"Let me know if I push you too far," Nyssa said. "I'm training you hard, like we did at the Order."

"Do you...do you miss it?"

Do I miss it? A sigh eased out of her, and she leaned forward, running her hands through her hair. "I do miss my time with Athen and Eron. And strangely enough, I miss working with the apprentices. I had been shunned for most of my time there by my peers, but the younger students actually sought me out when I was older. Well, one did. Juliana. The others always got the better of her while sparring. She asked me for advice, so I helped her out. Then the other apprentices came—one by one—some to spar, some to learn. It felt good to be needed; to be looked up to finally."

"Sounds like you found a place there after all."

"Strange as it is, I suppose I did. Eron and Athen made it a home, but it took years for me to earn an ounce of respect from any of the adepts." Nyssa tilted her face to the sun and squinted, relishing its warmth. "I'm struggling a little to understand my place in the world without the guild or my title. Without my family."

Quinn rubbed her hands together. "You must miss Eron."

Nyssa's breath caught in her chest. The death of her First Master—the man she considered her father—still made her ache. And made her angry. "He was the only person who never doubted me. I will kill Efla for what she did." Nyssa blinked back tears and cleared her throat, trying to re-center herself.

"I'm sorry, Nyssa," Quinn said, her tone somber.

Nyssa nudged her with her shoulder. "It's okay."

Quinn drummed her fingers on her thigh. "I gravely misjudged you at first. I thought the Emerald Order adepts were just a bunch of thick-skulled fighters. I didn't realize the skill or the...beauty behind the martial art."

"Is that an apology, Freckles?"

"I just wanted you to know that I have amended my judgment."

Nyssa cocked her head.

Quinn sighed. "Yes, it's an apology. I'm sorry."

"So, I'm no longer an ignorant brute?"

"Well, I wouldn't go that far," Quinn replied, offering Nyssa a sly smile that made the back of her neck grow hot. It wasn't that Quinn was flirting exactly, but sometimes...it did feel a *little* like flirting.

"Your turn to share. What was the Citadel like?"

A dark cloud passed over Quinn's face.

"It was cold and the food lacked variety," Quinn answered, offering no more than that.

Nyssa bit back her frustration. They were tied to each other now, by fate and circumstance, but it seemed their blossoming friendship would continue at Quinn's pace.

Nyssa took the hint. "We should resume training."

Standing with a groan, Quinn looked down at Nyssa. "Show me what I'm doing wrong?"

"First of all, you're fighting me. I'm really good. And I'm not being cocky, it's just fact."

A scowl passed over Quinn's face. "I'm starting to get a sense of what you'd be like as a guild Master."

"Pretty great, right?"

"Pretty frustrating."

Nyssa chuckled, turning her mind back to their training. "Look, you need to maintain your stance."

She stood and put her hands on Quinn's back, pushing her into the middle of the clearing. She moved behind Quinn and tapped her right leg. "Slide this back a bit and shift your shoulders slightly this way." Nyssa turned Quinn's shoulders to line up with her hips, and Quinn glanced back at her.

Nyssa stepped closer, placing her hands on Quinn's waist. "Remember to bend your knees. This is your center, your foundation. You start off solid, but you fall apart when you get flustered." To make her point, Nyssa flicked the back of Quinn's ear. Quinn jumped.

"See?" Nyssa said with a smirk. "Commit your stance to memory. After you attempt to strike me, reset your stance. Think about doing it. Take your time. Do it enough, and it will become second nature."

A frown crossed Quinn's face. "Why do you take such joy in rattling me?"

"Because it's so easy and I like to watch you blush," Nyssa said, as Quinn reddened. "Ah, see? You're so"—*stunning*—"predictable."

"Okay, let's go again," Quinn demanded, twirling the wooden sword in her hand, imitating Nyssa's habit. It was strangely flattering.

Nyssa shook her head. "No. I think you need to put the sword down. Let's work on the First Form."

Quinn frowned. "Again? I can do it in my sleep."

"You've memorized the steps, but your body hasn't learned the lesson that the form teaches. It's called the Bamboo Form for a reason. It embodies strength and flexibility, which is the foundation of your fighting stance. In the form, you move and reset back to your stance. Move and reset. It's the First Form because of the fundamental skills it imparts."

"So, you want me to stay rooted in one spot but be flexible? That's a bit...contradictory."

Nyssa moved next to Quinn, peered out into the forest, and pointed at a grove of bamboo trees. "Look at the top of the bamboo. It sways with the wind, but if you draw your eyes all the way down, the bamboo is rooted firmly in the ground. It's about being strong and maintaining balance."

Nyssa put her hand on Quinn's shoulder and shoved her. Quinn stumbled back.

"What the hell, Nyssa?"

"You should be back in your stance, not grousing at me." She pointed at the trees. "Like the bamboo."

Quinn took a deep breath and got into the basic stance. Wasting little motion, Nyssa went to shove her again, but she spun out of the way before resetting her stance.

"Shoulders aligned with your hips," Nyssa corrected, and Quinn adjusted. "Good."

For the next few minutes, Nyssa stalked Quinn, who dodged or blocked her soft strikes before re-assuming a basic stance. It was a fruitful exercise. Nyssa attacked Quinn from different angles, causing the woman to move and re-center herself quickly. Her body would continue to adjust and learn until it became instinctual.

"Now, understand that you can take the nine forms and apply them to Sakei's six tenets—justice, integrity, honor, loyalty, courage, and..." Nyssa looked at Quinn.

"Compassion."

"Good. Take the Bamboo Form and extend what you learn from it—strength and flexibility—and apply it to those six pillars." Nyssa sighed and scratched her head. "I wish I had Sakei's books to teach you from. I'm afraid I can't remember everything properly since I'm not Aryis by any stretch of the imagination."

"You're a good teacher, regardless," Quinn said.

The back of Nyssa's neck burned, and her cheeks grew hot.

A smile crept over Quinn's face.

"Are you aiming to become teacher's favorite?" Nyssa asked.

"Oh yes, I'm trying to beat out the log and that sassy rock over there," Quinn said, lazily pointing at a craggy stone sat at the side of the clearing.

Nyssa couldn't help but laugh. "You're funnier than you let on."

"I know," Quinn said with a shrug. "Okay, so Bamboo Form. How many times should I do it?"

"Until I tell you to stop."

"We're going to be here all afternoon, aren't we?"

Nyssa smiled and nodded. "Smart girl."

RECIPROCATION

As fully summer descended on Monk's Cove, Quinn found the water off their dock delightfully cool and refreshing, perfect for swimming. It was one of the few activities she was allowed at Arcton Citadel, a watchful guard always lingering in sight while she would swim in a small, cold reservoir fed by a mountain spring. She was allowed to go anywhere on the grounds as long as she had a guard with her. But freedom on a leash wasn't freedom at all.

She dangled her feet in the water and worked on her sketch of Hannah's Whisper from memory, missing the ship and its crew. Though only on the Whisper for a short time, it had come to feel like home.

She smiled at the thought. *Home.*

A shadow fell over Quinn, and she didn't need to look up to know it was Nyssa. She could sense the woman's presence in her core, feeling a warm buzz whenever she was close—another thing that had come to feel very familiar. Comfortable, even.

"That's rather good," Nyssa said.

"Thank you," Quinn replied, shutting her book before tossing her piece of charcoal in a tin and closing it, putting both in a rucksack. She popped up to her feet. "I'm here for you, actually. I knew it was your turn to fish."

"I'm not taking requests. We eat what I catch," Nyssa said, a twinkle in her eye.

Quinn laughed. "You're teaching me Ithais-Toru, so I thought, in return, I could teach you how to swim."

Without waiting for an answer, Quinn pulled her shirt over her head, revealing a tight, low-cut undershirt. She had debated leaving her shirt on, but she wanted to push herself to not be as self-conscious.

Nyssa looked away, obviously caught off guard.

"It's okay, I don't mind if you see the scars," Quinn said, shimmying out of her pants, leaving her in tight undershorts. She folded her clothes neatly and laid them on the dock before easing into the water with hardly a splash.

A frown planted itself on Nyssa's face. Any more severe and it would have been a pout. "I don't think this is a good idea."

"You'll be back on a ship soon enough, and swimming you obviously need to have. I won't always be around to dive in after you if you fall overboard."

"Oh no?"

"No. What if I'm in the mess, eating? I do love Buck's griddle cakes," Quinn joked. "Look, don't you think it's a bit ridiculous that a woman with the surname *Blacksea* and an affinity for the sea can't swim?"

Nyssa chewed on her lip. Quinn knew getting in the water wouldn't be a small thing for her after drowning. The memory of Nyssa's eyes growing still and distant as she succumbed to the sea was burned into Quinn's brain.

"We'll take it slow," Quinn said. "I promise."

Fear wasn't something she was used to seeing from Nyssa, who was fearless almost to a fault, even willing to die for Quinn when they barely knew one another. But now on the dock, Quinn watched Nyssa fight with herself.

Finally, Nyssa stripped down to her underclothes while Quinn tried not to stare. Nyssa had a warrior's body with muscles Quinn hoped to emulate, secretly secretly inspecting her own body in the mirror at the end of each day to see if she was getting stronger from their training. She certainly ached enough after practice to believe she had to be developing some muscles.

Nyssa's abdominal muscles alone were enough to spark jealousy. They descended down into her low-slung black undershorts, her thighs thick and powerful. Quinn blinked and looked away, her thoughts spilling over the border of mere admiration.

Shit.

Nyssa sat on the dock, swinging her legs over the edge and dipping them into the water. In the late afternoon light, the dark-gray poison scar stood out against her pale skin, radiating from her left shoulder, down her arm, and up her neck.

Quinn swallowed, trying to concentrate as she tread water. "Just lower yourself down."

Nyssa stared at the water and tensed up.

"Take my hand, I'll help you," Quinn offered, reaching up.

Nyssa shook her head and backed away from the dock's edge. "I'm sorry, I...I can't," she said, her voice shallow as she collected her clothes and hurried back up to the house.

Quinn sighed and pushed away from the dock, floating on her back, watching the clouds slowly pass in the sky.

She had hoped to help Nyssa learn to swim, to give something back. Nyssa was enthusiastic and patient with Quinn to a fault. Training seemed to make her happy, and it gave Quinn a chance to get to know her. She wondered if Nyssa even realized how much of herself she was sharing as they worked together.

Quinn had hoped to share the serenity she found in the water. Maybe it would help Nyssa understand her a little better in lieu of talking about herself. She simply wasn't comfortable letting anyone in, not after growing up with no one to trust at the Citadel.

With Nyssa, she felt she could offer maybe a little more, especially since she was finding it harder and harder to get Nyssa out of her head. Every time the damn woman even casually flirted with her or paid her a compliment, Quinn's stomach tightened and her face grew hot. It was disconcerting.

Footsteps on the dock roused Quinn out of her thoughts.

"Nyssa came in looking like she walked over her own grave. What happened?" Fontaine asked.

"I offered to teach her how to swim."

"I see."

"Was I wrong?"

Fontaine shook her head. "No, but Nyssa drowned, Quinn. You were with her; you saw what she went through. Some fears need to work their way out of the body at their own pace."

How had she been so thoughtless? Perhaps she had taken Nyssa's fearlessness for granted, thinking her strong in the face of everything. "I was cavalier about it. I should have been more careful."

"Your heart was in the right place. Nyssa knows that. Now get out of the water and catch us dinner."

Quinn sighed. She wanted to float more, to have some time alone to think. "In a minute."

Fontaine turned to go back to the house but paused. "Give Nyssa time."

AN UNTIMELY SLIP

"**P**unch me," Athen said.

The other man rocked back and let a fist fly, hitting Athen square in the chest, forcing him to take a step back. Athen could take a punch, his invulnerability giving him quite an advantage.

The gathered members of his newly-formed Lion's Guard voiced their approval of Athen's latest recruit. Out of the corner of his eye, he caught Aryis grinning as she took notes. His mother had asked for a fighting force, and he'd give her a small standing army.

Brick was the Ivory Triad's best fighter and the first person Athen had courted to join the Lion's Guard. And he took his sweet time coming around to the idea—four months. But at least he was here now. Four months behind the other recruits, but Athen would train him up.

"You definitely do hit like a brick," Athen said, praising the tall, muscular man.

He sighed and crossed his arms. "Is that a joke?"

"N-no. I can just see why they call you Brick. How tall are you, six foot nine?"

"Six foot ten."

Aryis whistled and made a note in her book. "You have four inches on Athen. Impressive." Athen eyed her. She responded with a bright smile.

How that damn smile made his knees weak.

"Brick, do you have a weapon preference?" she asked the large man.

Brick held up his fists. "These."

Aryis nodded, her light-brown eyes squinting in the sun that gave her rich brown skin a slight glow and her black hair a brilliant shine. Athen couldn't wait to get her in a bath later and just talk. They could talk for hours—her mind moved quickly and kept him on his toes. It was one of the things he admired about Aryis the most, and she had fast become a welcome fixture in his life. Every moment with her felt effortless.

"It's hard to believe you have no magick behind that punch," Athen remarked.

Brick raised up to his full height. "No magick that helps me throw a punch, anyway."

"I heard rumors that you used to be at Hazelspine?"

"Who told you that?"

Aryis raised her hand. "I recognized your given name from the guild rolls."

Brick frowned at her. "Who the fuck reads guild rolls from ten years ago?"

"I do," she said with that endearing smile.

"Look, I have nothing against ex-guildies. I'm just curious as to why you left," Athen said.

Brick scowled. "I was kicked out. Got into too many fights. I'm not Hazelspine material and being able to paint pretty pictures with light isn't Emerald Order material either."

Athen chuckled. Hazelspine produced some of the Empire's finest artists and musicians, but he could see how someone like Brick may not fit in. He reminded Athen a little of Nyssa.

"You'll find I don't care much for the guilds of late. The Order believes I'm a bit of a traitor."

"Yeah, I hear you're best friends with that Unworthy girl. Big row at the docks."

The smile dropped from Athen's face, and he stepped up to Brick. "Nyssa is family. And if you have something to say about her, say it now so I can toss your ass over the wall and be done with you."

Brick raised an eyebrow at Athen. They stared each other down. "You're a loyal son of a bitch. I like that."

"Nyssa is a good person stuck in a very bad situation."

"Unworthy bring bad fortune," Brick replied. "If you're a superstitious git, that is. Which I'm not."

"Thank you, I appreciate that." Athen smiled up at Brick. "Now, what do you know about Ithais-Toru?"

With a shrug, Brick sighed. "I'm not much for formal martial arts. I punch things."

"Well, Ithais-Toru is flexible. We'll find what works for you."

"And if I'm fine with the way I fight?"

Athen shook his head. "You'll learn Ithais-Toru like the rest of the Guard. That scrappy, dirty fighting style of the Triad is good for street fights, but if you want to be a proper fighter, you'll let me teach you. I'll turn you into a weapon."

Brick's bravado and prickly exterior fell away for a moment. "Enough to fight off wraiths if they ever come back?"

The change in Brick's demeanor clued Athen in. "Did you lose someone at The Masthead?"

"My cousin Alfie. A good man. My aunt's only kid. The Triad is looking after her now," Brick said, avoiding eye contact.

"Oh, Brick, I'm so sorry." Aryis lay a gentle hand on his arm. Her kindness teased a small, sad smile out of the big man.

"Thank you, Queen Aryis."

"I'm not a queen yet, Brick, but I appreciate the respect."

Athen stepped forward and held out his hand. "I'll teach you how to fight, Brick. More importantly, I'll teach you how to protect this city and its people. *Our* people."

Brick hesitated before reaching out and shaking his hand. His grip was as impressive as his fists.

"Brick, go join the rest of the Lion's Guard," Athen said. He turned to Aryis. "This is a good core group to grow from." He was finding a measure of happiness in his work. Teaching people how to fight was a job he was built for, and the Lion's Guard was coming along nicely.

"Well, I'm hardly a good evaluator of warriors, but you're starting strong," Aryis replied.

Athen glanced down at her. "I do enjoy when you join us to continue your training that we started back on the Sea Stag." He had done his best to give her the basics to defend herself while on their original journey to capture Quinn.

"You would make me a warrior queen?" Aryis asked, grinning.

"Couldn't hurt!"

"I do enjoy joining when I can."

"I like knowing that you can protect yourself." Athen watched as Brick fell in line and the other recruits started practice. "We have twenty-two members now. Now that Brick is here, I suspect we'll get more faction members joining up. I hope to have fifty by the end of the year."

Aryis scratched down a note in her book and smiled. "Okay. I'll budget for fifty members and adjust as it grows."

Athen smiled and moved closer to her. "I love when you talk numbers. It's sexy."

"Well, remember that for tonight, then," Aryis replied with a wink. "I'll talk all the numbers you like."

Athen loved her flirting, but he turned serious. There was something he needed to do, but he didn't know how to tell her. She valued honesty, so he just dove right in.

"Look, when you and the others are at a level where we can bring more in and train them, I'm going to leave Ocean's Rest to find Nyssa and Quinn and help them."

The smile disappeared off Aryis's face, and she grabbed him by the elbow and pulled him away from the others.

"You are going to do no such thing," she said, her voice low. "Leaving would garner a lot of attention, and you'd lead the Empire right to Nyssa if you even managed to find them. Your heart is in the right place—my gods, what a big, lovely heart it is—but you need to stay put."

The admonishment was sharp and clear, but he pushed forward. "I can't just do nothing."

"Doing nothing protects them. All eyes are on us. We cannot falter. We *will* find a way to help them, but it has to be from afar." Her eyes pleaded with him. "Promise me you won't do anything rash."

Nyssa's absence was like a persistent burr in Athen's boot, but Aryis was likely right. And he could hear Master Eron in his head as well, preaching caution and patience. Even for Nyssa.

Especially for Nyssa.

"Okay. For you, and Nyssa, I'll stay." He sighed, gesturing to the Lion's Guard. "Nyssa should be the one doing this."

Aryis rubbed Athen's back, her warm, comforting touch soothing his lingering frustration.

"Nyssa and Quinn are alive and well. I believe in Nyssa," Aryis said.

"I miss her."

Aryis leaned up against him, and Athen wrapped an arm around her. "Me too," she said. "I kick myself every day...we should have listened to her and Quinn."

"I ended up losing Nyssa instead of protecting her. We need to do better, Aryis," Athen said. "Stand up for what's right next time, even if Anelos is the one we have to fight."

"I agree, but we need to be careful. Our two Houses don't exactly hold a lot of political sway outside of Ocean's Rest or Frosland. Hopefully our Justiciar friend will stick to her word."

"She better or Reece will rip her to shreds."

"I would consider paying to watch such a thing." Aryis kissed him on the cheek and slipped out of his hug. "I wish I could stay, but I have to help your mother mediate a faction meeting. I'll see you later for dinner."

"Great," Athen said. "I love you."

He froze. The words just slipped out of his mouth.

Aryis turned around, fighting back a smile. "Is that so?"

"I-I'm sorry, that's not how I wanted to say it for the first time. It just sort of...happened."

"Come here."

Athen pushed off the brick barrier and walked over to her. She pulled him down for a kiss. A long kiss. One that made his face go hot. When she stepped away from him, she spun around to head back inside the Keep.

"I love you too!" she called out.

Athen burst into happy laughter as his trainees teased him with wolf whistles.

"Back to work!" he yelled, clapping his hands.

His heart felt lighter for the first time in months.

DINNER WITH THE QUEEN

S uvi took a languid swallow of her wine—a long drink for a long week—and shared a look with her brother. She had once ridden into battle and fought tooth and nail for days on end against the Areshi Empire, and she still would prefer the exhaustion of war over the tedious, draining weeks of treaty negotiation. If only she weren't so damn good at it.

Conversation around the dining table bored her, but this dinner was for a specific purpose: to send a message to the four military commanders exchanging pleasantries over a roast and her finest wines. She directed her gaze to Commander Feng, her military's most senior leader. He had turned down a glass of wine, preferring instead her rather expensive honey liquor.

A *fucking* waste of a good drink.

"Commander Feng, I would love to hear your opinions on our recent alliances," she said.

Feng smiled politely, his dark eyes unreadable. A stern man, Suvi's father had elevated him to commander during the Mire War despite his youth, and ever since, Feng considered himself to be the leader of

Thu'Dain's military, though that title resided with Suvi as queen. The man's arrogance rankled her.

"My Queen, your vision is certainly a...drastic change from your father's legacy," he replied.

"My father's legacy? A legacy of losing? Of dying in another useless war against the Areshi Empire?"

Matthys chuckled while Feng's face didn't flinch.

Suvi continued, "Tell me, Commander Feng, is it you who is whispering your discontent with my decisions into the ears of Houses Swain and Dalpati?"

"My Queen, I would never—"

"You'd be surprised how generous our trade agreements are to their interests. They seem unreceptive to your desire to remove me from power."

Feng went white. *There he is. There is the man.*

"Your problem, Feng, is you cannot envision a future where you and your ilk are merely a threat, an arrow in a quiver that is hopefully never drawn by a bow. You rely on a nation at war, its people under constant threat, real or imaginary. Therein lies your power: fear."

Suvi stared down the table at her other three military commanders. "Hopefully tonight's events will extinguish any thoughts of questioning my leadership."

She set her eyes on Feng and reached out to him with her mind, slipping over his consciousness.

In an instant, Suvi's perspective flipped. She saw herself across the table, eyes completely black. A smile spread over her face and she became fully aware of this new body—aged and male and buzzing with a cold dread. Feng's mind churned under her control, thoughts of a woman immediate and sharp. His wife. His concern for her safety hollowed him out, no moment spared for his own welfare.

If only Suvi cared.

"What should we do with him?" Suvi asked, her voice layered in her ears and Feng's.

"Yes, what should we do with me?" she asked again through Feng.

"You know I hate when you do that, sister," Matthys said, grinning.

Suvi stood and slowly walked around the dining table. It was a challenge to maintain control of Feng and move her own body at the same time, but she had become somewhat proficient at it over the years. Though the sensation of occupying two different spaces simultaneously would forever be strange.

"I will not be questioned about my decisions. Nor plotted against by my own *fucking* military," she said, laying her hand on Feng's shoulders. The sensation of touching a body she controlled sent an eerie chill of unease through her.

Suvi had Feng draw the dagger from the sheath at his belt and place the butt of the weapon on the table in front of him.

"I am your queen. You would do well to remember exactly who you answer to."

The panic inside Feng's mind as he stared down at the point of his dagger didn't concern Suvi. The man wouldn't think twice about cutting her throat and installing himself on the throne.

Fuck him.

"Your wife will die tonight, Feng. A reminder that there is more to lose than just one's life for crossing me," Suvi said before she drove his head down the dagger, its point bursting through his eye and into his brain, driving her out of his head as death came swift.

She closed her eyes and re-centered herself. When she opened her eyes again, Feng was slumped over. His blood spread across the dining table and seeped into the bright-white tablecloth. The perfect punctuation to a dinner she hoped none present would soon forget...for their sakes.

Suvi raised her gaze to the remaining three commanders. None of them moved.

"I want to reassure you that our military will remain as strong as ever. As such, I believe we could do with a few more weapons. I am putting a bounty on Nyssa Blacksea and Quinn's heads. Seven hundred fifty thousand gold each. Put your best trackers on them."

The men nodded, their faces slack. No glimmer of protest.

They were hers. As they should be.

"Thank you for the company tonight. You may go." Suvi smiled as the men all but ran from the room. She sat back down and poured another glass of wine, sighing at Feng's body.

Silence from Matthys clued her in to a change in her brother's mood. Usually he didn't mind a bit of spectacle.

"What?" she asked.

He cleared his throat. "I thought you were doing everything you could to extricate yourself from any future conflicts with the Empire, and now you want to compete for the Cursed Gods?"

Suvi swirled her wine glass, its sweet aroma calming her. "Quinn is rightfully mine. Her parents promised her to me over twenty-five years ago in exchange for a very generous payout."

"It doesn't seem like she wants to be controlled. She and the other one killed how many Justiciars?" Matthys grabbed the bottle of honey liquor off the table and drank straight from it.

"That is of no matter. Quinn was promised to me and I want her back. And Blacksea...we'll see if she'll heel."

He scoffed. "And anger Kalla in the process? Ah, that Rell entitlement of ours."

Suvi clucked her tongue. "Cursed Gods are dangerous. That makes them valuable. Kalla would capture and kill them to prove some sort of regressive point. Her lack of vision is stunning. I would have them be mine...and who would dare oppose us? We'll have countries at our doorstep, hounding us for alliances, knowing the power we wield."

Matthys leaned forward. "Do you truly believe this will be to our benefit?"

His caution was well placed—one of the things she loved about her brother. Matthys never failed to look out for her. He was truly the only person she could trust.

"Consider if Kalla decides that they're far better as her pets than lying in a grave. I will not put our future at risk to her whims. The Cursed Gods will be my weapons, not hers." Suvi reached over and took her brother's hand. "Trust me. I am doing this for our future."

"This is ugly business," he replied, but he squeezed her hand in return.

Smiling, Suvi leaned back and drank more wine. "Let's leave for the winery early this year. Put this behind us and spend an extra week getting drunk. I've invited that vintner you like to fuck. He will put a smile on your face."

Matthys clinked his honey liquor bottle against her wine glass. "Indeed."

THE EMPATH AND THE JUSTICIAR

Medias growled at Reece's messy bookcase and picked a collection of essays on Escostian art off a pile of books haphazardly stacked on a shelf, placing it where it should go. Reorganizing was easier when Reece was late getting back from The Feather. At least when alone, she didn't have to pretend to be perusing a tome before placing it back in its *proper* place.

The door to the office opened. Medias did her best to look nonchalant, leaning against the bookcase as Reece entered. Reece's dark-red velvet dress and short black jacket were a sharp contrast to her pale skin and silver hair, though her cheeks were flushed with color. Summer had turned to autumn, and with it came the first cold spell of the season.

"Empath," Medias greeted. "I took the liberty of ordering tea."

"Have you heard about the bounty Suvi Rell has put on Nyssa and Quinn?" Reece asked.

"I heard."

Reece frowned and tossed her rucksack onto her desk, likely full of paperwork from The Feather. It didn't escape Medias's notice that she was spending less and less time at the establishment with its consorts and gamblers, preferring to be in the Keep. Perhaps to keep an eye on her.

Medias gestured to the pot of tea and mugs sitting on a side table between two well-worn leather chairs close to the bookshelves.

Reece dropped into a chair and rubbed her forehead. Taking a seat across from her, Medias poured tea into their mugs and handed one to Reece, who stared down into the hot, sweet beverage and scowled.

Trying to gauge and adjust for Reece's preferences so that their working relationship would grow smoother proved difficult. On days where the empath was stressed—and today appeared to be one of those days—Medias found herself ill-equipped to offer much solace.

"Are you not concerned about this bounty?" Reece asked.

"Yes, but this wasn't unexpected. Other countries will likely follow suit, looking to exploit Nyssa and Quinn any way they can. Or kill them."

Reece blew out a breath. "How are you so...even-keeled about it?"

"Shall I wind myself up and get unduly upset over circumstances I cannot control?"

The look on the empath's face would have wilted someone else, but Medias remained unaffected. "You disagree?"

Reece leaned forward, her tea careening about her mug, setting Medias on edge, wary of a spill.

"I'm worried for their lives. I don't know how to make you care more," Reece said.

"Your implication that I don't care is incorrect."

"Do you merely care about keeping your word or do you care about Nyssa and Quinn?"

"A distinction without difference to me."

Reece shook her head and sighed. She obviously didn't appreciate Medias's answer, a strained, thin smile fighting off a frown. "Duty? Is that all this is, Medias? How can you be loyal to people you have no feelings for?"

The ease with which Reece dropped Medias's title and addressed her only by her name was irritating. "I keep my word, that's the important detail here."

Another sigh. Another impatient smile. "I'm loyal to the people I love. How can I trust you'll stay loyal when you feel nothing?"

"Just because you cannot sense my emotions doesn't mean I don't have them. My word should be enough. Have I done anything to make you doubt me?" She didn't care to explain that emotional attachments complicated her work—made things messy. Impartiality was part of her job as a Justiciar, something others could never understand.

Reece tapped her fingers on the arm of her chair, her dark eyes on constant alert. "Not yet, but duty is a poor reason to do anything. Nyssa tried to adhere to duty, and she found it untenable. Mind you don't find yourself in the same position, Justiciar."

"Your concern is noted," Medias said, trying to keep the sarcasm out of her voice, but the empath was right. And smarter than expected.

Medias slipped her hand inside her jacket and pulled out an envelope, placing it on the table between them. "These are the current locations of two Obsidian Rule operatives on Nyssa and Quinn's trail."

Reece glanced down at the envelope and nodded. "I'll see what false information we can leak to them."

The partnership between the two of them had proved successful over the past months. Credible sightings of Nyssa and Quinn had the Empire chasing ghosts. Now, with Thu'Dainian agents in the mix, they would have to be very careful. But mercenaries could be played against each other. If they were busy stepping on one another's toes, their pursuit of the Cursed Gods would become further complicated by ego and greed.

Reece sipped on her tea and smoothed out her dress. "You should send more frequent updates on your progress here to the Arch Justiciar and Ceril. And express your frustration in that stiff, restrained style of yours."

Medias glanced at Reece and ran her finger along her bottom lip, thinking. The empath was pushy, unapologetically so. Telling Medias her business amused her, but Reece was right.

"Noted," Medias replied, standing. "You should get some rest. You're looking frayed."

Reece frowned. "Your pleasantries need work."

The Justiciar grunted and left Reece's office.

A SECOND CHANCE

Goosebumps pricked up on Quinn's skin as she floated in the cove's peaceful waters. It had become a refuge for her, a way to soothe aching muscles after her sessions with Nyssa. Fall was coming, and she lamented the change in the seasons. Soon it would be too cold to drift and have a think.

Her mornings were completely dominated by Fontaine's training. Then, after lunch, Nyssa would train Quinn relentlessly for hours. But she was improving. And beginning to understand not just the martial art, but the philosophy behind it—and the code of honor that drove Nyssa. Along the way, Nyssa would share her memories of Athen and Eron, often involving troublemaking and a requisite punishment from their First Master.

Nyssa's face would light up when she told those stories, and Quinn laughed whenever one of the tales involved a fight because Nyssa would spring to her feet and re-enact the skirmish with dramatic flair. But a melancholy clung to her at times like gossamer threads, especially when recalling her lessons with Eron.

Most of their time, however, was spent drilling and sparring, Nyssa attentive and exacting. By the time they were done, Quinn was exhausted. Nyssa had encouraged her to meditate to still her mind and body, insistent it would help her with both her magick and her Ithais-Toru training. The time spent floating in the water was her reprieve, giving her pause to reflect on what she had learned that day from both Nyssa and Fontaine. There was a tranquility about the water that enveloped her; it made her feel safe.

It was also a perfect time to practice sensing the ambient magick in the world around her, barely detectable until she relaxed and let her power flow as Fontaine had taught her. How strange it was to become aware of more than just herself or Nyssa or even Fontaine, but of the water, the forest, and the sky above it.

Energy tingled around her, vibrating, alive and pulsing like fireflies. The edges that separated her body from the world fell away, and she became something more, if only for a slight moment of time as the deep drone of magick filled her ears, all of it a strange symphony of sound and sensation.

The resonance of the sea's magick was familiar—it matched the buzz in Quinn's chest when Nyssa was near, her mere presence warm and comforting.

A splash in the water pulled Quinn out of her trance, and she shot to attention. Nyssa was half in the water, clinging to the edge of the dock, her arms visibly trembling. Quinn hadn't felt her get close, too deep in her meditation.

She couldn't help the smile of pride that plastered itself on her face as she swam toward Nyssa. It had been two months since she first offered to teach Nyssa to swim. Since then, she hadn't mentioned it again. Didn't push.

Her patience had paid off.

"Nyssa?"

"Teach me to swim, please?" Nyssa asked, her fingers gripping the dock so tightly they were white.

Quinn held out her hand. "Let me show you how to tread water. We won't move from the dock in case you need to steady yourself. I promise."

Nyssa took a deep breath and nodded, peeling off the wood to grab Quinn's outstretched hand. Quinn squeezed and smiled. Nyssa's deep-blue eyes didn't leave her face.

"I've got you," Quinn said.

"I'm sad we won't be swimming anymore," Nyssa said with a dramatic pout as she lay back on the dock. "I'm rather good at it."

Quinn rolled her eyes. Typical cocky Nyssa. Before the weather turned too cold to swim anymore, Quinn had turned Nyssa into quite the competent swimmer. She was rather proud of how Nyssa had overcome her fear, not that she would admit to such a thing. She did miss dangling her feet in the water, but it had become too brisk to do it for long. Nyssa, however, was in her element. She loved the approach of winter.

Behind them, Fontaine paced, uncharacteristically nervous. "He should be here by now."

"You should really sit down and relax," Nyssa suggested. "Shall we bet on Elias's facial hair? I say he's grown a beard."

"I'll take that bet," Quinn replied. "A week's worth of fishing?"

"Deal." Nyssa offered a handshake.

"I trust you," Quinn said.

"Ha! I don't trust you." Nyssa winked, and Quinn slapped her hand away.

"Asshole."

"There he is!" Fontaine said, bouncing on the balls of her feet.

Hannah's Whisper shimmered into view, dropping its invisibility veil once inside the bay. Nyssa scrambled to her feet and laughed, waving her arms over her head. The crew appeared at the rail of the ship and waved back. Despite her short time on the Whisper, Quinn was happy to see the ship again. It had become something of a home to her, much like Monk's Cove.

The women waited as a tender approached. Elias's beaming—bearded—face was the first thing that greeted them.

Nyssa threw an arm around Quinn's neck and pulled her close, gesturing to Elias. "I win! But if you're nice to me, I'll keep you company while you fish."

"I've already lost once, why the need to torture me further?"

A laugh rumbled out of Nyssa, and she beamed a bright, warm smile. Quinn flushed with happiness.

When the tender got to the dock, Elias jumped out to give Fontaine a big bear hug. Jerrin and Yuha followed him out of the boat.

Elias let go of Fontaine and put his arms around Nyssa and Quinn. "How are my little gods?"

"It's good to see you, Elias," Nyssa replied, kissing him on the cheek.

"Come, let's get some rum into me while these guys stock you full of supplies," he said, winking at Jerrin and the others.

"Blacksea." Yuha stepped forward and grabbed Nyssa's shoulder, staring down at her. "I left word with Athen that you were alive and well. He was much relieved."

Nyssa exhaled, her face teetering a moment before she put her hand over Yuha's. "Thank you, my friend."

Yuha grunted and turned to help Jerrin with the supplies. Nyssa glanced over at Quinn, returned her happiness with a smile.

That night, over roasted chicken and vegetables, Elias gave them news of the outside world. Quinn listened intently, concerned about the danger she and Nyssa had brought upon the crew.

The Whisper had been forcibly boarded a few times by Imperial agents, and Jerrin stood up and gave a dramatic re-enactment of a tussle he had with an Areshi naval officer, demanding they get off of his damn ship. Elias clapped him on the back and tipped a generous glug of rum into his cup.

The Empire quickly lost interest in Elias when rumors of sightings of the Cursed Gods on land proliferated. Mostly from the Eastern continent, but a few rumors had them back in the Empire or even in Thu'Dain. Quinn sighed, pleased that their pursuers were chasing their tails and not harassing the Whisper anymore.

"Athen and Yuha, with the help of Medias it seems, got rumors floating around about where the two of you were, and those rumors are now pinging about in all directions," Elias said. "A ruse to get everyone off our tails and I suspect your friends in Ocean's Rest are continuing to pull the strings."

"Thank you—all of you—for helping," Nyssa said. "Now, tell me more about Medias. I need to know if I'll have to kill her when I see her again or if she's remained loyal."

Elias laughed. "She's living in Ocean's Keep, serving as the city's Justiciar."

"Well, fuck me. She kept her word, eh?" Nyssa replied, exchanging a look with Quinn.

"Seems like it. You collect strange friends, present company included," he said, slicing away at a large round purple fruit that Quinn had never seen before. He handed a slice to her. Its sweet, mellow aroma made her mouth water.

"What is this?" she asked.

"An ice melon."

"Melon? I've not had melon before."

Excited to try something new, she took a bite. *Holy. Fuck.*

The fruit was sweet and delicious, different from the berries, grapes, and apples on the island, and somehow tasted like sunshine and honey and airy spun sugar. A soft moan escaped her, much to her horror.

All eyes darted to her, and she quickly wiped the juice from her lips with the back of her hand.

"Have you discovered your new favorite thing?" Nyssa asked, a mix of amusement and joy on her face. Heat overtook Quinn's cheeks. Elias handed her half of the melon and his knife, and she ate her fill, Nyssa swiping the occasional piece and popping it into her mouth.

"Jerrin, on the next run back to the ship, pull all the melons we have and bring them over. They're imbued with preservation enchantments, Quinn, so no need to eat through them all in a week."

"That is not something I can guarantee, Elias," she replied.

He chuckled. "How I've missed your smart ass. The two of you should come back on the tender tomorrow and visit while we load you up with the last of the supplies. I'm assuming another six months and you'll be ready?" He looked over to Fontaine.

Quinn stopped mid-bite, waiting for the woman's answer.

"Their progress is acceptable," Fontaine said. "They will have to continue to push themselves in order to be ready to take on Suvi and her mages. And her guards. And her equally dangerous brother—"

"Point taken," Nyssa grumbled.

Elias poured himself another large glass of rum. The man could toss them back like water. "Suvi has complicated things a bit by offering a seven hundred fifty thousand bounty for each of you. Kalla, of course, matched the amount."

Shit.

He continued, "In the meantime, I'll work on a way to get us to Thu'Dain and close to Suvi." He exchanged a look with Fontaine before continuing. "Understand, I cannot sail into Thu'Dainian waters. We'll find another way to get into the country."

"What? Why?" Nyssa asked.

A sadness passed over Elias. "I lost my wife, Hannah, in Thu'Dainian waters twenty-some years ago. We were attacked by Reavers, a deadly warning to stay out of their territory. I..." He swallowed.

Quinn frowned and glanced at Nyssa—this was new information to them both.

Fontaine reached over and took his hand. "She was the absolute best of us."

*Twenty years...*Quinn scowled. Fontaine had been a chicken for twenty years. Now it made sense. She was in mourning.

"Hannah's Whisper...the ship's named after her," Quinn said.

"A birthday present. I renamed it for her."

"I'm so sorry, Elias. We had no idea," Nyssa said.

"We'll find another way into Thu'Dain," Fontaine said.

"I'm sorry. Tonight is a reunion, let's not cast a pall over it," Elias said, brightening. He raised his glass. "To my loyal crew, two idiot fledgling gods, and ice melons!"

"Hey!" Nyssa softly objected.

"To idiot gods!" Yuha said, lifting her mug and laughing at Nyssa. Quinn couldn't stop her own laughter and Yuha winked at her.

They all raised their glasses and spent the rest of the night listening to tales of the Whisper's latest pirating conquests.

THE CALLING

Nyssa bounced on her toes, her breath hanging in the air as she exhaled and waited for Quinn to attack. Winter had set in nice and deep on Monk's Cove, but it didn't stop their training—in magick or Ithais-Toru.

Though Nyssa did her best to concentrate and stay in the moment, Winter's Fire was drawing close, and she found herself distracted, looking forward to celebrating the holiday with Quinn and Fontaine on the island. She needed the rest.

Finally, Quinn moved. Nyssa recognized the opening from the first movements of the Ninth Form—the Sea Form. But Quinn altered it, changing the angle of her attack and swiping her wooden sword across Nyssa's torso.

Smart girl!

It was one of the few times Quinn was able to get past Nyssa's guard in the nine months they had been training. Quinn shouted in celebration.

Nyssa dropped her practice sword and grabbed at her stomach, dramatically sinking to her knees.

"Oh, stop," Quinn said, rolling her eyes, though a smile gave her delight away.

Nyssa stood, brushing snow off her pants. "That was impressive. You must have a good teacher."

Against anyone else, Quinn landing a strike would have been superb as a novice fighter, but against Nyssa—who considered herself an exemplary swordswoman—it was a triumph. Her pride in her student clashed with the chagrin of Quinn sneaking through her guard.

A smile of victory lingered on Quinn's lips. Nyssa lit up with magick and sent a small spark of lightning at her, hitting her in the nose, drawing a happy yelp out of her. Gods, how Nyssa loved to make Quinn laugh, almost craving the sound of late.

"You could have negated or blocked that little shock, you know," Nyssa said.

With a shrug, Quinn replied, "I had to give you one small victory today."

Fontaine barked out a laugh from her seat on the log.

"Mind your business, chicken!" Nyssa said.

The woman stuck her tongue out at her and went back to the spell she was weaving, creating threads of magick in front of her with increasing complexity.

Nyssa turned back to Quinn, but a gust of wind stilled her.

Something's wrong.

A cry from above pulled her eyes upward. Nyssa's mouth went dry.

Dark creatures hurled down from the sky.

"Wraiths!" she yelled, running toward Quinn. Black shadow whirled around Quinn as she braced for an attack. Nyssa followed suit, pulling her magick forth. "At my back!"

The first wraith landed in front of her. She shot a streak of lightning into its chest without a thought. It barely let out a shriek before dropping dead. Nyssa took aim at the two wraiths that followed behind it, hitting one in the shoulder with a bolt, only slowing it down.

Fuck.

The other wraith dodged her lightning and caught her with a fist to her chin. Nyssa reeled back into Quinn, and they both spilled to the ground.

"You okay?" Nyssa asked, blinking through her pain.

Quinn scrambled to her feet. She sent a spear of darkness through the head of a wraith bearing down on them before grabbing Nyssa by the collar of her jacket and tugging her up to her feet.

More wraiths landed, surrounding them. Nyssa lunged forward, crushing the head of the closest monster with her wooden sword before grabbing another and sending a shock of lightning through it. The beast fell; dead.

"We have to help Fontaine!" Quinn yelled, pulling Nyssa's arm toward the log where Fontaine had been sitting. Two wraiths lunged at them. Quinn spiraled her darkness around the monsters, trapping them in a whirlwind of shadow that ripped them apart.

Wraiths filled Nyssa's vision, coming quick. She pushed the fear in her gut down and attacked, sending out a wide shock wave of lightning, putting every bit of power behind it. The wraiths screeched, their ear-piercing cries making her heart pound.

Quinn shouted. A wraith had her by the wrist, but she lashed out, forcing it off of her with a vicious palm strike to its chest. A swath of shadow poured out of her, darting toward the wraiths surrounding them and striking with swift precision, spikes of black sinking into their flesh.

Nyssa whirled around, breathing heavy, heart thumping in her chest. The log where Fontaine had sat was empty, her spell book spilled open on the ground.

"Where's Fontaine?" Quinn glanced around frantically, a thin trickle of blood tracing down her chin.

"Fontaine!" Nyssa shouted.

No response. Nyssa choked down bile. *She can't be dead.*

A bellowing cry echoed on the wind, chilling Nyssa's blood.

"No," she whispered. *No, no, no—*

A large, dark form ripped out of the forest, and Nyssa froze. *Blood wraith.* Its size, speed, and ferocity made the normal wraiths seem tame in comparison. One had almost killed her—twice.

Her eyes went wide as the blood wraith stalked toward her. It was almost ten feet tall and short, broken horns twisting out of its forehead. And those fucking red eyes Nyssa would never forget.

Quinn moved first, hurling a shard of darkness at the massive creature. It dodged the strike, its preternatural speed far quicker than their reflexes.

Nyssa gathered herself and sent a streak of lightning into the blood wraith. It stopped and shuddered, shirking off the blow.

How?

It shot forward and was on her in a heartbeat, backhanding her across the face. She staggered aside but somehow stayed on her feet, the familiar taste of copper flooding her mouth. Lightning sparked on her fingertips and sputtered. "Fuck," she hissed as her magick slipped away, her focus shattered.

The creature grabbed her fist, yanking her forward. It wrapped its massive hand around her throat, lifting her off the ground. She shouted in a panic and thoughtlessly sent a shock wave through the wraith. Its thick legs wobbled, but it held up.

How is it still alive?

Quinn rushed at the blood wraith, darkness spiraling around her hands, but a last remaining wraith grabbed her and threw her to the ground.

"Quinn!" Nyssa yelled. She clawed at the blood wraith's wrist, blue energy crackling around her hands. The wraith's arm began to vibrate, becoming blurry before it shattered. Nyssa dropped to the ground, landing on her feet.

What the hell?

The wraith reared up to its full height and roared at Nyssa. Even missing an arm, it was deadly. Hot rage spiked through her, replacing her fear, and a guttural cry ripped from her mouth.

Thunder bellowed across the sky, and a thin bolt of lightning struck the blood wraith, shattering it immediately. The force of it knocked her to the ground. Her eyes shot upward. A storm roiled overhead, blue lightning sparking under its dark clouds.

"Nyssa?" Quinn scrambled next to her and wrapped an arm around her, grabbing the front of her jacket. "Are you hurt?"

Thunder crashed overhead, and they both jumped, Quinn pulling Nyssa closer. "What's happening?"

"Nyssa!" a woman called out. Fontaine stalked toward them, looking up into the sky.

"You're not dead!" Nyssa cried.

Fontaine's finger pointed to the sky. "Is that you?"

"I don't…I don't know!"

Fontaine crouched in front of her. "Nyssa, you need to calm down."

"I don't understand," Nyssa stammered.

Fontaine grabbed her hand and grimaced. Lightning sparked around her fingers as bolts streaked across the sky. Thunder roared in her ears. "The storm, Nyssa, will it away."

How the fuck…

"I'm not doing it!"

"Yes, you are. Now will it away!" Fontaine yelled over the wind whipping around her. "Reach out, sense the storm, and will it away. Pull it back, like you do with your magick."

Nyssa looked up, concentrating on folding her magick back inside her, furling it like the sails of Hannah's Whisper. The storm slowly calmed, the lightning receding to a few sparks before the clouds dissipated and the winter sun became visible again.

Fontaine let go and fell back on the ground, panting.

"What…. What was that?" Nyssa asked, her mouth bone dry.

"Impossible," Fontaine whispered. Her face was pale and blank. "You called a storm. It shouldn't be possible…you created it without thinking."

Nyssa's brain chugged, unable to process what had just happened.

"Fontaine, did the wraiths hurt you?" Quinn asked.

"My dear, look around you."

The bodies of the wraiths were slowly turning into dust and blowing away on the winter wind.

"They weren't real. I constructed them, including the blood wraith," Fontaine said.

Nyssa sat up and grabbed the front of Fontaine's sweater, growling. "Why would you do that?"

"You know why."

A test. A *fucking* test.

Quinn laid a hand on her wrist. "Nyssa, let her go. Please."

"That was a dirty trick," Nyssa breathed, releasing Fontaine.

"Yes, it was. But I had to see how far you two had come; to see how you would fare when threatened. But Nyssa...what you just did...you called a storm. Do you understand how amazing that is? It's unbelievable." Fontaine shook her head, a smile forming on her face. "Get cleaned up for dinner. We'll talk about this over a meal. Then it's off to bed early for plenty of rest."

"Wait. Why?" Nyssa asked.

"Because I want to see if you can do that again tomorrow."

STORM AND SHADOW

Nyssa shifted her weight back and forth, trying to stay warm and shake off her nerves.

Practically laughing with excitement, Fontaine clapped her on the back. "This will be an extraordinary day."

The storm Nyssa conjured up the previous day was an accident. She had no idea how she did it. What brought it forth? Anger? Fear? Calling a storm on purpose was a completely different beast, though Fontaine had assured her if she could do it once, she could do it again.

The women stood at the end of the dock facing the cove. "Everything you need to create a storm is inside you. Remember, magick is magick, just the size and complexity changes," Fontaine said. "You just need to will it to happen. Extend your magick outward and mix it with the natural magick in the world. Don't worry about how to assemble the pieces. This isn't about shoving building blocks together or an equation your brain can solve. This is instinctual. Trust your gut. Find the calm in the chaos and you'll grasp your control."

Nyssa swallowed. *Calm in the chaos? That doesn't even make sense!*

She looked down and pulled her magick forth, letting lightning ripple across her skin. With a deep exhale, she looked up into the cloudless sky. How was she supposed to conjure a storm on a clear day?

"Reach out with your senses and feel the ambient magick in the world, just like I taught you. But instead of observing it, now it's about controlling it. Once you feel it, direct it. The storm is there, *you* just have to bring it into being," Fontaine said, her voice low in Nyssa's ear.

Nyssa closed her eyes and calmed herself, slowing her breathing. Extending her senses beyond her body, her bubble of awareness growing, she reached up into the sky.

And found nothing.

No magick to spark into a storm.

"I can't…"

Fontaine's hand settled on her shoulder. "Remember that time on the Whisper when you stayed out in the winter storm. It called to you, didn't it? Transfixed you. Now, you call to it. The storm is waiting for you."

Nyssa opened her eyes and flexed her fingers, curling her hands into fists at her sides. She didn't understand how she was supposed to call to something that didn't exist.

Closing her eyes again, she found her center and waited for the world to still around her. She reached back out. It was easier this time to sense the sky. Energy began to shimmer and pulse as she narrowed her focus and let herself feel the power instead of think about it.

Will it to happen. Just…will it to happen.

Nyssa imagined a storm forming, picturing faint flashes of lightning as the harbinger of a greater force, the thunder bellowing the storm's power.

The more she imagined the components of a storm, the less confined she felt by her own body. The barrier between herself and the rest of the world seemed to fade, and her magick unfurled, stretching up into the sky and wrapping around the power, waiting for her.

Thunder rumbled in the distance, and Nyssa's eyes flew open. A dark, angry sky roiled above them and blue lightning tickled the bottom of the ashen clouds.

"Holy shit," she whispered.

"Don't stop, Nyssa. Feed it. Make it roar," Fontaine said, squeezing her shoulder.

Nyssa did as she asked, imagining more strength. More violence. Minutes passed as she slowly built up her storm's intensity. She focused and maintained control, feeling the power of the storm build as she gathered more magick. Thunder rolled across the sky in an angry growl.

"Quinn, close your eyes. Extend your magick out and see if you can sense Nyssa," Fontaine said.

"A-are you sure?" The hesitation in her voice mirrored Nyssa's nervousness.

"Find her in the storm."

A crack of lightning made Nyssa jump.

"Maintain control, Nyssa," Fontaine warned.

Closing her eyes and refocusing, Nyssa extended herself back into the sky. Using her magick and flexing these very strange new muscles became easier the more she tried, but she knew not to get overconfident.

She let her magick flow through the storm. A gasp left her lips when she realized she wasn't alone. Nyssa could feel Quinn—her soul, her magick, her body. Everything. Quinn was simultaneously beside her and a thousand legions away, then inside of her—vibrating and still at the same time. The experience was bizarre and wonderful, but as Nyssa pulled Quinn's magick toward her, she could sense Quinn doing the same, their energy weaving together.

Threading their magicks brought them together, folding them into each other over and over again until Nyssa couldn't find the edges of herself anymore. Scared of losing control, she pulled back to her center—to her calm—until the boundaries between her and Quinn became tangible again.

Beside her, Quinn exhaled. Nyssa opened her eyes. Lightning streaked across the sky, but now Quinn's shadows coiled around the bolts, tendrils of bright blue energy and darkness twisting around one another. Streaks of blue electricity entwined with shadow flashed in the sky, stretching all the way down to strike the water in the middle of the cove.

The crisp scent of the storm hung in the air while thunder roared in Nyssa's ears and lightning crashed into the water. As they wove their power together, layer upon layer, Nyssa's heart beat faster and faster, though her excitement was tinged with fear. This was barely controlled chaos, fierce and destructive.

"Direct the lightning where you want it to go," Fontaine shouted. "It is a weapon."

Nyssa nodded and put her left hand up, feeling power thrumming through her, resonating with the storm above. She reached out and pulled a bolt of lightning out of the storm, willing it into the cove. The arc of energy streaked toward the water and hit, tendrils racing in all directions as thunder boomed, accompanied by umbral veins of darkness. Nyssa could swear she saw trails of ice in the magick's wake.

Despite the danger, working in tandem with Quinn was breathtaking.

Nyssa marveled at the storm. The things she could do with this power...she could make Ceril pay for everything he had done...

Make him *fucking* pay for Eron's death.

Lightning struck the water close to them, knocking the three women off their feet and sending them sprawling to the dock.

"Nyssa!" Fontaine yelled. "Careful!"

Nyssa's eyes went wide. *Fuck-fuck-fuck-fuck-fuck.*

She tried to get her legs under her, but her mind reeled, panic clamping down hard. Another bolt of lightning shot out of the sky and into the water next to them, thunder roaring overhead.

"Nyssa!" Quinn's voice barely cut through the noise. The thunder rumbled and grew louder, singing the danger of the storm across the sky. Before Nyssa could turn to Quinn, the world around her went dark. And cold. The storm above glowed with strange, shadowy luminescence.

The hair on Nyssa's arms rose, signaling another lightning strike. *Control.* She needed to regain control. Her heart thumped wildly in her chest, and she tried to stop the storm, but her magick wouldn't obey. Her concentration slipped further as panic set in.

A dark shape blurred next to her, and Nyssa was instantly surrounded by darkness. The rumble of the storm ceased. A sudden all-encompassing silence cut her off from the world.

She didn't move, the air around her heavy.

A fog of chilled breath left her mouth as she exhaled. "What's happening?" she whispered, sitting up.

Two glowing green eyes appeared in front of her, and someone grabbed her arms.

"Calm the storm," Quinn said, her voice low and thick.

"Quinn? Are you doing this?"

"Listen to her," a faint voice said. *Fontaine.*

Why does she sound so far away?

"Will it away," Quinn said, her presence burning bright and hot in Nyssa's chest.

Nyssa closed her eyes and expanded her senses, only this time she moved through a dense layer of Quinn's magick, its chill causing her to shiver.

Calm. Nyssa needed to stay calm and *concentrate*. Her magick unfurled into the darkness and into the sky, where the storm raged and crackled with untold power.

Her power.

She refocused and willed the storm away, yearning for a blue sky. *Needing* one. She kept the image in her mind, blocking out everything else.

Her whole body trembled from the effort, but eventually she sensed the storm receding. She exhaled and collapsed back against the dock, unable to stop shaking.

"Quinn," Fontaine said.

Nyssa looked up at Quinn. She seemed to shift like the wind, like the darkness that expanded out of her when she called her magick forth. Slowly, the darkness, like the storm, receded, and Nyssa blinked in the bright sunlight.

Quinn stood on the dock, staring down at her trembling hands. "What did I do?"

"Wrapped us in darkness and protected us from the storm, I'd guess, like that time you protected my hand in the kitchen," Fontaine said, her voice upbeat and a smile on her face, as if they all weren't almost incinerated by Nyssa's lightning strikes. "Nyssa can call storms and you...you can surround us with night."

Quinn lifted her eyes. "I have no idea how I did it."

"Instinct. Like raising your arm to protect against a blow, you called forth a great swath of darkness to protect us."

"I almost killed us," Nyssa choked out. *And Quinn saved us.*

Fontaine knelt beside her and grabbed her hand. "You did not. Those strikes were close, but we're fine. Remember, find the calm in the chaos—but you also have to *keep* calm."

Nyssa turned to Quinn and found her scowling. "You okay?"

"I'm just...trying to understand what I did."

"We'll explore that together and I'll help you understand," Fontaine said. She stood and wrapped an arm around Quinn. "This is new for all of us. I promise you we will figure this out together."

Quinn exhaled and nodded. "I didn't know creating all that darkness was possible."

Fontaine laughed. "Imagine my surprise!" She pulled Quinn close and gave her a gentle kiss on the temple. Quinn seemed to relax. "Now, tell me, what was it like when you joined your magicks together in the storm?"

Nyssa shook her head, struggling to find the words. "I've never felt that much power before, especially when we got tangled up. It felt wild and dangerous. I lost myself a little in Quinn. The beginnings and endings of myself got...blurred." She hesitated. "It was kind of like really great sex." It was the only analogy she could conjure in the moment.

"Nyssa!" Fontaine grinned and shook her head.

"You asked! I don't know how else to describe the indescribable."

"Fair enough. I asked for your impressions and they are indeed uniquely yours. Quinn, your thoughts?"

"It was...strange. So much energy and power..." Quinn glanced out to the sea, her face pale. She didn't seem willing to offer more.

"I'm so proud of you two," Fontaine said. "Take the rest of the day—you both need to rest. But we'll start exploring these new skills tomorrow." She smiled at the women before turning to head back to the house.

With a groan, Nyssa pushed herself to her feet. Exhaustion was beginning to set in deeper than usual.

Nyssa turned to Quinn. "You coming?"

"I'll be along, I just need a moment."

"You want me to stick around?" Nyssa asked, frowning.

"No," Quinn replied.

Nyssa crossed her arms, frustrated. Sometimes she made inroads with Quinn, but then the woman could just close herself off entirely. "Are you okay? You're shutting down on me."

"I'm not. I just need a moment to myself, okay?"

"Look...you...you did good today. You saved my ass."

Quinn opened her mouth but didn't say anything. As much as Nyssa wanted to stay with her, help her with whatever she was struggling with, she knew it was best to back off.

"Alright." With a sigh, Nyssa slowly turned and headed back to the house.

Quinn sat on the dock and flopped onto her back. The look on Nyssa's face, disappointed that she needed to be alone, pained her. She didn't want to hurt Nyssa, but she had to slow down and think.

How had she become a Cursed God with strange, potent magick? What exactly did she do to deserve these powers? All she wanted—long before she ran away, long before she met Nyssa—was to be free of the Citadel and Ceril. To live a life of her own choosing. But now...

Quinn covered her mouth, an awkward, unexpected laugh escaping her lips.

This is insanity.

Turning day into night...how was that even possible? She had wrapped Fontaine and Nyssa up in darkness and shielded them without thinking, without knowing what she was doing.

Power was never something Quinn craved, but this was different. Protecting her friends made her feel strong.

If Ceril could see me now. She gritted her teeth and shook her head. "No," she whispered to herself. *I won't ruin this with thoughts of that monster.*

When Fontaine had her find Nyssa in the storm and entwine their magicks, she felt the thunder and lightning thrumming in her chest. And a heartbeat lay on top of her own.

Nyssa's heartbeat—vibrant and strong.

In the sky, Quinn could feel Nyssa drawing her out, pulling Quinn to her. Quinn responded in kind, pushing and pulling, feeling the edges of their magicks entangle, creating something stronger and more fearsome. More dangerous.

Lightning and darkness. Storm and shadow.

Combining their magicks was exciting, but there was an undercurrent of something else. Something unexpected. The experience was *intimate.* She could feel Nyssa's magick running through her, as if she was a ghost inhabiting Quinn's body as they twisted and wove their energies together. The sensation was wild and exhilarating.

Quinn sat up. She closed her eyes and tried to recapture the feeling of getting tangled up with Nyssa. There were faint wisps of thoughts and emotions—some her own, some she knew had to be Nyssa's. Quinn didn't even know how it was possible to sense Nyssa so deeply, but part of her was sad when it ended. She wanted more. But that meant giving more of herself and letting Nyssa in. And that scared her to no end.

Quinn sighed and slowly rose to her feet, slouching from exhaustion.

"This godling needs a nap," she murmured, before heading back to the house.

A LATE NIGHT VISIT

A knock on the door stirred Medias from her reading. She stood and slipped the book under her pillow. This was only the second time anyone had dared come to her room, though Medias suspected who it might be as she slid her arms into her jacket and put her mask on. She opened her door to find Reece frowning at her.

"Empath," she sighed. "Shouldn't you be preparing for Winter's Fire rather than interrupting my evening?"

"I understand you chastised Athen and Aryis today?" Reece asked, inviting herself in.

Medias closed the door and leaned up against it, folding her arms across her chest. She wanted to be annoyed at the empath disturbing her reading but, strangely enough, she found herself welcoming the company.

"I warned them about speaking too freely about Nyssa or Quinn when not in private. The son of a Regent and a Queen-in-Waiting...one would think they'd be far smarter about protecting secrets."

Medias had found Athen and Aryis in an alcove that morning, stealing a moment together and talking in hushed tones. She was angry to hear them mention Nyssa and Quinn. Voices carried, and Medias was certain that Ceril had spies among them, even in the Keep.

"Point taken," Reece acquiesced as her eyes surveyed the room. She rounded on Medias with a frown. "Have you acquired nothing in your time here to decorate your room? Not even a little trinket from one of our many shops in Ocean's Rest?"

"This is a temporary arrangement. One in which I think it best not to put down roots."

"You've been here for nearly ten months and nothing has changed. One little personal item wouldn't kill you."

"You shouldn't concern yourself with the private affairs of a Justiciar."

Reece scoffed. "I'm sorry, but suggesting you personalize your room a *wee* bit is not interfering in your private affairs."

"Perhaps I like things the way they are."

"Interesting. You don't seem to take that into consideration with me."

Medias raised an eyebrow, curious.

"You think I haven't noticed that you move the books in my office around, one by one? You take one down, make a show of browsing its contents, then put it in an entirely different place on my shelves."

Medias scowled. "I do not."

Reece sighed, but a small smile tugged at her lips. Medias found the disarray of Reece's library maddening. She couldn't be expected to stare at those messy books and *not* do something.

Medias suspected that Reece exacted her revenge by barging into the small corner office Medias occupied to water its plants. When pressed, she claimed that Medias wouldn't bother with their caretaking. A correct assumption.

On those plant-watering occasions, she would often linger and talk about her day. Or ask Medias about hers. Medias's responses were always measured—a good balance of what she was comfortable disclosing without being too standoffish.

Initially, their meetings were meant to be weekly, but the frequency had increased. It struck her that the empath had firmly inserted herself into her life. If Reece were desperate for a friend other than Athen and Aryis, Medias found herself a poor alternative.

"Did you really come here tonight to yell at me for cautioning Athen and Aryis?" Medias asked, pushing off the door to trail Reece around the room.

Reece ran a hand through her hair. "You rarely say two words to them. Would it hurt to get to know them?"

Medias wasn't very good at niceties—the small talk, the feigning interest in the banal details of the lives of others. It was torture. "I will give it some consideration."

"You don't have to make it sound so distasteful."

"Small talk doesn't interest me."

Reece tossed her hands up. "Small talk doesn't interest anyone, Medias! Especially not Athen and Aryis. They're more than happy to have a deeper conversation. Besides, you have no problem talking to me."

"I mostly listen," Medias replied. "I might as well be one of your plants."

With an exaggerated sigh, Reece rolled her eyes.

"Let me ask you something, empath. A curiosity I have."

Reece shook her head, her eyes wide. "The plant speaks!"

A low hum rumbled out of Medias, a halfhearted sign of frustration that Reece ignored. "Lilliana is obviously expecting Athen to be the next Regent of Ocean's Rest, though he seems wholly uninterested. Why does she insist on forcing the office on him? He has taken to his Lion's Guard duties and spends very little time on governing. Certainly you recognize that."

Reece's dark eyes searched the Justiciar's face. Even though Medias knew the empath couldn't sense any of her emotions, she felt uncomfortable nonetheless—there was something unsettling about her gaze. Medias wondered if she practiced it in the mirror.

"An odd question from you. Why do you care?"

"I said it was a curiosity I had. Nothing more."

Reece's face softened. "Lilliana spilled a lot of blood, some of it her own, to control this city. She wants to keep it in the family."

"Are you not a part of the family?"

Surprise flickered over Reece's face. "I'm not blood."

"I watch you study everything Lilliana does. The Feather's continued success bears testament to your intelligence. Tell me, don't you wish to be something more than a brothel mistress?"

Reece frowned. "It's not...it's not my place."

Medias narrowed her eyes at the woman. "Mmm." Did the empath seriously not consider herself a worthy candidate for the Regency? Reece's cunning while helping Medias pretend to play the dutiful Justiciar was proof of her prowess. Very much in the same vein as Lilliana. Though with a kinder touch.

And loath as she was to admit it, Medias had come to depend on Reece. She was creative and clever, well versed in creating plausible lies to keep Ceril chasing his own ass trying to hunt down Nyssa and Quinn.

How Lilliana could overlook her was confounding.

"Do you wish to be more than a Justiciar?" Reece asked.

"You know very well that I never had a choice. But you could be so much more than a steward of a glorified whorehouse."

"Excuse me? Is that all you think it is? How the fuck do you think our whisper network operates? From years of building relationships and loyalty. The information that moves through The Feather gives House Fennick power and influence. What we're doing to help Nyssa and Quinn...it doesn't work without the place."

"Lilliana's whisper network is far larger than The Feather now. Its tendrils extend all across the Empire, and she's the one in control. You could be her one day. If only..." Medias shook her head and walked toward her door. She couldn't make Reece recognize her value and was not in the mood to argue. "I'm sure I'm keeping you from some important work. Brothel books that need balancing. Decimal points that require proper placement."

The look on Reece's face belied something Medias had only seen early on in their arrangement—anger. She looked about to protest, but instead followed Medias to the door and cleared her throat. "Have a most pleasant evening, Justiciar."

Medias caught Reece's arm as she brushed past her, the gentle scent of lavender filling her nose. "Anyone can keep The Feather running. Your talent doesn't belong behind a desk, pushing papers around." She let go. "Goodnight, empath."

Reece left without another word, and Medias watched her walk away, dipping in and out of the pools of golden illumination cast by the hallway's lights before disappearing around a corner.

The next day, after her morning activities, Medias returned to her room to meditate. She found a plant sitting on the windowsill. A smile curled up the corners of her mouth.

WINTER'S FIRE

Quinn circled Fontaine, the other woman whipping her head around, trying to find her in the darkness. How strange it was to stand in front of her mentor and not be seen. Glancing up, she marveled at the dim disk of the sun in the sky, completely obscured by the dome of darkness she created over them. Everything around her glowed with an eerie under light, her shadow creating its own peculiar purplish illumination.

"I can't see you," Fontaine said, her breath hanging in front of her, the chill in the air caused by the shadows rather than the winter air.

"I'm right next to you," Quinn said.

Fontaine jumped and clapped her hands. "Marvelous! You sound like you're coming from all directions, like you *are* the darkness itself."

Ever since Nyssa called a storm and Quinn turned day into night, Fontaine had been drilling them. Hard. Nyssa had gotten proficient at creating a storm, though she refused to call down lightning. She seemed scared to lose control again, and Fontaine, though clearly frustrated, didn't push.

Quinn found herself able to cast a wide swath of darkness—Fontaine estimated her biggest circle was two hundred yards wide. Inside the dome of night, the temperature dropped to freezing, which Nyssa seemed to enjoy, and Quinn was able to manipulate a larger volume of her shadows.

She could move without being seen, her body somehow blending in with the darkness as it flowed around her. The problem was, she was utterly drained by the end of their drills, barely able to summon a wisp of shadow to poke at Nyssa.

Arms wrapped around Quinn's midsection and lifted her off her feet, the familiar scent of verbena teasing her nose. Nyssa's laugh rumbled next to her ear. "Found you."

Quinn sighed. She was *almost* able to move without being seen. Nyssa could find her no matter where she was within the shadows. Their bond was like a beacon to one another and seemed to amplify when they used a great deal of magick.

"You got me," Quinn admitted, patting Nyssa's arms, missing her warmth when she set her down. Nyssa suddenly appeared in the darkness, illuminated by azure arcs of power sparking across her skin and in her eyes. She sent out harmless ripples of lightning in all directions, the blue light eerie and beautiful.

"Okay, that's enough for today," Fontaine said.

Exhaling and closing her eyes, Quinn pulled the shadows back. Sunlight flooded her senses in the absence of the dark.

"I think for our next lesson, I'll see how many orbs tainted with a little forbidden magick you can detect and destroy when you call down the darkness," Fontaine said, her eyes lighting up.

"Should be easy," Quinn said, confident.

"Simultaneously find *and* destroy them, my love. Over a wide area."

Quinn groaned while Fontaine looked rather pleased with herself. "But," she went on, "that's a test for another day. Today is Winter's Fire, and we have a dinner to make for tonight's celebration. Good friends and good food!"

The mention of food seemed to light a fire under Nyssa, who threw an arm around Fontaine. "I cannot wait!"

"You can go inside and clean. I would like to welcome the heart of winter with an orderly home. You two leave books strewn about like children."

An exaggerated huff came from Nyssa, but they had truthfully been a bit messy of late, spending more time on training than picking up after themselves.

Fontaine continued, "I'll take care of the meal, and Quinn has volunteered to make dessert."

"Oh?" The widening of Nyssa's eyes didn't put Quinn at ease, who was nervous about getting the pie right. Nyssa's love of dessert just added another layer of stress, and her sly smile needled Quinn further.

"Blacksea, do as you're told and get inside," Fontaine ordered.

Nyssa let her go and bowed. "As you wish, my liege." She gave Quinn a wink before heading back to the house, a noticeable bounce to her step.

Quinn and Fontaine sighed at the same time, sharing a smile. "Every time I'm rather close to killing that woman, she gets me with that smile," Fontaine admitted.

Me too.

Raising an eyebrow, Fontaine asked, "Don't you have some winter apples to pick for your pie?"

"Yes, I do, my liege," Quinn replied with a bow and a smirk.

She was met with a heavy eye roll. "You are so lucky you're somewhat charming. Now go on. Happy Winter's Fire!"

Quinn turned, gathered her basket, and hummed to herself as she followed the trail through the forest, more excited than she cared to admit to celebrate the holiday.

Fontaine had prepared a Winter's Fire feast that made Quinn's stomach growl as she worked on her own contributions—a passable loaf of bread and a pie. She worked hard at the dessert, spending the afternoon picking winter apples, her fingers going numb as she tried to select the best-looking fruit. When she finally pulled the pie out of the wood-burning oven and laid it on the counter to cool, she broke out into a wide, beaming smile, proud of her creation.

Nyssa leaned on the counter. "That smells amazing. Athen would be jealous," she said with a smile. "And here's the part where you blush."

Heat rose in Quinn's cheeks.

Dammit.

"So predictable," Nyssa said, chuckling.

"Nyssa, make yourself useful and set the table," Fontaine admonished, setting the roast chicken down, its golden brown skin glistening. Though the bird looked delicious, it smelled even better, lying on a bed of potatoes, carrots, and turnips.

As the women sat down and enjoyed their meal, Quinn thought back to the previous Winter's Fire. It had been her first outside of Arcton Citadel, and she'd wandered around Ocean's Rest to celebrate with the rest of the revelers. It was a risky decision, but a taste of freedom proved too tempting. She had been close to getting caught, but she had managed to escape during the wraith attack that almost killed Nyssa.

The thought of it, and Nyssa's distress over recollecting the events of that night, still haunted her. She had run, escaped the attack, and left the others behind to fend for themselves. She owed Nyssa and the others nothing at the time, but she still felt the guilt of leaving them. How strange a year it had been to come to feel such a way. To actually *care* about others.

"Hey, you okay?" Nyssa asked, a concerned look painting her features.

"I...was just remembering last year's Winter's Fire."

Nyssa uncorked a large bottle of spiced cider and poured the drink up to the brim of Quinn's mug. "Let's make memories we can look back fondly on this Winter's Fire night, yeah?"

Quinn smiled, thankful that Nyssa didn't seem to hold a grudge. Fontaine tapped the rim of her mug, and Nyssa filled it before attending to her own.

"What shall we toast to?" Fontaine asked, raising her mug.

Nyssa smiled. "To the patience of a great mentor. To unexpected new friends. And to making new Winter's Fire memories."

The three women clinked their mugs together.

The dinner was as good as any Quinn had eaten, the chicken juicy and the vegetables charred to perfection. Fontaine could coax flavor out of any ingredients with the right mix of herbs. Quinn waited and worried as Fontaine and Nyssa tried the pie she had baked, hoping that she got the mix of apples, sugar, cinnamon, and earthy spices right. Fontaine had given her a basic recipe to follow, but like her magick lessons at times, it lacked specificity. She preferred the women figure things out for themselves.

The tension in Quinn's shoulders released when Nyssa broke out in a wide smile after a first bite.

"This is really special," Fontaine said.

Nyssa enthusiastically nodded, taking another big bite. "Delicious! Can you make this every day?"

Quinn's cheeks grew hot again, and Nyssa must have noticed—her smile turned into a sly grin.

After dinner, the women sat and listened to Fontaine's stories of her Winter's Fire memories. One involved a drunken tryst with a prince who turned out to not be a prince—he was pretending to be royalty to get into a luxurious party in order to drink his fill of rich people's liquor.

"He could charm a snake out of its skin," Fontaine said wistfully, winking at Quinn and Nyssa. "We ran off with a few bottles of very rare whiskey and spent a week together, throwing around money we didn't have on the 'prince's' credit at the poshest inn in Cardin. We barely left the room."

Quinn chuckled at the story, not at all surprised that Fontaine had lived a long and interesting life. Though it reminded her that she had barely lived at all.

"It was one of the best Winter's Fires I've had," Fontaine said. "Right up there with this one."

Nyssa scoffed. "Surely you're joking."

"Not at all. You two have become wonderful companions. Who knew hijacking a ship and taking you both for ransom would lead us here? Serendipity, one might say."

"I know a Justiciar who would call it fate," Nyssa replied.

"Why quibble over terminology?" Fontaine replied. She raised an eyebrow in Nyssa's direction. "I bet you have some fun stories."

The sly smile that overtook Nyssa's face made Quinn curious.

Perhaps *too* curious.

Nyssa took a long pull of her drink. "I may have had some fun back at the Emerald Order."

"With men and women, correct?" Fontaine asked.

Nyssa leaned back and narrowed her eyes. "Correct."

"You know, as old as I am, I have never been with a woman."

"At some point, you'll go through all the men the world has to offer."

"Then I shall simply start over from the beginning."

Nyssa threw her head back and laughed. Quinn wished she could be joyously free like that.

Fontaine shrugged. "Women are undoubtedly beautiful, but I will stick to men. For now."

"Pity," Nyssa said. "I could have some fun with you."

Quinn nearly choked on her spiced cider. The small, strange spark of jealousy she felt disconcerted her.

Fontaine gave her a little bow. "Oh, my love, I'm flattered."

"Men are fun, but women are..." Nyssa bit her lip, teasing a smile, "a uniquely amazing and exhausting experience, limited only by stamina."

A flicker of a glance from Nyssa made all of Quinn's blood run hot. She often had cause to curse her pale skin and propensity for blushing far too easily, and this occasion was no different. Certain that all her confused feelings were playing across her face, she looked away from Nyssa.

A deep, rumbling laugh came from Fontaine. "I am truly glad to be in your lives, for as frustrating as you may sometimes be, you are rather entertaining." Fontaine stood up with a groan and stretched. And then began to remove her clothing.

"Fontaine!" Nyssa said, her eyebrows popping up.

"You humans are so shy about naked bodies! I'm going to go dance among the trees. Would you two like to come with?"

Nyssa laughed and gave Quinn a puzzled look. Fontaine had her ways, and they didn't question her—Quinn was even getting used to seeing the woman traipsing around naked.

"I think perhaps we'll stay here where it's warm. Have fun with the trees," Quinn said.

Fontaine waved her hand dismissively at the women, folded her clothes in a neat pile, and left the house.

Nyssa burst out laughing and fell back on a pile of pillows. "I honestly don't understand that woman sometimes." She gave Quinn a broad smile and sprang to her feet. "I have something for you. A little Winter's Fire gift. Be right back."

Quinn watched Nyssa retreat to her room and quickly stuck her hand in her pocket, fingering a small item wrapped in paper from her sketchbook. She was certain Nyssa would hate it. Her palms started to sweat.

Nyssa returned with a small paper envelope and handed it to Quinn. "Open it."

Quinn tried to ignore her damp hands and tore open the envelope, eager at receiving her first-ever present. She pulled out a woven strand of blue, black, and white leather.

"It's a toldoku—a talisman awarded for achievement in Ithais-Toru. It's a tradition that predates the Emerald Order. Warriors would proudly display their talismans, incorporating them into their armor or weapons. Mine are woven into the grip on Winter's Bite," Nyssa said.

Quinn turned the cord over in her hands. It was braided tightly, comprised of multiple thin strands of leather. It was elegant in its simplicity, but knowing what it meant to Nyssa made it truly special. When had she had the time to make this?

Nyssa cleared her throat. "Fontaine and I had a devil of a time dying the leather, but she remembered some enchantments. It's blue and black, the colors of our magicks, with a little white for contrast...I guess I got a little literal with *forever entwined*."

For all her confidence and bluster, Nyssa was now blushing herself—a rare occurrence—and seemed nervous.

Quinn swallowed. "It's beautiful...but I can't possibly accept it. I haven't earned it."

"That's not for you to decide."

"Nyssa—"

"As your teacher, I have deemed you worthy of this toldoku. You're tenacious. You never back down; never ask for mercy. This recognizes your fighting spirit. It's the first one I've ever given, so the honor is mine," Nyssa said, her voice light, almost...shy?

Despite feeling she was not worthy of such an honor, Quinn accepted the talisman. "Thank you. Can I wear it on my wrist since I don't have a proper weapon or armor?"

"Certainly. I'll tie it on," Nyssa offered. "We'll need to find you a proper sword at some point."

Nyssa affixed the toldoku to Quinn's left wrist, tying the knot tight to keep it on. Her fingers lingered for a moment, and Quinn had to look away to avoid blushing again as her stomach tightened.

"Thank you," she said, her voice quiet.

Nyssa seemed to relax, her smile big and bright.

"I...I have something for you too," Quinn said, pulling the small package out of her pocket. "It's silly."

"Let me be the judge of that," Nyssa said, plucking the gift out of Quinn's hand with a sly grin. She ripped the paper away to reveal its contents—a small, flat river rock no bigger than a gold coin, deep blue and almost a perfect circle. As perfect as a river rock could be, anyway. Quinn had spent hours finding the right rock, pulling stone after stone out of the river that ran through the woods and inspecting each one, comparing them to each other, trying to get as close to Nyssa's eye color as possible.

"Is this from the river with the snapping turtles in it?" Nyssa asked, turning the stone over in her hands.

"Yes."

"And you still have all your fingers?" Nyssa asked with a laugh.

"I may have warned off a few turtles with a little poke of darkness here and there," Quinn said with a smirk, holding up her hand and coiling wisps of shadow around her fingers. "I remember you telling me that you collected smooth rocks from the Emerald Lakes with Eron. He would let you fill your pockets with them and take them back to your room. I thought maybe you'd like it?"

A small strangled breath escaped Nyssa's lips. Quinn looked up, finding Nyssa's eyes shiny. She turned the stone over in her hand, swallowing hard.

Perhaps reminding Nyssa of her dead father wasn't the best idea.

"The rock matches your eyes. Oh, and this side has a bit of a scratch," Quinn said, pointing at the stone. "It reminded me of your scar."

Nyssa closed her fist tight around the rock.

"I know it's a stupid gift," Quinn said, her mind fumbling awkwardly to find something to say.

"No, it's not, it's perfect. I love it. Thank you, Quinn."

Nyssa stepped forward, but Quinn turned toward the kitchen, avoiding eye contact, retreating from what likely was going to be a hug.

The feelings she had for Nyssa were getting more complicated. Scary. So avoiding them and not getting too close to the woman was her plan. A poor plan, considering they were stuck together on an isolated island, but one she needed to stick to.

"I'm going to make some tea. Want some?" Quinn asked.

When Nyssa didn't answer, Quinn turned around, catching her smiling down at the rock in her hand, her silly grin charming. Everything about the woman unbalanced Quinn, pushed her into an equally exciting and uncomfortable corner.

"You know," Nyssa said after a bit of silence, "this Winter's Fire sure beats last year's. You're far better company when you're not a fugitive."

"Mm-hmm," Quinn said.

Nyssa slipped the rock into her pocket with a smile and joined Quinn in the kitchen, pulling mugs down from a shelf for their tea. "I've talked your ear off about how I grew up, the Order, Eron, Athen...but you never tell me about your life at the Citadel..."

Nyssa was opening a door, inviting Quinn to share. Most of her upbringing was lonely. Solitude and Ceril's cruelty had cut scars deep into her. Even when she attended classes and lectures, the other adepts steered clear of her, scared of her magick.

She didn't want to share the ugliness and pain she hid. She wasn't bold like Nyssa, who kept her scars to remind her of her past.

Quinn wanted hers forever locked away.

"I would prefer to leave the past in the past," Quinn said.

Nyssa scowled, which wasn't an uncommon reaction whenever Quinn sidestepped a question. "I just wanted to get a little peek into that head of yours."

Quinn fell silent as Nyssa watched her.

"Hey, when is your birthday?" Nyssa finally asked.

"I don't have one."

"What?"

Quinn shrugged and turned to retrieve the sugar bowl. "I was never told my birth date. What about you?"

"Eron asked me to choose a day, giving me the approximate timeframe he figured I was born, so I picked the first day of winter. I actually forgot this year with no one to remind me...Athen was always good at that."

Quinn clucked her tongue. "Nyssa, you should have told us. That was fourteen days ago!"

A shadow passed over her face. "Ah, fuck, I always hated my birthday, anyway. It's a reminder that no one really knows anything about me. They gave me a surname to honor where they heard I was born. I had to pick a random day to celebrate my birth. Everything about me is borrowed. Nothing feels like mine."

"I'm sorry. I happen to think Blacksea is a very noble name. Fitting." Quinn cleared her throat and poured tea into the mugs, pushing one toward Nyssa. "Happy birthday. And happy Winter's Fire."

Nyssa regarded her before sipping on her tea. Were those eyes trying to peer into Quinn and figure her out? And if she dug too deep, would she hate what she saw?

"May all your Winter's Fire wishes come true," Nyssa said softly.

Quinn smiled, hiding her sadness. She missed not having a lantern to whisper a wish into and release to the skies. Last year's wish had been desperate and lonely.

She closed her eyes, recalling the chill of that night, the lantern in her hands, and the words she had whispered into it...

I wish to disappear.

THE LION AND THE QUEEN

A then kissed the inside of Aryis's thigh, waiting for a reaction. Nothing. Frowning, he tried again. The papers in front of her face wavered a bit as he ran his tongue along her skin, but she seemed intent on finishing her work, propped up against a pillow in his bed. She had been getting to sleep later and later recently. Athen often found her asleep under a pile of papers.

He glanced up at her. The soft, flickering flames in the fireplace across the room danced across her face, glowing in her light-brown eyes. She scowled and put pen to paper, scratching something out with fervor.

With renewed determination, he gently bit her inner thigh.

"Hey!" She giggled, swatting his head with the papers in her hand. "I'm working here!"

"So am I," he replied with a wink. "May I continue?"

Raising an eyebrow, she replied, "You may."

Athen continued with his kisses, trailing them closer and closer to the one spot guaranteed to get her attention. He pulled her underwear aside. The moan that escaped her lips let him know his efforts were working. But she was still intently staring at her work.

He sighed and stopped, resting his chin on her thigh. "It's hard to go down on you when you're not entirely here with me."

Aryis tossed the papers aside and frowned. "I'm sorry. I've just been trying to figure out a problem Lilliana has me working on. Goods have gone missing from the docks. I want to figure this out before I leave."

"And that's more intriguing than my tongue between your legs?" Athen asked, feigning offense.

"Never," Aryis said, reaching forward to stroke his head.

With a sigh, Athen drew lazy circles on her stomach, her silky camisole smooth under his rough fingers. "I'm going to miss you when you're at Wayland."

"It's only for a couple weeks. I think you and I both know this invite to be a guest lecturer is the Empire calling me to heel, to see if I'm still a good little adept."

"Regardless, I'm proud of you. And who deserves such an accolade more?"

The smile on Aryis's face never failed to make Athen's heart flutter.

They had been together for over a year, and his love for her only seemed to grow. And that love moved him closer to making a decision on his future, one rooted in happiness rather than duty. A decision his mother wouldn't like. Aryis was to be queen, a reality that loomed in the future, and he found his heart open to leaving Ocean's Rest to be with her when she had to return home to Frosland.

"I'm going to miss you, Athen. I'm sure by the time I get back, your hair will be halfway down your back."

"Oh, you'd like that, right?" Athen asked. He hopped up on his knees and bent his head upside down over her, pulling up her camisole and dragging his shoulder-length hair over her naked torso. It had the desired effect as she melted into a fit of giggles. She sat up and pulled him in for a kiss, her taste still on his lips. Athen ran his fingertips over her skin and she laughed under his lips.

She put her arms around his shoulders and ran her fingers through his hair. "I wish you could come watch me teach. I'm nervous."

"You're going to be great. You've practiced on Pol, Reece, and my Lion's Guard. Brick said he found you mildly interesting. That's a compliment coming from him!"

Aryis leaned back and laughed. Athen wrapped his hands around her waist, taking the opportunity to admire her body. It was hard to believe this woman, this glorious woman, would be a queen. She constantly astonished him with how she effortlessly moved through the world with kindness and intelligence, never once making anyone feel lesser. One day, it would be an honor to stand by her side as her partner, and he couldn't wait for her to get back from Wayland to ask her to marry him. The thought of it filled him with a giddy nervousness.

"Are you happy, Aryis?" Athen asked.

A bright smile overtook her face. "With you, always." She ran her hand along his face, tender. Her face turned from joyous to wistful.

The shift in her mood worried him. "What is it?"

She raised her eyes to his. "I haven't been able to be completely honest with you. And you might just kick me out right now and never want to see me again...but I need to tell you before I go."

Aryis's throat bobbed up and down. He gently rubbed her waist while trying to ignore how the back of his neck went cold. "Out with it."

"Empress Kalla promised my father that her successor for the throne would come from Frosland. And that successor...is me."

His breath caught. Aryis? The next Empress? He shook his head and searched for something to say. His mind reeled at the complexity added to their relationship in the very instant.

"I know I have a terrible habit of keeping big secrets from you, first being the Queen-in-Waiting, now this. But I was forbidden from sharing because Kalla hasn't announced her decision yet, and I'm sure some of the Great Houses are unhappy given my association with Nyssa and, well, you and House Fennick. I understand how awkward this is, and I understand if you're mad—"

Athen stopped her with a kiss, pulling her into an embrace. He needed to show her that he loved her and let her have no doubt. She grasped at him, deepening the kiss. He ran his hands up under her camisole, trailing his fingertips gently over her warm skin. She arched her back into his touch.

His body responded to their closeness, her heat. Finally, he pulled away. "I'm not mad."

"You're not?"

"This changes things for us a bit, but I understand why you had to keep it a secret." Imperial politics were messy and oftentimes dangerous. This news would complicate things, make their lives more difficult to navigate.

But it changed nothing about his feelings towards Aryis—he would stand by her whether queen or empress or just Aryis Devitt. "Empress." He smiled. "Do you know how much good you're going to do?"

Aryis sighed and ran her fingers along his cheek, scratching his beard. "Kalla has no intention of retiring any time soon, so it'll be years before I ascend to the throne. I just wish I could be Empress tomorrow and lift Quinn and Nyssa's bounty. But if I say anything now, she'll know I'm colluding with them. I have to be careful...I want to help them, but I need to keep us safe." She sighed. "I feel useless. Queen of nothing. Empress of nothing. Able to *do* nothing."

Athen caressed her cheek. "I understand more than anyone. But you're right, we have to be careful. I won't do anything to jeopardize Nyssa's safety or yours."

She took his head in her hands. "Understand this: if Nyssa needs us, we go. No questions asked. No throne is worth abandoning my friends for. We go, and we deal with the consequences later."

"And that's why I love you," Athen replied, staring into her eyes.

She kissed him gently and gave him her warmest smile. "When I volunteered to help find Quinn, I thought I was just having one small adventure before buckling down and becoming a bureaucrat. Instead, I got blindsided by a very handsome, strong, intelligent, kind—"

"Handsome..."

"I mentioned that already."

"It seemed worth repeating." Athen grinned, pulled Aryis close and kissed her. He left her lips to trail kisses down her neck.

She sighed, humming under his touch. "All that to say, you're the one person I trust with all my heart. I love you more than I thought possible."

"You're not the only one that was blindsided, woman!" Athen leaned forward and nipped at her neck. "I honestly don't know how I'd navigate this whole mess without you at my side."

She ran her fingers through the top of his hair. "I am a rather good partner," she replied with a cheerful smile.

"Still have work to do or can I keep doing this?" he growled, flicking his tongue against the hollow of her throat.

"You definitely have my attention," Aryis said, her voice a low purr. She pulled her camisole over her head and tossed it off the bed.

Athen caressed her breasts before moving his hand down her body. "Are you sure?" he asked as he inched his fingers into her underwear. He bent his head, flicking his tongue against her nipple, making her gasp and arch into him. "Because I understand if you have paperwork to do…"

"I think I'd prefer manual labor right now," Aryis whispered as she reached between his legs. Athen's breathing deepened and his body eagerly responded to her touch. He gently leaned Aryis over and removed her underwear. When she sat back up, Athen pulled her onto his lap.

"I love you," Aryis mumbled, her breath hot against his neck. She moved against him in slow, languid strokes. Athen wanted to stretch the moment out and bask in Aryis's warmth. The scent of her skin clung to him, and he groaned as they rocked together, their bodies fitting perfectly.

THE WAYLAND CONSERVATORY

Aryis stood behind her desk, waiting on her students. How nervous she had been walking back onto the grounds of the Wayland Conservatory, but the ivy-covered buildings and adepts hurrying about to their next classes cheered her up.

Sun streamed in through the peaked glass ceiling of the classroom, filtering against the worn brick walls. This room was one of her favorite places in the whole Conservatory. Its thick windows gave her a perfect view of the deep-green hedgerows and purple winter lilies in full bloom in the South Gardens.

Laughter pulled Aryis out of her thoughts as adepts filed into the room. A boy younger than the other students hurried in, his arms full of books. "Master Aryis, here are the rest of the books the librarians pulled for you."

"Rustam, I told you I'm not a Master," Aryis replied, smiling at the boy as he dumped the load of books onto the desk, then went about tidying them up.

"Would it be okay if I stayed for the lecture, Mast—Lady Devitt?"

"You want to listen to me talk about the transitive nature of ethereal magick? Isn't that a bit advanced for you?"

Rustam shook his head, his shaggy blond curls bracketing his eager face. "I've picked magick research as my specialty."

"You're too young to pick yet."

The boy began pointing at the books on Aryis's desk. "I've read this one...and this one...and I'm halfway through this one."

"How old are you?"

"Eight."

Impressive. He was half the age of the students she was about to lecture, and she herself hadn't read the same books until she was at least ten. Suppressing a smile of admiration, Aryis made a show of sighing. "Fine, you may stay, but do not disturb the class. If you have questions regarding concepts I cover that you don't understand, we can discuss them over dinner."

A smile almost as bright as the sunshine streaming through the windows lit up Rustam's face. Aryis remembered being his age, incessantly curious about the subject of magick. It was her first field of study, and it remained her first love. A little encouragement and mentorship couldn't hurt, and she didn't mind indulging Rustam's enthusiasm for his studies.

Aryis pulled at her dark leather jacket and smoothed out the scarlet wool skirt she wore over black leggings and sturdy boots, the latter two a habit now. Lessons learned from Nyssa and Athen—always dress for a fight. Lilliana had ingrained the same message when it came to governing.

"Everyone take your seats. We'll get started shortly." Aryis turned to the massive chalkboard on the brick wall behind her and began writing out a light orb enchantment. Diagramming a rudimentary spell served as a good starting point for the day's lesson.

The class was full when she turned back. Small groups of students conversed in hushed tones, their eyes darting her way. Aryis had become somewhat of a celebrity, according to her brother Vykas. Aside from everyone now knowing her Queen-in-Waiting status, her adventures at sea and scandalous association with Nyssa and Quinn had gotten her a small reputation of being a rebel.

From invisible bookworm to renegade…Nyssa would roar with laughter at the absurd notion.

Aryis dove into her lecture. The adepts sat quietly, save for the occasional questions which would spur conversation amongst them. In the corner, Rustam scribbled furiously in a notebook. She was once exactly like him, head down, capturing every drop of knowledge her teachers could impart, her hand popping up whenever her mind conjured up a question.

A quarter hour in, she turned back to her chalkboard to transcribe another spell, one containing far more complexity—the spell that created floating messenger orbs. Murmurs sprang up behind her, dying out as she worked, silence replacing the side conversations. When Aryis turned back to the adepts, one sat with her hand raised.

Aryis smiled. "Yes, Jomante? A question?"

The girl blinked slowly. "Can I show you something?"

Aryis strode across the room and stopped in front of Jomante's desk. The girl stared up at her and turned her notebook around for Aryis. The page was covered with thick, dark pencil scratches.

"What is this?" Aryis asked, reaching down for the notebook.

Jomante drove her pencil into Aryis's left hand.

Aryis cried out. Jomante tilted her head, staring at Aryis before pulling the pencil out.

Aryis cursed and snatched her hand back, her mind reeling. Blood flowed out of the wound in the middle of her palm. "What is wrong with you?" she hissed.

Jomante blinked at her, expressionless.

Another student's hand went up. "Can I show you something?"

Aryis stepped back, her hand throbbing, blood dripping on the floor. She swiveled her head around. The adepts stared at her, their eyes unblinking, unmoving. No anger, no surprise. Nothing.

Her blood turned to ice.

What the hell is happening?

"Can I show you something?" Another adept held up his notebook. More black, angry scratches. Aryis's eyes darted around the room, her students holding up their notebooks. All the same.

"This is madness..." she whispered.

Jomante stood up. In concert, chairs scraped against the floor as the other adepts rose to their feet all around Aryis. Heart pounding, her hand flew to her dagger, Talon, at her waist.

No...they're just children.

Aryis spun around, desperate for an escape route, but she was surrounded by at least twenty students, all of them watching her, their eyes still. They had to be under some mass enchantment, perhaps a mass delusion. Or compulsion. There were forbidden magick spells that could—

"Can I show you something?" Jomante asked and smiled. Her smile grew wide until her face was contorted and grotesque. Her teeth chattered, then stopped, and then she took a step toward Aryis. The other adepts followed suit.

"Stay back," Aryis warned, holding her hand out. As if that would stop them.

Another step brought the children closer. One reached out and touched her. Aryis gasped, pulling away from him. Another student reached for her, and she shifted back, now closer to Jomante. The girl grabbed at Aryis, slow and deliberate. Aryis fought her off, pushing her back, but the other adepts drew nearer, one step at a time, their faces contorting into hideous smiles.

Words weren't going to work. Aryis resorted to her fists, fighting the adepts off, trying her best to remember Athen's lessons. She needed to get out of the middle of them, cut off their angle of attack.

Aryis shot forward and caught a male adept across the chin. He crumpled, her punch doing exactly what she wanted, but another girl advanced, taking the boy's place. Aryis gritted her teeth and buried a boot in the girl's midsection, driving her back. She slid out of the reach of another adept, his fingers brushing against her jacket.

"Can I show you something?" Jomante asked, advancing on her. The other students spread out, cutting off all avenues of escape.

Except one. Aryis scrambled forward to grab a chair and whirled around, smashing the window behind her. She could climb out and run—

"Aryis!" a tiny voice cried out.

Rustam.

Aryis twisted away from the window, and hands descended on her. Jomante buried a fist in her hair, driving Aryis's head down toward the jagged glass that remained in the frame.

"Can I show you something?" she asked, pushing Aryis into a shard of glass. It sliced into her face across her jawline, and she let loose a scream.

I'm going to die here.

Aryis pushed away from the window, throwing Jomante off of her. A boy with dark-blond hair grabbed at her face, his hand coming away red with blood when she kicked him back from her. Unrelenting, he came for her again.

Aryis gritted her teeth and drew Talon. If she could just get to Rustam, get him out of the room and to the Conservatory guards...

She drove her dagger into the boy's shoulder, hoping to slow him down. Hot blood splashed over her hand. The boy didn't make a sound.

And he didn't stop.

How...

"Please..." Aryis whispered. The boy grabbed at her again, his hands tearing at her eyes. Panicking, she thrust Talon into his chest, and he stilled. She looked into his face, and he smiled, blood pouring out of his mouth. "Can I sh-show you..." he stammered before his shoulders sagged and he dropped to the ground. Dead.

Bile rose in Aryis's throat. A girl with red hair pushed forward, the smile on her face eerie. Hateful. Aryis tried to shove her, but the girl persisted, her fingers scrabbling across Aryis's throat. More hands sought her out, the faces of the adepts blank and staring. She raised Talon and drove it into the hollow of the girl's throat.

No choice. She had no choice.

That's what she kept telling herself as she fought off adept after adept, forcing her way forward. She needed to get to Rustam and get out. Tumbling forward, she separated herself from the pack of slowly advancing adepts, and scrambled toward Rustam.

She grabbed his hand. "I'm getting you out of here."

A line of adepts stood between her and the door. She charged forward, shoving her fear aside and fighting her way through hands that clawed and scratched and grabbed. Talon bit into flesh, slowing the mindless students down. She needed to get Rustam to safety.

A large student stepped in front of her, and she slashed his throat, then ran to the door, pulling Rustam behind her, vaguely aware that he was crying, his grip tight around her wounded hand. Aryis ignored the pain and whipped the door open, ready to escape.

Rustam tugged at her. "Aryis, help!"

She whirled around, keeping her grip tight on him. Rustam struggled as a student held on to him, wrapping his hand around the boy's throat.

"No!" Aryis yelled. She slashed at the adept, cutting a deep gouge across his face. He pulled on Rustam and smiled. More students moved in, pawing at Rustam, moving toward her.

An arm encircled Aryis's waist and hauled her back. Rustam slipped out of her grasp. She tried to lunge for him, but she was yanked through the door and it slammed shut.

Rustam wailed and screamed for Aryis, the only sound that came from the classroom.

Aryis rushed at the door, but a stiff arm stopped her. She whirled toward its owner.

Vykas.

"Aryis, no!" he said, shoving a key in the door to lock it.

"I have to help him!" she cried, clawing at Vykas, trying to get to the doorknob.

He wrapped his arms around her, pulling her back. "No, Aryis."

"Vykas, please, I have to help him," she begged as he hugged her tight. He wouldn't budge. "Please."

Rustam screamed her name, over and over, each cry slicing into her heart like hot glass.

Until the boy went silent.

Aryis's legs gave out, and Vykas slid to the floor with her, refusing to let go. She cried into his chest, her heart pounding. Breaking. Talon tumbled out of her hand.

Fists pounded slowly on the door. "Can I show you something?" a cold voice asked from the other side.

Aryis sat in sunlight that failed to warm her. The Empress's sunroom was bright, the hard lines of its walls meeting cold white marble floors, chilling her as she retreated farther into her wool coat.

"We have narrowed the incident down to a spell that creates murderous mass delusion. It could have been whispered into the ears of the students by an unknown aggressor or through poison introduced through their food...we don't know for certain. A rare spell and of soul magick origin, most likely," Ceril said. "The magick of coercion and control, long forbidden. I suspect, as with the wraith attack, the blame lies with Suvi Rell."

A small gaggle of Justiciars nodded in agreement. Aryis wished, odd though it seemed, that Medias was here. She could use a friendly face among all the severe-looking men and women that glanced her way and whispered to one another. She tried to gauge Empress Kalla and Arch Justiciar Decia's reaction, but they sat stoic, their eyes on her.

After the Wayland attack, Aryis and Vykas had been summoned to Cardin for questioning. Ceril Anelos asked most of the questions. The guilds were his responsibility, after all, and while he showed the requisite amount of outrage and sorrow over the incident, Aryis knew in her gut he was responsible.

Worse yet, she was certain that *she* was his target.

"Twenty-six students dead," Ceril said, shaking his head. Aryis gritted her teeth, willing herself to not call out his fakery. He didn't care about those adepts.

She wanted to scream until her throat bled.

Aryis put her hand to her face, her fingers running over the raised edges of the scar along her jawline. The healers had made a fuss when she refused to let them erase it from her smooth skin.

What Aryis had seen at Wayland—and the aftermath of the students turning on her—left her hollow. The banging on the door eventually stopped, and when the guards opened it, the room was bathed in blood. The adepts had turned on each other, ripping one another apart. Aryis caught sight of Rustam's sweater before Vykas pulled her away and cleaned her up as she sat numb and motionless in his office.

Everything after felt as though it were happening to someone else: The healers tending to her wounds. The questions from the Masters at Wayland. The trip to Cardin. The questioning for hours under the watch of Arch Master Anelos and Arch Justiciar Decia.

Even when Athen arrived, his face fraught with worry, she felt a million miles away, like she was merely observing everything through a pinhole. He had held her and rocked her to sleep, murmuring comfort into her ears, but she couldn't feel him. The only thing she felt, the only real thing, was Rustam's fingers slipping through her own as he was torn away from her. Losing him played over and over again in her nightmares.

When her father arrived in Cardin from Frosland, she sat still. He had knelt in front of her and rubbed her hands, his gray eyes full of worry against his dark-brown skin. The only person that elicited an emotion from her was Anelos. His lies, his fake concern—he made her simmer with anger.

She sat in the sunroom, surrounded by her father, brother, and the highest-ranking individuals of the Areshi Empire, all eyes on her, and never felt more alone.

Empress Kalla stirred. "I would have a moment alone with King Devitt."

In that second, Aryis knew something more was at play. A greater concern in the balance beyond the Wayland attack. Her father's eyes grew cold and steely, making her stomach constrict. She was certain her future—and Frosland's—had been irrevocably changed in that classroom.

Outside the Empress's sunroom, in a hallway of endless bright-white marble, Aryis sat down on a bench, joined by Athen, who took her hand and said nothing. He had likely come to understand that words turned to dust as soon as they left his mouth—they held no meaning for her.

Minutes passed before her father stepped into the hall and approached Aryis, Vykas at his back.

"Aryis, I want you to return to Frosland with us for a time. Your mother aches to see you after all that's happened," her father said.

"What's wrong?" Aryis asked.

He gave her a faint smile. "The Empress and I think it best you come home to heal. And then we'll re-evaluate your future."

"What does that mean?" Athen asked.

"It's okay," she said, turning to him and taking his hand. "This is for the best." She didn't have the will to argue.

The look on his face was enough to break her further.

She turned from him, biting the inside of her cheek. Anything to not cry. Not now. Not while Ceril lurked about, glancing at her as he spoke to Arch Justiciar Decia down the hallway.

"I...I can come with you. Help you get settled at home," Athen said, his voice soft. How tempting it was to lean on him, ask him to come back with her. Maybe he could heal her.

"No," she replied. She didn't have the heart to drag him down with her. "You should return to Ocean's Rest."

"Aryis, I can—"

"Athen, I thank you for your help, but I think it's best you listen to my daughter," her father said. "Come, Aryis, we're slated to depart."

"W-wait, you're leaving already?" Athen stammered, his eyes pleading with her. He appeared lost. Before he could say one more word, something that would wear her down, convince her to let him come with, she hugged him and let him go.

She turned to follow her father, trying to swallow back the dark lump of regret as Vykas put his arm around her.

HOMECOMING

Tiny hints of spring, green and fragrant, popped up on Monk's Cove by the time Hannah's Whisper returned. Seeing the crew again brought an unabashed smile to Nyssa's face. Elias gathered her and Quinn in his arms for a suffocating embrace before lifting Fontaine off her feet and giving her a long hug.

The homecoming aboard the Whisper was jubilant. Familiar faces surrounded the three of them, and Nyssa reveled in the attention. One familiar yet unexpected face stuck out in the crowd.

"Mina?" Nyssa said, hugging the woman. "Does your father know you're here?"

Nyssa had gotten to know Mina Surk a little when they sailed aboard House Fennick's ship, the Sea Stag, captained by Mina's father. She lit up when she saw Nyssa, her dark-brown eyes smiling. She looked good in the black wool coat of the Whisper's crew. It complemented her short black hair and tanned skin.

"He knows. Is he happy? I'd say not, but I wanted more...adventure. Maybe I'll find it out here on the Whisper," Mina replied.

"I'd say you found at least one thing," Jerrin said, sidling up to Mina and putting his arm around her shoulder.

Nyssa reared back and laughed. "You two are together? Jerrin, you red-headed devil. You know, he flirted *shamelessly* with me when we first met."

"Oh, you wish," Jerrin said with a smile. He grasped Nyssa's hand and gave it a hearty shake. "Welcome back, Blacksea. You two have been missed." He winked at Quinn.

Nyssa turned to Yuha. "What, no hug?" She received an eye roll in return. Frankly, she expected nothing less.

Elias and the crew let Nyssa, Fontaine, and Quinn settle back in, Nyssa and Quinn retaking their old stateroom. It was as if they had never left. One of Quinn's sketches of Fontaine as a chicken was still tacked up above her bed.

Later that day, the crew gathered in the mess and shared a feast. As they ate, Buck placed a plate down in front of Nyssa full of pieces of roast chicken, crispy rice, and pickled vegetables.

"I understand this one was givin' you—mmm—trouble?" Buck asked, eyeing the roasted bits of meat.

"Is this...is this that bitch that pecked at me every fucking day?" Nyssa asked. "The hen that Fontaine forbade me to kill?"

"You bet it is."

Nyssa stood up and threw her arm around the short man. "You're the best, Buck!"

She tucked into her plate and as the meal wore on, Elias caught them all up on the news of the world, including Frosland's withdrawal from the Areshi Empire and its return to being an independent nation.

"What about Aryis?" Nyssa asked.

"She's back in Frosland, it seems. Perhaps she'll become an ambassador and return to the Empire in that capacity. Such is the strange way of politics," Elias said.

"And Athen?" She swallowed, hoping for the best.

"From what I hear, he's in charge of training up a defense force for Ocean's Rest. Doing a right fine job of it too."

Nyssa chewed her bottom lip. "He's got to be missing Aryis something fierce." But he was doing well. "And Reece? Medias?"

"To the best of our knowledge, your friends are well, Nyssa. And missing you terribly, I imagine."

Sighing, she sank back into her chair. The safety of those back in Ocean's Rest had been her only concern at the start of this whole mess, when she first learned of what she was. Maybe once they had Suvi, she could find her way back to them all.

Elias leaned forward and drummed his fingers on Nyssa's forearm. He gave her that charming smile of his. "I've been doing some asking around with my old contacts from when I used to buy and sell rarities."

"Oh, like forbidden spell books?" Nyssa asked, raising an eyebrow.

"I did once trade in illegal items, but most of the goods were perfectly legal, love. I think I have a way into the Whitefield Vintner's Festival. It's a semi-private event, but if you bring something that would pique Suvi's interest, well, the invite is a mere formality."

"What exactly could we find that would interest a queen?" Quinn asked, eyeing a bowl of strawberries in the middle of the table. Elias pushed the bowl her way, knowing exactly how to please her.

"A case of Kannis Winter Reserve—a very rare and expensive wine from the Eastern Continent that any wine expert covets. I found a case and have reached out to Suvi's vintners to gauge interest, posing as a reclusive and wealthy wine trader with my wife, Fontaine. The invite came quick. Suvi's vintners are always desperate to find something to please her. We'll have to plan carefully how to pull this all off, but this is our way in."

"How did you manage all this?" Nyssa asked, happy to hear Elias's efforts while they were training had garnered results.

He raised an eyebrow. "I have cultivated some...alternative identities over the years. So, when people look into one, it has some history. The hard part is getting the wine. It's exceedingly rare. But a friend of yours has it for sale, though I find him quite detestable. A preening, cocky asshole."

Scowling, Nyssa said, "Most of the cocky assholes I know are seated at this table."

After a long, drawn-out sigh, Elias said, "Mox the Whip."

Fontaine snorted.

"Oh, *that* preening, cocky asshole. He likes me." Nyssa grinned.

Elias's eyebrow perked up. "Of course he would. I've been in contact with him and have negotiated a price for the wine. He and I don't get along, so he's twisting the knife a bit to get as much money as he can from me. Fuckin' Mox."

"When can we get the wine?"

"He'll have it in a couple weeks. I gotta plunder more ships in that time to scrape a few more gold marks together. When we do, you two are going to hunker down and stay below deck, got it?" Elias pointed a finger at the two women as a warning.

Quinn sighed next to Nyssa. "I'd like to plunder too."

"Freedom first, then plunder," Fontaine said with a chuckle. "You'll make a fine pirate, Quinn."

Nyssa grunted and reached for a strawberry. Quinn grabbed her hand and squeezed—a rare gesture that took Nyssa aback. "Can I not have a strawberry?" she asked, trying to not get distracted by Quinn's berry-stained lips.

"We're going to kidnap a queen," Quinn said with a faint smile. "We're really going to do this."

She nudged Quinn's shoulder. "Yes, we are."

A FAMILIAR FACE

Nyssa tightened her scarf around her chin, an extra precaution in addition to the bit of makeup she used to cover the Mark of the Unworthy. Getting caught now as she and Quinn made their way through the busy streets of Jejin would be a disaster. Every step they took to get closer to snatching Suvi out of Thu'Dain needed to be wrapped in care and diligence. No getting lazy and letting her identity slip.

The city was just as Nyssa remembered but far more lively and vibrant with the advent of spring, its rows of brightly colored banners spanning the streets, flapping gently in the wind.

The grand market of Jejin sprawled in the city square next to The Lash. It buzzed with magick, a sensation that pricked against Nyssa's skin. A mix of talisman symbols and advertisements for shops, eateries, and pubs flashed at their feet, a magickal map leading shoppers to various stalls and businesses.

The bright-neon magick reminded Nyssa of Aryis. She could touch a treasured possession and send out a thread of red energy that led to the owner, just like she'd done in these very streets when searching out Quinn. Nyssa smiled at the memory. Quinn had caught her with a punch, dropping her where she stood. The first of many surprises concerning Quinn—some aggravating, others delightful.

"It's strange being back here," Quinn remarked as they browsed stall after stall of spices, fruits, vegetables, art, and weapons stretched out before them. Street musicians played stringed instruments and danced around those who milled about to watch the performances, hoping to coax coin from the audience. The smell of roasted nuts and meats made Nyssa's stomach rumble at every turn, each new tempting treat drawing her attention like a child chasing a floating toy.

"I suppose we should keep browsing," Nyssa replied, fingering the gold marks in her pocket, dropped in her hand by Fontaine before they left the Whisper, insisting they explore a little before meeting Elias at The Lash. Nyssa didn't know if it was smart to be out in public, but with her mark covered and hoods over their heads, they were just like anyone else out for a day of shopping. She felt *normal*.

They stopped at a drink vendor, and Quinn ordered them chilled sweet milk tea spiked with almond oil. It was a perfect treat for an early spring day.

"This is delicious," Quinn effused, humming to herself as they walked and browsed the stalls.

Nyssa often forgot how little of the world Quinn had experienced. Truthfully, she wasn't well-traveled either, but Quinn was stuck at Arcton Citadel for twenty-five years, eating the same food, seeing the same faces, surrounded by the same walls. That she never tasted a strawberry before meeting Nyssa was a sad thought.

She sipped at her tea and eyed a blacksmith's collection of blades. The quality wasn't half bad. She picked up a sword, testing its heft and balance. Perhaps it was time to get Quinn a sword that wasn't scrounged from the Whisper's storage room.

She turned to Quinn. "You like this blade?"

Quinn shook her head. "I like the sword I have." She moved closer and pulled Nyssa's scarf up a bit. "Just in case." Her eyes seemed to linger a bit too long on Nyssa's lips.

Or did Nyssa imagine it?

"Thank you," she said, trying to ignore the flutter in her stomach. "Let's head over to The Lash and wait for Elias."

As they walked through the square, Nyssa stopped by a small cart and bought a bag of roasted chickpeas. She always loved them as a snack growing up at the Order, but these were laced with a spicy coating. Utterly delicious.

She held the bag out to Quinn as they walked, and Quinn coughed after popping one in her mouth.

"A little warning, please! My tongue is on fire!" Quinn said, sniffling and shaking her head when Nyssa offered her more.

"They hurt so good." Nyssa shrugged, crunching on another chickpea. "Let's go around to the back alley."

Quinn raised an eyebrow. "I tend to get accosted by very rude women in back alleys."

Nyssa burst out laughing. "True." She kept enjoying her spicy roasted chickpeas as they headed around to the back of The Lash to wait for Elias. They didn't have to wait for long before he showed up with Yuha at his side.

"Ladies," he said.

"I'm offended that you brought extra muscle," Nyssa remarked, winking at Yuha. "I thought we were enough."

Yuha snorted. "I've seen your arms, Blacksea."

Nyssa put on a show of pouting. "Rude." She happened to have very nice arms.

Elias stepped close. "You two are here to smooth over any rough edges with Mox. Like I said, he and I don't get along. We get in, get our wine, and then get back to the ship and out to sea."

"And he'll be discreet...regarding us, I mean?" Quinn asked.

"One thing about Lilliana's pleasure houses, discretion is rule number one. She wouldn't be in business with Mox if he didn't keep his mouth shut."

They walked through the back entrance to The Lash, its narrow hallway leading to the main salon of the establishment. Nyssa was struck instantly by the scent of cloves and tobacco. Like outside in the square, magick buzzed all around her. She wondered with a sly grin what types of enchantments Mox employed to keep his customers happy and coming back for whatever he and his consorts offered.

The salon was dim, and the bartender cleaning glasses behind the main bar nodded at them as they entered. Security guards dotted the empty room, hugging the outskirts. At least they'd have some privacy.

Mox sat at the same booth Nyssa met him at over a year prior, his blue skin a shade or two lighter than Elias's. His horns were shorter than Nyssa remembered, though heavily adorned with silver bands studded with jewels, and his jet-black hair hung at his shoulders now. Handsome as ever and by his demeanor, flaunting it at every opportunity.

A wooden crate sat on the table, *Kannis Winery* burned into the side. He smiled and slid out of the booth, approaching them, his arms wide. "Nyssa Blacksea. I've heard some nasty rumors about you being an scurrilous outlaw."

Elias stepped next to Nyssa, his hand on her shoulder. He leaned into her ear. "Why is he not surprised to see a wanted fugitive? I never told him you were with us."

Nyssa glanced back at Mox, and the smile slipped from his face. *Shit.*

"I'm sorry," he said.

"What the f—"

Blurry figures took shape next to Mox, seven in total. A woman drew Nyssa's focus, turning her blood ice cold.

"Juliana?" she whispered.

The young woman stepped forward. "Surrender to the authority of the Areshi Empire, Unworthy, and you will be unharmed." Behind Juliana were six adepts. Nyssa recognized them all from the Emerald Order.

"You sold us out, Mox," Nyssa growled.

He shrugged. "Just business, gorgeous. I took a chance you were still hanging around the Ghost of the Sea despite the rumors they had kicked you off their ship a year back."

"I'll fucking kill you."

The Order adepts all noticeably stiffened, hands tightening on their sword hilts.

Nyssa turned her attention to Juliana. "You're not old enough to be outside of the guild." None of them were—they were just teenagers.

"I'm eighteen now, Unworthy. And more than capable of dealing with you."

The arrogance didn't suit her. It sounded put on.

"The Empire must be desperate if they're sending guild pups after us...you're not even Ashcloaks yet. You need to turn around and leave," Nyssa replied.

"You're wanted by the Empress, murderer," one of the adepts behind Juliana said. He gripped a large silver-black band.

A void collar.

Nyssa pulled down her scarf and wiped away the makeup covering the mark on her chin. *Let them all see it.* "Unworthy. A word you spit out like poison. But you know me, Juliana."

"I knew you once. But you killed our First Master, traitor."

Nyssa exhaled hard. "Is that the lie Ceril's telling? Go home and ask Ashcloak Fennick. He'll tell you it wasn't me. It was Efla Eld'on from the Obsidian Rule."

"Fennick is Order in name only. He dishonors the guild by being your friend." Juliana waved an adept on. "Collar them."

Quinn stepped forward, shadow swirling around her. "Leave now or I will drop you where you stand."

One of the adepts behind Juliana raised his hand and attempted to hit Quinn with a spike of light. The spike never got close to her, disappearing into Quinn's defensive shadow. She counterattacked with a single barb of darkness, crumpling the adept to the ground.

The other adepts gaped at their dead guildmate.

"Quinn," Nyssa said. "What did you do?"

"They'll never stop coming for us, Nyssa."

Fontaine and Elias had warned Nyssa that showing mercy only meant the same faces would turn up again trying to hurt them. Though these pursuers were far different—she knew them—Quinn was right.

Her stomach turned, knowing what they had to do. "Juliana, leave now," she said, her voice hard and insistent.

The adepts shifted into fighting stances.

Nyssa steeled herself. "Elias, Yuha, take care of Mox's guards. Move when we do."

"Got it," Elias replied, his voice low. Tension radiated off of him—he was ready for a fight, flames licking at his finger tips as he called his magick forward.

Nyssa glanced at Quinn, nodding her head once.

A beat passed.

Nyssa and Quinn attacked, Quinn driving a thick tendril of darkness into the chest of one of the adepts, killing him. Out of the corner of her eye, Elias flung a fireball at one of The Lash's guards and Yuha tackled another.

A torrent of air struck Quinn and Nyssa, and they tumbled over a gambling table and hit the ground hard, chips cascading to the floor around them. Quinn was quick to her feet, drawing her sword in time to parry a blow from an adept, his wooden staff colliding against steel. He whirled around and jabbed the butt of his staff into Quinn's stomach, sending her reeling.

Nyssa pulled herself up and sensed a flare of magick. She struck out instinctively in its direction, glancing a bolt of lightning off a male adept. He cried out, his arm sparking as Nyssa vaulted over the table and closed the distance to him, knocking his hand away before it could draw his dagger. She grabbed its hilt, drew the blade, and arced it up, slicing the adept's throat.

Quinn's attacker drove her back and took a swing at her with his staff. Nyssa gritted her teeth, fearing he'd knock Quinn unconscious, but Quinn ducked and shot forward, her sword sinking deep into his belly. She stepped back, and he slid to the ground, coughing up blood.

Pain exploded in Nyssa's chest, hot and sharp. She cried out, sinking to the ground.

"Nyssa!" Quinn yelled, running to her. She held her hand out. A torrent of green magick slammed into a swirling shield of her darkness and dissipated.

Nyssa glanced down—the same green magick fell away from her chest. Power that inflicted pain. Just like Tann Eld'on. The adept responsible bared his teeth and drew his sword, lunging forward. Shadow coiled around him and dove into his body. He struggled for a moment, pawing at his chest as if trying to pull the darkness out of himself, then stilled. Quinn let her magick fade, and he fell limply to the floor.

Two adepts remained on their feet—Juliana and another girl. The girl's hands burst into bright-yellow flames, and she started running toward Nyssa and Quinn.

I remember her. Her fists can melt steel.

Nyssa choked down the lump in her throat and hurled a bolt of lightning at the girl. The adept ducked out of the strike, bearing down quickly on the two of them.

"Don't let her touch you!" Nyssa yelled.

Quinn snaked shadow around her legs, and the girl tripped, sprawling in front of them, lunging for Nyssa.

Nyssa rolled out of the way and grabbed the back of the girl's neck, the adept's magick thrumming under her fingers like a river of power. Nyssa sent her magick into the girl's glowing soul and twisted, snapping it in two. The adept gasped and went limp.

"Nyssa..." Quinn whispered.

Nyssa stumbled to her feet, searching for Elias and Yuha, catching sight of Yuha bouncing the last guard's head off the bar.

"We're good, Nyssa," Elias said, panting.

She nodded at him before turning to the remaining adept. Juliana. She had never attacked.

Maybe I can save her.

Juliana stared at the dead bodies on the floor of The Lash. She reached for her sword and drew it.

That fragment of hope died in Nyssa's chest.

"What are you doing, Juliana?" Nyssa asked. "I don't want to have to kill you."

"I can't disobey an order."

"Yes, you can."

"Like you did to earn that mark on your face? You dishonored your guild. You dishonored *us*! You're a traitor."

Juliana set her jaw and stepped toward Nyssa, gathering herself into a stance Nyssa was all too familiar with—a variation of a defensive stance that Nyssa had taught her, altering it for Juliana's fighting style.

"Juliana, I'm begging you. Go." Nyssa's voice wavered as a lump rose in her throat. "Please."

Juliana was one of the few people who showed Nyssa kindness back at the Order, seeking her out for mentoring. She was too young to die for a guild that cared nothing for her.

"I've beaten you before," Juliana said.

Nyssa tilted her head back and exhaled a heavy breath. "I once warned you about mistaking confidence for skill. I *let* you win when we sparred."

Juliana shuffled forward, the tip of her sword aimed at Nyssa. "I'm not scared of you, Unworthy."

Nyssa looked down at her hands and pulled her magick back inside of her, watching the blue shards of lightning fade from her skin.

"I didn't kill Eron. I swear to you," Nyssa said softly.

"You're a liar and not worthy of Eron's trust."

The certainty in Juliana's voice shattered something within Nyssa. She started toward the young adept with purpose, anger surging with every stride.

They will never stop coming for us.

Juliana steadied herself, but her eyes betrayed her fear. Nyssa lunged and drew her sword. In one swift, decisive motion, it was done.

Juliana's sword clattered to the floor, and her hands flew to her throat. Blood seeped between her fingers, confusion and fear stark on her face. She tilted forward. Nyssa caught her and lowered her gently to the floor. Rivulets of blood flowed away in the seams of the wood beneath her.

Juliana stared up at Nyssa, tiny gasps of air leaving her lips. Nyssa leaned forward, taking the girl's face in her hands, and whispered the Emerald Order's oath:

> *"To my brothers and sisters, my bond.*
> *To my guild, my fidelity.*
> *To my Empire, my blood.*
> *Stand fast. Face the darkness. Fall without fear."*

Quick, shallow breaths gave way to one long, last exhale, and Juliana stilled.

Bile rose in Nyssa's throat. She drew her bloody fingers over the dead girl's eyes, closing them.

A hand settled on her shoulder. "Nyssa," Quinn murmured.

Nyssa looked up at Quinn. "She shouldn't have been here. None of them should have been here. They're too young."

"Come on," Quinn said, helping Nyssa to her feet. Quinn took Winter's Bite from her hand and cleaned the blade, resheathing it as Nyssa stood over Juliana's body, numb.

Elias pointed Yuha toward Mox's table. "Grab that wine. At least we've still got that. Now, we have to go. We can't be found here."

"Where's Mox?" Nyssa asked.

"Fled, like the coward he is," Elias spat.

Quinn put a hand on the small of Nyssa's back and gently pushed. "Let's go."

The Empire had sent her own guild after her. Worse yet, they'd sent unseasoned kids. Ceril had ordered them to hunt her down, of that she was certain.

They left through the back-alley exit. Nyssa didn't know how much time passed before they got back to Hannah's Whisper. She felt as though partially removed from the world, still trying to reckon with what she had done.

Elias quietly told the crew what had happened as Nyssa stood by, her head bowed, replaying the confrontation in her mind. Regret churned inside her, twisting her stomach. Despite all their precautions, they had been found.

Regret began to turn to anger, simmering, waiting to explode.

A RECKONING

Wind whipped through the sails as Hannah's Whisper slipped away from the docks, the ship's invisibility veil activated as they left Jejin's harbor. Nyssa stared over the side of the ship, gripping the handrail until she could no longer feel her fingers. She kept replaying the confrontation with the Order adepts in her mind, wondering what she could have done differently. If she could have saved Juliana.

Quinn stood nearby. Silent. Watching.

Nyssa turned around and slid down to the deck. What would Eron have thought of her killing her own? A sob escaped her. The eyes of the crew were on her as they went about their duties. What did they consider her? A traitor? A murderer?

Quinn knelt next to her. "Nyssa, I'm sorry."

Nyssa exhaled forcefully and looked over at Quinn. "They sent my own guildmates after me."

"It...it's not your guild anymore. I think that's clear now."

Nyssa's stomach churned. "They were innocents."

"They were there to arrest us," Quinn replied, scowling. "They held no love for you anymore."

Quinn couldn't understand. She hated every second at Arcton Citadel. Nyssa didn't hate everything about the Order. It's where Eron raised her. Where she met and became friends with Athen and learned how to stand up for herself.

"They thought I killed Eron. My own father."

"Nyssa, I...." Quinn looked down and shook her head. "The adepts hurt you; ostracized you because you didn't have magick. The Masters let your peers abuse you. You think you were earning your place in the guild through blood, bruises, and broken bones? That wasn't your trial by fire. That was abuse. Why do you feel *anything* for them?"

Nyssa balled her hands into fists. "It was my home. I wish I was home," she breathed, her chest tightening. Her admission felt damning. "I wish none of this happened."

Quinn stood up, towering over Nyssa. "You wish *I* never happened."

"That's not what I said."

Quinn's face turned hard. "Those aren't the words you used, but it *is* what you meant."

Nyssa shot to her feet. "No, it's not! I just...I thought I did the right thing...but look at us now. Hunted by the whole goddamn Empire. I don't even know if I'll ever see my friends again."

"The friends that hurt you?"

"What? Athen and Aryis didn't hurt me. I'm the one that put them in danger!"

Shaking her head, Quinn said, "When you needed them to believe you, to stand up for you, they failed. Where were they when you needed them most? They were going to stand by and watch me die. Watch *you* die."

Quinn's words dove into her like daggers. "You don't know anything about Athen and Aryis," Nyssa snarled. A flood of grief washed over her, a cruel punctuation to an already awful day. She swallowed and stepped away.

Her life was supposed to be *different*. Eron should be alive. She should be at Ocean's Rest, serving the Order as an Ashcloak.

Nyssa stared down at her hands. They pulsed with energy. Her magick had come to the surface. "Eron would be so ashamed of me. Of what I've done."

She swallowed back the lump forming in her throat. All this time, even in her quiet moments, she had turned her thoughts away from her father. It was too painful to think of him. To mourn him with the blood of her fellow Emerald Order adepts on her hands and the Mark of the Unworthy marring her face would be a cruel betrayal of his trust in her.

Quinn grabbed her arm. "Nyssa, he wouldn't be ashamed. You saved us."

Nyssa looked up at Quinn. "No, my *anger* saved us. I lost control and this happened." She held up her hands, lightning rippling across her fingers.

"Your anger set us free!"

"It gets people killed! Do you think I've forgotten those people on the docks?" She stepped forward and pointed at her chin. "Is this what freedom looks like, Quinn? This mark means I'll never be truly free."

Thunder rumbled overhead, Nyssa's anger reflected in the sky.

She didn't care. *Let the storm come.*

Fontaine and Elias approached, the concern on their faces evident. Or was it fear? "Nyssa, please calm down."

Nyssa held her hand up as a warning. "You stay out of this."

"You blame me for being marked, don't you?" Quinn asked. "Saving me made you a traitor in their eyes."

"I keep telling you I don't," Nyssa said, pulling out of Quinn's grasp. *Do...do I blame her?*

Quinn stepped up, poking a hard finger in Nyssa's chest. "You're lying. I think at least part of you blames me. You have a code of honor and you act on it. But when you do something driven by that code and harsh consequences follow, you don't get to be angry at *me* for your choices."

Nyssa twisted her fist in Quinn's shirt. "Where do you get the fucking audacity to say that to me?"

A crack of thunder echoed her anger.

Quinn snarled back, "You thought that doing the noble thing would *mean* something? That the people who had always put you down would finally acknowledge you? You're so *fucking* naïve. The Empire, the guilds, Ceril, Athen, Aryis—hell, even Eron—they all failed you in the end, and that's my fault?"

"Don't talk about Eron. You didn't know him. I lost everything to help you," Nyssa breathed.

"You fucking gave me *back* to them!" Quinn cried, her voice breaking, eyes lighting up with green fire. She shoved Nyssa as darkness began swirling around her. "You saw the scars. You knew what Ceril did to me. And you gave me back to them, anyway!"

Nyssa rushed forward and grabbed Quinn. "You don't think I hate myself for handing you over? But I came for you. I thought I could make things right. Instead, I lost my father, my friends. Everything!"

Quinn grabbed Nyssa's wrists. Nyssa sent a pulse of lightning through her, making her cry out, driving her to her knees. Nyssa moved over her and balled up her fists. "I lost everything!" she yelled.

Thunder boomed overhead. A split second later, lightning crashed onto the deck of the Whisper behind Quinn, splintering wood. Alarmed shouts rang out from the crew. Fontaine yelled over the storm, begging them to stop fighting.

Nyssa didn't care.

The sky opened up and dumped down rain. Lightning flashed overhead, illuminating Quinn's face in an eerie blue glow. Nyssa reached down and grabbed her, yanking her to her feet.

Thunder boomed overhead, shaking the Whisper with its force. The crew scattered, running for shelter.

"You had nothing to lose, but I lost my *family*!" Nyssa snarled, spiraling into a dark pit of anger and guilt, her magick slipping out of her grasp.

Quinn sent a barb of darkness into the center of Nyssa's chest.

Nyssa flew off her feet and landed hard on the deck, skidding away. She gasped for air, the cold shock and pain of the blow causing her body to curl in on itself.

Lightning struck the deck only a few feet away from Nyssa. Panic gripped her as the crew yelled, their voices filled with fear.

She was causing this.

Scaring them.

Endangering them.

Nyssa clawed at the deck, trying to gain purchase, to anchor herself to something so she could try to pull her magick back, but it raged out of her control. A pure, primal fury driven by her anger. How easily she had lost the thin thread holding her power back from raging. Panic flooded every crevice of her body.

Quinn stood over Nyssa and sent a fist across her face. Shadow coiled around her, biting into her, its chill sending ripples of pain through her body.

"Is this what you want?" Quinn yelled, her face a mask of anger. "Is pain all you understand?"

Nyssa had lashed out and pushed Quinn to her breaking point. She hadn't expected Quinn to push back.

She dug her fingers into Quinn's leg, desperate. "Quinn, please..." Nyssa begged. "I can't make it stop." The hairs rose on Nyssa's arms, and a thick streak of cobalt lightning blazed into the water next to the ship. "I can't control it. Please help me!"

Quinn dropped down and pinned Nyssa's shoulders to the deck. A dizzying wave of magick washed over her, fighting with her own power. Another wave followed, stronger. More painful. Nyssa's body tensed as Quinn sent nullifying wave after nullifying wave through her, bringing her back from the brink bit by bit. The storm overhead began to calm, and the rain petered out. Moonlight flooded through the dissipating clouds, illuminating the deck. Quinn sat back and exhaled a grunt, her shoulders slumping.

They had gotten lucky. They could have torn the ship apart. Nyssa's grief and rage and lack of control had risked everyone's lives.

She scrambled to her feet and barely made it to the rail before she threw up over the side of the ship. She collapsed to her knees, clinging to the handrail, afraid to let go. Her whole body shook.

The lore of the Cursed Gods came into sharp focus—*Two souls, forever entwined, clash with fists and blade, dragging the tips of their swords across the world.* Nyssa could raze the earth, kill so many with so little effort.

If she could lose control with Quinn, what would she do *for* her?

"Nyssa?" Quinn said, her voice low and cautious.

Nyssa choked back a sob. "Is anyone hurt?"

A hand on her back pulled Nyssa's gaze up. Fontaine bent over her. "No, Nyssa. No one is hurt."

Nyssa buried her head in her hands. "I'm sorry. I'm so sorry. I couldn't control it...."

Quinn sat down hard next to her, her back against the rail. "It's my fault. I antagonized you."

"You both lost control of your tempers and your magick. This is why I insisted on a year to train you at Monk's Cove. Now I regret leaving. You both need a lot more work," Fontaine said. The anger in her voice made Nyssa flood with shame.

Quinn put her hand on Nyssa's arm. "Nyssa, what you said...you haven't lost everything. You have family here. You...you have me."

"Then why do I feel so alone?"

Quinn exhaled a shaky breath, her face pained. "Nyssa—"

Nyssa raised her head and looked at Quinn, whose eyes were shiny with tears. "When I reach out, you recoil. Retreat behind your walls."

"I don't want you to lose anything more because of me," Quinn whispered.

"I said I don't blame you." Nyssa reached out to her, but Quinn stood and stepped back, silent. That was all Nyssa needed. She sighed. "I only want what's best for you, and I don't think that's me."

Nyssa shook her head and slowly got to her feet. Around the deck, the crew had come out of their hiding places. "Fontaine, I'm sorry.... I...I'm sorry," she said, her voice catching.

"No lives were lost. The ship can be repaired," Fontaine replied. "But I think you two need a break from one another. Nyssa, stay in my room tonight. I will speak to you both separately about what we can do to avoid this happening again. Elias, take Nyssa below deck."

Nyssa hung her head and avoided looking at Quinn as Elias put an arm around her. "Elias, I'm so sorry," she whispered.

"We'll get you and Quinn sorted out, love. You've had a really awful day and it got to you. I'd be lying if I said I didn't have a couple of those myself. Fontaine and I can help," he said, his arm tightening around her. Nyssa hid her face as the tears came.

Quinn kept to herself, brooding in her room while Nyssa stayed with Fontaine. They were kept apart at Elias's orders until the sting of their confrontation on deck waned. She was achingly lonely even though Nyssa was only a few doors down.

Elias didn't want to chance going into port so soon after Quinn and Nyssa's trouble in Jejin, so Hannah's Whisper dropped anchor near the city of Merra, the northern-most island in the Basai Island chain and a two-day trip from Jejin. Fontaine wove a protective ward to be extra safe—it would keep anyone from coming aboard the ship, and sound an alarm if breached.

The next day, Nyssa had disappeared before sunrise. A tender was missing, and she left a note.

> *Need to clear my head. I'll be back in a few days.*
> *— Nyssa*

Quinn's stomach dropped. "She's gone," Quinn said, fingering the paper in her hand.

Nyssa just...left.

"A break will be good. You can breathe and figure out who you are apart from Nyssa," Elias said.

"I thought I was doing that."

Fontaine laughed softly. "You two are always together. Now you can cast your own shadow, as Nyssa would say. For a few days, at least."

Quinn sighed. Fontaine was quoting Sakei at her, as Nyssa had several times as she taught Quinn Ithais-Toru.

"What if...what if she doesn't come back?" Surely she was being paranoid. Nyssa said she'd be gone for a few days and her leaving for good was unthinkable. But Quinn's stomach still twisted at the thought. The night before, she recoiled from Nyssa, furious and hurt. Now, all she wanted was her back on the ship.

"Oh, my sweet thing. Maybe next time you see Nyssa, tell her how sad you were in this moment. I think that's all she needs from you," Fontaine said, "a little glimpse at your heart."

"I don't think she would care."

Fontaine groaned. "I think your fight proved otherwise."

Quinn frowned. "All it did was bring resentment to the surface."

"It brought the truth to the surface. At least you showed her something of yourself. You were honest about your pain."

Honest? Everything she had said hurt Nyssa.

Elias clapped her on the back. "Get on deck and have Jerrin put you to work. We'll keep you too busy to mope."

Quinn nodded. She needed something to occupy her mind. Nyssa's absence was a heavy, cold stone in her chest.

AN UNEASY PEACE

Quinn hissed at the burn of alcohol after a generous swallow from her flask and cast her eyes up at the stars. Her restlessness brought her to the deck where she went to work polishing the quarterdeck's metal rail.

Nyssa had said she'd be back in a few days, but seven had passed since she left. Seven fucking days. Even Elias was beginning to wonder if she'd return. He tried to stay positive, but a worry had crept into them all. He seemed poised to dock in Merra and go look for her himself.

What if Nyssa had gotten herself in trouble or hurt? Or worse?

The thought was too dour. Quinn tossed her cleaning rag on top of the can of brass polish and looked down at her hands, running her thumbs along the callouses on her palms. Only a month as a true member of the crew, and her hands showed the wear of honest work. Far better than the scars she earned at the Citadel.

A warm breeze swept across the deck, and Quinn stood up and closed her eyes, drinking in the night air. She strode over to port and drank in the shimmering city of Merra as she took another generous swig of whiskey. She wasn't prone to drinking, but she didn't much care of late.

Sighing, she turned and sat on the deck, her back to the rail, and closed her eyes.

A low drone woke Quinn, slow to rouse. She hauled herself up by the handrail and listed to her left. Too much damn whiskey. She rubbed her eyes and found a hooded figure facing her. Instinctively, she summoned her shadow, coiled it around the figure's throat, and squeezed.

"Q-Quinn," the stranger croaked, pawing at their throat.

Quinn gasped and willed her magick away. "Nyssa?"

Perhaps it was the whiskey or being startled awake, but she hadn't noticed the warm buzz in her chest. A spark of excitement flooded through her, along with a dark anger that stirred in her stomach, creating a confusing mix of happiness and resentment.

Nyssa flipped back her hood and pulled down the black scarf that covered her chin. Her hair was partially braided with threads of leather woven through, same as when they first met. And she now wore a thick black leather band around her left wrist.

Footsteps thundered toward them as Elias, Fontaine, and two crew members approached. Fontaine was naked. Once again.

Elias eyed Nyssa, his sword pointed at her neck. "What do you think you're playing at, sneaking on my ship?"

Nyssa pushed away his sword. "Sneaking aboard? I came aboard and got stuck in some sort of spell before I ripped it open."

Fontaine clucked her tongue. "My ward? You damaged my pristine ward?"

"Can't you just fix the hole I made?" Nyssa asked sheepishly.

Elias sheathed his sword and pulled her into a hug. "We were worried about you. Did you bring my tender back in one piece?"

"No, it's got a massive hole in it," Nyssa quipped. "Of course I did! How do you think I got back to the ship? I had to follow the magick, though, being invisible and all. Felt the Whisper buzzing like a billion hornets' nests."

A satisfied smile pushed Fontaine's frown to the side. "That's my magick."

"I'd know it anywhere now. It's got a distinctive feel to it."

"You stir up any trouble? Anyone figure out who you are?" Elias asked.

"Nah. I laid as low as one can and found a little inn near a bookstore to stay. I drank tea and read and ate more pastries than should be legal." Nyssa made a show of patting her stomach before turning serious. "I'm sorry I left like that. I just needed..." Nyssa glanced at Quinn, the blue in her eyes glinting in the deck lights.

Quinn crossed her arms.

"Alright," Elias said. "I would order you to not leave the ship again without my permission, but I know how well that would go over."

Nyssa shrugged.

A warm breeze ruffled Elias's hair, and he moved closer to Nyssa and Quinn. "You two are my responsibility, as is everyone on this ship. You're not guests or tourists, you're pirates. And members of my crew."

Quinn couldn't fight the soft grin inching onto her face. Part of Elias's crew. *A family.*

Nyssa bowed her head. "Thank you. I don't know if I deserve a second chance after endangering the ship, but I'll do my best to honor and protect this crew."

"I'm holding you to your word," Fontaine said, crossing her arms across her pale breasts.

Nyssa beamed at her before scrunching up her brows. "Naked again, Fontaine?"

"I sleep naked, you know this! You woke us all up!" Fontaine threw her hands in the air before she walked down the deck and began to weave magick to fix her ward.

"I don't even get a welcome back hug?" Nyssa asked.

"Feh! You ripped my beautiful enchantment," Fontaine grumbled. "Shut your face and let me work!"

Elias waved the two crew members with sleep in their eyes back to bed. "I'll give you two some space," he said before retreating back down below.

Nyssa stepped closer. "Quinn...I..."

Quinn backed away. Nyssa's return left her conflicted, happiness and anger roiling within her like a storm. Those piercing blue eyes seemed to be searching for a sign of warmth, but Quinn resolved to give her nothing.

"Are you okay if I return to our room?" Nyssa asked.

"Your bunk is as you left it." Quinn gestured to the stairs leading below deck, as if Nyssa didn't know the way.

Nyssa frowned. She gave Quinn one last look before walking past her toward the stairway.

Everything about their exchange confused Quinn, especially her own reaction. Her whole body ached when Nyssa was gone, but now that she was back, within feet of her, the ache only deepened. It made no sense. Fucking *maddening*.

Quinn turned and sat on a crate to calm down and think. The swirl of emotions was stronger than she realized, and the cold, darker ones were winning out.

She felt Fontaine watching her out of the corner of her eye, but thankfully the woman was busy reweaving the protective veil around the ship, her lips and hands moving as she spoke the spell into the night air.

Nyssa shed her jacket and boots and sank onto her bunk with a happy sigh. Even though only gone a week, it was good to be back aboard the Whisper. When she boarded the ship, a familiar feeling crept back into her body and settled into her bones. Quinn's presence. The absence of that warm glow had become an ache Nyssa found harder and harder to ignore as her time away from the ship wore on.

Forever entwined, Nyssa thought, glad to sense Quinn again even though there was an icy divide between them. Not that Nyssa expected anything different. She'd left instead of resolving things. It was a moment of pure selfishness—her need to get away—to think without Quinn in sight.

After a long soak in the tub, her fingers numb from working the braids out of her hair, Nyssa lay reading in her bunk when Quinn returned to their room. She disappeared behind her privacy screen and changed for bed.

Nyssa tapped her finger against the leather band she found in a little shop in a dark corner of Merra. Its owner was an old man with gnarled fingers and a deft hand at making excellent handcrafted leather gear. The cuff had a little pocket perfect for Quinn's Winter's Fire gift to Nyssa so the smooth rock sat safely against her pulse.

She took a deep breath. Nyssa hated the resentment that had shot to the surface during their argument. She didn't blame Quinn for her choices. Saving Quinn was the right choice. It would *always* be the right choice.

She swallowed. "I'm sorry for…what I've done and I know you're mad at me. Can we talk about this?"

Quinn appeared from behind the screen and tossed her clothes on the floor near her bed. Nyssa scowled. Quinn was never messy or careless with her belongings.

"The time to talk all this out was a week ago. Instead, you left. And I didn't know if you'd come back."

Nyssa swallowed. "I wouldn't leave you like that. But I thought we could both use some time alone."

Nyssa neglected to mention that she needed time away from Quinn to sort through her emotions. Not that a week made much of a difference. Hell, a year wouldn't have helped. She found no new insight in what to do about her feelings for Quinn.

"You left because you lost control," Quinn said.

"Yeah. I…hated what I did and what happened between us."

Quinn looked her square in the face. "You're scared of me."

"I…" Nyssa floundered. It was true, she *was* scared of Quinn. No one made her feel as deeply, as sharply, as Quinn did. All of her emotions were heightened around her—joy, protectiveness, loyalty, anger.

Affection.

And Nyssa didn't know how to explain herself without admitting her feelings and risking everything for a woman who didn't seem to return those sentiments.

It could end so badly.

"I'm scared of *us*. The lore of the Cursed Gods and the damage we could do is always in the back of my mind," Nyssa finally answered. "Look what happened when we fought. Thankfully no one got hurt!"

Quinn finally looked up at her. "You got hurt."

Nyssa swung her legs off her bunk and stood. She crossed over to Quinn, who was tightening and loosening the cap of her flask. Nyssa crouched down and put her hand on top of Quinn's, stilling her fidgeting.

"The two of us fighting like that—it can never happen again," Nyssa said. "We could have ripped this ship apart."

Quinn pulled away. "I already got this lecture from Fontaine and Elias. The thing is, Nyssa, I'm not scared of what I am. But you are. You're scared to push yourself because you might not be able to stop." Quinn raised her flask to her lips and took a deep swallow. "Why did you even come back?"

The truth came tumbling out; "I...I missed you."

The admission hung between them. Quinn sat, silent.

Nyssa continued. "We made each other a promise to go after Suvi and gain our freedom. That's what I want."

"I want more than that now." Quinn sighed, her shoulders sagging. "I've had some time to think and...I need to find out who I am. Who my parents are. There's one person who has those answers."

Nyssa nodded. She understood. Fear had stopped her from asking after her parents for so many years until it came to a head when she finally talked to Lilliana. The memory of that time made Nyssa ache. She didn't know what Quinn would find out, but she was determined to be there for her.

"After we get Suvi," Nyssa said, meeting Quinn's eyes and giving her a smile, "I'll help you get Ceril. You deserve your answers from him."

Quinn's gaze flicked down to Nyssa's lips before rising and settling back on her eyes. Nyssa couldn't ignore the small flutter in her stomach. Despite the glance, Quinn's face was cold. "Assuming the Empress agrees to our terms, I will go after Ceril on my own."

Nyssa frowned. "You know I won't let you face him alone, Freckles."

"Stop with the pet name."

"I...I just—"

"You can't come back and just assume things are back to normal between us. Whatever the fuck normal used to be," Quinn said, her voice cold. "Once we trade Suvi for our lives, I think it would be wise to go our separate ways."

Nyssa swallowed and stood, gutted. *Separate ways?* "Quinn, I don't want that," she whispered.

"Well, you're not the center of the universe, Nyssa. I get a choice too."

The deep ache that she felt being away from the ship—away from Quinn—came roaring back with a vengeance. She couldn't believe what she was hearing. "I'm...I'm sorry," was all she managed to whisper before returning to her bed, hollowed out.

She had fucked everything up.

A GROWING DISTANCE

Athen leaned into a large ball of dough and hummed to himself, a habit he had while baking—the one thing he could lose himself in and forget his problems for a time. Of late, it was a retreat he desperately needed.

Four months had passed since Aryis left and communication between the two of them had ground to a halt. He had half a mind to get on a ship and go to Frosland himself, but he knew it would only make things worse. Still, he sat with Reece for hours, time and again, and made her talk him out of doing it.

Soon after Aryis had returned to Frosland, the country withdrew from the Empire, citing a need for sovereignty. Athen knew better—he learned that Kalla had reneged on her promise to make Aryis the next Empress. He could only guess that the Wayland attack changed everything. None of it had been her fault, but when did that ever matter in the politics of perception? Ceril had to be involved somehow, dripping poison in Kalla's ear. Ker Devitt left the Empire rather than swallow down the dishonor of rejection.

Athen hated that Aryis was caught up in the web of messy politics. She deserved far better.

A presence drew Athen out of his thoughts. Medias leaned against the wall, watching him from across the kitchen. "You sneaking up on me?"

"I do not sneak, Fennick."

Athen grunted a laugh. The Justiciar didn't sneak so much as just...appear. He rarely spoke to her, instead letting Reece deal with the woman and, to her credit, Reece didn't seem to mind. A far cry from their first reaction, when her anger was palpable at the thought of allowing a Justiciar to live among them. If Reece trusted Medias...well, that was enough for him.

"What brings you here?" he asked.

"Can I simply not desire a pastry?"

Athen smirked and cut his dough ball into quarters, putting each in an oiled bowl and covering them with a towel so they would rise. "I'm making bread for the Guard. I've been working them hard lately and thought they could do with a show of appreciation."

"Thoughtful."

"What do you truly want?" Athen wiped his hands and leaned against the counter.

Pushing off the wall, Medias walked over to him, lifting a towel to peer inside at his dough. "Your mother has put a price on Mox's head—an apt response to his betrayal."

Mox was the least of his concerns. That asshole would get what was coming to him for selling out Nyssa. But when Athen heard that Order adepts had been sent—young ones, not even Ashcloaks yet—his heart dropped into his stomach. That Nyssa had to kill them...it was unthinkable. And he knew she wouldn't have done so if she had a choice.

"Aryis. Nyssa. Quinn. I can't do anything to help them," he said aloud before he could stop himself. "I'm letting down everyone I love."

Medias stood straighter and considered him, her red eyes narrowing. "Athen, that simply isn't true."

"What the fuck do you know?" The anger came quick, as did his regret.

The Justiciar drew in a breath, her face unreadable under her mask, though her lips formed a thin, humorless line. Lashing out was not a habit of his. He prided himself on his patience and even temper.

"We have all made choices to place us in the circumstances we find ourselves in. None of it is ideal, but Nyssa and Quinn are feeling the worst of it."

Athen hung his head. He was being selfish, dwelling in his own thoughts and lamenting his failures. "What am I supposed to do? I can't help Nyssa. Aryis is gone, and I don't know when...or if...I'll ever see her again. Everything is fucked," he said, not raising his eyes to Medias. The last thing he wanted was a Justiciar's pity.

"Athen, I'm...sorry that Aryis isn't here. I can see that pains you. I know she misses you just as well."

Athen's eyes shot up. "How do you know? Have you seen something in your visions?"

Medias shook her head. "Her feelings for you were obvious."

Athen had no way to know if she was lying or withholding information from him, but he wasn't about to push. Reece had warned him a while back to let the Justiciar offer information in her own time and in her own way.

"Have you...have you heard anything about Aryis?" he asked.

"I know your heart is heavy without her here," she said. "You will see her again, but you will need to be strong."

His stomach did a flip. How could good news sound so ominous? "You *have* seen something."

With a sigh, Medias shook her head. "There is a reason I don't share the details of my visions with anyone. Just know I don't do it to vex you. My seer sight can be confounding. But if you trust me, I will try to steer you away from danger and toward the people who need you."

Athen sighed. "Reece has encouraged patience and trust with you, so I'll do my best to honor that."

"Has she?" The lilt in Medias's voice gave away her surprise.

"She has."

"Interesting." Medias gave him a nod and walked away.

WATERING PLANTS

The scent of lavender that lingered in the hallway near her door left Medias with the distinct impression that her room was not unoccupied. No one would dare break into a Justiciar's room...save for one person.

Medias opened the door and exhaled an exasperated breath. Reece sat on the windowsill across the room, talking to the plant she had brought the Justiciar five months prior. It still remained the only decoration added to the room since Medias began living in it.

"Are you having a conversation with my plant?" Medias asked. Reece's habit of talking to plants was odd, but slightly endearing.

Gods, I'm going soft.

Reece frowned. "You mean the plant that I'm letting you borrow? *My* plant?"

"I don't recall asking to borrow a plant."

Were it anyone else in Medias's room without her permission, she would have been incensed. No one else would dare steal into a Justiciar's room, let alone just to talk to a plant. Reece cocked her head, a gesture that Medias had learned usually preceded a probing question.

"You've been here a little over a year now. It's time you told me exactly why you helped Nyssa and Quinn. You've risked your life and entrusted us with knowledge that could get you executed. I need to understand why," Reece said, crossing her ankles and slowly swinging her legs.

"My life is in your hands. One word from you to the Arch Justiciar and my life would be forfeit. Is that not enough?" Medias asked, starting to unzip her jacket. She caught herself and stopped. Had she really become so comfortable around the empath that she would forget herself? She knew in her heart she barely held on to the Justiciar title, but still a Justiciar she was, nonetheless.

"Actually, no, it's not enough." Reece hopped down from the windowsill. She crossed over to Medias and took her by the arm, steering her toward a chair.

The forwardness of the woman annoyed Medias at times and Reece damn well knew it, insistent on pushing boundaries.

Medias sat down with a huff and crossed her arms. Reece sat opposite from her on her bed. Another boundary pushed.

"You know the news out of Cardin isn't good. They're nipping at Nyssa and Quinn's heels. I don't know how much longer we can continue this ruse. At some point you're going to have to declare sides. You'll either go back to the Empress and serve her or you'll stay on this road you're on, wherever it leads."

"You still don't trust me, do you?"

"I want to, but…" Reece exhaled, "I can't read you. My abilities give me an edge, an insight on where others stand. But with you, there's nothing. And I can't trust that. I've been burned by someone like you before."

Someone like me? Curious.

"When we don the mask, we are changed forever. Our hearts and minds are shrouded by Amberis to protect Imperial secrets. You may not be able to read my emotions but trust that I do have them."

Reece's eyes bored into Medias. "I need more than that, Justiciar. Repay my faith. Tell me why you're doing this."

Medias folded her hands in her lap. This moment wasn't unexpected—she was just surprised it hadn't happened sooner.

"My father also possessed foresight. He hid it, like I do, but we're not like other seers. Most seers have but a few visions in a lifetime. I've had twenty or more in a year alone."

"You and your father shared a very unique ability," Reece said.

"He had visions of Nyssa and Quinn starting a few years after I was born, around the time they were born. He spoke of the marked god, driven by honor and anger. And the raven-haired god, her scars and her heart hidden. He saw far into the future, including visions of his daughter taking a knife to Nyssa's face to mark her a traitor."

Reece sucked in a breath. "Your father saw that?"

"Yes, and to his credit, he never shamed me for it."

"Medias...I..."

Medias shook her head, a sad smile briefly pulling at her lips. "My visions of Quinn and Nyssa began when I was a girl. I would watch them die. Then watch them ascend. Suffer and thrive. I didn't know why I saw conflicting fates for them. My father's visions weren't confusing like mine."

"Do you have any idea why your visions were different?"

"My father believed it's because Nyssa and Quinn and their magick can slip the bonds of fate. He was convinced I had a gift, a connection to them, and he urged me to trust my visions and to trust the two of them. I'm here because of him."

Reece exhaled, narrowing her eyes. "Is that what you meant the day Nyssa and Quinn escaped? You said they shattered a strand of fate."

"I thought for so very long that my visions were immutable; that nothing could change them. I foresaw my father's death and nothing either of us did changed his fate." Medias dug her fingers into the arms of her chair to steady herself and avoided looking at Reece.

"After he died, my visions of Quinn and Nyssa ceased. It wasn't until I came here to investigate the Winter's Fire wraith attack and saw Nyssa for the first time that I realized she was real. Seeing her took my breath away. Soon after, the visions returned. I decided to try one more time to alter the future, to see if my father was right. You, though, were the first strand of fate I had to pluck. I needed you to find Nyssa. And for that, I'm sorry."

Reece's throat bobbed. Medias had told Master Justiciar Elken that Reece had a connection with Nyssa and could find her. It was necessary, but Elken had not been kind. Medias had a lot of regrets, but watching Elken hurt the empath and bend her to his will was one of her biggest.

"I've done some awful things behind the authority of this mask, Reece. By helping the Cursed Gods, and helping you, perhaps I can make up for some of my sins."

She released her grip on the arms of the chair and looked down at her hands, flexing her fingers, her leather gloves creaking. She had come to love the sound. It grounded her, kept her in the moment.

Reece sat silent, staring at her.

"I only see things in my visions that are important to me. But they can also be dangerous, so I keep them to myself. My father died knowing exactly how it was going to happen, powerless in the end to stop it. I can't imagine what that was like...I don't want to do that to anyone else."

"I didn't realize that. I'm sorry, Medias," Reece said, her voice low and soothing.

"Maybe I can change the things I see and maybe I can't, but my father didn't believe in sitting idle, waiting for the future to pass. I want to honor him."

Medias swallowed back the lump forming in her throat. It had been years since she thought of her father's death, but it never ceased to stop her in her tracks.

"What of your mother?" Reece asked.

"A modest woman with a small bookshop. We don't speak."

Reece looked about to ask a follow-on question, but Medias cut her off. "Do you have what you came for?"

"Yes. Thank you for your candor."

Medias stood and pulled at the bottom of her jacket, smoothing the leather down. "There's something I think you should have." She opened the drawer of her nightstand and pulled out a small, round metal pin, handing it to Reece.

"That's Nyssa's guild pin. I know you visit her father's grave. Perhaps he should have this?"

Reece closed her fist around the pin. "You didn't have to give this back."

"It belongs with Eron Greye." Medias looked away, suddenly uneasy in Reece's stare. "It's been a long night, empath."

Reece stood and headed to the door. "Have a good evening, Medias."

She slipped out the door, and Medias let out a heavy sigh, slumping forward. She put her hand to her face, the Justiciar mask smooth and warm to the touch.

THINGS ARE NOT OKAY

Nyssa tossed a line to Mina to unfurl the sails. They were two months away from their attempt to capture Suvi, and Nyssa found working hard on deck calmed her nerves.

Fontaine had doubled up on their training to prepare for the wine festival in Thu'Dain. Nyssa and Quinn would wordlessly follow her instructions as she drilled them on all things easy and hard—the first to underpin their basic magick discipline, the second to advance their skills and control. Nyssa was cautious, reluctant to do anything too risky. Frustration was plain on Fontaine's face, but Nyssa didn't want another incident.

Despite their icy relationship, Nyssa insisted on resuming Quinn's Ithais-Toru training. It was awkward, but Nyssa hoped a crack would appear in Quinn's armor and she could maybe work her way back into Quinn's good graces. A month had passed since her return and no opening availed itself.

After helping the crew with the sails, Nyssa turned to find Quinn waiting for their sparring session, watching from the rail. The sun beat down on the deck, and Nyssa upturned a bucket of cold water over her head, shivering as it cascaded over her and cooled her down.

She threw caution to the wind and flicked a spark of lightning at Quinn. It hit Quinn and she jumped, meeting the spark with a frown instead of laughter.

Nyssa shook her head—she wasn't going to cater to Quinn's mood today. She bounced on the balls of her feet and rolled her shoulders to get loose. "Let's dance, Freckles. I want to kick your ass quick and get lunch."

The frown on Quinn's face turned to a sneer, and she pushed off the rail to stalk toward Nyssa. With a cock of her head, Nyssa beckoned Quinn forward, taking a casual stance instead of the ones she used to drill Quinn with. She knew it looked lazy and disrespectful.

She didn't care.

A small contingent of the crew gathered in a semicircle around them. Some of them barked out encouragement for their fighter of choice and called out their bets to Jerrin. Wagering on their sparring sessions had become something of a pastime for the crew. It wasn't lost on Nyssa that Jerrin would alternate betting on the two women, unwilling to pick a favorite. This fight he cheered on Quinn. Nyssa vowed to lose him some money this morning.

Quinn attacked fast, not waiting for a signal to start. Nyssa blocked her flurry of punches and shifted back. Quinn was on her again quickly with another flurry of fists followed up by a vicious kick to Nyssa's knee. It landed with a sting.

A cheer went up from the crew, who had been used to Nyssa getting the better of Quinn during their sessions, making Quinn a riskier bet but with greater reward. Quinn pressed her advantage, but this time Nyssa avoided her fists and shot forward with a palm strike to Quinn's chest. A gasp went up from the onlookers.

Quinn stumbled back from the blow. She exhaled and got back into her stance. If Nyssa weren't concerned with winning, she would be proud of her student.

The crew cheered them on as they went back and forth, trading blows, with Nyssa landing more strikes. While she pulled her punches and kicks, she noticed that Quinn did not. Quinn landed another kick on the same knee. Nyssa limped away.

Quinn resumed her stance. "Do you yield?"

The fucking audacity. Nyssa shook her head.

Quinn smirked and closed the distance between them. Nyssa shifted forward and hit Quinn with a roundhouse kick to the gut. Quinn cried out and dropped to her knees. Nyssa cursed under her breath and moved in to check on her.

Quinn rolled forward and hooked a leg around Nyssa's knee, wrenching the injured joint in a leg lock. Nyssa fell onto her back with a grunt. She grabbed at Quinn, but Quinn leaned out of her reach and continued to apply pressure to the knee.

It wasn't the first time Quinn faked an injury, playing on Nyssa's concern. Nyssa snarled, pulled her free leg back, and kicked Quinn's shin with her heel, drawing forth a yelp of pain. Feeling Quinn's grip loosen, Nyssa yanked her injured leg free and lunged forward, grabbing and trapping Quinn's arm. She applied leverage, putting pressure on the elbow. Quinn tried to pry her arm loose, but Nyssa punched her in the nose, feeling it crunch under her knuckles.

Nyssa's stomach dropped as blood spurted from Quinn's nose. "Yield!"

The crew fell silent.

Quinn gritted her teeth and shook her head, grunting when Nyssa put more pressure on the trapped arm.

Quinn didn't budge.

She'd rather I break her arm than relent.

Nyssa let go, shoving Quinn away from her. Winning no longer held any attraction.

"I didn't yield," Quinn hissed.

"I do," Nyssa growled, standing. Her knee throbbed. "This is over."

Murmurs of confusion spread through their audience. "Who won?" Jerrin asked.

"She did," Nyssa said, taking a towel offered by Mina to wipe the sweat off her face.

Quinn stared angrily up at her. "But you were winning."

"Yeah, winning," Nyssa muttered and threw her towel at Quinn. "Your nose is broken."

Thunder rumbled overhead, and Nyssa flinched. The morning sun had disappeared, replaced by gray clouds.

"Nyssa?" A gentle, soft voice called from behind her. She turned to find Fontaine approaching in a flowing green dress, the wind whipping the fabric around her legs.

Nyssa lifted her hands. They sparked with shards of blue magick. It was happening again. Without any effort, without realizing it, she had started to summon a storm.

Destruction could come so thoughtlessly.

She looked to Fontaine as another low growl of thunder bellowed in the sky. Nyssa's heart skipped. She closed her eyes and, with a deep breath, centered herself, clawing back her magick.

"It's okay, Nyssa," Fontaine soothed.

"I'm sorry," she mumbled, hurrying to the stairs that led below deck.

"Nyssa, wait," Fontaine called after her, but Nyssa didn't stop, needing to get away from Quinn and the rest of the crew as fast as possible. Hot tears burned her cheeks as she retreated to her room.

"Nyssa?" Quinn closed the stateroom door behind her and waited for Nyssa to respond. Nyssa lay on her bunk and stared up at the ceiling, not acknowledging her.

Quinn had avoided their room, going to see Buck to have him look at her nose. He'd grumbled angrily at her for interrupting his cooking to tend to her injury, and she'd let out an embarrassing yelp when he reset her nose and strapped a bandage over it.

During the sparring session, she threw all her anger and frustration at Nyssa. She wanted to push, to see if she could draw anything out of the woman other than a resigned sigh. Quinn knew she bore a lot of responsibility for their estrangement, cutting off Nyssa's attempt to reconcile. She had given in to her anger in the moment, and it led to them barely speaking.

Quinn walked over to her bunk and plopped down to lament her throbbing nose. Nyssa had punched her in the face endless times before, but until today, Quinn didn't realize how much she pulled her punches. She had been restraining herself all this time. Part of Quinn resented her for it—she didn't need to be coddled.

She glanced at Nyssa, who seemed content to ignore her, hands on her stomach. "Nyssa, look, I'm sorry about earlier. I got carried away."

Nyssa's index finger began tapping on her stomach. After a few moments, she sat up and swung her legs off her bunk, her face red.

Was she crying? Quinn's chest grew heavy.

"I started teaching you Ithais-Toru so you could become a proper fighter," Nyssa said, her voice low. Measured. "So when we go after Suvi, you're ready to stand at my side as a warrior. And fuck if you're not good at it. You're quick and savvy. But sparring is about putting what you learn into practice. It's a dance. A give and take between two combatants. We spar so you can see the flow of combat, how your opponent moves and responds to you. What happened today was not sparring. It was a fight. You were taking out your anger on me.

"What I don't understand is that you were willing to let me hurt you. I can't...." Nyssa dropped her head. "That can never happen again." She raised her eyes to meet Quinn's gaze, pinning her in place with a rare seriousness that chilled Quinn. "There is a code. You cannot make the training about your personal vendettas or resentment toward me, do you understand? Or the training ceases."

"I didn't mean to—"

Nyssa held up her hand. "I don't want to hear anything other than you understand."

Quinn's stomach dropped. "I understand." Her anger had driven her to take out her frustrations on Nyssa. And those actions reflected poorly on Nyssa—Quinn had dishonored her teacher. Worse than that, it was painfully evident she had hurt her.

"We are going to be face-to-face with Suvi Rell in two months. That is the moment we are training for. And once we have her and win our freedom, you will be done with me. I'll go my separate way."

Quinn wanted to argue and erase the notion that she wanted to be apart from Nyssa, but she couldn't. Stubborn pride had grabbed hold of her, and she found herself unable to break free.

Nyssa stood and crossed over to Quinn, putting her hand under Quinn's chin to lift her face up. Quinn swallowed, not expecting the contact to feel electric in a way that had nothing to do with Nyssa's magick.

"Your nose doesn't look too bad," she said, peering down at Quinn, her face inscrutable.

When Nyssa moved her hand away, Quinn swallowed, her nerves vibrating. "Buck says it should heal fine, maybe be a little off-kilter. He yelled at me for interrupting lunch."

Nyssa let out a low, rumbling chuckle. Quinn wondered what it would feel like to put her hand on Nyssa's chest and feel her laughter, the vibration of an unguarded moment of happiness that seemed rare of late. The laughter quickly faded, and Nyssa sighed, her shoulders drooping. Without another word, she turned from Quinn and left the room.

Quinn lay back on her bed with a deep sigh. The gulf between her and Nyssa was becoming untenable. The awkward silences and strained politeness made Quinn's nerves buzz with unease. And Nyssa's mere presence was a distraction, her existence lazily draped over Quinn's body.

She turned and buried her face in her pillow, crying out as her nose flared up in pain. She rolled on her back, letting her nose throb.

"I'm a goddamned idiot," she moaned.

A HEART TO HEART

Quinn took a long pull of whiskey, the liquid sloshing in the bottle as she put it back down on the deck, her eyes turned up to the stars. She had taken to spending time at night out on the deck rather than in her room. Avoiding Nyssa had become her way of coping with the tension between them.

At least out here, under the stars, Quinn could listen to the sea and the ship creaking underneath her instead of being so damn keenly aware of Nyssa's presence. The warmth in Quinn's chest when Nyssa was near had become a sort of passive torture, a reminder of how poorly they had both handled the aftermath of their fight.

Soft footsteps approached, and Quinn found Fontaine pulling a wooden crate over to sit with her. Quinn tipped the bottle of whiskey back before handing it over.

"You going to listen to the sea's song again tonight?" Quinn asked.

"Yes, child," Fontaine replied before taking a swig of the whiskey.

"Can you at least put some clothes on while dancing? I worry you'll catch cold."

Fontaine reared her head back and laughed. "You are so oddly concerned about me getting sick. I can count the days I've been sick in my life on one hand." She focused on Quinn. "I see you and Nyssa have resolved nothing."

Quinn sighed and held her hand out for the bottle. "No, we haven't."

"You're both fools, you know that?"

Quinn snorted. "Your pep talks need work."

Fontaine poked her in the knee. "The strange thing with you two is you're both dying to ask the same question of each other but afraid to receive the answer."

"And what question is that?"

"You both wonder if you could be something more to each other," Fontaine said, smiling.

Quinn sputtered out whiskey and clamped a hand over her mouth. She struggled to find an objection that Fontaine wouldn't immediately sniff out as false.

"Let me save you the embarrassment of making a fuss out of denying your feelings," Fontaine said. "The thing is, Nyssa's afraid you'll reject her if she tells you how she feels. And you...you're the puzzling one. You're afraid she'll say yes if you wanted more out of her."

Quinn scowled. This conversation was the last thing she wanted. But she couldn't deny Fontaine had the insight that she lacked. She was hardly experienced or worldly by any stretch. "Even if I wanted something more—and I don't even know what that would be exactly—tell me why you think I'd be scared she'll say yes." Quinn bit the inside of her cheek and waited for the answer.

"You were raised by a cruel man who locked you away, feared you even when you only had a small fraction of the power you have now. He put a void collar on you so he could rest easily. You were made to feel less than. What in the world did you ever consider yours? What in the world did you ever think you deserved?"

Quinn dropped her eyes. Fontaine had dived into her memories—she knew things about Quinn she was scared to share with anyone, even Nyssa. Her time at Arcton Citadel was lonely. And painful. It had filled her with a cold darkness that threatened to overwhelm her at times.

"Quinn, you fear telling the world what you want because, in your mind, what have you done to truly earn it? And how do you keep it? You're just an orphan. You don't even have a surname. Nothing in this world is truly yours. You think you're not worthy of what you desire."

Quinn tensed. The truth was raw and unforgiving. She wanted to curl up and cry.

Fontaine saved her by continuing, "But you're a goddamned fool because you could not be more wrong."

Quinn exhaled a short, unsteady breath. "You had a brief glimpse of my memories. How could you know all this about me?"

"I don't have to see your past to know any of this. I observe you every day. You have maybe three sets of clothes, despite a storeroom full to choose from and endless shops at the ports we dock at. You tried your damnedest to turn down the sword that Nyssa insisted you should claim as your own from our armory. You have one tea mug that you favor, the dark-blue one with the chip on the handle. You make yourself small and barely leave a footprint anywhere on the ship, as if you don't exist. Your sketchbook and that talisman you wear around your wrist are the only things you treasure."

Quinn ran her finger along the toldoku. She had taken to touching it absentmindedly, finding the habit soothing.

"Tell me I'm wrong, Quinn."

Quinn opened her mouth to object but just stared at Fontaine. *Dammit.*

Fontaine gave her shoulder a squeeze, offering a gentle smile. "You are not small. You are a god, so be a fucking god. You deserve everything you were ever denied. You deserve your heart's desire. Have the courage I know you possess to take what you want in this world. And maybe stop being scared to let people know how you feel. How you *truly* feel."

Quinn sat for a moment with Fontaine's advice. She had learned to shrink around others to protect herself; to not draw the attention of those at Arcton Citadel. Those habits were hard to break. Fear and distrust could settle into one's bones and never leave.

"It's hard for me. I don't want to get hurt...or hurt anyone else."

"You have to let people get close." Fontaine laughed and shook her head, a wistful expression on her face. "Here I am giving you this rather sage advice and I ended up as a chicken for over twenty years of mourning."

Tears rose in Quinn's eyes, and she wiped them away, but Fontaine had taken notice.

"What happened?" she asked. "There's something more, isn't there?"

Quinn swallowed, hesitant. "When I was sixteen, there was a kitchen assistant, Filip. He was my age, and he was kind to me. The first and only friend I made. The guards that always shadowed me must have told Ceril because one day, Filip was just gone. I can't help but think Ceril did something to him because of me. And I...I touched Ceril to see what his magick felt like, to cut him off from it and make him feel small, like he made me feel. That's when he put the void collar on me."

Fontaine placed her hand to her chest and let out an exasperated sigh.

"I'm so sorry. You shouldn't live in fear of having everything taken from you."

Quinn rubbed her palms together. Before she could think better of it, she said, "I'm pissed that Nyssa and I aren't talking. And just so damned sad. Sometimes my whole body aches because I miss her friendship so much."

"That was a very good start."

"Fontaine, I barely understand friendship. Anything beyond that with Nyssa scares me."

Fontaine laughed. "Here's a little secret: It scares everyone."

Quinn scowled, annoyed. "That doesn't help."

"Too bad. You will figure things out, in your own time—and not a moment before. Trust your instincts."

My instincts. They were all mixed up and conflicted, tangled in the one person that she couldn't bring herself to talk to.

Fontaine stood and stretched, peering up at the clear night sky, the moon shining brightly. The salt in the air tickled Quinn's nose.

"Ah, I love how early spring just breathes new life into these old bones. It will be a good night for dancing." Fontaine twirled around. "Are you sure you don't want to come hear the sea sing?"

Quinn stared at her.

Fontaine shrugged and began stripping off her clothes. "Fine, I will go dance alone."

A FRIENDLY FACE

N yssa and Quinn hurried up to the deck, their swords strapped to their backs. Jerrin had called for them, and Nyssa soon saw why. A heavy fog covered the deck of the Whisper. She could barely see more than ten feet in front of her. More concerning, however, was the buzz of magick emanating from the fog.

"When did this happen?" Nyssa asked Elias.

"Visibility's been shit for a day, but this heavy fog just rolled in," he said.

"It's magick," Nyssa said.

"No shit."

Something else made her blood run cold—the clatter and dings of nearby ships were unmistakable. It was the same sound she fell asleep to every night aboard the Whisper. She touched Quinn's arm and exchanged a glance.

"We're surrounded, aren't we?" Quinn asked, her eyes fraught with worry.

"We are," Elias replied.

"Who is it?"

"Not a clue, beauty." He stepped forward and called down to a crewman from the quarterdeck, his voice low but strong. "Weapons at the ready, make the call."

A murmur of voices traveled outward from the quarterdeck as the crew spread the word to be ready for a fight.

"You two ready for anything?"

Nyssa glanced at Quinn, who gave her a stern nod. "Yeah."

Elias looked over at Quinn. "Then show them your power and let's see who we face."

Quinn raised her arms. Shadow exploded from her hands with a loud crack like shattering ice. A massive shock wave of darkness shot out in all directions, dispersing the magickal fog.

Nyssa sucked in a breath. Six warships surrounded Hannah's Whisper.

Shit. This is bad.

Elias moved between Quinn and Nyssa, pointing toward one of the ships. A thin ribbon of red magick rose up and snaked toward Hannah's Whisper, headed directly for the quarterdeck.

Quinn raised her arm, ready to negate the threat, but Nyssa stopped her. "Wait," she said, a spark of hope rising in her chest.

The red tendril rushed toward them and slowed to a stop just before it reached Quinn. It hovered in front of her face for a moment before recoiling.

"Aryis!" Nyssa said, releasing a tense laugh. She smiled at Quinn and Elias. "It's Aryis!"

"Aryis and her six warships, Nyssa," Elias said. "Do you know if you can trust her?"

"Of course we can trust her. It's Aryis!" Was Athen with her? The thought of seeing him again made her beam with happiness.

"What do we do?" Quinn asked Elias.

"We wave our reds at them and hope they're not here to kill us all." Elias barked orders down to his crew to wave the red signal flags to indicate that Hannah's Whisper was standing down. The warships waved reds in response, drawing a heavy sigh of relief from Elias.

One warship closed the distance to the Whisper. As it drew closer, Nyssa spotted Aryis at the rail, and her smile grew wider. The Frosland deck crew tossed ropes from the warship to Hannah's Whisper, and as they slid a walkway from one ship to the other, Nyssa shifted nervously from one foot to the other.

Elias, Quinn, and Nyssa lined up to welcome the Froslandians aboard, with Jerrin and a small cadre of the Whisper's crew behind them.

The captain of the warship boarded first, followed by a contingent of guards. He crossed over to Elias and shook his hand.

"I'm Commander Velis of the Frosland Navy," the older man said. His ice-blue eyes scanned the deck, lingering on Nyssa and then Quinn. He seemed to stiffen in his uniform, the cut of it flattering for a man of his tall stature. His regalia was mostly black, save for accents of dark red and silver. It complimented his cropped white hair and weathered dark skin.

"Commander," Elias said. "Quite an honor to meet you, sir."

"The honor is mine, Captain Elias. You are a legend on these seas. For a pirate," Velis remarked with a tight smile. The backhanded compliment didn't escape Nyssa's notice. Velis's manner was stiff and reserved, as befit a military man, his eyes darting around to take stock of the crew.

"You flatter me, sir. I am but a humble sailor," Elias said with a bow, drawing a low laugh from Nyssa. *Humble* was not a trait she'd ever use to describe him. "If I may cut to the heart of the matter—as you can imagine the sight of six warships can make a man a bit nervous. Why are you here?"

Commander Velis offered him a thin smile. "I am here at the behest of his royal highness, King Devitt."

Elias nodded. "And what business does Ker Devitt have with us, if I may ask?"

"I will leave that to Her Royal Highness to explain," Velis said. "I present to you our honored Queen-in-Waiting, Lady Aryis Devitt of the First House of Frosland." The guards behind Velis parted, and Aryis walked through them, stopping next to the commander. Nyssa burst into a smile.

"Aryis!" she exclaimed, rushing forward. Several of the guards stepped between the two women, their hands on their swords.

"Stand down!" Aryis ordered as she strode through their ranks. Without hesitation, Nyssa threw her arms around her.

"I've missed you, my friend," Nyssa breathed.

"It's so good to see you," Aryis said.

Nyssa stepped back to get a look at Aryis. She seemed older than her twenty-four years. Her clothes carried a seriousness that didn't seem to befit the young woman—her dark cloak covered an embroidered jacket, leather pants, a heavy split overlay skirt, and boots. All black. The only colors on her were the silver and red metallic threads woven throughout her black hair, which she wore in an intricate braid with her temples shaved, as was her style. Silver and red—the color of House Devitt.

Nyssa's eyes were drawn to the weapons at Aryis's waist—a sword on one hip and Talon on the other. She looked every bit the royal scion of her family.

But a weariness clung to her.

Nyssa's eyes were drawn to a jagged scar running along the right edge of Aryis's chin. "Aryis, what happened?" she asked as she gingerly touched her face.

Aryis smiled, but her light-brown eyes held a sadness that made Nyssa's chest grow tight, her usual enthusiasm replaced by a dour seriousness.

"Things have changed a great deal since you've been away," she said. "I'm so happy to see that you're safe."

Nyssa put an arm around Aryis and gently kissed the side of her head. "Little Hawk," she said with a soft smile.

Aryis gave Nyssa a squeeze before she looked toward the rest of the welcoming party.

"Elias!" she said, walking toward the man and giving him a hug.

"It's good to see you again, my Lady Devitt," Elias said pulling away from her with a bow.

Aryis grinned and shook her head. "No need for such formalities, Elias. I'm just Aryis."

Nyssa chuckled, recalling the time Aryis tried to use her Queen-in-Waiting status to persuade Elias to release them. It didn't work one bit.

Aryis turned to Quinn. "How have you been, Quinn?"

"I've been well," Quinn replied. Aryis gave her a smile, but Nyssa noticed it didn't reach her eyes. There was a tension to the woman that raised the hackles on the back of Nyssa's neck. She looked past Aryis toward the Frosland military on their deck. More had crossed over the temporary bridge between ships, spreading out. They eyed her, their faces stern.

"Why have you come, Aryis?" Nyssa inquired.

"If I could speak with you and Quinn, I can explain why I've sought you out," Aryis said, walking back toward her commander and beckoning Nyssa and Quinn to follow.

"You don't know how much I've missed you. Is Athen with you?" Nyssa asked as they walked with her.

Aryis turned to them. "I'm afraid not, Nyssa."

"Are you two still together?"

Aryis looked down and slowly shook her head. "No."

Nyssa's stomach dropped. "Why not?"

"As I said, a lot has happened since you left." Aryis stepped closer to Nyssa and Quinn. "There's a lot I have to explain." She swallowed hard and glanced to her left. There was something *off* about her.

Quinn let out a hiss, and her hand flew to her neck. Frosland guards rushed forward and pushed her down to the deck. Hands grabbed at Nyssa, pulling her away from Aryis.

Jerrin cried out and charged at the men around Quinn, his sword at the ready. Steel flashed toward him, and he hit the deck with a sickening thud, blood spurting out of his neck.

Nyssa gasped, not believing her eyes. *No. No!*

"Jerrin!" Quinn cried out as she fought against the guards holding her down.

Nyssa roared with rage. "What did you do?" She lashed out with a bolt of lightning, striking Jerrin's murderer. The air filled with a sickening crack as the man fell dead to the deck.

"Nyssa, stop!" Aryis yelled.

Nyssa hissed at a sharp sting on her neck. She whirled around.

Aryis held a small dart in her hand.

Rage flashed again, this time directed at Aryis. She snarled, ready to strike, but her magick fizzled out. "No."

She stumbled forward, head spinning.

Cold metal clamped around her neck. Everything went dull.

She tried to draw Winter's Bite, but a hand grabbed her wrist, stopping her. Guards forced her down to the deck.

She struggled to shed the hands restraining her as the world began to fall away, her vision growing dark around the edges. She heard Aryis choke back a sob.

"Please forgive me, Nyssa."

IN CHAINS

Nyssa startled awake from a loud *POP!* next to her ear. Her eyes flew open.

"Fuck!" Quinn hissed, pulling back and shaking her hand as if she had been burned.

Nyssa groaned, her head pounding as Quinn helped her sit up. "What happened?"

"Aryis betrayed us," Quinn growled.

Nyssa glanced around. They were in a brig, no doubt. Two small cots lined the back wall, a small porthole above each letting in dim light. Outside of the bars was a small enclosed area sealed by a heavy wooden door.

She put her hand up to her throat, touching the collar around her neck. A dull heaviness pressed down on her whole body. The cold, stark absence of her magick left her feeling hollow. It was hard to imagine Quinn lived like this for ten years.

"Careful touching that. I've been trying to get it off of you for an hour now, but the locks have a ward. Gives me a nasty shock when I try to pick it."

The events that led them to this cell snapped back in her mind. "They killed Jerrin."

Quinn swallowed hard and sat back on her heels. She nodded.

Nyssa ran her hands through her hair, trying to push her grief away. Jerrin was family. He looked after Nyssa and the others when they were first taken aboard the Whisper, and he taught her everything she knew about sailing. His smile could cut through the coldest winter on deck. Her hands curled into fists. "Fuck. What about Elias and the rest of the crew?"

"I don't think they're on board, but I can't be certain. They drugged us. I don't even remember being taken off the Whisper."

"I hope they're safe." A ball of guilt sank into the pit of Nyssa's stomach at the thought that she put the crew in danger, lulled into complacency by the face of a friend.

Friend...that no longer seemed to be the case.

"Why would Aryis do this?" Quinn asked.

Nyssa's eyes grew heavy with tears. She wanted to rage. None of this made sense. Aryis betrayed them. It was unthinkable. Anger and confusion welled up inside of her.

"I have no—"

A heavy bolt slid back in its lock, and the wooden door to the brig swung open. Aryis stepped into the small area outside their cell. "Stay outside," she commanded and closed the door behind her.

Nyssa stood and stumbled backward, her head still foggy from the drug. She grimaced and clutched her forehead. Quinn got on her feet and steadied Nyssa.

Aryis took a few steps toward their cell. "I need to explain—"

Nyssa shot forward and crashed into the bars of the cell, stretching her arms through the cold steel to grab at Aryis, wanting to rip her apart.

Aryis flinched back, out of reach. "Nyssa please..." she said, her voice trembling.

"I'll fucking kill you for this," Nyssa growled as she clutched the cell bars, shaking with thick, wild rage. "Why did you do this? Why?" Her voice broke, hot tears falling on her cheeks. Quinn pulled her back.

Aryis shook her head, her eyes pleading. "You are both part of a very large, complicated treaty my father made with Thu'Dain to secure an alliance with them. I'm sorry about this. I fought against it, but Suvi Rell insisted."

Nyssa's stomach coiled into a knot. "You're making deals with that bitch? Suvi Rell killed my parents, Aryis! She killed my—" Her voice broke with a sob, her heart pounding. Quinn put a steadying arm around her waist.

"I didn't know that," Aryis replied. "So much has happened in the last few months, Nyssa. My nation is independent now and forging alliances so that we never have to bend a knee to the Areshi Empire again."

"I don't fucking care about your country or your alliances. We were friends!" Nyssa spat.

"What is Suvi going to do with us?" Quinn asked.

Aryis stiffened. "That I do not know."

Quinn let go of Nyssa and stumbled back to one of the cots, dropping down on it. "I told Reece to give you my book so that if you needed to find me—find us—again, you could. And you used it to put us in chains."

Aryis approached the bars. "I will figure this out. I'm your friend, despite what this looks like."

"You're the same person that stood by and watched as Ceril and the Justiciars tried to take my head. Your love for Nyssa recedes the moment you're asked to be brave," Quinn seethed.

Nyssa hung her head. "You can't let them do this, Aryis."

"Suvi is a reasonable woman, Nyssa. I will reason with—"

Nyssa snarled, "Queen-in-Waiting? You're powerless, aren't you? They used you to find us, like an obedient dog."

Aryis stepped forward and held Nyssa's gaze. "I'm doing what I need to do to help my people. I don't expect you to understand. Maybe if it were Athen in my position—"

"You keep his name out of your *fucking* mouth. He would *never* do this to me," Nyssa hissed, her glare unwavering from Aryis's face. "I will make you pay for this, our friendship be damned. You collared us. And you killed Jerrin."

Aryis swallowed. "No, I never meant for that to happen. My guards got overzealous—"

"Did you kill the rest of the crew?" Nyssa asked, her stomach churning, fearing the worst.

Aryis blinked back tears. "Elias and Fontaine are alive. They've been warned not to follow us."

"How many of my friends did you kill?"

Aryis's face collapsed.

Jerrin wasn't the only one. Fuck.

Nyssa coiled her hands around the bars of the cage and gripped hard until her knuckles turned white. "You better hope this collar never comes off me because I will make you pay for this." She rattled out a breath as her heart fractured. "I will kill you."

Aryis stepped away from the cell, her lower lip trembling. She retreated out the door.

Nyssa turned around and put her back to the cell's bars, slowly sliding down into a crouch. The hope of a chance at freedom died with the thud of the brig's heavy wooden door. She buried her head in her hands as tears fell, her body shaking as she broke apart.

Quinn's concern grew as Nyssa became more distant, not eating or sleeping, caught in a daze that Quinn couldn't break through. On the morning of the third day, with Nyssa looking gaunt, rings under her eyes from the lack of sleep, Quinn had had enough. She crouched in front of Nyssa and pulled a tray of uneaten food next to her.

"Nyssa, you need to eat. You can't just sit here all day and night like this." Quinn searched her face for a reaction. For one inkling of the stubborn fire she knew was below the surface of Nyssa's dark mood.

"The fuck I can't," Nyssa whispered, slowly blinking, refusing to look Quinn in the eye.

"Please. I need the headstrong asshole back. The fighter. This version of you is for shit."

Nyssa didn't respond.

Her patience gone, Quinn stood and grabbed Nyssa by her jacket, yanking her up to her feet.

"What the fuck?" Nyssa snarled, pulling away.

Quinn didn't relent. She couldn't. She needed Nyssa to fight. A rough shove sent Nyssa into the bars of the cell. Nyssa let out a low growl from the back of her throat and grabbed Quinn, forcing her back against the wooden wall of the cell. Quinn grunted from the blow as Nyssa pressed her forearm into her neck, meeting the resistance of the void collar.

"Do you want me to hurt you?" Nyssa growled.

Quinn balled up a fist and punched Nyssa in the jaw.

Nyssa stumbled, shaking her head. She doubled her efforts and shoved Quinn even harder against the wall, knocking the air out of her.

"What do you want from me?" Nyssa demanded.

"I need you to fight!"

"Why? I failed! Elias and Fontaine helped us, and I failed. I didn't see the danger because I trusted Aryis. I just...I don't have anything left." Nyssa's shoulders drooped, whatever burst of energy her anger had given her seemingly gone.

"I can't fucking do this without you!" Quinn said, her breathing ragged. "Please, Nyssa, I can't—" Her voice broke as her eyes filled with tears.

"Quinn, I'm sorry," Nyssa whispered. "I don't know what to do." Her bottom lip began to tremble.

Quinn had never seen Nyssa like this—so utterly lost. It frightened her to her core. She stepped forward and pulled Nyssa into a hug, clutching her tight. She was always reserved around Nyssa, always hiding her feelings behind a sarcastic remark and keeping Nyssa at arm's length.

But she couldn't do that now.

"You don't need to have any answers, I just can't have you disappear on me," Quinn whispered. "I need you, understand? We're in this together."

Nyssa exhaled and grasped ahold of Quinn, trembling in her arms.

"I've got you," Quinn murmured.

Nyssa buried her head in Quinn's shoulder and wept.

A MEETING AT SEA

Nyssa blinked in the brightness of the sun. Almost a week had passed since their capture, and they'd been hauled out on deck, but for what, she didn't know.

She spotted Aryis, who stood with Commander Velis, deep in conversation. A raging heat flooded Nyssa. She jerked away from the two guards holding her and spun around, bashing one in the side of the head with her shackled wrists, dropping him to the ground. She spun again and lunged toward Aryis.

A fist collided with her temple, causing her legs to waver. Aryis's guards were on her quick.

"Teach the Unworthy bitch a lesson!" one of them yelled.

Nyssa dropped to her knees as another fist struck her head. Then another. She raised her arms to protect herself.

"Stop!" Quinn cried out, trying to shove guards away.

Aryis raised her voice. "Stand down!"

But more fists rained down, again, and again, and again.

Until they suddenly stopped.

Nyssa sat on her heels, head lolled back, blood trickling down her chin. Aryis had her dagger to the throat of a guard. "You'll do as I say or I will spill your blood," she said, her eyes gleaming with anger, her voice steady.

She stepped away from the guard and sheathed Talon. "Get her up."

Two guards hooked Nyssa under her arms and hauled her up. She spat blood at Aryis's feet. "Will they listen to you when you become queen, or will you have to threaten them at every step?"

Aryis gestured at a guard, and Nyssa and Quinn were quickly gagged.

"Is this what passes for security on your ships, Aryis?" a blonde woman asked, striding toward them in a long black coat lined with fur. She was slightly taller than Nyssa with sharp, hawkish features and an air of superiority.

A man accompanied her—Vykas Devitt, Aryis's brother. He was just as Nyssa remembered, dapper and haughty, if not appearing a little weary.

The woman stopped in front of Nyssa and Quinn, her pale-green eyes scrutinizing them. The hairs on the back of Nyssa's neck pricked up, and her stomach churned, somehow knowing exactly who was standing before her.

"Your Majesty," Aryis said with a slight bow.

Queen Suvi Rell smiled at Aryis in a way that chilled Nyssa's blood. Though she had to be at least fifty, she looked only a few years older than Nyssa thanks to the longevity magick the Rells had in their bloodline. Suvi turned her attention back to Nyssa and Quinn, her self-satisfied grin a thin dash of deep red on an otherwise pale face.

"You have done as I asked, Aryis, and for that, I thank you. Ours is going to be a long and fruitful alliance. Your brother has entered into even more negotiations on your country's behalf, including a marriage to establish a tighter bond between our nations."

Aryis scowled and eyed her brother.

Suvi continued, "An open marriage, of course. And no children, not from my body, at least. I suppose you two should choose which one of you would like to take my bond in marriage on whatever gods-forsaken windswept sea this is."

"The Black Sea, Your Majesty," Commander Velis offered.

With a smirk, Suvi glanced at Nyssa. Nyssa bit down on the gag in her mouth.

"If I may have a moment with my sister?" Vykas asked.

Suvi nodded at him once and moved closer to Quinn and Nyssa as he and Aryis stepped to the side.

"They are discussing the issue of marriage." Suvi turned to Nyssa. "Rather banal, don't you think? Which one of the siblings should I pick? Aryis was with the Fennick boy for a while, wasn't she? Tell me, Nyssa, do you suppose she's any good with her tongue?"

Nyssa lunged at Suvi, but the guards behind her clamped down on her shoulders, holding her in place.

"Ah, doesn't matter. This is a political marriage. I insisted on it to bind our countries even closer. Negotiation is a fascinating dance. I never dreamed I would be good at it. Statecraft isn't exactly in my family's blood. But as it turns out, I'm a natural at extracting what I want at very little personal cost to myself. Your poor friend Aryis, though...she got caught in a game she had no idea how to play."

Nyssa snarled underneath her gag, which drew a soft chuckle out of Suvi.

"The information about you two is ragged at best. Let me see what your abilities are," Suvi said. Her eyes turned completely black.

Quinn shuddered next to Nyssa and her eyes flooded with darkness, like Suvi. Both women stood completely still. Nyssa had heard of the Queen's powers—she was able to mesmerize others for a short period of time and see through their eyes. But most terrifying of all, she could bend people to her will.

"Interesting," Suvi said, her black eyes empty. "Lightning and darkness, and the ability to manipulate and negate magick. No wonder the Empress wants you both dead. You're extremely dangerous. *Perfect*."

Suvi released her hold on Quinn, who sank to her knees. Nyssa swore behind her gag, drilling hate into Suvi with her eyes as guards yanked Quinn to her feet.

"I would love to get in that head of yours, Blacksea. I could make you do unspeakable things," Suvi whispered to Nyssa before smirking at Quinn. Nyssa trembled with anger, desperate to get her hands on the Queen and wipe that wolfish grin off her face.

Vykas and Aryis walked back to them, and Suvi put on a pleasant smile. She was faking respect for the Devitts, of that Nyssa was certain.

Suvi was pure predator, waiting to feast.

"My Queen, I would like to offer you my bond in marriage," Vykas said, his face flat. Aryis held her head high, but she was clenching her jaw.

Suvi clapped her hands together. "Excellent! Commander Velis, will you perform the ceremony? Let's make this official and be on our separate ways."

Commander Velis nodded. In a few unceremonious minutes, papers were signed and sealed, and Suvi Rell and Vykas Devitt were married. No roar of congratulations or toasts accompanied the exchange of words. It was as heartless as the midday sun that offered no warmth.

After the vows, Nyssa and Quinn were taken into Thu'Dainian custody. Suvi's ship waited off the portside of their Froslandian vessel. As Suvi and her guards moved them to the gangway slung between the ships, Aryis stepped in front of them, her face inscrutable.

"I'm coming with you," she said.

"You will do no such thing," Vykas insisted. "Your place is back in Frosland."

"My place is where I determine it to be, Vykas, and right now that is in Sarisan."

Vykas stayed silent, but it was clear he wasn't happy.

Suvi crossed her arms, peering over her nose at Aryis. "Why?"

"I would like to see the nation we've allied with," Aryis said. "And to see to Nyssa and Quinn's welfare."

Suvi chuckled. "The Cursed Gods are mine now. If I choose to drop them into the sea and let them drown right now, you couldn't stop it."

"Understood," Aryis replied curtly.

Nyssa didn't know what Aryis was playing at, but she wanted the woman gone from her life. Being in Suvi's custody was bad enough, but Aryis tagging along was a dagger in the gut.

Suvi waved her hand. "I will extend my hospitality to you. Perhaps you'll learn a bit of what it takes to be a queen."

THU'DAIN

"Hold your head up high," Nyssa said, locking eyes with Quinn before they set foot on Thu'Dainian soil. "They might have us in chains but we are not their property."

The capital city of Sarisan lay before them, its buildings comprised of shades of ivory and gold, quite unlike the dark reds, blues, and greens of Ocean's Rest. Earthen colors became more prominent on the outskirts of the large, sparkling city—where the working people live, Nyssa was sure.

Men and women lined the streets as Nyssa and Quinn were marched down the docks and through the city, their hands bound. Hundreds, if not thousands, of eyes bore witness to their captivity, the onlookers growing silent and gawking at them as they passed.

All the dark things Nyssa had imagined of Thu'Dain seemed to be exaggerated in her head, her own fears and prejudices coloring her beliefs. The men and women lining the streets could easily be transplanted into Ocean's Rest and wouldn't look out of place. The scent of flowers and deep earthy spices hung in the air, reminding Nyssa of Eron's pipe tobacco that permeated the hallway outside his office at the Emerald Order. She swallowed and raised her head higher.

They continued their slog through the streets for over an hour before a large gold and white capitol building rose before them. Severe pointed spires soared into the skies, ivy twisting around the base of the building and crawling up the sides of the faded white stone that was overlaid with gold embellishments in the shape of leaves and birds. The large entrance of the building loomed in before them, but Nyssa and Quinn were pulled to the side and taken down a set of wide stairs into the belly of the building and shuttled into a remote cell.

Their guards untied their hands and gags before locking them in together. Quinn dropped down onto a cot and rubbed her wrists. Nyssa shrugged out of her jacket and sat next to Quinn, reclining against the wall. Even though they were in a seaside city, she missed the sting of sea salt and the rocking of the boat beneath her.

The two of them sat in silence until guards came and took Quinn away to Nyssa's objection. They returned her an hour later, cleaned up and in fresh clothes. Nyssa was also taken to a small private bath where she was allowed to clean up and change as well. When she got back to their cell, trays of steaming food were waiting for them.

They ate in silence.

Nyssa tugged at her void collar, hating the weight of the cold metal that never warmed against her skin. She pulled on her leather jacket to fight off the chill, thankful for its comfort, her fingers finding the outline of her small notebook tucked in the inside pocket. Losing her poems didn't concern her, but losing the chromoimage of Eron would break her.

After dinner, Nyssa sat next to Quinn and closed her eyes. It had been a while since she quieted herself and meditated. Now it seemed like the only thing to do. Even when Quinn fell asleep against her, her head on Nyssa's shoulder, Nyssa didn't move. Her mind searched for a solution, a way out.

When sleep finally claimed her, she was no closer to an answer.

A PALACE GUEST

Athen had been polite, he really had, before he began tossing Thu'Dainian guards aside. After being stuck in the hold of a cargo ship for a week to get to Sarisan as fast as he could, his patience was at its end.

The guards outside had rejected his request to see their queen, so he forced his way into the capitol building. As plans went, it was a bad one—and he knew it—but he didn't have the time for diplomacy.

Nyssa needed him.

He was halfway through the building when Suvi's elite guard of fire mages halted his progress. After he dodged the first fireball flung his way, he weighed the chance to help Nyssa against his need to hit things.

Choosing Nyssa, he put his hands up. "I'm Athen Fennick. Suvi Rell will know the name. I demand to see her. Now."

After low, urgent words were exchanged between the guards, and messengers were sent sprinting down the hall, Athen was eventually ushered to the throne room. The large wooden doors swung open, and his eyes swept from one side of the room to the other. Men and women milled about, mostly gathered around long tables off to the sides.

All activity stopped when he entered.

Floor-to-ceiling windows let in multicolored light, the very tops of them intricately stained, depicting a seascape. The space was bright and warm, light wood walls enclosing the room. A massive rug with a woven blue and red pattern sat in the middle of the room, leading to its center-piece—a gilded throne atop a platform, a wide set of stairs set before it.

A side door opened, and a woman strolled in, a blonde man trailing behind her. It had to be Suvi and, judging by their resemblance, her brother, Matthys. They shared the same sharp features, though the arch of Matthys's eyebrows suggested a perpetually amused expression.

"Rell! Where is Nyssa Blacksea?" Athen yelled.

Suvi stopped in her tracks and put her hands on her hips. "You assault my capitol, throw my guards about, and now you address me in such a rude fashion? You are truly your mother's son."

Athen's stomach turned. Handing himself over to a Rell could spell suicide. If Suvi wanted revenge against Lilliana for killing her father, he was making it easy for her. But he had to do something, and no one was going to stop him.

"Where is Nyssa Blacksea?"

"She is here. And safe, I assure you," Suvi said, resuming her walk to the throne, which sat at the top of a raised platform, a small flight of stairs necessary to reach it. Instead of ascending to the throne, she sat down on the first step. Matthys leaned against the steps beside her.

Behind him, a commotion erupted from the hallway. Aryis burst into the room, trailed by a few unhappy guards.

"Athen..." she said, coming to a dead stop upon seeing him. Surprise and sadness worked across her face at once. The exuberance that always clung to her was gone—she looked weary.

A chill washed over Athen's body, followed by an unexpected—and unwelcome—heat of affection. He wanted to yell at her for what she had done, but his heart remained conflicted. Sweat pricked his brow. "What did you do, Aryis?" He was amazed his voice didn't crack.

"H-how are you here?"

He swallowed, trying to maintain his composure. "Elias told us what happened and I hopped on a ship immediately. Did you turn on Nyssa for this bitch?"

"It's not that simple, Athen...I..." Aryis trailed off.

"Well, this is rather awkward," Suvi purred. "I don't know what you planned on accomplishing by coming here, Fennick, but judging by what you've done to my guards, you need to be tamed."

Athen turned back to Suvi, and her eyes went black. He stumbled forward, pressure building behind his eyes. The unsettling feeling of not being *alone* in his own mind crept over him. He tried to move, to speak, but his ability to control his body had evaporated.

"Guardsman Wilam, a void collar if you please," Suvi said.

"Your Majesty, is that really necessary?" Aryis asked.

"It's for his safety and mine."

Unable to stop himself, Athen bent down for the older guardsman, who snapped a void collar around his neck. The presence controlling him fell away, and he shuddered, trying to remain calm. He sneered at Suvi and took a step forward, balling up his fists.

"Where is Nyssa?" he growled.

"Athen, you shouldn't be here," Aryis said.

Athen whirled around and stomped toward her. "Why don't you slink back to Frosland?"

Tears sprang to her eyes and his chest tightened. Something in him wanted to wrap her in a hug, but he kept his face still and cold. Aryis had crossed a horrible, dangerous line, and he couldn't understand why she did such a thing.

"I'm here to help Nyssa," she replied.

"Fucking too late for that," he snapped before turning back to Suvi. "How much to free them? How much gold do you want for Nyssa and Quinn?"

Suvi frowned at him. "This isn't about money. I'm surprised the son of Lilliana Fennick doesn't understand that." She turned to Wilam. "Take him to a cell far away from Nyssa and Quinn."

"Please let me see them."

"In due time," Suvi replied, taking a few steps toward him. She held him in her pale green gaze. "Your mother killed my father. She put her fist through his chest as I watched. My soldiers pulled me away before we could recover his body, or I would have died with him. I will never forget that day, nor the look on Lilliana's face." She narrowed her eyes at Athen and it sent a chill through him. "I see her in you."

Wilam took Athen's arm and directed him away from the throne room. Athen glanced back at Aryis. She turned her eyes to the ground, her expression exactly the same when he last saw her in Cardin...

Lost.

Athen knew the footsteps belonged to Aryis before the woman approached his cell. He dreaded seeing her, scared of what he might say, his anger a deep well of bitterness that threatened to roar out of him like a tidal wave.

"Can we talk?" Aryis asked as she stilled on the other side of the bars.

"No."

"Please, I—"

Athen shot to his feet. "No!" His voice echoed off the walls of his cell.

"I'm sorry, Athen, I just..." The defeated tone of her voice made his heart ache despite everything that she had done.

But he needed resolve and couldn't afford his head and heart warring with one another. "Leave."

He sat back down and stared at his hands, unable to look Aryis in the eye. He knew she could break down his resolve, and he wasn't ready to talk to her. His anger was still too hot and deep.

How could she betray Nyssa? Betray him?

"I'm sorry. I love you and I'm sorry," she said before turning and walking away.

Part of him wanted to call after her, but he stopped himself.

Her betrayal was a dagger in his gut, and every word of attempted contrition twisted it deeper.

The attack at Wayland had changed her. She had pulled away from him as he tried to understand her pain, creating a divide between them. That distance widened further when she returned to Frosland and broke off contact. Now, the divide was a gaping chasm he didn't know if he could cross.

Or if it was worth crossing.

A CHASM CROSSED

Footsteps rang down the hall, growing louder. Nyssa sat up and swung her legs off her cot. Quinn gave her a worried glance. Aryis slowly approached and stood in front of their prison cell.

Nyssa tensed. "Why are you here?"

"I want you to truly understand why—why I did this."

The urge to lunge at the woman still roiled under the surface, but Nyssa lacked the will to do anything. She was tired down to her bones. "It won't make a difference to me."

"Then I will simply talk, and you will just happen to be in the vicinity as I do so," Aryis said, her dark eyes moving from Nyssa's face over to Quinn. "I want *both* of you to understand."

Aryis bit her lip and thought for a moment before speaking. "My country has sacrificed a lot since joining the Empire. Ships. Soldiers. We lost half of our navy in the Mire War. My father lost his first wife and my eldest brother. To make us whole, the throne of the Areshi Empire was promised to my family. And that promise was rescinded a mere week after the attack..." Aryis stilled, her eyes dark.

"You were meant to be the next Empress?" Nyssa asked, surprised. She glanced at Quinn, her eyes wide.

"Yes."

"Another secret you kept from us."

"Yes."

Nyssa gritted her teeth. Didn't the damn woman learn when she kept her Queen-in-Waiting status from them?

Aryis sighed and shook her head, a wry smile on her face. "Promises made. Promises broken. Kalla said my failure at Wayland tarnished me in the eyes of the Sun Council."

"Wayland? What happened at Wayland?" Nyssa asked.

Aryis lowered her eyes, her whole demeanor changing, as if she was coiling in on herself. She stood silent for a long while.

"Frosland has had a few very hard winters. Our food stores are depleted. When we asked for help, Empress Kalla gave us half of what we needed. She's not an unreasonable woman, but word got back to us from allies in Cardin that Ceril was in her ear, claiming our demands were driven purely by greed. That man has a black, putrid heart." Aryis paused and ground her jaw.

Nyssa had never seen her eyes filled with hate before that moment. It didn't suit her. "Aryis, what happened at Wayland?"

Aryis ignored her question. "Suvi Rell knew all of our problems with the Empire, of course. The Areshi alliance was poised to break. All she did was press her foot to its neck and offer us her hand instead. And the hard truth is our alliance with Thu'Dain is very beneficial to both nations."

Nyssa leaned forward, scowling. "But you sacrificed us."

"Suvi had a fleet of ships filled with food waiting off our shores. The food would be released to us in exchange for turning you two over to her. She knew I could track you. I tried to refuse, but my people faced starvation." Aryis swallowed. "I had no choice."

"You always have a choice, Aryis. I guess that's something your precious fucking books don't teach you," Nyssa growled, standing and approaching her. How could a woman as smart as Aryis be so fucking dumb?

Aryis wrapped her hands around the bars of the cell, her face painted with need. A need to be heard? Understood? Nyssa didn't care.

"Please, Nyssa, I was in a horrible position. I have a nation to protect. Every decision I make impacts my people. Every failure puts them in danger. I love you, Nyssa, but—"

Nyssa's last ounce of restraint snapped. "*Love*? You *love* me? Let's be honest, Aryis, we were barely friends. You make the mistake of thinking I care about you. The truth is, you're a girl I knew for a few scant months and who my best friend happened to fuck. I hold no love for you. You're still the naïve fool I met—just another weak coward I have no use for, Queen-in-Waiting. Go *fuck* yourself."

Aryis's face turned hard before she pushed away from the bars and hurried off.

Nyssa clutched at her chest as she listened to her retreating footsteps, pieces of her starting to crumble.

Hold it together...

"Why did you say that to her?" Quinn asked.

"She needs to hurt," Nyssa breathed. *Like I hurt.*

"You are many things, Nyssa, but you're not cruel or vindictive. Don't let this situation change that." Quinn stood, crossing her arms. "And now you hurt even more, don't you?"

"Shut up," Nyssa grumbled. Her anger wheeled toward Quinn, needing somewhere to go. "Why are you suddenly concerned about my feelings? I thought you didn't care."

Quinn's eyes dimmed. "That's—that's not true."

"Oh no? This past year, I could never really get behind those walls you've built around yourself. You'd let them down on occasion, and I'd see someone looking back at me that I thought—" Nyssa stopped before she exposed too much of her heart.

Quinn shifted her weight impatiently. "Thought what?" she asked, trapping Nyssa in her narrowed gaze.

Nyssa's chest tightened. "This isn't important right now. Not with—"

"Oh no, this conversation feels long overdue. Everything changed when we fought and you left."

"No, *you* changed. You could barely look at me when I got back. You were so cold and angry. Why?" Nyssa asked, trying to keep her voice steady. The thin thread that held her emotions in check threatened to snap.

Quinn shook her head and exhaled a shaky breath.

"Just tell me!" Nyssa said, balling up her fists.

"You left me!" Quinn yelled, stepping toward Nyssa, tears springing to her eyes. "I needed you to stay and you ran instead."

"I...I needed space to think."

Brilliant emerald eyes bore into Nyssa. "I have one person in this world and that's you. Don't you get that? And you...you left me."

"Quinn, I—" The apology turned to ash in Nyssa's mouth. How could she make Quinn understand what she would do for her? What she would do to be with her?

And how much they could hurt one another?

"You lost everything—Eron, your friends, your place in the world. And that's my fault," Quinn rasped. "You hate me, don't you?"

A mountain of hurt tumbled through Nyssa, but she only cared about the pain she had caused Quinn. She closed the distance between them, desperately needing to make Quinn understand. Twisting her fist in Quinn's sweater, her breathing quick and ragged, she pulled her close and kissed her.

After a painfully long second of nothing, Quinn responded, returning the kiss, slow and tentative. Her fingers came to rest on Nyssa's hips, tightening, and her lips parted to draw Nyssa closer.

Their bodies pressed together, and Nyssa's pulse pounded in her ears as she wove her fingers through Quinn's dark hair. Her heart beat wildly, and a deep thrumming desire coursed through her.

She had to pull away to regain control of herself, exhaling a gasp before opening her eyes. Quinn's gaze, beautiful and unyielding, threatened to break her apart.

"I don't hate you," she whispered, her voice trembling. This kiss was long overdue—Nyssa had ached for it but was so terrified of getting her heart shattered.

Quinn opened her mouth to speak—

Thick, glowing cords of energy coiled around her and yanked her away from Nyssa. A guard stood at their cell, orange energy pulsing off his fists.

"You have an audience with the Queen."

ULTIMATUM

Guards dragged Nyssa and Quinn into a large sun-soaked room. Nyssa blinked in the brightness of the daylight, her eyes slow to adjust after spending days in a cell. The room was filled with richly dressed men and women whose heads swiveled toward her and Quinn as they entered, followed by a small uproar of excited chatter. Servants milled about with bottles of wine to refill the glasses of Suvi's eager audience.

Nyssa's stomach sank. These people were gathered to witness a spectacle. And Suvi was serving them drinks like it was a goddamned garden party.

A throne sat in the middle of the room, and Suvi perched atop it, speaking to a man who leaned close. The resemblance was obvious—he must be the other last remaining Rell, Matthys.

Nyssa's eyes trailed down the throne's steps to find Aryis, her head bowed. A cold dagger of fear shot through Nyssa when she saw the man standing next to her.

"Athen!" she cried out.

Athen stepped forward, but the guards flanking him pulled him back. She ground her teeth at the void collar around his neck. The guard next to her tightened his grip on her arm. She could fight him, and the guard with Quinn, but they would be quickly overrun by the sheer number of guards that rimmed the room.

Why is Athen here? He's going to get hurt.

"Ah, our guests," Suvi said. Matthys descended the steps and joined a man watching from the side of the room. Their laughter drifted toward Nyssa, drumming anger through her veins. The guards stopped Nyssa and Quinn ten feet away from of the steps leading to the throne and released their arms.

"Athen, what are you doing here?" Nyssa called.

"Are you okay, Nyssa? Quinn?" Athen asked, his face fraught with worry.

"They are fine," Suvi assured from her throne. "Fennick came to buy you back, Nyssa. His and Aryis's combined political savvy could perhaps fill half a shot glass—and I'm being generous."

All Nyssa wanted to do was run to Athen and give him a hug.

He came for me.

She hoped he didn't pay for it with his life.

"I've missed you, big man."

Suvi raised her voice. "Esteemed Houses of Thu'Dain, may I introduce you to Nyssa Blacksea and Quinn...did they ever bother to give you a surname? Ah, I suppose it really doesn't matter now," Suvi said, her grin infuriating as she toyed with Quinn. She surveyed the crowd. "I've gathered you here to witness history. You've all heard the rumors of these two gods. *Forever entwined*—do I have that right, Aryis?"

Aryis looked up with a start. She blinked at Suvi.

"Do I have it right, Queen-in-Waiting? Are these two the gods foreseen by the Whitepeak Mystics?" Suvi asked. "You've witnessed their power. Verify who they are for my guests."

Aryis looked from Suvi to Nyssa and Quinn, refusing to answer.

Suvi brought her open palm down on the arm of her throne, and a loud smack rang through the room. "Do not look to make a fool of me."

Aryis swallowed. "It's true. These are the Cursed Gods."

Nyssa snarled up at Suvi. The woman killed her mother and father. She wanted to wrap her fingers around Suvi's throat and squeeze until she felt the life leave the Queen's body.

"The fruit of our alliance with Frosland stands before us. Their navy procured these Cursed Gods, a gesture of goodwill. Aryis Devitt, Queen-in-Waiting of Frosland, delivered them to me herself," Suvi said with a smile and a nod toward Aryis.

Nyssa glanced at Aryis, who avoided her glare.

"In Quinn, we have a god of extraordinary power. She is able to extinguish magick and the essence of life itself with a mere touch. I welcome you back to the nation of your birth," Suvi said, her voice loud and steady.

"What?" Quinn whispered.

An excited murmur arose among the onlookers. They grew quiet when Suvi held her hand up and directed her gaze at Quinn.

"Your parents promised you to me as a child. Sold you, actually, when a seeker sensed something different about you and thought you might be one of the gods foretold by the Mystics. I was willing to pay for the chance that he was right, but before I could take possession of you, you were stolen from me, kidnapped by a cruel nation that only wanted you for your power. They raised you as one of their own in Arcton Citadel. But you are a daughter of Thu'Dain. And now I have you back."

Quinn let out a hollow breath of air, her face going white. "My...my parents...sold me?"

With a sigh, Suvi nodded.

"Why?"

"If only you could ask, but I'm afraid they are long dead, dear girl."

"No," Quinn whimpered. Her legs buckled, and Nyssa rushed to hold her up. One of their guards grabbed Nyssa, and she shoved him.

"Keep your hands off me," she growled. The guard looked up at his queen, who waved him off.

Nyssa put her hand on the back of Quinn's neck. "I've got you."

Nyssa had lived through a moment like this, and Athen was the person who helped her through the grief and anger. She would do the same for Quinn.

She would do anything for her.

Trembling beneath Nyssa's fingers, Quinn took a few deep breaths before addressing Suvi. "What happened to them?"

Suvi tried to exact a sad expression, but Nyssa knew it was for show—a cruel display of fake sincerity.

"They promised me something, then failed to deliver. What do you think happened?" she replied.

Quinn lunged toward Suvi's throne. Nyssa struggled to pull her back.

"They are in beggars' graves now, unmarked and unremembered." Suvi sighed. "But look what they gave the world: A woman of unparalleled abilities. A god that will serve and protect the nation of her birth."

Suvi smiled coldly at Quinn before her eyes shifted to Nyssa. "But what of Nyssa Blacksea? You don't belong here in Thu'Dain," she said, standing up and descending the stairs from her throne. "But you could."

She approached the two women and gave Nyssa a smile she could only describe as predatory, a wolf stalking its prey. "Nyssa, pledge your allegiance to me and this nation. Imagine it...the unwanted, magickless orphan raised by the Areshi Empire, a fallen Ashcloak deemed a traitor, serving at my side. You would strike such fear—"

"No," Nyssa said, her voice low.

Mock disappointment settled onto Suvi's face. "I'm being very generous."

"You killed my parents!" Nyssa yelled, taking a step toward Suvi, murder in her heart. Guards immediately grabbed her.

Suvi's pale-green eyes narrowed, and she took a few steps until she stood mere feet from Nyssa. "Is that what they told you?" she asked, her voice low.

"Your warships sank the Demon's Wail," Nyssa choked out, her voice breaking. "Why did you go after them?"

"That's quite the story, but that's not what happened." Suvi paused, scowling. "Wait...you really have no idea what your parents did, do you?"

Nyssa swallowed hard. "What are you talking about?"

A laugh escaped Suvi's lips, and she looked pleased with herself. She shook her head slowly. "Who do you think stole Quinn from us, Nyssa? A smuggler of great skill and his pirate mate."

Nyssa let out a strangled breath. "You're lying."

"That's not all." Suvi turned away and walked back toward her throne, sitting on the first step of its platform, her gaze unrelenting. "I spent a lot of money trying to find your parents, Nyssa, but they disappeared into thin air. How is it possible that two of the most notorious pirates on the seas were suddenly nowhere to be found? Thing is, I love a good mystery and kept looking until I came upon a sailor with a bad gambling habit and the debt to match who was willing to talk. He was the bosun of the Sea Stag at the time. And he told quite the interesting tale. The Stag, with Lilliana and a cadre of Justiciars aboard, sailed out to meet up with the Demon's Wail. Lilliana returned with two infants in her arms. One, the stolen child from Thu'Dain. Who do you suppose the other infant was?"

Nyssa shook her head. "No...my parents left me in Ocean's Rest."

"*Two souls, forever entwined*...and given over to Lilliana Fennick before the Justiciars slaughtered your parents and set their ship on fire."

Nyssa's legs gave out, and she dropped to her knees. Quinn was quickly beside her, wrapping an arm over her shoulders.

"Two infants...two gods, forever bound to one another," Suvi said quietly. "Take solace that your mother's last act was to surrender you to Lilliana. She valued your life more than her own."

"My mother would never—" Athen yelled.

Suvi reared her head back and roared with laughter. "Oh, please, finish that sentiment, Lord Fennick! What would your mother never do, exactly? Kill anyone who stood in her way to rule Ocean's Rest? Put her fist through a king's chest? Sink the Demon's Wail and put Nyssa's parents on the bottom of the ocean? Your mother would do all that and more, make no mistake."

"Nyssa, don't listen to her," Athen pleaded.

"You're lying," Nyssa seethed. "Lilliana made me her ward and protected me. She gave me to Eron to raise."

"Lilliana unleashed the Justiciars on your parents after she retrieved the baby the Areshi Empire contracted them to steal. But why did your parents have to die?" Suvi said. "You'll have to ask Lilliana."

Quinn laced her fingers in the back of Nyssa's hair and leaned forward, her forehead touching the side of Nyssa's head. "Don't listen to her. She's trying to hurt you, to bend us to her will," she whispered.

"She already has us, Quinn. We're powerless," Nyssa replied, her eyes not leaving Suvi, who sat patiently. So casual, so in control.

Suvi stood and smoothed out her dress, her eyes scanning the room. "I will extend my offer one more time, Nyssa. Serve me and you will live the life you deserve. That Mark of the Unworthy on your chin will never stain your reputation in this nation. You will have the respect you've always wanted."

"No," Nyssa coldly answered, gathering her strength to stand.

"How unfortunate. What happens now is because of your stubborn refusal to cooperate. I don't need both of you and, frankly, given the history of the Cursed Gods, even just one of you is extremely dangerous. Two of you is asking for a great deal of trouble. I've had a peek inside Quinn's head. There's a...connection between you two, and I know neither of you will rest until you free each other. I can't fight that bond, but I can tame one of you and break the other."

Suvi's eyes shifted to Quinn. "We will take that collar off of you, Quinn, and you will extinguish Blacksea's magick."

Quinn gasped. "No. I would never!"

"What do you want?" Aryis asked, rushing forward. "I'll give you whatever you want, Your Majesty. Just let them go. Please. This has gone too far."

"Your desperation makes you stupid, Aryis. There's no treasure as remotely valuable as either of them."

Aryis shook her head. "There has to be something! Anything!"

Suvi laughed. "Your country doesn't even have enough food to feed its people. What could you possibly offer?"

Tears glistened in Aryis's eyes. "I'm...begging you. Please let them go."

A low rumble of laughter rippled through the room. The Thu'Dainian Houses were drawing some sort of sick pleasure from the whole spectacle of a groveling Queen-in-Waiting.

Suvi ignored Aryis and turned her gaze to Quinn. "Let me show you what I can do if you say no to me. Hold Lord Fennick steady."

The guards next to Athen grabbed hold of him.

Suvi's eyes glossed over, turning black. Next to Athen, Aryis jerked once, her eyes bleeding into pools of black, and drew Talon. She turned and in one quick movement, slashed Athen's face. Nyssa shouted and lunged toward him, but guards descended on her, pushing her to the ground. Athen fell to his knees and clutched at his right eye with his hands, a strangled cry of pain echoing through the throne room.

Aryis stood emotionless next to him.

"You bitch!" Nyssa screamed at Suvi. "I'll kill you!"

Suvi laughed and approached. "Quinn, you will destroy Nyssa's magick or I will continue to use Aryis to maim Athen, one body part at a time. And then I'll have Aryis peel off her own skin."

Nyssa choked out a sob, finally understanding her purpose in all of this. She was meant to be the lesson—the warning to others—that Suvi had a weapon in Quinn unrivaled by any other. And what better way for Suvi to demonstrate her power than than to have one god destroy another?

This whole sick thing was just a show, a spectacle to solidify Suvi as a woman to be feared not just for her family name, but her ruthlessness and cunning.

Gods, how Nyssa had fucking underestimated her.

Suvi cocked her head at Quinn. "Well?"

Quinn shook her head. "I won't hurt Nyssa," she whispered. "You'll have to kill me."

With a sigh, Suvi turned back to Aryis, who stood motionless, drops of blood falling off her dagger to the white marble floor.

"I suppose I shall have to take Athen's other eye, then."

"Stop! Please, don't do this," Nyssa begged. "Please."

"Only Quinn can stop this," Suvi replied with a casual shrug.

Nyssa swallowed. If there was a way she survived this day, she swore to herself she would gut Suvi and watch her die slowly.

"If Quinn does what you want, will you let Athen and Aryis go?"

"No, Nyssa, don't," Quinn breathed.

Suvi nodded.

"Swear it!" Nyssa growled.

"You have the word of a queen—I will let Athen and Aryis go once I get what I want."

As much as Nyssa hated taking Suvi at her word, she had no other choice.

She looked up at Quinn. "Do what she asks."

Quinn shook her head. She seemed lost, her green eyes searching Nyssa's face for an answer; a way out. "You'll die," she whispered.

"Destroy Nyssa's magick but leave as much of her soul intact as you can so she can make it back to Ocean's Rest to see the truth in Lilliana's eyes before she dies. An apt punishment for your parents' sins against me," Suvi said, waving her hand dismissively toward Nyssa.

"Please. Just keep her here. We won't hurt you!" Quinn begged.

A sullen expression weighed Suvi's face down. "Cursed Gods come in destructive, dangerous pairs. I'd rather not tempt fate. And she will pay for her parents' crimes."

Quinn shook her head and turned back to Nyssa, her eyes filling with tears.

"Please, Quinn," Nyssa whispered. "I'm begging you. Suvi will kill Athen and Aryis, and then me. At least this way they'll live."

"I *can't*."

"This is the only way," Nyssa pleaded.

Suvi waved her hand at the guards next to Quinn and they pushed her down to her knees in front of Nyssa. Suvi smiled down at them, her eyes returning to their pale green, releasing Aryis from her control.

"What did you make me do?" Aryis screamed. Talon clattered to the floor, and she sank down next to Athen.

Suvi strode over to Aryis and Athen, bent over to pick up the blade, and wiped it on Aryis's shoulder, staining her white shirt with Athen's blood. She knelt next to them and re-sheathed the dagger at Aryis's hip. A nervous rumble of whispers wove through the spectators.

Rising to her feet, Suvi reached down and stroked Aryis's head, as if she were a pet. Then she dug her fingers into her hair, and pulled her head back. Aryis let out of sob.

Suvi stared down at her. "You will see, in time, that what happened here today will be a new era for both of our countries. No one will move against me with a god in my possession, least of all you, Queen-in-Waiting." Suvi let go of Aryis and approached Quinn. "We're going to take your void collar off. You try anything other than nullifying Nyssa's mag-ick and my guards will kill her and her friends."

"Why not just use your magick on me, you bitch? Certainly that would be less risky," Quinn said, not taking her eyes off of Nyssa.

Suvi scoffed. "That would be too easy. Stripping Blacksea of her mag-ick because I tell you to—that's true power."

A titter of laughter spread through the room—the goddamned bas-tards were *entertained* by Suvi's cruelty.

Gods, she'll be unstoppable.

Nyssa exhaled and bowed her head. Once again, she was on her knees, at the mercy of a power she couldn't rival. She'd prefer to die fighting, with Winter's Bite in her hand, but Suvi would rob her of that honor.

Suvi's guards surrounded them, their weapons drawn. One of them positioned himself behind Quinn with his dagger an inch from her neck, ready to strike. He carefully removed her collar.

No one moved. Everyone in the room was waiting to see what hap-pened next.

Nyssa extended a hand toward Quinn.

"It's okay," she said.

Quinn's eyes brimmed with tears and began to glow a bright, stunning green as darkness coiled around her.

A HEART TORN OPEN

Quinn choked back bile, struggling to compose herself in the face of madness. Nyssa was willing to let Quinn destroy her magick to save the lives of her friends.

It was unthinkable, untenable.

Not an hour earlier, Nyssa had kissed her. A whirlwind of surprise and desire possessed her in that moment, and she'd dropped her walls down to let herself embrace what she had been holding inside.

Had it all been for nothing?

She extended her hand and Nyssa grabbed it. "I'm sorry," Quinn whispered as darkness began to coil around her skin.

"It's okay, Freckles." Nyssa smiled gently, perhaps to reassure Quinn and lend her the strength for this horrific task. They both knew Quinn's magick would spell a slow and inevitable death.

Quinn wanted to pull Nyssa into a tight embrace, wishing she could make up for all time time she spent keeping Nyssa at arm's length, letting doubt and fear drive control her. Now, there were no more chances.

Her magick rippled around them and sank into Nyssa, her void collar falling away. Nyssa's face was set with a grim determination. Quinn reached out and found her core, a jagged, glowing blue orb of magick surrounding the white flicker of her soul. Destroying Nyssa's magick would eventually kill her—the magick and the soul connected too intricately to be separated without tainting one with the darkness of death.

Something in Quinn rebelled and refused the destruction. Instead of strangling the magick within Nyssa, she tugged at it. A small bit peeled away and with a little effort, it moved through Nyssa and into Quinn.

She gasped.

Maybe if I don't destroy her magick, Nyssa won't die. A glimmer of hope unfurled at the insane notion, and tears streamed down her cheeks as Nyssa doubled over in pain.

Gritting her teeth and concentrating, Quinn extracted the magick from Nyssa and drew it into herself, the displaced magick coiling around her own power in the center of her chest. Its energy twitched and buzzed, like a thunderstorm filling her whole chest. As she dislodged the blue magick, Nyssa's screams of agony tore Quinn's heart wide open, filling it with anger and regret. She was destroying Nyssa, laying her open and taking the one thing she couldn't survive without, condemning her to waste away until she died.

The jagged pieces of Nyssa's magick scraped through Quinn as she worked, like she was breathing in shards of glass, but she stifled her cries of pain. She had to hide her agony or Suvi might know.

The acts of destruction Quinn had witnessed before were loud and boisterous, a cacophony of fire and tumult. Pulling Nyssa apart was deep and intimate, the only sounds her strangled cries of agony.

A sob choked out of Quinn's throat when she finished.

Nyssa's hand grew cold.

A HEART SHATTERS

S uvi Rell loomed over Nyssa. "Get her up."

Two guards pulled Nyssa to her feet but had to hook their arms under her to keep her standing. Her head bobbed slightly as she tried to gain some control of her limbs. She was hollowed out, her skin feeling like a fragile shell that could crack and crumble with ease, and her eyes refused to focus.

Suvi laughed. "My seeker confirms your magick is gone. You're back to what you once were—a mundane, magickless woman. I suppose there would be some strange comfort in that, if it weren't also a death sentence for you."

She stepped up to Nyssa and placed her hand under Nyssa's chin, running her thumb down the Mark of the Unworthy. "The Justiciars didn't realize what you were when they gave you this, did they? How strange and frightening that day must have been for you. First you were marked, then you became a god."

Nyssa tried to pull away, but her muscles refused to obey.

Suvi's eyes narrowed. "I want you to go back home, Nyssa Blacksea, and ask Lilliana Fennick what she did to your parents." She turned and pointed at Quinn, on her knees with silent tears streaming down her face. "This day will be spoken of in Thu'Dain for centuries. The day I condemned one god to an inevitable death and enslaved another."

Suvi let Nyssa go, and her head lolled forward. Her eyes found Quinn, who slowly met her gaze. A void collar was back around her neck.

Nyssa lifted her head, focusing on Suvi. "Please don't hurt her."

"She's no longer your concern."

Nyssa's eyes fell back down to Quinn.

"Nyssa?" Quinn's voice cracked. Her face was pale and etched with sorrow. The look on her face broke whatever thread of strength was holding Nyssa together—she felt untethered from the earth, a dull thud pounding in her head.

Suvi tapped on Nyssa's cheek. "Quite a shame, you saying no to me. You are unfulfilled destiny," she said, staring into Nyssa's eyes. She crouched next to Quinn, pulling her head up. "You will be tucked safely away now, my god on a leash."

Suvi turned to two guards. "Take her to my estate and lock her in the southern wing." The guards lifted Quinn off the ground. She pawed at the collar around her neck before they screwed her arms behind her, causing her to cry out in pain.

"Stop, you're hurting her!" Nyssa rasped. "Please—"

The two guards began to drag Quinn away. She bucked out of their grasp, lunging toward Nyssa. Her fingers clasped Nyssa's outstretched hand, squeezing hard, before they were pulled apart.

"I'm sorry, Nyssa," Quinn cried. She sagged and her captors dragged her away, disappearing through a door on the far side of the room.

Nyssa's heart grew cold, shattering like ice, as Quinn was torn away from her and her anguished cries grew ever distant until they dwindled into silence. A hollow ache settled into Nyssa, taking up the space that Quinn used to occupy. Tears fell down her cheeks, though she barely felt them.

Athen lay on the floor a few feet away with Aryis next to him, her arm protectively around him. He was scarcely moving, one bloodied hand clamped over his right eye, his other hand clutching at his void collar. He met Nyssa's unsteady gaze.

At least Athen is alive.

Something barely resembling hope fluttered in her chest before it, too, fell away to pain and emptiness.

She was cold. So very cold.

Suvi Rell turned her attention back to Nyssa. "You and Fennick will be put on a merchant ship bound for Ocean's Rest." She turned to the guards standing over Aryis and Athen. "Aryis Devitt is not to be harmed. She was foolish to insist on coming here, but since we are now family, she will be returned to Frosland as a courtesy to her father and my husband."

Aryis scrambled to her feet. "We are not family, you bitch. And I'm not leaving my friends. I'm going with them."

Suvi smiled with amusement and waved her hand. "As you wish, girl. Frosland is already bound to Thu'Dain. You are no longer my concern until you're actually queen. I hope you wise up between now and then."

She stepped toward Nyssa. "I truly wish Lilliana Fennick does you the courtesy of telling you the truth about what she did to your parents before you die." She turned around and walked to the door, pausing to look back at Nyssa. "If you live long enough to see her, that is."

"I'll kill you," Nyssa hissed.

Suvi's eyes bored into her. "We will never lay eyes on each other again, Nyssa Blacksea." She turned and left the room, her footsteps echoing down the long, dark hallway.

Athen, Aryis, and Nyssa were put on horses and escorted silently to the docks by a large contingent of guards. They had to strap Nyssa on her horse to keep her from toppling over. She tried to hold her head up, to not let anyone see her bowed and broken, but she found it impossible, exhausted and still reeling from the pain of her powers being stripped away.

Before they departed the capitol building, Aryis was allowed to clean and bandage Athen's eye and was given a bottle of tonic to fight infection. A small mercy.

Word of what Suvi had done spread through the city, and the streets were lined with citizens that came to watch their procession to the docks—a neutered god, a defeated Queen-in-Waiting, and the half-blind son of the woman who killed their once king.

They were escorted aboard a merchant ship and shown to a large storeroom in the belly of the vessel that would serve as their quarters for their journey back to Ocean's Rest.

As they sailed, Nyssa barely looked at Aryis or Athen, her eyes watching the sea move past them through a dirty porthole. Her thoughts were dark and sullen.

Aryis tried to help Athen, but he only let her replace the bandage over his eye. The bleeding had stopped, and he dismissed any questions about pain. When Aryis brought Nyssa food, Nyssa weakly pushed her away. Even her anger was dulled. The hate she felt toward Aryis mixed with the cold ache inside of her and settled into her bones and flesh like a disease, but it had no urgency or fire.

At night, when Nyssa would lie down, Athen wrapped her in a blanket and draped an arm over her while she shivered, unable to shake the cold from her body. He would murmur in her ear as she tried to drift off to sleep.

Whatever words he spoke were wasted, unheard and unheeded.

Nyssa's dreams were plagued by the moment Quinn took her magick. She relived the pain every night—a cruel reminder of her last moments with Quinn.

The agony that ripped through her when Quinn extinguished her magick had pushed her close to the edge of blacking out. Excruciatingly hot pain seared through her, followed by an unrelenting cold. Every fiber of her body had wanted to pull her hand away from Quinn, to stop the pain and the violation of her power, but she fought the instinct to let go. She curled in on herself, gritting her teeth, while Quinn's magick razed and destroyed.

For the first time in her life, she'd wanted to beg for death.

By the time it was over, she barely felt Quinn let go of her.

Nyssa would jolt awake every time Quinn's hand slipped out of her own in the dream, Quinn's cries echoing in her ears. Athen's grip would tighten on her, and he'd whisper his guilt to her, sorry he was unable to keep her safe. If she fell asleep again, the dream would return. Over and over, her sleep interrupted by that horrible moment.

And Quinn's cries.

When the ship reached Ocean's Rest and Nyssa's feet were back on Imperial soil, she felt nothing. And when the Keep grew closer and closer as they made their way up the road to Athen's home, she only felt contempt.

Lilliana Fennick waited in the Keep, and Nyssa would do anything to find out the truth about her parents, even if that meant wrapping her cold fingers around Lilliana's throat.

AN ICY RETURN

Nyssa woke, disoriented and groggy.

Where am I?

She let out a soft sigh. Low, flickering light and the fragrance of warm spices breached her awareness. And lavender—the beautiful scent of lavender.

"Hey," a woman said. "You're awake."

The voice warmed Nyssa's heart. *Reece.* She sat on the bed, holding Nyssa's hand.

"Where am I?" Nyssa asked, trying to keep her steady over the lump in her throat. She never thought she'd see Reece ever again.

"Your old room at Ocean's Keep. You passed out on the way here. Athen carried you back."

"Athen...is he okay?"

Reece squeezed her hand. "He's resting."

Movement from the foot of her bed caught Nyssa's eye. Elias and Fontaine smiled at her. They both looked frazzled.

"Elias? What are you doing here?"

"We had nowhere else to go to lick our wounds, love."

Fontaine rounded the bed and sat next to her. "Aryis told us what happened in Sarisan. I'm so sorry, Nyssa. I wish we could have stopped them, but they had mages with them. They killed Jerrin and three others. We had to stand down or lose everyone."

"Four died? Jerrin…" Nyssa squeezed her eyes shut, willing herself to not cry. "Elias, I'm so sorry. Quinn and I shouldn't have been on your ship," she rasped.

"Do not blame yourself for the actions of Aryis Devitt. That girl brought this upon all of us," Elias spat.

"Where is she now?"

"In the guest quarters. Lilliana doesn't know what to do with her, and she won't leave," Reece said.

Reece touched Nyssa's shoulder and offered her a mug of tea. She cupped the mug in her hands, relishing the warmth, and drank the hot, sweet liquid.

Once she had some tea in her, she sat up, feeling better. Though *better* was a matter of opinion, relative to her new state of being. Darkness swirled within her, hollow and cold, slowly overtaking what was left of her life. The dim, decayed edges of where her magick used to be would soon leech through her like a disease.

It was only a matter of time before it killed her.

"How are you feeling?" Fontaine asked.

"I'm…" Nyssa stared into her tea mug. *Dying.* Saying the word aloud would make it a reality. Inevitable. She quickly turned her thoughts to other concerns. "My presence in this city puts you all at risk. There's still a price on my head. If the Empress finds out I'm here, she'll come down hard on Ocean's Rest."

"Do not worry about the Empress right now, Blacksea," a voice echoed from the shadows of the small enclave in the corner of the room, startling her. Justiciar Medias stepped out of the shadows. "I will deal with the Empire."

Despite their rocky past, Nyssa smiled upon seeing Medias. "Did you foresee this, seer? What can you tell me of my future before this darkness sweeps me under?"

Medias frowned. "My visions never showed me Aryis betraying you or your current dilemma. But I highly doubt you will sink into a deathbed and waste away. That isn't who you are."

"Quinn was forced to destroy my magick. You know I don't have long to live without it."

Fontaine took Nyssa's hand. "You have weeks, maybe months. Right now, you're feeling the pain of the last remnants of your magick dying."

"Just long enough for the Empire to capture me."

"I won't let that happen," Medias said, her voice grave.

Serious as ever, that one.

Nyssa sighed. "I'm learning that nothing stands in the way of what the people in power want."

"Medias will protect you," Fontaine remarked, glancing at the woman. "Detestable creatures the Justiciars are, but this one holds some respect for you."

Medias frowned at Fontaine.

Nyssa normally would have laughed, but she couldn't find the energy. She let her head rest on her pillow before addressing Reece. "I need to talk to Lilliana."

"Can it wait until tomorrow? You should sleep."

"Yes."

"Tomorrow, then," Reece said before Nyssa surrendered to exhaustion.

The next morning, Reece and Fontaine helped Nyssa bathe and get dressed. Nyssa could have managed on her own, already feeling better than she had on the journey back, but she was thankful for the assistance.

She couldn't be bothered with being self-conscious when naked in front of them. Reece was already intimately familiar with every part of Nyssa's body and Fontaine would be naked all the time if she could.

Reece gently washed Nyssa's hair as Fontaine cleansed her body. Nyssa wished she could stay in the hot bath forever. It was the only thing that chased away the chill that had sunken into her bones since her power was stripped from her.

After Nyssa dried off and got into undergarments, Reece came out of her closet with an old outfit she had left behind—an extra pair of leather guild pants and a light cotton shirt.

"Are these okay?" Reece asked.

"They're fine. They fit me perfectly," Nyssa said. "Is it strange that I find comfort in that?"

"Not at all," Reece said as Nyssa stood up and the two women helped dress her.

"And this," Fontaine said, reaching for something lying on a table that Nyssa hadn't noticed earlier. Fontaine turned, Nyssa's sword and scabbard in her hands. "The Froslandian military took this off of you when they stole you from Hannah's Whisper, but Elias insisted they leave the weapon with us. Aryis made sure they did."

Nyssa took Winter's Bite from Fontaine and pulled it over her head, affixing it to her back. "Thank you."

Nyssa looked at Reece and moved to embrace her. "Thank you for everything. I missed you, you know that?"

Reece hugged her back with a chuckle. "Of course I do. Nyssa, I'm so sorry for everything. Including what happened to Quinn. I know you care deeply for her."

Nyssa swallowed and pulled away, trying not to think about Quinn. Thinking about her would make her shut down completely. "Thank you both."

"Lilliana is in her office, waiting for you."

Nyssa nodded and set her jaw. "Let's go."

BE FIERCE, MY LOVE

The atmosphere in Lilliana's office was icy when Nyssa entered the room. All eyes turned to her. She knew how she looked—pale and sunken in. Dark circles had taken residence under her eyes. She had only spent a few seconds looking at herself in the mirror, unable to meet her own gaze.

Death stared back at her.

Lilliana turned from the window that overlooked Ocean's Rest, meeting Nyssa's hard stare, sending a chill rippling through her.

Athen stood and crossed the room, a black patch over his right eye. He wrapped Nyssa in a hug that she desperately wanted to feel comforted by, but her heart was cold in the face of what she had to do. What she had to ask.

"How are you feeling?" he asked as he let go.

"That is a question I will never be able to find the words to properly answer," Nyssa replied.

Sadness and worry wove across his face as he looked down at her. His pain made her want to cry. "Your eye, Athen...I'm so sorry."

He smiled and tapped his finger on the eye patch. It shimmered for a moment, giving away the presence of the magick that held it to his face. "I look far tougher now."

Lilliana stepped forward. "Nyssa. We have asked that Aryis leave Ocean's Rest, but she has refused to return to Frosland. I'm at my wits' end."

Aryis sat in a chair across the room, keeping her eyes down.

"Let her fucking rot," Nyssa said, trying to control the tremor in her voice. "I'm here for you, Lilliana. Suvi told me what you did to my mother and father. Tell me it's not true. Tell me you didn't kill them."

Lilliana's face didn't waver, but her eyes flickered.

"No," Reece whispered, stepping back. "What did you do?" She must have sensed something shift in Lilliana's emotions, confirming Nyssa's worst fears.

Nyssa lunged at Lilliana, using what little energy she had. Athen wrapped his arms around her waist. She fought against him, though she could no more break his grip than put a dent into Lilliana's magickally tough exterior.

"You killed them!" Nyssa rasped. "Why?"

Lilliana exhaled but offered Nyssa no words.

"Mother, please. You owe her the truth. You owe *me* the truth," Athen demanded.

"How can I explain the indefensible?" Lilliana said, her voice barely above a whisper.

Fontaine stepped forward. "I can show you what happened," she said to Nyssa. "The truth will hurt you more than you can imagine, but I can show you the night Shana and Mikel died through Lilliana's memories."

Lilliana's eyes widened. "No," she choked.

"Don't make me force you," Fontaine said, her gaze carrying a dark threat that Nyssa had never seen before.

Nyssa swallowed. Fontaine was offering her something no one else could, and though she was scared, she nodded.

"Step forward, Lilliana Fennick. You have nothing to fear from me," Fontaine said, "but you owe this woman the truth."

After a moment, Lilliana stepped around her desk to come within a few feet of Nyssa. "Let her go, Athen."

Athen slowly unwrapped his arms, releasing Nyssa. Fontaine laced her fingers together and spoke the unknown words of a lilting spell. Golden magickal threads twisted around her fingers. "Take my hands and let me build the bridge between you. Concentrate on that night, Lilliana. Don't make me dig around in your head to find it."

Nyssa grasped Fontaine's hand, and Lilliana took the other. Warmth flooded through Nyssa, coiling around her torso and up her neck until she felt pressure build behind her eyes. She closed them, and the memories—Lilliana's memories—began to flood in.

Lilliana stepped onto the Demon's Wail, followed by six Justiciars and Ceril Anelos. Spring had begun to take hold everywhere but the Black Sea, and a deep chill seeped into her bones.

The crew of the Wail kept their eyes on the boarding party as a woman stepped down from the quarterdeck and strode toward Lilliana, her open wool coat and white shirt rippling in the ocean wind.

"Shana," Lilliana greeted.

Shana met Lilliana's gaze. "Why do you bring Justiciars aboard *my* ship?" she asked, her voice low and husky.

"Bring us the child," Ceril commanded.

Shana scowled at him. "I don't fucking know you. And you certainly don't give orders aboard my ship." Her eyes narrowed on Lilliana. "Our deal was with you, Fennick. I'll ask again...why are Justiciars on my boat?"

"I am here as a courtesy. This was always an Imperial contract. I don't control them," Lilliana said. The declaration felt like a door slamming, driving the point home.

Shana's face changed, annoyance replaced by trepidation. Fear.

"Bring me the child," Lilliana said.

Shana's eyes scanned the Justiciars behind Lilliana and Ceril. She swallowed and nodded, putting two fingers into her mouth and unleashing a shrill whistle. A minute later, Mikel emerged from below deck, holding a baby with a tuft of dark hair and brilliant green eyes.

Ceril stepped forward to take the baby from his arms, and Mikel reluctantly let the girl go. Ceril scowled. It was apparent he had never held a child before. His arms were stiff, as if he was afraid the infant would break.

"We don't know her name. We've been calling her Quinn, after the Pirate Queen from—"

"*The Cry of the Sea*. I'm familiar," Lilliana said, glancing at the baby. The infant smiled up at Lilliana, her bright-green eyes shining in the moonlight.

"What's going on?" Mikel asked. His eyes slowly took in the contingent of Justiciars behind her, and his expression changed, becoming grim. He put his arm around Shana and pulled her close.

Lilliana didn't answer.

Shana locked eyes with her, and her face grew hard after a few moments. The shift in her was clear—she knew what was coming, of that Lilliana was certain.

"Go get our daughter," she said quietly to Mikel. He stepped forward and kissed her, rubbing her cheeks with his thumbs, then left her side and disappeared below deck. A minute passed before he emerged again, another baby in his arms, her blue eyes matching those of her mother.

"Take my daughter with you," Shana said as she took the baby from her husband. The infant reached for Shana's face and giggled.

"No," Lilliana said.

"Please," Shana rasped. "When your child is born, you will realize you will do anything for them. I can't stop what you're going to do to us. But please, my baby doesn't deserve to die."

Lilliana was ready to refuse again, but she stopped herself. She was six months pregnant and knew in her heart she would do anything for her child. The baby in Shana's arms was innocent. The Empire was willing to go to great lengths for one infant, the one prophesied by the Whitepeak Mystics, but she couldn't bring herself to condemn the other baby to death.

Lilliana stepped forward. "I'll take her."

Ceril spoke up. "No. This pirate's spawn isn't our concern."

She rounded on him. "Our? You needn't worry, Anelos. I'll take the child in and give her a life."

He grunted his discontent but didn't press the matter further. Quinn squirmed in his arms, reaching out for Shana and fussing.

"What is your child's name?" Lilliana asked Shana.

A tear fell from her blue eyes. "Nyssa," she said, kissing her daughter. Mikel stood at his wife's side, and Nyssa wrapped a hand around his finger as she cooed at Quinn.

"Surname?" Lilliana asked.

"She was born on the Black Sea. Let that be her name so she's free of the stain of our crimes." Shana kissed the side of Nyssa's head. "Be fierce, my love," she whispered. Nyssa pawed at the pendant around Shana's neck—a demon's head.

"I know you hate me right now, but I swear to you, I will keep her safe," Lilliana said, holding her arms out to take the child.

With a sob, Shana handed Nyssa over to Lilliana. She removed the thick chain and its pendant from her neck. "Maybe one day you can give her this. Make up a story about how you got it but let her know it's from me."

Lilliana took the pendant and turned away from Shana to return to the Sea Stag, Ceril following with Quinn. Behind her came the sound of swords being drawn.

Her stomach twisted.

Lilliana didn't witness Shana and Mikel die, but she heard their sharp, desperate cries as the Justiciars cut them down.

Nyssa ripped her hands out of Fontaine's grasp and stumbled back. Athen steadied her. She curled into herself and let out a primal roar, her anger and rage needing an outlet. She lifted her eyes to Lilliana's face.

"Ceril was there? You and that bastard killed my family?" she whispered.

Lilliana's eyes grew heavy with tears. "It was Kalla's orders. I didn't want any part—"

"You had my mother and father steal Quinn from her parents. Then you killed them!" Nyssa snarled.

"I didn't kill them, it was—"

"As if it makes a *fucking* bit of difference if you drew a sword or not. *You* brought the Justiciars to my parents' ship. *You* condemned them to death!"

Athen took Nyssa's arm. "Nyssa, please—"

"Let go of me!" she yelled, pushing him away.

She turned and ran out of Lilliana's office. She wanted Lilliana dead, but that would fracture her relationships with Athen and Reece forever. She couldn't stand the thought of hurting them.

For years, Nyssa had dreamt of what her parents might look like. Now, she finally knew. But that moment would forever be stained by their deaths. The sound of their desperate cries as the Justiciars struck them down would haunt her dreams.

Nyssa retreated back to her room, her thoughts spinning. There was no way she could stay in Ocean's Rest, even though everyone she loved was in the city.

Almost everyone, she corrected herself.

But their love was suffocating. They would watch her slowly die, and the thought of seeing pity in their eyes made her want to scream. She walked to the closet, pulled out a few clothes, stuffed them in a rucksack, then returned to the main room where she found Medias waiting.

"You here to talk me out of leaving?" Nyssa asked, throwing the bag on the bed.

"No."

"Then what do you want?"

"Nothing."

Nyssa exhaled and rubbed her eyes. She didn't have the time or patience for the Justiciar's games. "No visions this time? No talk of breaking or bending fate?"

Medias drew her lips tight. "I will miss your obstinate lack of fear when it comes to me."

"I was a good faker," Nyssa admitted. "You scared the piss out of me the first time we met."

"You are brave and stubborn, Blacksea. You will need that for your next journey."

Nyssa scowled. "That sounds like you've seen something of my future."

Medias shrugged. "Unfortunately, no…but I know you'll find your way, wherever that lies. Now go, before Athen or Reece come to check on you."

Nyssa was about to pick up her bag but stopped. Instead, she lifted her sword strap over her head and tossed Winter's Bite on the bed, then she twisted the Kraken ring off her finger and placed it gently on the scabbard.

"I'm no longer this person—a warrior," she said, looking down at her sword and ring. Two of the four things of any worth she owned in the world. "See that Athen gets the ring. As far as my sword, have Elias toss it into the Black Sea when he next makes his way out there. Can you do that for me?"

Medias nodded. Nyssa picked up her bag and slung it over her shoulder. She fingered the inside panel of the leather band on her left wrist, feeling the thin lump secured in the hidden pocket pressed against her pulse. The blue river rock. That and the chromoimage of Eron stuck in the page of her notebook would be the only two things she would carry with her into death.

"Here," Medias said, unzipping her jacket. She reached inside and pulled out a sizable bag, then tossed it to Nyssa. It rattled with the sound of gold. "You'll need money. And this." She removed a small, heavy-looking red coin out of an inner pocket. "It is my marker, just in case you need more than what that bag of gold can buy. Give me your hand."

Nyssa did as she was told, and Medias placed the coin in her hand, resting hers on top. Nyssa felt a small pinprick pierce her palm. "It's blood-bonded to you now. Only you or I can use it, but don't go buying an island or anything too extravagant. I'm not that rich."

"Thank you for this. And thank you for protecting my friends. But you don't have to look after them anymore," Nyssa said.

"Yes, I do. I gave you my word. Your death doesn't release me from my promise. Besides, I somewhat tolerate your friends now. This Keep has become more of a home than any other place to me."

Nyssa smiled through her sadness. Medias made an odd addition to her small cadre of friends, and she was comforted by the idea that the Justiciar would still watch over Reece and Athen.

"Goodbye, Justiciar."

"Farewell, Blacksea."

MOTHERS

Athen squirmed, impatient and uncomfortable in a chair that was a bit too small for him. Nyssa's disappearance left him feeling hollow. Nyssa had always lived on her own terms, but the thought of her dying alone left him feeling hopeless.

Ocean's Keep seemed like a prison now. Betrayed not only by Aryis, but his own mother. The thought that she helped the Empire kidnap Quinn as an infant was unconscionable. But the knowledge that she had led Shana and Mikel to their deaths was horrifying. He knew his mother could be ruthless when she had to be—especially in defense of her family or Ocean's Rest—but nothing prepared him for the stark reality that she had a hand in the death of Nyssa's parents.

Now, in his mother's office, he simmered with anger, his helplessness giving way to a darker emotion. Pol stood behind her, hands clasped behind his back.

"I wanted to explain to you both what happened with Shana and Mikel. Why I did what I did," Lilliana started.

Athen glanced at Reece in the chair beside him, her face inscrutable.

Lilliana leaned forward and folded her hands in front of her. "The Whitepeak Mystics warned of Cursed Gods being reborn into the world. Anelos, Arch Justiciar Decia, and other First Masters convinced the

Empress that finding them as children and raising them as Areshi adepts was a prudent course of action."

"To control them," Reece remarked.

"Yes. To make these gods Imperial weapons." Lilliana ran her finger along the top of her desk. "Empress Kalla came to me, requiring my help to retrieve an asset out of Thu'Dain—"

"You mean Quinn," Athen said. "She's a person, not a goddamn asset."

"That's how they viewed her."

"She was an *infant.*"

Lilliana blinked. "I contracted Shana and Mikel to find and smuggle Quinn out of Thu'Dain. The Empire offered them an obscene amount of money. I didn't know that they were in danger until I saw Ceril and a contingent of Justiciars waiting to board the Sea Stag with me." She closed her eyes and let out a long, weary sigh. "Loose ends. That's all Nyssa's parents were to the Empire. I couldn't do anything to stop it."

Athen had always understood there were things that his mother had to do in order to control Ocean's Rest. It shamed him how willing he was to overlook the ugly reality of what those actions might have been and who Lilliana might have hurt along the way to becoming Regent.

Athen's chest tightened. "Did Eron know?"

"Only after the fact. He would never have approved."

Athen let out a breath. At least Eron was clean in the whole awful affair. "Why was Ceril involved?"

"Arcton protects the Empire's secrets, and Quinn needed to be secured, hidden away. He volunteered to raise her and teach her how to use her magick."

"And look at what he did to her. When her power didn't manifest and it looked like Quinn wasn't a Cursed God, he locked her up. Put her in a collar. Abused her."

Lilliana's eyes turned down. Of course she couldn't look him in the eye. He gripped the arms of his chair tightly, relenting only when they began to creak under his strength. "To think I helped return her to that monster. Nyssa saved her and was branded a traitor. And what did I do? My duty. My *fucking* duty. As I always do."

"As we all do. We're put in our place and expected to obey," Reece said, a rare edge of anger coloring her tone.

Athen looked to his mother. "You had Nyssa's parents kidnap an infant and then were complicit in their murders. Why did you do it? What sort of monster are you?"

Pol cleared his throat as a warning, but Athen didn't care if his words cut deep.

"The Empress and her Arch Justiciar at the time made it very clear that if I didn't do as they asked, they would have taken something precious to me." His mother's gaze shifted to Reece. "You were barely two years old, but word of your abilities spread quickly. Ambershine would have taken you, Reece, and turned you into a Justiciar because of your empathic magick. I did as they asked in order to save you."

Reece inhaled a deep breath. "I'm...I'm the reason Nyssa's parents are dead?"

"No. Don't you ever blame yourself for that," Lilliana replied. "Kalla asked for Shana and Mikel specifically, but she wanted to use my connections in the under world and keep her own involvement hidden."

"Why didn't you tell Nyssa any of this?" Athen asked.

"No reason would have sufficed. Not for what I've done, and certainly not in her eyes. I don't expect pity or understanding from either of you, but I do care about how you regard me. Please keep this knowledge to just the three of us, as it does no good to anyone." Lilliana shifted in her chair. "I've done things I'm not proud of, but all of it has been to build a legacy for our family and to leave Ocean's Rest in your capable hands, Athen."

Athen steeled himself. He had never addressed his concerns with his mother for fear of disappointing her deeply. But now, her plans for him didn't matter. Not anymore.

"No," he declared. His mind had been made up for a while, but the words and the courage had eluded him. "I'm done pretending I want any of this."

"What does that mean?" Lilliana asked, her face darkening.

"I won't be the next Regent of this city."

Lilliana narrowed her gaze. "You're my son. I expect you to—"

"I don't want the job. I can train the Lion's Guard, as you asked, but let's not pretend that you haven't realized I don't have it in me to be a politician."

Lilliana leaned back in her chair. Color rose in her cheeks. "What are we to do, then?"

Athen glanced over at Reece. "The answer has always been right in front of you. Reece should be the next Regent."

Reece snapped her head in his direction. "Athen, what are you—"

"She isn't blood," Lilliana said. "The Regency stays in the family. You *will* take over for me."

Reece shot to her feet. "I will not be talked about like I'm not even in the room. You overlook me, Lilliana, even when I'm standing right in front of you. You always have."

"That's not true. You know how much I value you. You see what I've done to protect you."

Reece let out an exasperated breath. "Don't use your actions against Nyssa's parents as proof of your love for me. *Ever* again."

"I'm sorry, I—"

"I don't want to manage The Feather forever," Reece seethed. "Do you know what it takes out of me to play counselor all the time to clients? I'm done feeling all their pain. No one comes to me when they're happy. I have been loyal out of love for you, but I can't do it anymore."

Lilliana scowled, and Athen ground his jaw. This wasn't going the way he had thought it would. His mother was too damn stubborn and Reece had reached the end of her patience.

"Reece, you're an important component of this family and this city," Lilliana said, "but you have to understand, I built this for Athen—"

"No. I'm done," Reece replied. "I'm nothing to you." She turned, tears brimming in her dark eyes, and left Lilliana's office.

Athen shook his head, his heart aching for his adopted sister. He had never viewed her as anything other than family. He would die for her. How his mother could be so cruel in the face of Reece's loyalty shocked him.

"Reece is far more capable than me. Yet you dismiss her and take advantage of her. You took her in after her mother died, and she thinks she owes you for that. Now she's finally asking for what she wants, and you tell her she's not blood, as if that's more important than the family we made for her here. How could you?"

A heavy sigh from Pol drew Athen's attention. "Do you have something to add?" Athen asked, his voice tinged with frustration and anger.

Pol drew in a sharp breath, and his eyes darted down to Lilliana. "I don't disagree with you, Athen. Reece is smart and cunning. She would be an excellent Regent."

Lilliana glanced back at Pol. Athen had never in his life seen them disagree. It didn't cross his mind that Pol would ever have a differing opinion from Lilliana. Yet he knew Pol loved Reece deeply, a father to her in his own way.

Athen straightened. "Reece is well respected, even by the factions. No one would question naming her as the next Regent. But you're a hypocrite. Ocean's Rest accepted you as its leader, a low-born brothel mistress, but won't do the same for Reece? She has rare magick, is far smarter than I am, and knows how to handle herself in a room of men and women puffing out their chests. How are you this fucking stubborn? Or this fucking stupid?"

Lilliana brought her fist down on her desk, the wood splintering under the blow. "How dare you! Everything I've done was for us...for you."

"Don't presume to tell me who I should be anymore. I don't want this office or Pol standing behind me as I move pieces on a shadowy game board. That's not me. That's not who Eron raised me to be."

The desk creaked under Lilliana's fist. "Eron didn't raise you, I did."

Standing, Athen shook his head. "I spent twelve years at the Order. Eron fucking did his part. Don't dishonor his memory."

"Athen, you—"

"I've already lost Nyssa. I can't lose Reece. You pushing her away and denying she's family because she's not blood is bullshit. And if you lose her, you lose me. And you lose this city. Do you understand that?"

Lilliana blinked at him.

Athen put his arms in the air before letting them fall to his sides. "Gods, how can you not see the priceless jewel right in front of your eyes that you have in Reece?"

He turned and stormed out of Lilliana's office, slamming the door behind him.

He had finally stood up to his mother for what he wanted. It was a long time coming—a moment he would love to share with Aryis.

He hung his head. Every time he thought of her, the pain of her betrayal dug its claws deeper into his heart. The one person he wanted to share everything with was under his roof, yet never more distant.

DAUGHTERS

Medias leaned in the shadows of an alcove, watching Lilliana's office, and rolled a toothpick around her mouth. She wasn't in the habit of fidgeting. She wasn't in the habit of spying either, but it was worrisome that Lilliana had called upon Reece and Athen for an unscheduled meeting late at night.

The concern Medias felt for the two was unsettling. A year in the Keep had engendered a fondness for them. She was doing the exact thing her Justiciar upbringing had warned her against—forming attachments.

When Reece hurried out of the office on the verge of tears, Medias flicked away her toothpick and silently trailed the empath, sticking to the shadows. Reece reached the hall that led to Medias's guest room. She took a step in the direction of the room but stopped. Bowing her head, she retreated in the opposite direction through a pair of double doors that led to a dark courtyard.

Social graces may have prescribed that Medias should leave Reece to her thoughts, but she didn't care about protocol and followed Reece outside.

"Reece?" she called out softly, her eyes adjusting to the night. The moon hung in the sky, illuminating the courtyard. Its bare trees cast spindly shadows across the stones under her feet. The cool air carried the scent of crisp dried leaves.

"Are you following me?" a voice asked from a dark recess across the yard.

"I was concerned when Lilliana called you to her office, so yes, I followed and waited. But now you are upset. I can leave you alone if you wish."

"I found out that Lilliana agreed to help the Empire get Quinn in order to save me from being taken by Ambershine and turned into a Justiciar."

Medias stilled. The news didn't exactly come as a surprise. She had always wondered, after meeting Reece, how an empath of her abilities was passed over by her guild. Now it made sense.

"I am not surprised. Neither by the Empress' actions or Lilliana's," she replied.

"She's a monster," Reece said, her voice low.

"No, she's a mother. And mothers will do anything for their children."

A low, rueful laugh drifted out of the darkness. "Am I her daughter though?"

"She considers you such."

"Does she?" Reece stepped out of the shadows of the alcove, her silver hair catching the moonlight. "You were right. I'll never be more to Lilliana than a brothel mistress."

"I'm sorry."

Reece crossed her arms and lowered her head. "I don't know what I expected."

"What will you do?"

"There's no future for me here. I see that now. Even after Athen turned her down, Lilliana refused me."

Medias crossed over to Reece, pained by the tears rimming the empath's eyes. She had never seen Reece so openly hurt. Lilliana's rejection was raw and biting, the sting of it written all over Reece's face.

"I can't presume to tell you what to do, but I don't think you should leave. I can't protect you if you go running off," Medias said, offering Reece a rare smile.

Reece rumbled a low, rueful laugh. "What would you have me do, be the obedient servant? There's no reason to stay. Not anymore."

Her admission felt like a slap across the face. "I don't want to see you get hurt. Under this roof, you're protected."

"I feel like I've disappointed Lilliana simply by not being her blood daughter. Is that silly?"

"Mothers are exacting creatures. I know that all too well. And daughters, by blood or not, are often in the strange position of feeling as though they haven't lived up to unreachable standards," Medias said. From her own experience, trying to fulfill her mother's expectations was a losing proposition.

Reece shifted her feet. "I should go."

Medias reluctantly stepped aside to let her pass.

A hand came to rest on her arm. "I fear things are falling apart. It was slow at first, starting with that night the wraiths attacked. But there's a growing danger, I can feel it in my gut. And Nyssa is gone, dying. I can't..." Reece set her jaw before continuing. "What will Kalla do to you when she finds out you're not hers anymore?"

Medias closed her eyes and inhaled the crisp night air that carried a faint hint of lavender, taking a moment before answering. "You know what she'll do."

"Athen and I will help. With our connections, we can get you off the continent."

A sad smile crossed Medias's lips. "I won't run."

"If you get caught..." Reece took a deep breath. "You're no good to me dead, Medias."

Medias lowered her head, and Reece held her in her gaze, dark and unwavering. As always.

"Don't put me in a grave so quickly, empath. There are still plenty of battles to fight and win." She swallowed, thankful that Reece couldn't sense her fear.

Reece pulled her hand back with a soft smile. "I hope you're right. Goodnight, Justiciar."

PILES OF BOOKS

A soft click startled Aryis awake. She shot up in bed, desperately trying to remember where she had left Talon, her fingers twisting up in the bedsheets. A figure walked out of the darkness, into the small halo of light surrounding her bed. Red eyes stared down at her.

"Medias? Are you here to kill me?"

"No, Queen-in-Waiting. Put your mind at ease."

Nothing of late could offer Aryis solace. But didn't she deserve this pain now, after what she had done?

She swallowed. "Why are you here?"

Medias stepped to the side of the bed and, without asking, sat down next to Aryis. She placed a sword between them.

Aryis rubbed her burning eyes and focused. "Is...is that Winter's Bite? Why do you have it?"

"Nyssa left it behind. Along with this." Medias held up a silver ring between her thumb and forefinger, a Kraken etched into its metal. "Give me your hand."

Aryis reluctantly held out her right hand, and Medias slid the ring onto her middle finger. It warmed against her skin and resized itself to fit snugly.

"Why are you giving me Nyssa's ring?" Aryis asked, sitting up straighter.

"Why haven't you returned to Frosland?"

"Answering a question with a question is not..." She shook her head and sighed. There seemed no sense in trying to extract an answer from the Justiciar. "I'm not going back."

"I expected as much." Medias picked up one of the books surrounding Aryis. "You've been at this for days. Have you made any progress?"

It had been a week since Nyssa disappeared. Aryis had holed herself up in a guest room, refusing to leave as she researched herself into exhaustion, surrounded by stacks and stacks of books. But no matter how many she summoned to herself, none held a solution to Nyssa's problem.

No, 'problem' is too frivolous a word. Nyssa's dying. Because of me.

"I haven't found the answer yet," Aryis admitted, swallowing hard.

"Helping Nyssa isn't through these books. It's by her side," the Justiciar said. She tapped her finger on Winter's Bite. "And now you have the means to find her."

Aryis shook her head, confused. "What can I possibly do besides anger her? She'll push me away, if she doesn't kill me outright."

Medias shrugged. "I only know what I see, and your individual journeys converge soon. You can't accomplish anything hiding in this room."

Aryis leaned forward. Medias must have had a vision. And maybe she was right. Researching had gotten Aryis nowhere. "Where do I go? What do I do?"

With another shrug, Medias stood. "There's a Rare Collections Room at Wayland, correct?"

"Yes, but—"

"Then that's where you need to go."

The thought of returning to Wayland after what had happened to all those adepts...to Rustam....

"I...I can't go back."

"Don't you wish to serve a purpose after your betrayal? Get to Wayland, Aryis. There, a fat little bird awaits."

"Wh-what does that mean?"

"I don't know what it is, only what I saw," Medias replied, narrowing her red gaze. "You're the smart one, you figure it out."

She bowed her head and left Aryis to fume, the door hushing shut behind her.

Ayris sprang out of bed and began pacing, mumbling to herself as her thoughts tumbled around her head.

The Rare Collections Room?

She had never been allowed inside, where all manner of powerful, rare, and forgotten items lay within.

Fat little bird?

Aryis stopped in her tracks as her thoughts clicked into place.

"*That* fat little bird?" Her eyes went wide. "Shit."

The Hummingbird. She barely remembered it existed, locked away in the Rare Collections Room. There was only one use for it—one that would likely get her and Nyssa killed.

Aryis ground her teeth. The damn Hummingbird wasn't a cure for Nyssa's dilemma. *There isn't a cure.* Aryis had tried and failed to find an answer. Book after book offered nothing, not even a glimmer of hope.

No, helping Nyssa was perhaps no longer about saving her life, but saving another. And the Hummingbird was the way to do it...though admittedly unconventional. And dangerous.

Aryis got busy packing.

CONSEQUENCES

Medias hurried down the chilly, dim hall that led to Lilliana's office, willing herself to not break into a run. She had to maintain some semblance of calm, despite the fear churning in her gut. When she got to the office, she stopped cold and put on as stoic a face as she could muster before opening the door.

Ceril Anelos stood no more than ten feet from her, arguing with Lilliana. Though her face was red, a taut level of restraint radiated off of her. They were surrounded by a small pack of Imperial Guards and, to Medias's surprise, an Obsidian Rule adept. Ashcloaks were meant to protect government officials, not assassins.

"Arch Master Anelos, this is a surprise," Medias said, keeping her voice steady. Her stomach dropped when she saw Athen sitting on a bench near the spacious window, a void collar around his neck. Reece stood next to him, her face pale—a stark contrast against the dark night sky behind her. Medias swallowed hard. "Lord Fennick in a void collar? House Fennick is an important contingent within the Empire. Empress Kalla will not be pleased with this ugly spectacle."

Ceril sighed. "Your loyalty is to the throne, not House Fennick. Your association with them is making you weak."

Anger was rare for Medias, but it now coursed through her blood like liquid fire. She stepped toward Ceril. "Do not ever question my loyalty again, Arch Master, or you will witness the full power and authority of an Imperial Justiciar unbridled by the formality of your petty title. I answer to one woman and I do not see her here."

The smallest flinch escaped his buttoned-up exterior, enough to let Medias know he still respected a Justiciar's power.

"Justiciar Medias, why did I have to hear from someone other than you that Nyssa Blacksea was in this Keep two weeks ago?"

A cold lump caught in Medias's throat as she considered her response. "That's impossible," she lied.

"You had no idea Blacksea was in the Keep?"

She gritted her teeth and narrowed her eyes at Reece and Athen, doing her best to act angry toward them. "Is this true?"

"They hid her from you," Ceril said. Anelos didn't come to the Keep for a polite chat. He expected answers only a Justiciar could extract. To fool him, Medias needed to be that Justiciar.

If she didn't respond correctly, she could put them all in jeopardy.

She approached Athen. "Who helped you?"

"No one. My mother and Reece didn't even know she was here."

"Where is Blacksea now?"

"Gone."

A beat passed. "Where?"

Athen fell silent.

Silently hoping that Lilliana wouldn't kill her for what happened next, Medias held up her hand and summoned a burst of white light inside of Athen's chest. He grunted in pain.

"Stop!" Reece stepped in front of Athen and shoved Medias, her eyes close to tears.

Dammit, woman! I have to hurt him to save you all.

Medias grabbed Reece's wrist and pulled her to the side, whispering "I'm sorry" before pushing her back toward the window. "Do not interfere, empath, or I will hurt you."

Medias's magick—the only ability the Justiciars knew about—made her a valuable interrogator. Bursting her light inside a body caused a great deal of pain but did no lasting damage. She could interrogate someone for hours; days even. She had broken people. And with the stress the pain put on the body and mind...she had killed as well.

"We will get answers out of you, Fennick," Medias warned.

A feral smile graced Ceril's face, his spite worn nakedly. "Finally. You will do what you were made to do, Justiciar."

"My son doesn't know where Nyssa is," Lilliana said.

"Stay out of this, Regent Fennick," Medias said, hoping Lilliana would trust her in this moment. If she interfered, everything would go to hell. There would be no way to protect House Fennick from Ceril or Kalla. They would be arrested, or worse. She swallowed and turned back to Athen. "Where is Blacksea?"

He attempted to stand. She summoned another burst of light in his body. He doubled over, hissing in pain. Lilliana started to protest again to Ceril, and Medias took the opportunity to push Athen down onto the bench, leaning close. "Play along or we're dead."

Medias circled his chair and stood behind him. "Where is Blacksea?"

"Fuck you," Athen spat.

Medias glanced at Ceril, at the displeasure obvious on his face. Placing her hand on Athen's shoulder, she summoned a burst of light in his chest again. He cried out.

"Please stop!" Reece begged. Medias exploded light in front of her face, disorienting her. Reece stumbled back, blinking.

"Stay back, empath, or you will be next," Medias warned, hoping Reece would do something completely antithetical to her nature—back down.

"I don't know where Nyssa is," Athen seethed, his skin slick with sweat.

"Why did you go to Thu'Dain?" Ceril asked.

"Answer him," Medias said, giving Athen's shoulder a light squeeze.

"Because Nyssa needed to answer for her betrayal. She failed Eron and made a fool of me. I left without telling anyone where I was going."

Good. He's playing his part.

Ceril glanced at Medias. "And you weren't curious where Fennick disappeared to, Justiciar?"

"I was told he sailed to Frosland, running after Aryis Devitt like a lovesick puppy."

"And he brought Nyssa back in this Keep? Under your nose?"

No one had seen Medias with Nyssa. She was careful to stay out of sight and use the Keep's hidden passages to visit Blacksea.

"House Fennick keeps its secrets," Medias replied. "I don't have to tell you that, Arch Master."

Ceril's eyes went back to Athen. "Why did you bring Blacksea back here?"

Medias squeezed Athen's shoulder again.

"She's dying," he replied. Ceril's eyebrows shot up. "I took pity on her and gave her a chance to make her peace with us. It was one last thing I could do to honor Master Eron after I failed to stop Nyssa from betraying her oath to the Empire."

Smart man.

Painting Nyssa in a negative light played directly into Ceril's contempt for her, but Medias knew it must kill him to lie about his best friend.

"Blacksea is dying?" Ceril asked, his eyes narrowing. "What of Quinn?"

"Suvi Rell has Quinn. Suvi forced her to strip Nyssa of her magick," Athen said.

"I had heard rumors about what transpired in Sarisan, but I didn't know its veracity." The corners of Ceril's mouth curled slightly. Of course he was taking pleasure in Nyssa's impending death and Quinn's imprisonment. "Justiciar, you must weigh judgment here."

"Blacksea is a walking ghost, likely dead already," Medias said, hoping she was wrong. "Fennick was overzealous in his pursuit of Blacksea, yet I cannot punish his House and jeopardize the stability in Ocean's Rest over a dead god. But he's dishonored his guild and will no longer be counted among the ranks of Ashcloaks."

Athen exhaled hard. Stripping him of his standing with the Emerald Order couldn't be helped—it was the only logical choice that a Justiciar could make that didn't involve imprisonment or execution.

The decision seemed to please Ceril, whose myopic hatred of Nyssa drew his ire, thankfully leaving little left for House Fennick. "A savvy political move on your part, Justiciar."

Medias nodded, though she wanted to shove his compliment down his throat and make him choke on it.

Ceril turned to Lilliana. "Consider yourself warned, Lady Fennick. Should Blacksea return to this city, you will arrest her immediately and send her to Cardin. She must answer for her crimes."

"That poor woman will never come back here," Lilliana said.

Ceril scowled and diverted his attention. "Justiciar Medias, I wish you to find Blacksea for me. I want her brought to Cardin, even if you only find a body. Once we have her, the Empire's citizens can rest easy."

"Your hatred for Blacksea is coloring your decisions, Arch Master," Medias chided.

The room went still until Ceril hummed out a chuckle. "My hatred? Blacksea stands as an affront to everything this Empire represents. The very things I've sacrificed for. She had no business being in the Emerald Order, and First Master Greye paid for his decision with his life. As long as Blacksea is alive, she is a threat."

Medias approached Ceril. "I will have Imperial agents look for her. My time will not be wasted on chasing a dead woman into whatever hole she crawled into. I will remain in Ocean's Rest. Blacksea may still find her way back here to die with the people she foolishly perceives as family."

She waited for an argument.

A thin smile graced Ceril's lips. "Very well. At least I return to the Empress with good news. Blacksea's death will lighten her burden."

Ceril took one last look at Athen before he and his guards left the office.

Medias exhaled. They had avoided a number of very negative outcomes. She turned to Lilliana. "I think we're—"

Lilliana seized Medias by the throat and lifted her off her feet. "I should never have trusted you!"

Medias struggled for breath, clinging to Lilliana's wrists. "Please..." she wheezed, her vision beginning to darken.

"Let Medias go!" Reece pleaded, rushing forward. "I think she just saved us all."

For an excruciatingly long moment, Lilliana's fingers tightened around the Justiciar's throat. "You didn't know Anelos was coming?"

Medias choked out a "No."

Lilliana let go and Medias tumbled to the ground, gasping for air. Reece crouched down and steadied her.

Medias rubbed her throat. "I swear to you, I had no idea. I had to play my part, as did Athen."

Lilliana strode over to him, his color pale and forehead slick with sweat. She crushed the lock on his void color with her fingers and removed it from his neck.

He grunted. "Those things I said..."

"For Ceril's benefit only," Medias said. "You are a true friend to Blacksea. Know that. I'm sorry I had to strip you of your Ashcloak title. I fear Ceril wouldn't have accepted anything less. And anything more would have been—" She stopped herself.

Athen glanced up at her. "I know. You saved my ass."

Lilliana helped her son to his feet. "Are you hurt?"

"Just a little sore," he replied.

"My magick does no lasting harm, only temporary pain. I'm sorry for my..." Medias clenched her jaw. She wasn't accustomed to apologizing for what she did as a Justiciar.

"Come on," Lilliana said, putting her arm around her son, even though he dwarfed her in size. Before leaving the office, she turned to Reece. "Though you quit my employ and wish to leave Ocean's Rest, I need you here."

Medias frowned. She knew Reece was thinking of leaving, but thought she'd reconsidered. The empath had failed to share her decision with Medias and it stung.

Reece narrowed her eyes. "I don't understand what you want from me, Lilliana, but I can't be your empath-on-a-leash anymore."

Lilliana's jaw tightened. "That's not what you are to me, Reece."

"What I am is immaterial. I have no future here."

Lilliana sighed. "Resign your post, that's fine, but don't leave Ocean's Rest. It's your home, and until things are resolved, I'd like you to remain and stay safe."

"Resolved? You mean when Nyssa is dead."

The room, heavy with tension, was suddenly the last place Medias wanted to be. She was intruding, watching a family expose its ugly parts.

Lilliana tightened her arm around Athen. "House Fennick needs to present a united front."

"Strange, *now* I'm part of House Fennick," Reece sneered.

"You always were," Lilliana said, her face softening. "Regardless of what you think of me, you *are* my daughter."

Reece swallowed, her expression settling into a hard glare. "Enough of a daughter to claim as a member of House Fennick, but not enough to lead."

"Please reconsider. I want you to be safe." Lilliana bowed her head and left her office with Athen in tow.

Reece turned and walked back toward the window, looking out over the sparkling city. She said nothing, her mood dark.

Usually, Medias would be content to exist in silence. It was comforting, not having to navigate conversations and feelings and the meanings behind things, but now the silence set her on edge.

She hated seeing Reece so hurt.

Words of apology didn't come easy to her, but these words needed to be true. "I'm sorry for what I did to Athen. And to you."

Reece spoke, her jaw tight. "I know you were trying to protect us. To keep your word to Nyssa."

Medias scowled. "It's not just the promise anymore. We're all tangled up in this mess. Together."

"None of this is going to end well," Reece replied, bowing her head. "Nyssa is dying. Quinn is lost to us. I don't even know who I'm supposed to be anymore, and I..."

A sadness clung to Reece, and Medias didn't know what to say, grinding her teeth at her own social ineptitude. Lilliana spurning Reece had taken its toll.

Medias hesitated before crossing over to Reece, standing closer than perhaps she should, brushing her fingers over Reece's shoulder for a moment. "We...we will figure this out."

Reece turned, her face dark and unreadable. "Will we?"

"Do you trust me?" The question tumbled out, full of hope and danger.

Without hesitation, Reece said, "Yes."

"Then—then stay in the city. But not for Lilliana. Stay so I can keep you safe."

The second that Reece took to consider her words felt like an eternity. "Okay."

"Good," Medias said, doing a poor job of suppressing a smile. She turned and looked out the window, the lights of Ocean's Rest alive with warmth and promise.

AN ESCAPE

Quinn scrambled to her feet as a guard entered her cell. He put a tray of food down on the small table near the bed. It had been almost a month since they brought her to this room and she was careful to mark the days with small scratches in the wall below her lone window. In that time, she'd only seen two guards: Durlan and a woman. Quinn had asked the other guard her name but received no answer.

The female guard took Quinn to bathe and change her clothes three times a week. Quinn hated it, having to strip naked in front of a stranger and expose her scarred back, but she was thankful to be clean and have fresh clothes. It wasn't much, but it made her feel human, her freshly scrubbed skin pink and warm.

At night, Quinn tucked under her thin, scratchy blanket, trying to ward off the chill. The room had no fireplace, and Sarisan was taking a slow turn from winter to spring. When she asked Durlan for an extra blanket, he came back with a tattered cloak. Quinn pressed again and asked for a blanket, receiving a stiff punch in the gut as her answer.

It was that moment she learned Durlan was an asshole.

This night, as he put the tray down on the small desk, eying Quinn, his gaze drifted to her hands. She fidgeted with the toldoku on her wrist—a small, comforting habit.

"What is that thing?" Durlan asked.

Quinn let the sleeves of her cloak fall over her hands. "Nothing."

He strode over to her and grabbed her wrist, twisting it up for him to see. "It doesn't look like nothing." He tugged on the toldoku. Quinn pushed him away, fearing he'd take it from her. He grabbed at her again, catching the ring and little finger on her left hand instead of her wrist. With a sneer, he wrenched her fingers until they snapped.

Quinn cried out in pain and snatched her hand back, counterattacking with a strike to his chest, sending Durlan stumbling back. She had put force behind it, turning her hips as Nyssa had taught her.

Durlan snarled and came at her again, but she sidestepped him and punched him in the kidney. The man grunted and grabbed at his back. One more punch to his jaw put him on the ground.

Ignoring the throbbing pain of her broken fingers, Quinn darted to the open door and peered out.

No one was outside.

She ran.

Quinn slowed at the first cross hallway and peeked around the corner. An empty, dim corridor lay before her. She had no idea which way was out, but she had to keep moving to even have a chance of escaping.

She bolted down the hallway, her heart pounding in her chest.

Doors flanked her on both sides as she ran, slowing as she neared the end of the hallway. It terminated in a large, brightly lit room. Voices and laughter startled her, drifting from the room ahead of her. She pressed herself against the wall, scared of getting caught.

"Stop!"

Quinn cursed under her breath as Durlan limped down the hall, shouting after her. Her punch hadn't quite done the job. She wryly thought Nyssa would be so disappointed in her.

Without a second thought, Quinn pushed off the wall and ran into the large room.

The air left her lungs.

Suvi Rell sat on a stool in front of a large canvas, wine glass in one hand and a paintbrush in the other. Matthys sat on the opposite side of the room at a desk.

Quinn sprinted toward Suvi and tackled her, both women spilling to the floor. The wine glass shattered, red wine splashing on the pristine white marble floor beneath them. Matthys stood and yelled for the guards.

Quinn wasted no time, her rage driving her forward. "I'll fucking kill you!" she growled, scrambling on top of Suvi, glass crunching under her knees. The Queen's eyes began to pool black. Quinn reared back and slammed a fist into Suvi's jaw, breaking her concentration. Another punch bloodied the Queen's nose.

An intense gust of wind smacked into Quinn, and she tumbled off Suvi. She covered her eyes as the wind continued to crash against her, the force of it sending her sliding across the smooth marble floor and into a wall.

The wind let up for a moment, and Quinn staggered to her feet, using the wall to brace herself.

Footsteps echoed against the cold floor as guards ran in to help their queen.

Quinn centered herself. Escaping now wasn't an option, but she could still fight.

As a guard rushed at her, she sidestepped and let his momentum carry him into the wall. Then, she brought a vicious foot down on the back of his knee, and he cried out, crumpling to the floor.

Another guard went for his sword.

"Do not kill her!" Suvi shouted. "Take her alive, goddammit!"

Quinn slid to her left, keeping the wall behind her and the fight in front of her as Nyssa had taught. The guard stalked her and finally lunged forward. She seized his wrists and brought a knee up into his stomach, quickly followed by an elbow to his face.

"Matthys, will you kindly stop her so I don't have to bother?" Suvi asked, wiping the blood off her face. She glanced up at Quinn and smirked.

Matthys raised his arms, and Quinn rushed forward, hoping to catch him before he could call his magick forth, but he was too fast. Wind slammed into her, knocking her back against the wall with a loud thud. She pushed off, and Matthys hit her again with a torrent of air. Her skull slammed into the wall's stone surface, the breath completely forced out of her body.

Though wobbly and blinking stars out of her eyes, Quinn waved Matthys forward.

Nyssa's words rang in her head: *Use your words as weapons. Insult your opponent, get them off their game.*

Quinn didn't think herself much of a shit talker, but she tried to summon her best Nyssa impression.

"I'm in a void collar and you won't fight me with your fists instead of your magick? Fucking coward," Quinn spat.

Another gust of air hit her and her whole body vibrated from the impact. She crumpled to her knees. Guards grabbed her arms, yanking her to her feet. Her head lolled against her chest, darkness creeping in, threatening to pull her under. She shook her head, willing herself to stay conscious. *I need to fight...escape.*

She lifted her head and found Suvi's pale-green eyes staring at her.

"I had hoped to enjoy a rare bottle of wine tonight and paint, but here you are, in my sitting room." Suvi ran a hand lazily through her blonde hair and gestured behind her to the canvas that had been knocked to the ground. It was splattered with wine, paint, and ichor. "You've ruined what was going to be a lovely seaside landscape. Rather annoying."

Quinn grinned and spat blood on Suvi's expensive-looking dress, happy to further ruin her day.

Suvi sighed and struck Quinn with a short, cruel jab that bloodied her nose. Didn't break it, though.

"Just kill me," Quinn mumbled through a fog of pain.

Suvi shook out her fist and raised an eyebrow at Quinn. "Never. You're far too valuable. Did you really think you could escape?"

Quinn exhaled, a fine mist of crimson peppering the air before her. "Escape? I was just looking for an extra blanket."

Suvi let out a caustic laugh. "Does anyone find your smart mouth amusing?"

"No," Quinn breathed, then smiled. "Well, maybe one person."

"Blacksea? I can't imagine she's doing well. Rumor has it she's disappeared from Ocean's Rest. She's not long for the world, your friend. Or was she more than that?"

Quinn gritted her teeth. "Keep her name out of your mouth."

"Ah, so she was. Intriguing."

"She's probably on her way back here to kill you."

Suvi shrugged. "It would be best if you put such silly notions out of your head. And Blacksea out of your heart."

"Fuck you."

The self-satisfaction was evident on Suvi's face. So smug.

"Your friends are scattered to the winds and Blacksea is likely dead. You are alone in the world."

"Any more alone than you?" Quinn asked, her stomach tying itself into knots at the thought of Nyssa being dead.

For a moment, Suvi's mask of conceit slipped, revealing a small flash of anger. "A brazen assumption."

"I can recognize my own kind," Quinn replied.

The Queen sighed. "You are rather tiresome and need to be taught a lesson." Suvi's eyes ran over the guards, and she smiled at the largest. "You will do nicely."

The guard exhaled and jerked slightly, his eyes turning black. Suvi turned to Quinn, her eyes pools of ink.

"I won't break anything, Quinn. But I will make you regret this day."

Suvi stepped away and the large guard took her place. Before Quinn could brace herself, the guard buried a fist in her midsection, forcing the breath out of her lungs.

Quinn gasped for air.

Another punch slammed into her temple, and stars filled her eyes.

The punches kept coming, one after another after another.

Quinn's legs gave out quicker than she would have liked. The guards next to her had to hold her up. More strikes rained down, layering pain on top of indignity.

She refused to make a sound.

When Ceril had whipped her, she held out as long as she could before crying out in agony. She wouldn't give Suvi the satisfaction.

"I think that's enough," the guard and Suvi said in concert. The man's eyes faded to normal again, and he stepped aside, blinking rapidly in the wake of being controlled by his queen.

Quinn stared at Suvi through her pain, refusing to look away.

Suvi met her gaze, her red lips a thin, unwavering line. She turned and walked to her ruined painting, picking up the canvas and *tsking* at it. "At least your day is now worse than mine, Quinn."

"You think you can't be broken the same way you break others?" Quinn mumbled.

"Take her to her room."

The guards dragged Quinn through the halls. She hung her head and watched her blood drip to the floor as they pulled her along.

Once back in her room, the guards threw her on her cot.

After they left, she abandoned any pretense of showing strength and groaned from the pain in her ribs, her pride buckling. She had taken kicks from Nyssa that had hurt, but nothing like this. She pulled her flimsy blanket up around her, hissing from the pain. It had only been a month of captivity, but she knew she wouldn't survive like this for long.

As she breathed, she felt a slight twinge of pain in her chest, a small, dark ache separate from the pain in her ribs. She lay back and stared at the ceiling, avoiding closing her eyes. Her dreams since imprisonment were shattered and desolate, filled by the moment she took Nyssa's magick—her power twisting up inside of Nyssa, ripping the magick out, condemning her to a slow, agonizing death.

Now Quinn felt death inside of her, growing.

Nyssa's displaced magick was killing her.

Tears streamed down her temples, into her hair, her mind drifting back to the one place it frequently revisited: her last argument with Nyssa as they awaited their fate in the depths of the capitol building. Quinn remembered how Nyssa crossed the vast chasm between the two of them and kissed her, wildly turning everything upside down.

An ache careened through Quinn. She would never see Nyssa again. She would never be able to tell Nyssa what she meant to her.

Quinn tried to take a deep breath, her ribs twinging when she did. She winced, causing the split in her bottom lip to throb. But she didn't mind the sting. Pain was good. Pain distracted her. It turned her mind away from Nyssa and that kiss.

Pain was an escape.

THE HAWK AND THE HUMMINGBIRD

A proper, upstanding adept—with royal pedigree, no less—would never dare break into the Wayland Conservatory. It was not an act Aryis had ever seen herself doing. But there were many things she hadn't considered doing—like leaving Athen, betraying Nyssa and Quinn, and turning her back on her birthright.

Aryis swallowed hard as she crouched low and zipped from tree to tree through the Orchard Courtyard near the back-left wing of the sprawling Conservatory estate. Leaves crunched under her feet, each one bringing a wince to her face.

Getting caught was out of the question.

Getting caught meant an arrest for trespassing and an end to her attempt to help Nyssa.

Her heart beat faster as she ran, sweat popping up on her brow. By the time she reached the wall of the Grand Library, she was struggling to breathe. She slid down the wall and fell forward onto her hands.

Being at the Conservatory brought back that day and the horror of watching adepts turn on her, able to do nothing but barely stop them from killing her.

That day...that *horrific* day...

White static noise roared in her ears, and she clutched at her chest, her heart now thudding against her rib cage.

Why did I think I could come back here?

Aryis squeezed her eyes shut against her stinging tears and sat back on her heels, trying to get her breathing under control.

Passing out would spell disaster.

Voices nearby startled her. She pressed up against the wall, retreating as far into the shadows as she could, cushioned by the ivy that clung to the brick. Two guards came up the path beside her, so close that if they turned to their right, they would spot her.

Every muscle in her body tensed, and her mind screamed for the guards to continue on their rounds, willing them not to notice her. She held her breath as one of them lit his thin cigar, his face illuminated for a second by the flame. Sweet tobacco smoke wafted over Aryis.

Seconds seemed to stretch on for an eternity, but finally, the guards resumed their rounds.

Twisting around to face the wall, Aryis closed her eyes and concentrated. She had held her brother's key in her hand on numerous occasions, but it wasn't like a book. She always stuck to summoning books. Books were safe.

Warmth tingled across her hands as she focused on the key, remembering the cool, smooth feel of it under her fingers.

Aryis sensed the key, impossibly far away. It was likely tucked away in a drawer in Vykas's room back at her father's estate in Frosland, a relic of his time at the Conservatory. She had ended his tenure as well on that one horrific day last winter.

She opened her eyes, doing her best to use her body to hide the cascading shower of golden sparks that accompanied summoning an item. A round metal disk appeared in her palm, its golden surface bearing an evergreen tree, the seal of the Conservatory. Aryis exhaled, closing her hand around it, and searched along the wall until she reached a slight indentation in the stone with a round metal plate in the middle. She pressed the key against it.

A second passed before the outline of a door began to glow with a deep-blue luminescence.

Aryis pushed the key deeper into the plate, and the door clicked and swung open. She slipped inside, taking one final look behind her to ensure no one had spotted her.

Once inside, she closed the door and stilled, her ears on alert. Tucked in the corner of the library, only a few people knew about the hidden door. Like Ocean's Keep, the Conservatory had its architectural secrets. And as with Ocean's Keep, Aryis had memorized every single one.

She moved forward and poked her head out of a small nook situated in the corner of the library. The familiar, comforting scent of books brought a smile to her face. Hours upon hours had been spent in the Grand Library, its books her best friends for over a decade.

The library lay quiet. Rows upon rows of tall bookshelves rimmed the room, with tables and chairs filling the middle. Overhead, moonlight streamed through the windowed ceiling. She mouthed the names of the constellations she recognized from years of study, their formations imperceptibly changing as the seasons shifted from one to the next.

She lowered her gaze, focusing on the adepts dotting the room. They sat at dark reddish-brown mahogany tables, the surfaces worn from centuries of study. Aryis had her favorite table, the patterns of its wood and scratches etched into her memory. The same dark wood paneled the walls and comprised the shelves. At night, the wood reflected the soft-yellow glow of the light orbs, bathing the library in a warm orange radiance.

Aryis pulled her hood up to obscure her face. She would have to cross through the main library to get to the Rare Collections Room, in full sight of anyone spending all night studying. She crossed over to a line of bookshelves, removing several books. No one would take a second look at an adept with a load of books in her arms. Taking a deep breath to settle her nerves, she set about walking across the room, tightly hugging the edge of the bookcases. They seemed to stretch on forever. When she was an adept, she welcomed the endless bookshelves and all she could learn from their contents. Now, she relished getting past them as quickly as possible.

Finally, Aryis reached the end of the room and turned to her right, following the worn brick wall into the narrow corridor that led to the Rare Collections Room. Before going any farther, she stopped and waited, listening to see if anyone had followed her. She gave it two minutes, just to be sure, before continuing down the dim hallway.

Aryis exhaled and pressed Vykas's key against the door. It unlocked and she slipped inside. The Rare Collections Room was the one place she was never allowed to see. Now, after desperately breaking into the Conservatory, she'd finally lay eyes on the one room she always wanted to explore.

She found a light orb and slid her hand across it, spilling a golden glow over the room.

When she got a good look at the vaunted Rare Collections Room, her shoulders slumped forward. Maps and loose papers lay strewn about on tables, and books were stacked in sloppy piles everywhere, including the floor. Dust tickled Aryis's nose, and she stifled a sneeze, letting out an exasperated sigh.

The one room at the Conservatory she was dying to explore was a disordered mess.

"Fuck," she breathed.

Aryis glanced around to get her bearings before rifling through a loose stack of maps. She found maps of Thu'Dain and Sarisan far quicker than she had anticipated, given the disarray. The map to Suvi's estate was very detailed—save for the grayed-out areas that were filled with question marks and guesses from the mapmakers. Areshi spies were good but hadn't been able to get a full layout of the house and its surrounding buildings.

Good enough.

She rolled up the maps and secured them with twine.

Old wooden cabinets spanned a wall, each one filled with a column of drawers, their brass knobs rubbed dull through years of use. The Hummingbird had to be in one of them, but there seemed to be no discernible cataloging system.

Aryis sighed. She could be at this all night, and if she wasn't done by the time the sun came up, she'd be trapped.

"How did this room just...get like this?" she groused. Such priceless items shouldn't be treated so carelessly.

She took a deep breath, stifled another sneeze, and got to work, moving from cabinet to cabinet. She pulled out drawers and carefully poked through the contents, wary of setting off any wards or traps. The Hummingbird was a rare trinket, rumored to have been crafted and enchanted at Ellanholme over the course of several years. How it came to be in Wayland's possession was a mystery.

Several times during her search, Aryis had to remind herself to focus and not get distracted by an item that sparked her interest. After many opened drawers and a handful of stifled sneezes, she opened a box stuck in the back of a drawer. Inside lay a small silver object in the shape of a hummingbird.

She indulged in a relieved sigh.

Aryis closed the box and picked up the book next to it—details about the Hummingbird's construction and instructions for its use, the handwriting inside inelegant. She put the box and the book into her bag, made sure the maps were snuggly wrapped up, and slung the bag over her shoulder. Giving the room one last look, she turned off the light orb and slipped out the door.

The main room of the Grand Library was thankfully empty since she had been searching into the early morning. She hurried across the room and back out the side door she had entered, careful to check for guards.

Outside, the waning night was cool and still, the only sound the chirping of insects. Aryis pressed against the door and exhaled before darting into the night, silently whispering a final goodbye to the only home she'd known.

HOLLOW

Nyssa tossed her cards down. The assholes around her shouted, slamming their fists on the table and sloshing their drinks about. She quickly rescued her pint of beer, taking several deep swallows before she raked a pile of gold coins her way.

The beer dulled her pain and winning gave her a short-lived buzz of victory—the only two escapes she had left. She had hopped on a train, got off at Whitreach, and found the seediest tavern in the darkest part of the city, one with cheap but passable beer. She'd settled in for a long—or short—stay, intent on drinking and gambling herself to death.

Though a new face, the bar's clientele deemed a drunk stranger with plenty of gold to lose not worth killing. Their thin tolerance endured as Nyssa kept turning up to drink and gamble night after night, her chin covered with makeup to hide the Mark of the Unworthy. It was far less expensive than the temporary and illegal face-altering enchantments that floated around the black market and only lasted an hour or two.

Ossie, the owner of the bar, rented Nyssa a sparse room above his less than fine establishment. She overpaid for the dim, drafty room, but she didn't mind. The convenience of stumbling up to her bed at night was worth every gold mark she spent.

On this night, the tenor of the bar was slightly off. She was winning too many hands, but she wasn't sober enough to care if someone saw fit to slide a knife into her gut.

Die now, die in a month, what did it matter? Dying was dying.

Nyssa exacerbated the gamblers' anger by running her mouth, and their begrudging coexistence turned surly.

"A round for the table!" she yelled to the bartender. "These assholes keep shoveling their gold my way, I should give a little back."

The men and women around the card table grumbled about her.

Nyssa laughed and downed the rest of her beer. As fresh pints were brought to the table, a man sat down next to her and draped his arm across the back of her chair.

"You been in here a lot, lovely. You lonely?" he asked.

The scent of earthy tobacco wafted off of him. He was somewhat attractive, if a bit skinny for her tastes. At least he was clean—which was saying a lot for this part of town.

"Your boss sent a woman yesterday," Nyssa replied. "Same answer. I'm not looking for company."

"You sure? You look like you could use a good fuck. I could put some color back in those cheeks."

Nyssa sighed and drained half of her beer. The ache in her bones waned, and the cold receded slightly as the alcohol warmed her stomach.

It wouldn't last long.

"I'm fucking sure," Nyssa replied.

The man turned to leave, but Nyssa grabbed his crotch under the table and twisted. He grunted in pain.

"Return my coin purse or I'll snap your dick clean off," she slurred.

Nyssa felt the man slip her coin bag back inside her jacket. She shoved him away. "Tell your boss that the next one of you he sends is coming back with broken fingers." The prostitute hurried away, walking gingerly.

By the end of the night, Nyssa was still up in winnings, even after playing several poor hands, trying to give some of the money back to her unfortunate opponents. Groaning after drinking herself into oblivion, she stumbled up to her room and fell face-first onto her bed, trying to will the room to stop moving.

As the room spun, so did her mind. She had left so much of herself behind—pieces here and there.

Part of her was left at the Emerald Order with Athen, laughing at his silly jokes as he worked on a new recipe in the kitchen.

Part of her left in Ocean's Rest with Reece, in her bed, curled up and safe in her arms.

Part of her on Hannah's Whisper, working among the crew and trying to learn their sea shanties.

And part of her left behind in Thu'Dain, trembling in pain on the floor of Suvi Rell's throne room, her magick destroyed by the woman she....

Nyssa scrunched her body into a ball and pushed Quinn out of her head. The hollow loneliness that accompanied thoughts of her was too difficult to bear.

Everyone around her had gotten hurt—Athen, Aryis, Reece, and Quinn had all suffered because of her. She just wanted to let go of the world as it slowly let go of her.

What had Suvi called her? *Unfulfilled destiny.*

Clasping her eyes tight, Nyssa pulled her blanket around herself and hoped to fall asleep before she started shivering again.

Nyssa groaned awake, her head pounding. She opened her eyes, and the world shifted beneath her. It took her a moment to realize she was hanging by her wrists, her toes barely touching the floor as she swayed back and forth.

"What the fuck?"

A copper taste lingered in her mouth. She lolled her head back and peered up. Her wrists were tied by a rope that led into the rafters high above her. Light orbs dotted the beams, shining down in patches, making her eyes sting. Cold, hard steel encircled her neck, an unwelcome yet familiar feeling—a void collar. Whoever put it on her had wasted their time. There was no magick left to suppress in her rickety body.

"The Unworthy bitch awakens!" a man said, stepping into a ring of light. Middle aged and paunchy, he wore a sword at his side.

Two more men stepped from behind him and smiled. "We're gonna be rich if you be right about this one, Bowman," the younger man said. The other one, dressed in a dark suit, tossed Nyssa's rucksack on the ground.

Bowman pulled a crumpled piece of paper out of his back pocket and unfolded it. Her pulse quickened at Quinn's face on the paper.

"That's not her," the young man said over Bowman's shoulder.

"No shit."

Bowman placed his hand on the paper and drew his fingers down the page. The surface shimmered, the drawing morphing into a sketch of Nyssa's face, her name coalescing in large black print under her likeness. A dual bounty notice.

He held it up to Nyssa. The reward for her had increased to an insane amount of one million gold marks.

"You been lucky up until now, girl. Whorin' and gamblin' underneath our noses," Bowman said.

"I haven't been whoring," Nyssa clarified.

Bowman buried a fist in her ribs. She sputtered out a cough through a strangled gasp of pain.

"That's a big bag of gold you got. That and the price on your head will set us up for life."

Nyssa snorted. "The bounty for me went up? One million now? I'm impressed with myself."

The men shook their heads. They were unmoved.

Pity.

She continued, "Aren't you fuckin' lucky? Maybe you could splurge on a hot bath. I can smell you from here."

Bowman punched her again. Her muscles convulsed as she gulped for air.

"You got a mouth on you, Unworthy. And you get careless when in your cups. Bit of face paint rubbed off—enough for Ossie to see that mark. Imagine his surprise to have a wanted traitor under his roof."

"I'm sure that bastard will get a nice fat cut of your bounty," Nyssa grunted.

"Finder's fee. We don't mind taking care of Unworthy trash." Bowman slid his hand over the bounty notice, and Quinn's face shimmered into view. He held it up to her again. "Where's the other cunt?"

Nyssa snarled. "None of your fucking business. And watch your fucking mouth when you talk about her."

The man in the suit stepped up and unsheathed a knife from his belt. "Another million gold marks says she's very much our business." He was tall and skinny, like a blade of overgrown grass. Dapper, unlike the other two, with a wolf's smile. He passed his blade in front of Nyssa's eyes before he reached down, pulled her shirt up, and pressed the tip of his knife against her stomach. "Shush now," he hissed.

Nyssa gritted her teeth as he slowly pushed it into her skin, trying hard not to jerk away and make it worse. Sweat popped up on her brow, in odd contrast to the cold wracking her body.

"I won't kill you, but I know where to cut to make it hurt," he said quietly.

Nyssa let out a pained groan as the man pulled the blade along her flesh, widening the cut. Hot blood ran down her skin.

"Where is this Quinn?" he asked.

Nyssa bared her teeth. "*Fuck. You.*"

The man withdrew the blade and moved around to her back. He pressed the tip of the knife against her skin. She closed her eyes and waited for the pain.

"That's the thief that stole my gold!" a voice shouted.

Nyssa's eyes flew open. A woman walked into the ring of light as the men took a step back.

Aryis *fucking* Devitt.

Aryis stared up at Nyssa and frowned, then thrust her chin out. "This one here offered me a good time the other night, then stole my coin purse. I thank you gentleman very much for returning it to me."

Nyssa wanted to laugh. The damned idiot was going to get herself killed.

"You know what she is?" Bowman asked.

"A thief, I dare say!" Aryis replied.

"Unworthy scum," he said, spitting at the ground at Nyssa's feet. "That traitorous bitch, Nyssa Blacksea."

Aryis glanced at Nyssa with interest. "I heard about the Unworthy. First one in forever...and supposed to be some sort of weird god? This...this is her?"

The man nodded. "Murdered a gaggle of Justiciars, and now the Empress wants her bit o' skin."

"Oh, that doesn't sound pleasant. I will just take my coin purse back and you can have her to yourselves." Aryis tried to put some authority in her voice.

"Sorry, girlie, we took the gold off her. You have no claim to it."

Aryis swallowed, her eyes flicking about the room, likely trying to find a solution to being outmanned. Talon hung on her belt, but the blade wasn't hefty enough to cut the thick ropes around Nyssa's wrists quick enough. The bounty hunters would be on her in a second if she tried.

Aryis cocked her head. "Very well, but I want one shot at this bitch before I leave. I think breaking the nose of a god will make for a good story. What say you, boys? Just give me a taste?" Aryis smiled at the men, and Nyssa saw a look in her eye that she had never seen before. It was almost...seductive?

The men grinned at one another and Bowman gestured at Nyssa. "Have a go. Just don't break your hand, darlin'. You don't look like you know how to throw a punch." The men walked over to a table, perching atop to watch.

"Oh, you'd be surprised what I know how to do." Aryis smirked and approached Nyssa, picking up a small crate and planting it in front of her. She stepped on top of it to meet Nyssa at eye level, and the bounty hunters laughed.

Aryis scowled, hissing "Stall!" at Nyssa under her breath.

Nyssa grunted, meeting Aryis with a cocky grin. The woman must be insane, but she'd play along. "I bet you punch like a sickly child," Nyssa mocked. "I knew from the looks of you that you and your gold were easily parted."

The men chuckled.

Aryis shook out her hands and held them in front of her stomach, tight to her body. "Oh really? You won't be so smart with a broken nose," she taunted.

Nyssa laughed, trying to buy time for whatever Aryis had planned. She hated the woman, but she didn't deserve to die in some dusty warehouse. And undoubtedly, that's where this foolish charade was headed.

Aryis's hands began to spark with golden magick.

"Are you seriously summoning a goddamn book right now?" Nyssa hissed through her teeth.

Aryis closed her eyes, and a form began to take shape. Only it wasn't a book. Nyssa couldn't believe her eyes.

"Hey, girl, what ya playin' at over there?"

Aryis opened her eyes. She held Winter's Bite in her hands.

"Gods, I did it!" she gasped, beaming at Nyssa.

"Cut the goddamn rope!" Nyssa yelled.

Aryis took a wild swing at the ropes above Nyssa's head. An instant later, Nyssa dropped to the ground, her hands free and thankfully still attached to her body. She scrambled to her feet and moved next to Aryis, reaching to take Winter's Bite.

"I did it." Aryis smiled.

"You did," Nyssa said, thankful that the gambit paid off. The bounty hunters hopped off the table and advanced on them.

"Does your little bounty paper there tell you I was once an Ashcloak?" Nyssa asked. "What chance do you think you have of living past your next heartbeat?"

Nyssa paused before lunging forward, Winter's Bite singing through the air. Two bodies dropped to the dusty floor. She turned to Bowman, who fumbled for his sword. With a smirk, Nyssa struck at him quicker than he could respond, his sword never leaving its sheath.

He toppled over with his hand clutching at his slit throat and Nyssa stood watching him for a moment, his blood pulsing slower and slower out of his neck until his heart stopped. She picked through his jacket pockets, finding the key to the void collar. She turned him over with her foot and pulled the bounty notice out of his back pocket, sliding it into her jacket.

After fishing her coin purse off the other man, she knelt next to him and wiped Winter's Bite clean on his pants.

Nyssa slumped forward and sucked in air, exhausted from the effort of killing. Her body wasn't up for it. She grunted as she rose to her feet and turned around.

Aryis blinked at her and took a step back. A flicker of hate burned inside of Nyssa, but she was too tired and cold and weary of the burden of her anger to do anything about it.

She broke the silence. "How did you call Winter's Bite to you? You've only done books before."

Aryis swallowed. "I've been expanding my skill set, though never with an object as big as a sword."

"Where's my scabbard?"

"Back in my room at a nearby inn."

Nyssa scowled. "Then how did you pinpoint where I was if you didn't have the sword on you?"

Aryis held up her right hand. Nyssa's Kraken ring sat on her middle finger. "Medias gave me your sword and ring. She told me I needed to do something other than read myself blind trying to figure out how to cure you."

"Fucking Justiciar," Nyssa said, tossing the void collar's key to Aryis. "Get this goddamn thing off me."

Aryis approached Nyssa slowly, her hands trembling as she turned the key in the lock. When it clicked open, Nyssa tore the collar off her neck and flung it across the room.

"Why are you here?" she asked, advancing on Aryis.

Aryis swallowed and stepped back. "I think I know a way to rescue Quinn."

Nyssa contemplated punching the woman—her betrayer—but thought better of it. She didn't have the energy. Instead, she picked up her rucksack and slung it over her shoulder.

"Fuck you," she mumbled before walking out into the night.

STALEMATE

Nyssa shuffled along, trying to put distance between her and Aryis, but she wasn't strong or fast anymore. Her body rebelled, aching. Creaking like a rotting floor.

Aryis ran after her. "Wait! I have a room in a quiet inn. Let's just go there, get some rest, and I can tell you about my plan. Please, give me a chance."

Nyssa wanted nothing more than to leave Aryis behind, but a warm bed that wasn't above a loud, smelly tavern sounded tempting—plus, she had nowhere else to go. If Aryis needed shutting up, a swift punch in the mouth would do.

"Where is this inn?" she asked.

Aryis pointed toward a building on the next block.

"Fuck," Nyssa sighed. "Okay."

She followed Aryis to the inn. The room was small but cozy—a couple chairs, a table, and a large bed with a number of thick blankets on it. An upgrade over the thin mattress and scratchy bedding in her room at the bar. She spotted her scabbard on the bed and tossed Winter's Bite down next to it before turning back to Aryis.

"Why are you really here?"

"I need to make things right between you and I."

"You don't get to work your penance out through me. I don't owe you that."

"I'm going to help you regardless."

Nyssa lunged forward, twisting her fists into Aryis's coat and throwing her down on the small table. She reached between them, snatched Talon out of its sheath, and held it to Aryis's throat.

"I'm dying. Athen is half blind. Quinn is Suvi's prisoner. All because of you! Why would I ever trust you again?" Nyssa pressed Talon against Aryis's throat. A bead of blood formed on the tip of the dagger.

Aryis gritted her teeth. Her eyes wavered, filling with tears. The woman Nyssa had once known—the naïve, enthusiastic adept who had endless questions and a bottomless pit of curiosity—was gone. Nyssa felt a pang of sadness for that friend, the one who got lost somewhere along the way.

But that sadness was washed away by something far darker. An ache for revenge.

Aryis didn't fight back. "Kill me if you need to, but I'm here to help. I swear on my life."

"Your life is meaningless to me," Nyssa whispered. The insult spawned an immediate pang of regret. Her need for revenge clashed with whatever affection remained in her heart for her estranged friend.

Bowing her head, she backed off and tossed Talon down on Aryis's chest.

Aryis slowly stood up, her breathing ragged, and walked to the bed to pick up Winter's Bite and sheathe it, her hands trembling. She placed both her dagger and Nyssa's sword down on the bed, sitting next to them.

Nyssa spotted a bottle of whiskey on the bedside table and picked it up, wrenching the cork out with her teeth.

"If you could use a—"

Nyssa spat the cork out and took a swig of the dark liquid.

"—glass," Aryis finished.

When the whiskey hit Nyssa's stomach, she closed her eyes and savored the temporary warmth that snaked through her body. She lifted up her shirt and splashed a bit of the liquor on the gash the bounty hunter left in her side, hissing at the sharp burn.

Nyssa dropped into a chair, resting the bottle on her thigh. She locked Aryis in her gaze.

"What did Medias tell you to get you chasing after me?" Nyssa finally asked.

"She said that our journeys converge. But that was all. She's not…terribly forthcoming about her visions."

Nyssa rolled her eyes. "No, she is not."

"I know I'm the last person you want to see. I'm sure you'd much rather kill me than listen to me, but I think I know a way to—"

"Shut up. I just want to sit here and drink."

Nyssa reached into her jacket and pulled out the bounty notice she took off of Bowman. Her own face stared back at her—a remarkably accurate rendering, though the woman on the paper was healthy. Full and ruddy. A far cry from her current state.

She hovered her hand over the paper before drawing her fingers down the page. Her likeness shimmered and faded, replaced by Quinn's face. Nyssa's breath caught. Quinn's green eyes stared up at her, her dark hair falling in waves, framing her face.

Nyssa gently touched the paper before folding it back up and putting it in her jacket. She took a long pull of whiskey and leaned her head back against the chair, her soul and body weary down to her toes.

Aryis rubbed the small nick on her neck where Nyssa had pushed Talon up against her skin, and her fingers came away bloody. How her stomach had plunged in that moment, fearing the worst.

But even after everything that had transpired, Aryis still trusted Nyssa. Trusted her code of honor. Her unfailing heart.

Nyssa had fallen into a cold silence, the weight of Aryis's betrayal hanging in the air between them, presenting a yawning chasm that Aryis had no idea how to traverse.

"I didn't want things to end up this way," she said. "You didn't like me when we first met, but we sparked a friendship. Now I've jeopardized our bond."

Nyssa stared at the bottle in her hand. "We don't have a bond. Not anymore. Not after what you fucking did."

"I didn't have a choice...but I'll fix it. I'll fix us."

After a long pull of whiskey, Nyssa whispered, "There is no fixing us. I'll *never* trust you again."

Aryis wanted Nyssa to understand how everything had spun out of her control and gone so wrong. She knitted her fingers together, leaned forward on the bed, and started talking.

"You asked me how I got this." Aryis touched the scar that ran down her jawline. "I was giving a lecture at the Wayland Conservatory when...something unspeakable happened."

Aryis swallowed and quietly told the story of her students turning into mindless killers, compelled by some forbidden magick. As she dove into her story, dread churned in her gut. The horror of that day was so close to the surface. Too close. As she neared the end of her retelling, she found her hands trembling.

She balled them into fists.

"I had to kill innocent children, Nyssa. They were going to tear me apart. And there was this boy, Rustam...he was the only one not affected. I tried to get him out of the room. I tried...but he slipped from my grasp. He was pulled away from me by the other adepts. I...I cannot get his screams out of my head." She swallowed back the cold lump of guilt that stuck in her throat. "I failed him. And I'm scared I'll fail again and those that I love will suffer—my family, my friends, my people...I'm supposed to be a queen, but all I can do every day is not fall apart from the thought of letting something slip through the cracks; of letting someone slip out of my fingers..."

Aryis stopped. She put a shaky hand to her chest and cleared her throat, tears in her eyes. She hadn't even said this much to Athen, preferring to suffer alone so he didn't know her shame.

Nyssa's face was tense, her jaw clenched, eyes dark.

"I didn't know Suvi would hurt you like that," Aryis said. "Or imprison Quinn."

Nyssa exhaled a shallow breath. "How are you so naïve? What did you think she was going to do with us?"

Aryis placed her elbows on her knees, resting her head in her hands. She was exhausted. The stress and guilt of what she had done seeped into the fibers of her being, plaguing her with sleeplessness.

"I love Athen. And I love you. But I also love my home and my people. My heart is pulled in so many directions, and I can't make everyone happy at the same time. My nation was facing starvation. How could I betray my father, my people, by saying no to Suvi? I saved Frosland, but I failed the ones I love the most. My heart aches so badly I want to rip it out." Aryis wiped the tears that streamed down her face. "I lost you and Athen." She buried her face in her hands.

The two of them sat there for a long while, the only sound Aryis's sobbing.

Then Nyssa finally spoke. "My actions—what I am, being a Cursed God—put you all in danger. It's my fucking fault." Nyssa's eyes dropped from Aryis's face. "You shouldn't have come here. I have nothing left to give you."

Aryis's heart ached. Nyssa looked lost. Had she really intended to just drink herself to death?

"Nyssa, this isn't you. You're a warrior. You fought for Quinn's freedom once before despite the risks. Help me free her again."

Nyssa raised her eyes to Aryis, the darkness in her expression gone, replaced by sadness. "Your heart has always been the biggest out of all of us. It was bound to end up shattered. And now we're all broken."

Aryis held Nyssa's gaze. "I'm so sorry Nyssa. I...I didn't know until I saw the way you look at Quinn." She hesitated, scared of saying what she suspected, but she pushed forward. "You're in love with her."

Nyssa shot to her feet, the bottle of whiskey clattering to the floor. She closed on Aryis, twisting her fists into the woman's sweater and yanking her off the bed.

"No!" Nyssa said, shaking with rage. "You don't get to know that. You don't get to say those words to me." Her face fell, pain and sadness replacing her anger. She shook her head as her eyes filled with tears. "You don't get to know that."

"I can help you get her back. You'll see her again. I won't leave your side until you do, I promise. And then you can do whatever you want to me."

"I didn't even tell her," Nyssa whispered.

She collapsed against Aryis, sobbing into her shoulder. Aryis didn't know what else to do but hold on. She couldn't imagine the churning emotions Nyssa felt on top of the slow, creeping pain of death.

Finally, Nyssa pushed away and wiped her eyes. "You did this to us," she murmured, before crawling onto the bed. She pulled a blanket around her and turned her back to Aryis.

No apology was ever going to close the chasm between them.

Aryis hung her head. She sat down on the opposite side of the bed and stayed still for a long time, listening to Nyssa's soft labored breaths.

AN INSANE PLAN

Nyssa woke up late, startled out of slumber by the sensation of falling. Her dreams of late were dark, fragmented. The familiar dream of being underwater, of feeling Quinn's presence, eluded her, replaced by slivers of nightmares. Night after night, she relived Quinn destroying her magick.

She sat up, grunting from the wound on her stomach, and reached down to check if she was bleeding again. A bandage was affixed to her side. Her boots were placed neatly by the bed. Aryis had taken care of her the night before, it seemed, and wrapped her in blankets, the chill in her bones somewhat abated by the layers of fabric.

As she buckled her boots, Nyssa patiently listened to Aryis launch into her plan to rescue Quinn. Her anger from the night before settled into a dull ache. No matter what Aryis had done, if there was a chance of getting Quinn back, Nyssa would hear her out before deciding what to do.

Aryis sat at the room's small table, eating her breakfast and going on about maps of Thu'Dain and a device called the Hummingbird she found in a dusty drawer at Wayland.

"Suvi's mansion is up on a cliffside and highly guarded. Unassailable. No way to get in using magick, as the Rells have traps for that," Aryis said around mouthfuls of egg. Nyssa's stomach growled, and she joined Aryis at the table.

Aryis pushed a full plate of food in front of her. "Eat. It'll keep your strength up. It's better than whiskey."

"Debatable," Nyssa grumbled before chewing on a piece of bacon. It would be her first decent meal in weeks. The tavern had barely passable food that Nyssa would pick at, preferring the drink. She tucked into her eggs. They were warm and fluffy and sorely needed.

Aryis continued, "So, with the estate protected by every ward imaginable, getting in is impossible. Unless we take a slight detour."

"Secret passageways, like in Ocean's Rest?"

Aryis shook her head. She placed a small black box on the table and opened it. On a bed of black velvet sat a round, silver object about two inches long. Nyssa took it out of the box.

Aryis sucked in a breath. "Please be careful with that…"

"Calm your tits," Nyssa groused. She turned the fat little bird over in her hands, bending its small metal wings forward and back. Thin, delicate lines were etched onto its body, and as Nyssa looked closer, she realized they were feathers. She tested the sharpness of its long, pointy beak, hissing as it almost pricked her finger. A thin silver chain was attached to its underside. In all, a very fine piece of metalwork.

"May I?" Aryis asked, picking up the Hummingbird from Nyssa's palm. She held on to the silver chain and twisted part of its body. The Hummingbird whirled to life with a metallic buzz and floated into the air, its ascension stopping when its chain tether drew taut.

"So, it's a flitter?"

Aryis pursed her lips. "Similar, but this isn't some shiny bauble that rich men and women adorn themselves with." She poked at the bird with her finger as it hovered, its wings a blur. "Another twist opens the portal."

Nyssa didn't like where this was going. "Portal?"

With a sigh, Aryis twisted the Hummingbird again, deactivating it. "Yes. A portal to the Realm of Shadows."

Nyssa stopped shoveling eggs into her mouth and stared. "Aryis, you have *got* to be fucking—"

"Hear me out!"

Nyssa tried to protest, but Aryis barreled on. "The Realm of Shadows lies on top of this world. You can move within it, leaving our world in one location and returning in another. For instance, if one wanted to break into an impenetrable mansion on a hill, you could enter the realm at a safe distance, traverse through the realm, and exit inside the estate. It's called shadowstepping. I read about it when I was a kid, but I just thought it was a fantasy. But it's not. It's just...not done anymore."

Nyssa stared at Aryis. "Are you fucking serious? This is forbidden magick."

"Partly, yes. Its magick creates tears in the Shimmer. The Humming-bird is specifically attuned to the Realm of Shadows. I think...I think it was created to attempt to control the realm."

Nyssa sat silent and tapped her finger against her coffee mug.

Only a fucking idiot would try to control a realm. No wonder the magickal bauble was left in a drawer.

Aryis cleared her throat and continued.

"If we do this, there are rules"—she placed a small book on the table—"outlined in here, but the gist is you keep your eyes front and center. You don't look down, you never look back. You just keep moving forward. The, uh, inhabitants of the Realm of Shadows won't bother you if you don't...uh...antagonize them."

Nyssa blinked. "Inhabitants?"

"Yes. They're not well-documented, so I don't exactly know what they are..."

With a boisterous laugh, Nyssa poured herself more coffee, dousing it with cream and sugar. "We're going to get killed, aren't we?"

Aryis exhaled heavily through her nose. "Nyssa, this is serious. When we go inside, you and I must be tethered to one another. If we get separated, one of us could get lost in there, and—this is *fucking* impor-tant—those who get lost never come back out."

Nyssa arched her eyebrows. Aryis rarely swore and only used it to punctuate rather important points. Duly noted.

"Well, I'm already dying, so it doesn't make much of a difference to me," Nyssa said, omitting her concern about Aryis's safety. "How do we know where we're going once inside the shadowy place?"

"This Hummingbird has a light that shines into our world. I think it's like looking through a dirty window. With the maps and the Hummingbird, we can navigate the estate, walking through solid objects that exist in our world, like walls. I...think. I don't exactly know if that's true. There's very little *actual* documentation."

"Well, what does the documentation *actually* say?"

Aryis shifted in her seat. "The Hummingbird was only used one time, so—"

"You're kidding me, right? This is a joke. A big, fat fucking joke. You want to do something that's only been attempted *once*? Do we even know if anyone lived?"

Aryis glanced at the Hummingbird. "Well, someone brought this back to our realm, so at least one person?"

Nyssa grunted. "Oh, so a *brilliant* success." She fell silent.

"So," Aryis said, a bit hesitant, "do you think you're willing to give this a try?"

"No." Nyssa waved her off. Shadowstepping was absolutely out of the question. They would certainly die. "You're fucking insane. You want to go into a dark realm full of scary, unknown things with rules like '*don't look back*' and you think this is doable?"

Aryis's face fell. Then she scowled and held Nyssa in an insistent gaze. "You know what, this was the best I could come up with given our constraints. Very little time, no allies to speak of, and a well-guarded estate that's impossible to get into. I'm trying here. And, this is the last damn thing anyone will expect." Aryis leaned back and crossed her arms.

She was proving to be rather spirited today. Back before her betrayal, it might have been a source of amusement.

Nyssa drank her coffee and considered Aryis's crazy plan. She could stay in Whitreach and drink until she passed out each night, waiting for death. Or she could give the Realm of Shadows a try and likely die a horrible death in some pit of terror. There would be screaming, but at least then it would be over quickly.

Though...if the plan actually worked and they got inside Suvi's estate...they could save Quinn. It gave Nyssa a spark of hope. She could do one last good, honorable thing before she died, even if it meant accepting Aryis's help.

She sighed. Saving Quinn was now the only thing that mattered. "Alright, let's give it a try."

Aryis smiled. "Thank you."

"Maybe I can make up for my parents' sins." A lump of regret choked Nyssa up. "And my own. We should never have brought Quinn back from Jejin. We should have let her go."

Aryis cast her eyes down. "I know."

Nyssa refilled her coffee mug. She didn't want to dwell on her own self-pity, nor indulge Aryis's.

"We need to get a message to Elias. Have him meet us at Avarest, then sail as far south as he'll take us," Nyssa said.

Worry passed over Aryis's face, but she nodded in agreement. No one on the Whisper would want her aboard, that was for certain, and that realization seemed to hit her quickly. Nyssa wasn't even sure if Aryis wouldn't be killed on sight.

Part of her didn't care.

"I'll get a message out to him, but how do I make it known it's from us without giving us away?" Aryis asked.

Nyssa thought for a moment, tapping her finger against her coffee cup before a smile spread across her face. It felt good to finally smile—and have purpose—after weeks of resignation.

"Say the message is from Stitches."

Aryis nodded and sat up straighter, her mood obviously brighter. She thrived with a mission, it seemed. "If I may suggest—respectfully—a hot bath? And give me your clothes so I can have them laundered before we leave?"

Nyssa sat back. Truthfully, hygiene had fallen by the wayside of late. Only drinking and gambling had concerned her. "Fine," she mumbled.

"We'll set out for Avarest tomorrow, then."

Aryis went about gathering clothes for the laundry service. Nyssa would suffer her long enough to rescue Quinn and then decide what to do with her betrayer.

BLOOD AND STONE

Quinn woke up and peeled herself off the floor, sliding over to the cold, gray wall. Her body protested every movement. Her last three escape attempts were all failures, each one earning a progressively more violent punishment until she was left unconscious and bloody on the floor of her cell at the end of her last beating.

She ignored the pain that wracked her body as she kept dipping her finger in the pool of blood on the floor. It would have to do as impromptu ink. Asking for a blanket had gotten her beaten, so requesting a sketchbook and charcoal was out of the question. Blood and stone would have to do. After a long while, Quinn stood up and limped back to examine what she had drawn.

The head of a buck with exquisite, twisting antlers stared back at her, its four eyes burning through her. Whatever the creature was and whatever it meant, it was the one image, aside from Nyssa, that had invaded her fractured dreams of late—a beautiful stark-white Caracor stag, its eyes burning white and a blaze of onyx fur on its massive chest. Darkness, not unlike her own, swirled around it and threaded through its antlers, rising into a night sky that shimmered with stars.

The door to Quinn's cell opened, and she jumped, bracing for another confrontation with Durlan. The female guard—who had finally revealed her name to be Krysh—entered and sighed at the sight of Quinn. She crossed the room and grabbed Quinn by the arm.

"No, don't—" Quinn objected.

The familiar warm vibration of healing magick wove through Quinn as Krysh mended her wounds.

"Do you heal me so Durlan can beat me again tomorrow?" Quinn asked with a sigh, pulling away from Krysh when she was done.

Krysh folded her arms across her chest. "You provoke him. Why don't you try to get past me?"

Grunting out a short laugh, Quinn replied, "It's best to know when some fights are already lost before they begin."

Krysh grasped Quinn's chin and examined her face. "You need to stop this. The Queen will be displeased at how much I have to heal you."

"We can't break Suvi's playthings, can we?" Quinn asked, dropping her eyes to the floor to hide her resigned anger.

Krysh cocked her head at the rough painting on the wall. "Not bad. What is it?"

"I wish I knew."

The guard turned, her dark eyes unreadable. Was this her job, keeping Quinn healed? Keeping watch to ensure she not die by her own hand?

"Let's clean you up." Krysh slipped a hand around Quinn's arm, her grip strong but not crushing, and steered her to the door.

Quinn glanced back at the stag's head on the wall, her blood already dried and black in the dim evening light.

INK AND SKIN

The crew of Hannah's Whisper ceased their activities when Nyssa stepped on the deck. They rushed forward to greet her. Elias swept her up in a hug, pulling away when an angry murmur rippled through the crew.

"What the fuck is that murderer doing on this ship?" Mina asked, pushing past Nyssa to give Aryis a rough shove.

Nyssa fought the impulse to stop the woman. She understood the anger. Jerrin was her man and was now dead because of Aryis. The crew gathered, raising their voices to object to her presence on their ship.

Elias looked on, his arms folded. Fontaine was nowhere to be seen.

"I'm sorry," Aryis said, pulling her cloak tight.

"Sorry? That's it, you're sorry?" Mina spat. "Jerrin is dead because of you!" Mina cocked a fist and let it fly, striking Aryis across the chin. Aryis spilled to the ground, her teeth bloody. Mina reared back and landed a kick in Aryis's mid-section.

Aryis let out a grunt of pain, but she didn't make a move to defend herself. She tried to get her arms underneath her to push back up to her feet, but she collapsed. Mina made to advance on her again, but Nyssa moved between the two women.

"Stop," she said, voice still and quiet, placing a hand on Mina's chest.

"Her people killed four of ours!"

Nyssa could tell Mina was teetering between rage and sorrow, a strange mix of emotions she herself was all too familiar with of late. "I know. Aryis has much to answer for, not the least of which is Jerrin's death. But she's got a plan to get Quinn back, and I'll kill anyone who gets in the way of that."

Mina's warm-brown eyes searched Nyssa's face. Finally, she nodded.

Nyssa put an arm around her. "I'm sorry for your loss, Mina. Jerrin was a stand-up man and a good friend. Tell me what I can do to honor him."

Mina wiped tears from her face. "Just bring Quinn back to us. You're both family."

"I will do my best." Nyssa let go of Mina and walked over to Aryis, bending over to help her to her feet.

"Thanks," Aryis mumbled, casting her eyes down.

Part of Nyssa hurt to see Aryis defeated like a whipped dog. But didn't she deserve every bit of pain and insult thrown her way? Four lives had been lost because of her.

"Get below deck. You'll stay with me," Nyssa said, her eyes drifting over the crew as they got back to their work.

After Aryis headed to her stateroom, Nyssa walked back to the quarterdeck with Elias, his arm around her.

"Where's Fontaine?" she asked.

"Finishing up some business in town. Once she's back, we're off."

"I owe the both of you a debt I will never be able to repay. You're mixed up in this mess my life has become. I never wanted to be a burden like this."

"You're one of us. We go all-in for our own."

A lump formed at the base of Nyssa's throat. "Well, I appreciate you all more than words can express."

"I can't say I'm happy to see Aryis on my ship again."

"I need her."

He grunted, his eyes troubled. "Careful with that one, Nyssa."

"I don't trust her, but she's the key to rescuing Quinn. Nothing is more important to me."

"Understood. It's important to me too. You should go below and get some rest."

Nyssa shook her head. "The sea air is good for me. It makes me feel a little less like I'm dying."

"Then stay here with me and keep me company." Elias smiled, bending over to gently kiss her forehead. "I won't complain, child of the Black Sea."

Settling in for the night, Nyssa attempted to ignore the constant dull pain that wracked her body. With her eyes closed, she let her mind wander, hoping to drop into sleep quickly.

Only sleep let her escape the pain and the hollow ache where Quinn's presence used to be.

"I noticed something when flipping through this," Aryis said, startling Nyssa. Aryis stepped over to her bed and crouched next to her, holding Quinn's book in her hands, a collection of poetry entitled *Songs of the Sea*. It was book Aryis used to track them down and capture them.

Nyssa clenched her jaw while Aryis thumbed through the pages, many of them filled with drawings in pencil and charcoal.

"Quinn loves to draw," Nyssa mumbled to herself.

"I read the whole book on the boat ride over to Jejin and this sketch wasn't here when we first went after her. I think she drew this after I returned the book to her in Ocean's Rest."

Aryis turned the book, and Nyssa's breath caught in her throat.

A massive Kraken filled the page, drawn in dark charcoal, fierce and imposing. A true god of the sea, its eyes colored a hue as blue as her own eyes. Nyssa blinked back tears at the beauty of the creature of the deep, drawn by a careful hand. *Nyssa Blacksea* was written in Quinn's handwriting underneath the drawing.

"She drew this for you," Aryis said.

Nyssa put her hand to her mouth, fighting back tears. Aryis stood and returned to the other bunk to lie down. Nyssa laid back and clutched Quinn's book to her chest, settling into an uneven sleep.

The next morning, Nyssa sought out Ebe, a senior member of the Whisper's crew. Nyssa had watched her tattoo some of the men and women on board. She was a talented tattooist and proud that she used the old methods of needle and ink. When Nyssa asked once why the crew didn't wait for painless tattoos from onshore mages who could imbue them, Buck had laughed at her.

"Ink and blood is the way of the—mmm—sea, Stitches. You gonna get one from Ebe?"

Nyssa had been intrigued at the time, her body already marked and scarred, but she could never settle on what tattoo to get. She smiled at the recollection as she sought out Ebe in the mess.

The room grew quiet when Nyssa entered. She sighed. "You all need to stop with that. I'm not dead yet. And I'm still a member of this crew. I need your bluster and bullshittery to make me feel normal. You won't offend me."

"Fuck if we won't try," Max said, drawing laughter from the crew. Nyssa smiled, appreciating him speaking up. He was the new boatswain after Jerrin's death, and the crew would look to him for guidance.

Nyssa sat down at Ebe's table and slid Quinn's book toward her. "Can you tattoo this on me exactly as it appears?"

"This one a' Quinn's? I've always liked her art."

Nyssa nodded.

Ebe squinted at the drawing and grinned. "'Course I can tattoo it, sweetheart. Where's it goin'?"

"Upper back?"

"When ya want it?"

"Ebe, I think you know the answer is as soon as possible," Nyssa said, flashing a half smile at the woman. She had leaned on that cheeky smile for years, knowing it could get her what she wanted a good deal of the time.

"You don't need to charm me, girl," Ebe said. "Get some food in you, and I'll get my needles and inks. Meet me up on the deck. Dress appropriately. I don't need you flashin' a tit at the crew while they try to work."

Later, underneath the mid-morning sun, Ebe worked her needle into Nyssa's skin, pausing to switch out colors, using black and shades of blue and gray to match Quinn's drawing. The pain was shocking at first, but turned strangely cathartic as Ebe tattooed her upper back. Nyssa's skin buzzed beneath the relentless vibration of the needle.

Ebe hummed as she worked, reminding Nyssa of Quinn. She was glad she faced the sea as Ebe inked her, not wanting the crew to see her cry like a baby at the ache Quinn's absence left inside of her. She had never felt so goddamned helpless, scared for Quinn's welfare. If Suvi had done anything to hurt her...

Ebe let Nyssa cry, taking a few breaks to give them both a rest. When she finished hours later, she wiped Nyssa's skin clear of excess ink and led her to a mirror below deck. Nyssa choked up when she saw her tattoo, unable to speak. Quinn's art, replicated painstakingly down to the last charcoal smudge, graced the skin between her shoulders. The Kraken rippled as Nyssa moved, its strength evident in the powerful tentacles that stretched over her shoulder blades. Intense blue eyes completed the tattoo, staring into her soul—a soul that was slowly dying.

"Ebe, it's...amazing. It's perfect," Nyssa whispered. She broke down, unable to contain the sadness roiling inside of her. Ebe wrapped her arms around her and let her cry.

"I'm turning into a weepy, sentimental fool," Nyssa said when she pulled away from the woman, wiping her tears away.

"You're not a fool, girl. You're allowed to hurt."

Nyssa smiled with gratitude. "Thank you, Ebe."

Settling back in her room, Nyssa flipped through the pages of Quinn's book, stopping at each sketch, trying to commit the artwork to memory.

When she got to the page with the Kraken, Nyssa scrounged up a pencil. She hoped Quinn wouldn't mind as she slowly added words to the page before closing the book and drifting off to sleep.

The morning after they sailed into the port of Le'Caal—as far south as Elias was willing to sail—Nyssa woke Aryis up and told her to pack to leave immediately. She wanted to slip off the ship and forgo the goodbyes. Honestly, her heart likely would break if she had to endure the sad faces of the crew one more time.

She and Aryis were halfway down the gangplank when Fontaine's voice cut through the dark, damp morning fog. "You're getting rather good at sneaking off the Whisper."

Nyssa turned, and Fontaine padded down the wooden ramp with bare feet, a blanket wrapped around her body.

"I'm sorry," Nyssa said, "but I can't bear to say goodbye."

Fontaine smiled and pulled Nyssa into a hug. "Then I will not say it. When you find Quinn, bring her back here to Le'Caal. We will look after her. I will make sure she's safe."

"Thank you for everything," Nyssa breathed, pulling away from Fontaine, her eyes filling with tears—she didn't much care to hide her emotions anymore. It seemed like such a waste of time now. "Say good-bye to everyone for me."

Fontaine murmured under her breath, weaving a spell, a lumines-cent glow flushing her skin. The golden shimmer took Nyssa's breath away. Fontaine braced Nyssa's face with her hands, her fingers warm and buzzing with magick.

"I hope this will sustain you for a bit." She placed a gentle kiss on Nyssa's lips.

Nyssa tensed, a surge of warm energy flowing through her, spreading to her fingertips and toes. She gasped as Fontaine maintained contact, her chaste kiss transferring life.

When Fontaine finally pulled away, her complexion was ashen.

Nyssa's heart sank. "Fontaine?" She touched her lips. They still buzzed with magick.

"I will be okay, sweet girl," she said, smiling weakly. "I'll just need a nap."

Fontaine's eyes darted over to Aryis. "I have no love for you, traitor, but look after Nyssa, keep her safe. Earn your way back to those you love." She focused back on Nyssa, touching her cheek, her fingers light and warm. "Until I lay my eyes on you again, stay strong, my love." She smiled before returning to the ship.

After they disembarked, Nyssa stood on the dock and regarded Hannah's Whisper for a moment. Even with Fontaine's gift of life coursing through her, Nyssa very much knew this was the last time she would see Elias, Fontaine, and her friends aboard the Whisper.

THE UMBRA WOODS

T he quickest way to cross into Thu'Dain was through the Umbra Woods, a two-day ride from Le'Caal. The cursed woods were on the side of the border closest to the coast and stretched a hundred or more miles inland. There were far safer places to cross, but they'd have to travel weeks out of the way.

And Nyssa didn't have weeks to spare—her body was telling her that much. And she needed to get to Quinn as quickly as possible.

Nyssa and Aryis sat on their horses and scrutinized the path that entered the woods. The hairs on the back of Nyssa's neck stood at attention.

"Do you suppose the stories are true?" Aryis asked.

Nyssa tried to put on a brave face, but the woods had a reputation. According to stories, the Umbra Woods lured travelers deep into the trees and dark gullies where no animals stirred, and they never returned. "Before I came here, I would say no, it's all just silly superstition, but now? There's something strange here." Something *other*. A presence that made her feel decidedly uneasy.

The gravel path through the woods was wide and clear, the trees curling up and over it, looming above them, casting a dim, hazy pall over the ground. A bright, evergreen scent hung in the air, undercut with the earthy stench of damp, decaying leaves.

Nyssa caught Aryis shivering out of the corner of her eye. The temperature dropped as they crossed into the Umbra Woods—even the occasional shafts of sunlight feeling oddly cold.

A few days into the five-day trek, they hadn't encountered any other travelers, nor had they expected to. Regardless, Nyssa kept her scarf around the bottom half of her face as they rode. Anything she could do to add a measure of warmth.

She hated to admit it, but the spark of life that Fontaine granted her was beginning to wane. A chill had crept back in, her fingers turning cold and stiff, her joints faintly aching.

At night, they'd camp just off the trail, careful to stay out of the trees.

Nyssa woke up three nights into their journey with a tightness in her stomach. Something pulled at her. Something from deep inside the forest. Her head buzzed with its presence, making her dizzy.

She got to her feet, head swirling, and stumbled into the dense trees, letting the moonlight guide her into the woods. She didn't make it far before she knelt next to a tree trunk and lost the contents of her stomach.

In the trees, Nyssa spotted a small glistening stream that cut through the dark woods. She staggered over and sank to her knees, cupping her hands in the icy water and lifting them to her lips, savoring the crisp, refreshing gulp. She leaned her head back and exhaled a pained breath, raising her eyes to the sky.

Branches swayed back and forth, the leaves rustling on the breeze, lulling her as her eyes followed the mesmerizing movement. The sky and its stars twinkled in and out of view while the trees obeyed the wind, the night air cool on Nyssa's skin, raising goosebumps.

Despite their repute for danger, the Umbra Woods possessed an aching beauty, silent save for the sound of the water and the rush of the wind through the trees lightly blowing Nyssa's hair away from her face.

Not a bad place to die.

Nyssa considered standing and going back to the campsite, back to safety, but her body wouldn't respond. She didn't know if she was enraptured by the forest or if the exhaustion of her creeping death stopped her from leaving, but she lay down in the soft, yielding grass.

Drifting off to sleep, Nyssa's breathing deepened, and the world pulled away, replaced by something else. Something dark but comforting.

She opened her eyes, and the shadowy colors of the forest had grown darker, glowing dimly with a deep-blue light. She recognized the color. It once stirred within her...

It was the color of her magick.

Though her mind told her it was impossible, that her magick was gone, Nyssa could feel it thrumming around her; within her.

Familiar and calming.

Small green lights floated above her, and the forest, so quiet and foreboding before, came alive with the sound of insects and birds and creatures she didn't recognize.

Nyssa drifted somewhere between awake and asleep—or between this world and another, she really couldn't say—and found it strange that after living twenty-five years without it, magick had become precious to her. She never felt more alive than when she vibrated with it.

I miss it.

When her power twisted up in Quinn's, the experience was breathtaking...and terrifying.

A deep loneliness beat in her chest. The absence of Quinn left a rift inside her—an endless, unyielding darkness.

I miss her.

Then Nyssa sensed it. A presence. It moved through the forest, reaching out with a power that took her breath away. She stood up, barely aware of her body, and looked around her. Everything blurred and slowed.

The stream at Nyssa's feet danced with currents of lightning. She bent down and ran her hand along the surface, gasping at the power flowing under her fingers.

Suddenly, she felt eyes on her.

She rose to her full height. Across the water stood a towering white stag with a blaze of black fur on its chest. It stared at Nyssa with four white, glowing eyes, its body shimmering like stars.

A memory tugged at her brain—had she seen something like this before?

She let the thought drift away, her attention completely rapt by the beast.

The stag stepped into the water. Currents of blue lightning crept up its legs and crackled across its body, all the way up through the tips of its massive antlers, where darkness swirled and coiled around the beast.

As the stag came closer to Nyssa, she tried to step back, a dull and distant fear clawing at her gut. But she found herself rooted in place, like the trees that twisted up to the sky.

A dark, shimmering shadow rippled off the stag and cascaded around Nyssa's legs. Power thrummed and pulsed through her body like a symphony. She recognized it—the song of her magick, and Quinn's, ancient and vast. Throatless voices layered one upon the other, deep and droning, and hammered into her chest. Its echoes raced away from her in waves and shot back, flicking across her skin, the sound transforming into shining blue light.

A different, familiar resonance began to vibrate inside her. Another song twisted and entwined with her own. Nyssa recognized Quinn's magick mixing with her power, flowing off the stag and rippling through her.

"Please," Nyssa whispered, reaching toward the creature. All fear had vanished, replaced by an infinite, unyielding need to feel *more*. To feel not only her own magick once again but Quinn's presence as well. Even if it wasn't truly her, it *felt* real enough. Nyssa yearned for the sensation to seep into her bones and linger, a small, merciful reprieve from the cold, snaking tendrils of death that infected her body.

The white stag stopped in front of her and stretched forward, its nose nuzzling into the palm of her trembling hand.

With a touch, Nyssa's world went white and everything—her magick, Quinn's presence, the life of the forest itself—spiraled through her. She slowly fell backward, each second stretching and moaning into eternity.

She was sinking again, plunging deep into the night.

Nyssa closed her eyes and let go.

Aryis grunted under Nyssa's weight. She fought to keep Nyssa upright and moving forward, though she was barely conscious. They trudged through the forest and gradually made it back to their campsite. Aryis had woken up to find Nyssa missing and her gut knotted up in fear. But a trail of trampled underbrush and snapped twigs was easy enough to follow through the Umbra Woods.

Aryis found Nyssa unconscious next to a stream and struggled to get her semi-awake and on her feet. Aryis had let her fighting and weapons training lapse in the many months after she left Ocean's Rest, and she had lost some of the muscle she had once possessed. She cursed herself for being so lax.

After an excruciatingly long time, she stepped out of the line of trees with Nyssa in tow and unceremoniously tumbled onto a bedroll. Aryis pulled her arm out from under Nyssa—who had passed out again—and flattened onto her back, breathing heavily. She lay there for a good long while, thankful to be alive and amazed that her legs didn't give out on her on the trek out of the woods.

The stars above dotted her vision through the trees. It had been a long while since Aryis had simply rested; stayed still long enough to appreciate the world moving languidly around her. Lying on her back in the middle of a cursed forest, staring up at the stars, felt freeing.

But she knew it couldn't last.

Aryis looked over and tapped on Nyssa's cheek. "Wake up."

No response.

She tapped harder.

Nyssa's eyes fluttered open, and Aryis sighed with relief.

"What happened?" Nyssa mumbled.

Aryis pushed herself onto her elbows and sat up. The effort was exhausting, but she was in a mood to lecture Nyssa.

"Why did you go into the woods? I told you not to! I had to go in there after you. Gods only know what could have called me off to my death. Or I could have been enthralled by some wood witch and become her slave for the rest of my life or—"

"I felt something," Nyssa whispered, tears filling her eyes. "Then I saw something. A giant white stag with four eyes. I felt my magick flowing through it. And I sensed Quinn there too."

Aryis stared at her, excitement replacing her anger. It wasn't possible. Or was it?

Poring through her memory to find a book she had once read, she envisioned it in her mind's eye and gave it a tug. She felt the book's presence shift and held her palm out, and the tome appeared within a shower of golden sparks. She thumbed through the pages, hunching close to the waning firelight.

"I thought the Realms were inaccessible without something like the Hummingbird…" Aryis scanned the book, moving her lips as she read. People found it a strange habit, but she didn't care. She kept flipping through the book until a passage leapt out at her. She let out a gasp. "I-I think you saw a Caracor named Koras, the Ancient God of the Realm of Night. Nyssa, you were in the fucking Realm of Night!"

Nyssa peaked an eyebrow at her.

Perhaps the profanity was a bit much.

Aryis buried her gaze back into the book.

"Oh, here's an interesting bit: *Koras is an Ancient God that reigns in the Realm of Night, a spirit realm that stands as a reflection of our world. The Realm of Night is rife with magick, both dark and light, and rarely seen—or survived—by mortals.*"

Aryis read a bit farther before looking up at Nyssa. "Amazing. You were visited by a powerful god, Nyssa, and he let you go," Aryis breathed. "This is ancient magick. Before the Empire. Before the Old Folk. Your magick could be as ancient as the world itself."

Nyssa looked up at Aryis. "What does it mean?"

"The Realm of Night welcomed you in and then let you go, Nyssa."

"I wonder what Koras made of me, a neutered god teetering toward death." She scowled. "Why did I just...wander into the Realm of Night and we need the Hummingbird to get into the Realm of Shadows?"

Aryis frowned. It was a damn good question. All the rare books with comprehensive information about ancient magick, the realms, and their gods were kept under lock and key at Arcton.

"You look like someone peed in your tea, Aryis," Nyssa remarked.

"I wish I could tell you more, but the books that delve deep into the realms and their gods were never at my disposal. I can only assume that not all realms—and how they interact with ours—work the same way. One thing I do know is that some Ancient Gods are friendly and others...aren't."

Nyssa shrugged, pulled her cloak tighter, and shivered. She looked tired and sunken in.

I did this to her.

"Let me make you some nice hot tea," Aryis said, moving to put the teapot over the fire. She glanced back to find Nyssa watching, the fire dancing in her eyes. Nyssa slipped her hand into Aryis's and squeezed.

Aryis stopped herself from gasping. There was no warmth to Nyssa's flesh.

"Thank you," Nyssa said before letting go.

They sat and drank their tea. Aryis wrapped her hands around her mug, blowing on the hot liquid. "How do you feel?"

Nyssa offered a weak smile. "Better. Thank you."

"Good. Now let's get some rest. No more wandering off to cavort with Ancient Gods, please."

Aryis lay back and let the night air drift over her. She knew she would sleep with one eye open for the rest of their journey to make sure Nyssa was safe and sound.

A VISION INTERRUPTED

Medias stumbled into a table with a gasp, her plate slipping off her tray and clattering to the floor. Conversations hushed as heads turned her way in the dining hall of Ocean's Keep. She closed her eyes. Her visions were coming quicker of late, and at some rather inopportune moments.

This vision, however, set her heart pounding. She whirled and ran from the dining hall to the stables, appearances be damned.

A startled stable boy wordlessly pointed to a horse when she asked for the fastest steed. She threw a bit and reins in its mouth, swung up on its saddleless back, and tore out of the front gate of the Keep, her heels biting into the sides of the horse.

Medias rode wildly through the streets of Ocean's Rest, heading to the casino she knew to be controlled by the Razinu faction, carefully avoiding rickshaws, bicycles, and the tram as it rattled by. When she got to The Thirteenth Oak card house, she barely stopped the horse before sliding off of its back and sprinting toward the entrance. The two guards out front, rough-looking with slicked-back hair, blinked at her but didn't make a move to stop her.

The card room was busy, the air foggy with smoke. Gambling chips chinked onto tables, adding to the cacophony of voices and laughter that filled the crowded casino.

Medias grabbed a floorman by his arm. "Where's Reggie Cox?" she growled.

The man pointed to a corridor in the back of the large room and squeaked out, "Office."

Medias pushed him away and stalked back to the office, doing her best to calm her heartbeat. Voices drifted out of the askew door, and she stopped to listen, tamping down the raging desire to kick the door open.

"...long enough and I've been patient, but I want what you owe me," a man said. "Or you can come work for me here and pay off your debt."

"I don't have the money, Reggie. And I'm certainly not going to work for you," a familiar voice insisted.

Reece.

"One or the other, girl. You owe me."

"I've paid you five thousand marks and somehow my debt keeps going up?"

The man laughed. "You wanted a loan that's off any books Lilliana can see, so you pay the price."

"I can't give you what I don't have." The strain in Reece's voice made Medias tense.

"And you're not fucking leaving this city without giving me what I want."

"You don't get to tell me—"

The smart *smack!* of skin against skin, followed by Reece's surprised cry made Medias's blood run cold.

She kicked the door open.

Reece wiped blood from her mouth and blinked at Medias. A tall man with dark, beady eyes and close-cropped black hair barked an order to the guard in the room. "Put her down."

A flash of metal caught Medias's eye. She flinched, instinctively raising her left arm over her eyes. Hot, piercing pain ripped through her skin. She ignored it and attacked with her magick, aiming a light explosion at the guard's head.

He lunged forward, dodging the magick, and rushed at her, his long dagger arcing toward her. The curved blade barely missed her stomach.

She stumbled back and let loose another explosion of light. This time, she found her mark.

The guard cried out and swung his blade wildly.

Medias slid to the side and grabbed his hair. With a violent twist, she snapped his head back. His body twitched once, then fell to the floor.

Panting, she raised her eyes to Reggie. It took him a second to consider his options, picking the wrong one when he scrambled behind his desk and pulled a dagger from underneath.

She attacked with an explosion of light. He fell back into his chair, and she rushed him, sending a leather-gloved fist across his face. Then another. And another. She grinned when she felt his nose shatter under her blows, only stopping when Reece put a hand on her arm.

"Are you hurt?" Medias asked, gently pushing the hair away from Reece's face. A bruise was already starting to bloom on her jaw.

"I'll be fine," Reece said, her face softening. "Medias, your arm—"

Two throwing knives stuck into the leather of her jacket and her flesh underneath, gleaming with blood. Her blood. Medias gritted her teeth and steeled herself. She plucked the dead guard's knives out of her forearm and tossed them to the ground, pushing past her dizziness, embarrassed at how the sight of her own blood sickened her.

"How much money do you owe this man?"

Reece swallowed. "Ten thousand gold marks. I've already paid him five."

Reggie spat out blood, slurring, "You forget interest...you owe me fifteen thousand."

Medias cradled her left arm close to her body and reached into her jacket, pulling out a heavy red coin—her replacement marker for the one she lent Nyssa. She turned to the desk and tore a page out of an open notebook. She took off her glove, palmed the disk, and pressed it down on the paper. The coin burnt a shining blue mark onto the paper, its magick activated by her touch. Medias wrote *5,000 gold marks* and added her signature in black ink, leaving a smear of blood on the stark-white parchment.

"Medias, what are you doing?" Reece asked.

"Paying off your debt." Medias pulled her glove back on, tugging at it with her teeth.

"I didn't ask you—"

Medias stopped the empath with a look, not in the mood to argue. Turning back to Reggie, she slapped the paper against his chest.

"Her debt is paid off."

Reggie blinked up at her. He didn't look sufficiently swayed.

Medias reached forward and pulled her magick forth, sending bursts of light through his body, doing what she was built for and what the Masters trained her to be at Ambershine—the perfect Justiciar inflicting perfect pain.

Medias relented when Reggie's soft whimpers convinced her he was ready to comply.

"Come after Reece Ae'Shen ever again and I will have Justiciars crawling all over you. I will destroy your life and see your faction dismantled. And do not think, for one moment, that House Fennick will protect Razinu after you threatened its only daughter. Your whorehouses and card rooms only operate with Lilliana Fennick's permission." Medias leaned forward, locking eyes with Reggie. "Do you understand?"

"Yes," he mumbled.

She straightened up. A wave of dizziness struck her, and she stumbled back into his desk.

Reece put an arm around her. "I need to get you to a healer."

"Yes, I would like to feel my fingers again," Medias replied, loath to acknowledge she was in pain. She clutched her injured arm to her chest and avoided looking at her wounds.

"I know where we can go. We'll slip out the back so no one sees us." Reece took Medias's arm, slung it over her shoulder, and grabbed on to her wrist to steady her. "I've got you."

"Thank you," Medias murmured as Reece maneuvered them out of the office and through a back-alley exit.

Medias lay her head back against the cool, worn leather of the chair she sank into, enjoying the warmth of the pain-killing tonic the healer had given her after tending to her arm. When she was gone, leaving Reece and Medias alone in a small room above Crae's Alehouse, Medias finally felt as though she could breathe.

Crae's reaction to seeing her again was as expected—fearful. But the clinking of gold coins on his bar seemed to ease his discomfort enough to get a private room.

"You care to explain why you owe Reggie Cox and the Razinu faction all that money?" Medias asked. "And why Lilliana doesn't know about it?"

Reece wrung out a cloth over a bowl, the water inside turning pink from Medias's blood. She smoothed out the Justiciar's jacket on her lap and resumed cleaning the blood off the dark-red leather. She scowled. "It's not what you think."

"I assume nothing."

"It's embarrassing," Reece admitted. "Someone I...trusted stole ten thousand gold marks from The Feather's account using my bank marker. It was my fault, and I didn't want Lilliana to know how foolish I'd been."

Medias let loose a soft, amused grunt. "So you covered your foolishness with more foolishness by borrowing money from a black market money-lender?"

Reece stared down at Medias's jacket and scrubbed aggressively. "I was desperate."

"You borrowed money from a direct competitor to the business you oversee."

A huff of air escaped Reece. "I said I was desperate. And believe it or not, Reggie and I have a mutual respect. Or so I thought."

Eyeing Reece, Medias pushed for more information, her curiosity piqued. "This person who stole from you—"

"None of your business."

Medias frowned and lolled her head back against the chair again, closing her eyes. Could she fault the empath for keeping her secrets to herself?

"I'll pay you back, I promise," Reece said.

"At your leisure. I don't give the money with any expectation of recompense."

"I pay my debts."

Medias hummed out a chuckle. "Not in a timely enough fashion for Reggie Cox, it seems."

"Are you taking the piss out of me, Justiciar?"

Medias shrugged and had to stifle a groan, her arm still sore.

"When we get back to the Keep, I can have one of our seamstresses fix the damage to your jacket. Magick mending, good as new," Reece said, sighing. "You...you didn't have to follow me. Or rescue me like I'm a helpless woman who can't defend herself."

Medias opened her eyes and trained them on Reece. "You're the furthest thing from helpless that I could imagine. I had a vision..." She stopped and swallowed as the images came flooding back. Images that made her blood run so cold she almost shivered remembering them. "I saw you lying in a pool of your own blood, dead on the dusty floor of Cox's office. I..."

The intensity in Reece's gaze forced Medias to look away. For so long, she had told herself that protecting Nyssa's friends was her sworn duty, a promise made that she wouldn't break.

But what she did for Reece had nothing to do with duty.

She glanced down at her gloveless hands. The knuckles on her right hand were bright pink, the remnant of beating Reggie senseless.

"What you saw today...what I did...you were right about me, empath. This is what I am." Medias stood and pulled her jacket from Reece's lap, slowly putting it back on, taking care not to jostle her tender arm.

Reece stood. "I'm not scared of you."

"You should be." Medias bowed her shoulders. She wanted to lie down and rest. And tear the mask away to hide her face in her hands after her display of naked violence against Reggie.

"You saved me today," Reece said. Her dark eyes were unrelenting, prying Medias apart. "I'll never be scared of you."

Medias zipped up her jacket, trying to ignore how close Reece was standing to her. She breathed in Reece's lavender body oil—the fragrance warm and comforting. "We should get back to the Keep."

The silence stretched between them until Reece said, "I want to ask you something."

Medias waited.

"Will you take off your mask?"

She stared at Reece, startled by the bold request. "No."

"But I've already seen your face, briefly."

"That was an accident," Medias replied, a tightness in her chest forcing her to breathe quicker. Over the years, after everything she had done and the people she had hurt, she told herself that the mask was the monster. A convenient lie that Reece would certainly see past.

"I want to see you now, in this moment. As you truly are," Reece said.

Medias's gaze darted around the small room, desperate for escape. "I can't...please don't ask me to do that."

Reece's eyes filled with regret. "I'm sorry."

Medias stepped back. Rebuffing the empath felt like a violation of the trust they had tentatively built over the year. But Reece had already seen the ugliness that Medias was capable of. That ugliness made Medias feel unstable, ready to spin out of control, hating what Ambershine and its Masters had taught her to do.

She moved past Reece, heading to the door, but her vision went white. Images began to flood her mind. Grunting, Medias stumbled and grabbed her head, doubling over. Two visions in one day was rare—and painful. Her head pounded.

The sea flashed before her eyes, the brined air filling her nose. Seagulls bellowed, their loud cries piercing her ears. A ship's gangplank rose in front of her, and she found herself moving up it, magick tingling under her fingertips just before a protective ward bit and snared her.

Medias clung to every detail of the vision, committing it to memory as fragments of it drifted out of reach. A snippet of a wooden sign gave Medias a clue of the ship's location.

When the vision dissipated, Medias found herself on her knees with Reece steadying her. Blood dripped to the floor.

A damn nosebleed.

"What happened? Was that a vision? Are you in pain?"

"You ask too many damn questions, woman," Medias whispered, swallowing back bile.

"What did you see?"

Medias pushed herself to her feet with a strained grunt. "You know I won't tell you."

The disappointment in Reece's face drove a spike into Medias's heart. She was the only person that faintly resembled a friend, and Medias wasn't treating her the way she deserved.

Reece frowned but nodded. "I...understand. But if you need my help, you have to let me know," Reece said, squeezing Medias's arm to drive her point home.

"I will," Medias lied.

AN UNEXPECTED GUEST

Nyssa had breathed a sigh of relief once she and Aryis were clear of the Umbra Woods. Thu'Dain still posed dangers but didn't set her on edge like the dark forest. Now, they just had to get to Sarisan.

One step at a time.

The road to the Thu'Dainian capital was sparsely populated. Merchants dotted the journey, their small kitchens set up to sell meals to weary travelers, for which Nyssa was thankful. It was amazing how a steaming bowl of rice topped with grilled meat and vegetables comforted her, restoring her dwindling reserves of strength.

Nyssa tried to hide it, but she was getting worse—her body aches and chills pervasive and ever present. A shade was being slowly drawn on her life as her body failed her.

She only hoped to see Quinn one last time.

As they drew close to Sarisan, a mix of dread and excitement filled her. She hated the sight of the city but knew Quinn was there and soon would be within reach.

Once inside the city, they found an out-of-the-way lodge that seemed fairly private to rest and plan. Their room was far nicer than Nyssa expected, with two large beds that made her smile with relief. Sleeping on the road had been hard on her body.

"I've asked for food to be sent up later," Aryis said. "We can figure out our plan over dinner and maybe take a day to scout the outside of the Rell estate. We need to find a place to open the portal. Somewhere we won't draw attention to ourselves."

"Alright." Nyssa dropped her bag next to a bed and worked on un-buckling her boots. She wanted to rest before dinner and get warm under some blankets. She shrugged off her cloak and got into bed, pulling the comforter over herself. As soon as her head hit the pillow, her eyes grew heavy.

A knock on the door jolted Nyssa out of her slumber. She stumbled out of bed and drew Winter's Bite from its scabbard.

A man in the doorway smiled and winked at her with his one remain-ing golden eye. "Stand down, Blacksea."

"Athen?" Nyssa breathed, her heart racing.

He walked into the room and wrapped his arms around her. "Nice to see you still have some fighting instincts," he said before he pulled away from her. He put his hand under her chin and lifted up her face. "You've looked a sight better, but you're still alive."

"What are you doing here?"

"I got a message from a little bird that asked for help, so I came. I've been waiting for you two for days in a room down the hall."

Nyssa leaned against the room's small, rustic table, eyeing Aryis. "A little bird, huh?"

Aryis had planned all of this down to their accommodations, hadn't she?

"You made good time," Aryis remarked.

"I bought passage on a ratty merchant ship. They were transporting some of the stinkiest cheeses I've ever had the displeasure of sharing a hold with," Athen said. He smiled warmly at Nyssa. "How are you feeling?"

"I'm alright," she lied, trying to offer up a reassuring smile. She fished a fresh shirt out of her bag. "Give me a moment, I'm going to clean up."

In the bathroom, she splashed water on her face and chanced a look in the mirror. Dark circles had long since settled in the hollows below her eyes. Her skin lacked warmth and had become pallid. The scar running down the left side of her face was the only other bit of color aside from the Mark of the Unworthy, the raised skin gray.

Death was dragging her down at her and that fact was more obvious with each passing day. She stood back from the mirror and stripped off her shirt. The undershirt that once hugged her frame now hung loose.

A soft knock on the door snagged her attention. Athen slipped in after she answered.

"Do my breasts look like they're shrinking?" Nyssa sighed.

Athen raised an eyebrow. "If you pull your shirt up for me to look, I will throw you out the window."

"I feel like I'm...disappearing."

"You're sick, Nyssa. But I'm here to help now."

She smiled. "Athen...you don't know how much I've missed you. Ever since that fucking day I was marked Unworthy, I've missed your damn face."

He wrapped Nyssa up in a hug, and she went slack.

Athen let her lean into him. After a good long minute, she pulled away and wiped at her eyes.

"I don't know that it's a good idea you came, though," Nyssa said. "What we're going to do is very dangerous—"

"Nyssa, you're fucking insane if you think I'm not seeing this through with you." He took a deep breath, a stern bearing in his face and posture. "You and I are in this shit together now, got it? I'd rather careen headlong into my grave next to you than walk away again."

Nyssa fought the urge to break down into blubbery tears. The first time she had ever laid eyes on Athen, they were both ten years old. He'd pulled her bullies off of her as they gave her yet another beating and had stuck by her side ever since. He was the best damn friend she could ever ask for.

"I don't deserve you," she said, smiling up at him.

"Yes you do." He took a big breath, his demeanor growing more serious. "I have to tell you something."

"Is it bad news?"

His gaze dropped from her face. "It's about my mother."

Nyssa steeled herself. The last thing she wanted to talk about was Lilliana Fennick. Her parents died because of that woman's actions, but she'd hear Athen out, for his sake. "Out with it."

"Not that this justifies her actions, but I thought you should know that when the Empire asked her to hire your parents to...uh..."

"Kidnap Quinn. You don't have to try and soften that blow. I know what my parents did and it wasn't right."

Athen took another big breath and looked up at her. "The Empire all but threatened to take Reece away and hand her over to Ambershine if my mother didn't help them. She...she did it to save Reece from becoming a Justiciar."

Swallowing, Nyssa leaned back against the sink. "Fuck," she whispered. "Reece as a Justiciar...she would have been—"

"Dangerous. Nyssa, they would have broken her. Turned her cold. I love my sister and I would never want that life for her. I...I can't imagine what you're going—" he choked up and cleared his throat. "I'm sorry. I just needed you to know."

Nothing could absolve Lilliana of her crimes—the pain of Nyssa's parents' deaths was etched upon her bones. "Thank you for telling me."

"I know it doesn't change anything."

Nyssa shook her head. "It doesn't, but I guess in a twisted way, my mom and dad didn't die for nothing."

Athen didn't look convinced.

She stepped forward and gave his hand a squeeze. "You're carrying guilt for this, I can see it in your face. This isn't on you or Reece. Not ever. Understand?"

He did a poor job of convincing her with a weak nod of his head.

"Athen..." She put as much bass in her voice as she could muster. "Tell me you understand."

A slight smile broke through his dour exterior. "I understand."

"Good. You know I love you. And I love Reece. You two are family."

He nodded toward the door. "How is it going with Aryis? You two seem civil at least."

Nyssa scowled. "There are times when I want to just drive my sword into her heart and be done with it. And then...she does everything she can to help me and I see her hurting and it breaks me in half. I don't know how to feel about her, Athen. It's exhausting."

"Yeah, now you know where I'm at," he mumbled, leaning back against the wall and looking down at his feet. As hard as dealing with Aryis was for her, she couldn't fathom how his heart was coping.

"You still love her?" The question was like a boulder tumbling from her mouth, heavy and dangerous, but she needed to know—though she didn't know what she would do with the answer, whatever it may be.

"Yes," he admitted, not taking more than a beat to answer her question. Nyssa expected as much. .

"Of course you do," Nyssa said with no judgment. Athen was loyal and steadfast, despite the risk of getting deeply hurt.

"I don't trust her." He exhaled, a sadness clinging to him. "I wish I could turn my feelings off and just forget about what she means to me, but I can't."

"I understand, believe me." She smiled and squeezed his arm. "We need to be careful. I don't know what Quinn will do to Aryis when she sees her. And Aryis likely won't fight back. There are times..."

Nyssa swallowed and let go of Athen's arm.

"Nyssa?"

"I get this feeling that Aryis is ready to die to help me. And it scares me because I think I might be willing to let it happen," she whispered.

Athen put both hands on her shoulders and squared her up to look at him. "Your anger has always driven you, given you power and strength of will. It drove you to fight your bullies and to fight back against Ceril and the Justiciars. Gods know what else you had to fight while on the run. But it always guides you in the right direction. The situation with Aryis is complicated...but I know you care about her. We'll figure this out."

Nyssa looked up at her best friend. Sometimes she thought he knew her better than she knew herself. And he wasn't wrong. Anger and resentment burned deep inside her, alongside an ache of lost friendship and a desperate desire to find her way back to common ground with Aryis.

"I will do my best, but I'm not really *at* my best of late," she said. "I'm in pain all of the time."

"Nyssa—"

"You've always looked out for me. But I'll need you to look after Quinn when I'm gone. She'll need people to protect her. Promise me you'll help her. Don't make me come haunt you after I'm dead."

The look on Athen's face made her throat go dry—it was the same look of determination he had when he first helped Nyssa all those years ago when they were young pups.

"I won't let anything happen to Quinn." Athen pulled her into another hug, as if he were trying to hold them together. "I promise."

Athen watched Nyssa sleep, afraid to take his eye off of her. Her breathing was so shallow. Whenever she took a deeper breath, something wet rattled in her chest, and his blood ran cold.

When Aryis wrote to him and told him they needed his help, he didn't hesitate to pack and leave. Part of him was angry at Nyssa for disappearing. He feared that he'd never see her again. But this was harder—realizing he'd have to watch his best friend die, unable to do anything about it.

The first time Nyssa set upon helping Quinn, trying to save her from Ceril and the Citadel, Athen had failed them both. He hadn't believed Nyssa's suspicions, thinking Quinn had filled her mind with doubt.

He wasn't about to fail Nyssa a second time.

He sipped his tea, his eye lighting on Aryis, who sat on the edge of her bed, watching Nyssa too. They had said perhaps three words to one another before Nyssa fell asleep, settling into an uncomfortable silence.

Just looking at her swirled up a maddening mix of anger, hurt, bitterness, and love. *Fucking love.* But he needed to remain rational, for Nyssa, and to not dwell on Aryis and her betrayal.

It was Aryis who broke the silence between them first. "Athen, I can never apologize enough for what I did. But I wanted to thank you. I know you were sending food to my room at Ocean's Keep while I holed myself in there."

Athen sighed and nodded. It was true, he had looked after her, even from afar.

"I keep wondering what I would have done in your position," Athen said. "What you did—"

"But you're not in my position, Athen." Her face darkened. "I'm going to be *Queen*. You don't even want to rule over a city. There's an exceptional difference between our responsibilities."

Heat rose in his face. "You think I don't know what it's like to face responsibility like yours?"

Aryis lowered her head, her eyes on Nyssa's still form. "You most certainly do not. I don't say this to insult you or to be cruel, but I have a nation to answer to and a father expecting me to sacrifice everything to be a good leader to my people. Which is what I did. I sacrificed Nyssa and Quinn to keep my people fed."

He hated it, but there was no disputing the stark honesty of Aryis's words. He ran from politics, rebuffed his mother, and turned down his birthright. But the fact still remained that Aryis sacrificed her friends—to a Rell, no less.

The cup in Athen's hand softly popped, and a crack appeared in its side. He put it down, frowning. It had been years since he'd thoughtlessly broken something.

Nyssa stirred, and he held his breath, but she didn't wake up.

Aryis turned to Athen. "You have no idea how hard I fought to stop this from happening, but Suvi made it impossible. She would have starved Frosland out. That bitch knew exactly what she was doing, floating ships full of food off our shores. How could I say no?"

"You didn't need to face that decision on your own. You could have asked me for help."

"Athen..." Aryis sighed, "being a queen is a solitary position, a responsibility shouldered by one woman. How would it look if I ran to you for help every time I faced a difficult decision? I already looked weak after the Wayland situation and losing my position as successor."

Athen opened his mouth but lacked a response. Aryis looked away from him, back at Nyssa.

They sat silent for several minutes before Athen picked up another cup and poured himself more tea. "I was willing to give everything up and follow you to Frosland, to be by your side. I knew your life took you in a different direction than mine, but I was going to go with you. Now, I...I..."

"I'm sorry," Aryis whispered.

"I'm so mad at you," Athen admitted, "but despite everything, I still love you. I only hope that fades with time."

Aryis clamped a hand over her mouth and shuddered once, a small sob escaping between her fingers. Athen hadn't meant to cause her pain, and he fought the impulse to rush to her and take her in his arms.

"You'll forget about me," Aryis said, her voice wavering. "After this is over, you won't see me again."

Athen swallowed. Hearing those words made his heart ache. "Back to Frosland, then?"

Aryis blinked, her eyes shiny with tears. "I'm not going back."

"What? Why?"

"I'm not built to be queen. I don't have the stomach for it."

"Where will you go?"

"Far away from everyone."

In the bed, Nyssa groaned and mumbled incoherently.

Aryis looked over at him, her eyes shiny. "Nyssa has nightmares, but it's better to let her rest. She desperately needs her sleep."

She cleared her throat and stilled before standing up and moving to her travel bag, pulling out large swaths of paper. She approached the table and sat down, spreading the paper out between the two of them.

"Let's spend our time wisely and memorize Suvi's estate layout. The Realm of Shadows will be disorienting enough, we need to be prepared to pinpoint our location and know our exits once inside."

Athen nodded and swallowed back his pain as they sat and studied Suvi's estate.

THE REALM OF SHADOWS

Nyssa lingered in a dark alley several hundred feet away from Suvi's estate, watching and waiting. The city proper came to an abrupt end, as if forbidden from encroaching on Rell land. A wide stone street separated the city from a grove of trees that encircled the Rell mansion.

Past the grove, a high stone wall surrounded the royal mansion, hiding the house from view. Ivy crept up the pristine white stone but stopped about a foot from the top, an obvious sign of some variety of magick keeping anything living at bay. Nyssa didn't need her magick to know powerful wards were woven into the wall to protect the grounds.

The guards that dotted the outside perimeter and stood at the gate to the estate were staid, every last thread on their uniforms in its proper place. The small glimpse Nyssa got of the house far off in the distance rendered more of the same—white, sterile, impeccable. Its grounds were so well kept, they looked as if a leaf had never been moved out of place by an errant breeze.

Foot traffic near her was almost nonexistent, a perfect place to open a portal to another realm.

The Realm of *fucking* Shadows.

This is insane.

Nyssa had left Aryis and Athen behind, still asleep, and slipped out with the Hummingbird. There was no reason to risk their lives in the Realm of Shadows, if the stupid little device even worked. The danger to her was meaningless—her life was already forfeit. But the thought of Athen or Aryis getting hurt twisted her in knots, especially after what she had already cost them both.

Nyssa reached into her pocket and took out the Hummingbird. Cold and shiny, it was hard to believe that the little trinket could open up a portal between worlds. According to Aryis, it had taken several mages years to enchant, its magick extremely complex...likely some of the most complex ever woven. Exhaling, Nyssa began to rotate the back of the small body.

Suddenly, the Hummingbird disappeared from her hands. She turned to find Athen staring down at her, the little trinket between his fingers.

"What the fuck are you doing?" he asked, holding up the Hummingbird.

Nyssa's shoulders sank. *Dammit.* "Only one of us needs to go get Quinn."

"This is some misguided attempt to keep us safe, right?" Aryis asked.

"I don't want either of you to get hurt...I—"

"Goddammit, Nyssa!" Athen grabbed the front of her jacket and yanked her toward him until she was on her tippy toes. "You're stuck with me, understood? Pull another disappearing act like that and I'll—"

"Kill me?" Nyssa quipped, trying to smile.

Athen scowled down at her.

"I, too, am rather displeased you ditched us," Aryis piped up. "We go into the Realm of Shadows and get Quinn out *together.*"

Nyssa held her hands up. "Okay! Okay!" It seemed that despite her best efforts to keep her friends safe, they weren't about to let her go it alone.

Her heart would be gladdened if she weren't so scared for them.

Athen gave her one last warning look before releasing her. He slipped her bag off her shoulder and looped it over his head, adding it to his and Aryis's bags.

"How'd you find me?"

Aryis held up her left hand.

The damn Kraken ring.

"Give it back."

"I would prefer not to, given your penchant for taking off without us," Aryis replied, instead handing Nyssa a thin leather cord. "Tie this around your waist. Make sure it's secure. You'll go first, Athen second, and I'll head up the rear."

Nyssa did as she was told.

"Athen, tie yours around your waist and use the remainder to tie yourself to Nyssa's cord. I'll do the same to you so we're all latched to one another. No wandering off."

"Where did you get this stuff?" Nyssa asked.

Aryis cleared her throat. "A place that reminded me very much of The Lash."

Nyssa swallowed at the last memory of the pleasure house and what she had done. Betrayed by Mox and young adepts dead by her hand. All for what? So much senseless death, including her own soon. At least she could free Quinn, give her a chance at life.

When they were all tethered together, she turned back to Aryis.

Aryis wrapped the Hummingbird's chain around her wrist.

"So, you remember where they're most likely holding Quinn?" Aryis said.

Nyssa nodded. The maps Aryis had brought were detailed, and the area she referred to was fairly secluded from the rest of the house.

Aryis sucked in air and blew it out. "Alright. Time to go." She twisted the head of the Hummingbird. With a metallic click, the air in front of them began to shimmer. Aryis released the Hummingbird, and it floated up, anchored by the chain around her wrist.

The air in front of Nyssa churned and twisted, smoke and dark light dancing together. After a moment, the churning ceased and began to pulse gently, revealing a black hole in the world.

The void beyond the portal pulled at Nyssa, its invisible fingers sending a chill vibrating through her. She reached a cautious hand through the temporary doorway, the cold on the other side enveloping all the way down to her bones.

With one last glance back to Athen and Aryis, Nyssa took a deep breath and stepped into the Realm of Shadows.

Shadows engulfed Nyssa. An icy presence filled her up, something wholly different from the cold wracking her body. She took a hesitant step forward and felt herself move again a scant heartbeat later, as if time—and her body—was catching up with itself.

"We're in," Athen said.

Nyssa heard his voice once, then twice, like an echo. Her eyes slowly adjusted to the shifting shadows, the blackness underlit by a shimmery glow. That luminescence revealed a desolate landscape enshrouded in perpetual night. Nyssa lifted her hand in front of her face, able to see it as if it were outlined in deep purple light.

Nothing seemed alive or moving within the realm, but the gloom itself had shape and form, billowing like the sails on Hannah's Whisper. A shiver ran through her as the darkness rustled like dried leaves—she hadn't expected the shadows to make a sound.

"Let me turn on the beacon," Aryis said, her voice echoing into the shadows, sounding a million miles away and right next to Nyssa's ear at the same time.

A bluish-white light streamed out, illuminating the way in front of Nyssa. It took her a moment to understand what she was looking at. The grove of trees and tall stone barrier beyond it appeared, gauzy and dim. All of the world's color was drained away, replaced by shades of gray. Continuing forward, she entered the trees and reached her hand out, brushing her fingers against a tree trunk. Her fingers flowed through the wood, meeting slight resistance, as if dipping her hand into a stream of water.

"So strange..." she whispered, her words snatched away as they left her lips.

She shivered again, this time from the distinct feeling of being watched. She glanced to the side, ever so slightly, mindful of the rules. Something skittered out of sight in her periphery...or did it? She pressed her eyes closed and opened them again.

Sweat popped up on her brow despite the chill to the place.

"You guys ready?" she asked.

"Yeah," Athen replied into the echoes.

Taking a deep breath, she wove through the trees and led them to the wall surrounding the estate. The closer she got, the more the stone surface of the wall wavered, as if it were a reflection on the surface of water. She slowed to a stop once a few feet away.

"Push through it," Aryis said.

Reaching up, Nyssa met cold resistance under her fingertips. The wall gave way with more pressure, and she put her arm through it. Throwing caution and logic aside, she walked into the wall and continued to move forward, her whole body pushing against the resistance. When she stumbled out on the other side, it reminded her of wading into the water at Monk's Cove.

She fought the urge to look back, instead shuffling forward, tugging on the rope linking her to Athen. "You both okay?"

"Yeah. Felt like walking through oatmeal," Athen replied.

They navigated their way into the massive front garden of the estate, the greenery a dull, sickly dark-gray by the light of the Hummingbird. Guards milled about, and even though Nyssa knew they couldn't see her, she avoided getting too close. She didn't want to find out what moving through a living being felt like.

Nyssa steered them over to the south side of the estate. The rough stone of the mansion's surface was etched with runes of protection—symbols that focused and strengthened the magick they were imbued with.

Quinn was imprisoned somewhere behind those walls, and Nyssa didn't hesitate to walk through the exterior of the sprawling estate, finding it easier this time, her brain and body better acclimated to the experience. She reached the other side and found herself face-to-face with a strange woman.

Nyssa yelped out of surprise, but the woman walked through her and kept going down the hallway. It was quite unlike moving through a wall—the woman's body was warm and sparked like the embers of a fire as she passed through Nyssa.

"You okay?" Aryis asked.

Nyssa exhaled. "Yes, that was just...unsettling."

Her voice sounded thin and hollow, as if the shadows in this place were swallowing the words as soon as they left her mouth. A strong feeling of unease wound around her, tightening its grip. The darkness in the corners of her eyes seemed to creep oppressively closer.

Nyssa glanced left and right, trying to drive the darkness away. An undeniable pull kept nipping at her, a growing desire to explore the shadows. *Something* wanted her to veer off course. She shook her head, blinking hard.

Concentrate. Get to Quinn.

She started forward again, drawing on her recollection of the mansion's map. *Down this hallway and to the right.* Nyssa picked up her pace, reaching the end of the hall. Another long hallway faced them on the right, terminating at a door.

Nyssa's gut told her Quinn was behind it. She rushed forward until something brushed against her hand and she jumped.

"What was that?" she asked, her voice echoing in the darkness.

"Just keep moving. *Please*, Nyssa, we have to get out of here," Aryis said, the fear in her voice obvious.

Before Nyssa could take another step, something brushed against her again. She broke the rule and looked down. Just once.

Milky white eyes stared back at her.

Bile and fear rose in her throat. She rushed forward, keeping her eyes up. They had to get out of the Realm of Shadows *now*.

When she reached the door at the end of the hallway, she paused, took a second to calm herself, and walked through it.

A dark shape lay in the middle of the floor.

"Open the portal!" Nyssa ordered.

The air in front of her shimmered. Her hands twitched as she waited for the portal to open, her hair sticking to the sweat on her forehead. The strange sound of the realm—the rustling of dried leaves—grew louder. But then it changed...now like low whispering voices.

When the portal opened, Nyssa wasted no time dashing through it, pulling Athen and Aryis through with her. The last remnants of those shadowy voices lingered in her ears. Her blood ran cold when a whisper chased after her.

Nyssa.

SIGHING INTO THE DARKNESS

Nyssa sucked in a breath, happy to be free of the oppressive darkness of the Realm of Shadows. Her eyes scanned the dim room, finding a chair, a table, and a small cot, but not much else.

The figure curled up in the middle of the floor was covered by a ratty hooded cloak and lay in the small spot of sun afforded by the room's only window located high on the wall. Nyssa's heart dropped when the covered figure didn't move. She carefully approached, not knowing if it was Quinn or another hapless prisoner of Suvi's.

A faint warmth stirred in her chest, giving her pause. She crouched down and reached out with a trembling hand, gently placing it on the prisoner's shoulder.

"Quinn?"

There was an endless moment of stillness. Then the figure turned to her. Sleepy emerald eyes blinked, then widened in shock. Black hair tumbled out of the hood as Quinn sat up.

"Nyssa?" she whispered.

"Heya, Freckles."

Quinn shot forward and enveloped Nyssa in a hug, holding on tight as she shook with tears. Nyssa buried her face in Quinn's hair, her heart pounding in her throat, eyes closed, drinking her in.

Deep inside her, separate from the pain that wracked her body, a dull warm glow bloomed. Even without her magick, Nyssa felt Quinn's presence. It was faint, but it was there. Nyssa didn't know how it was possible, but she didn't much care.

Forever entwined.

"Is it really you?" Quinn asked, her voice rumbling against Nyssa's chest.

"Yeah, it's me," Nyssa rasped. Even though she knew they needed to get going, she didn't want to move. The one person she ever ached for was right there, in her arms.

Quinn pulled back and held Nyssa's face between her hands. "Is it really you?" she asked again.

Nyssa nodded, and her breath caught. "It's me, Quinn."

"You look like hell," Quinn said, breaking out in a smile. Those deep, beautiful green eyes sparkled with tears.

Gods, she was stunning.

"I've been better," Nyssa laughed, helping Quinn to her feet. The woman clung to her, face streaked with dirt, reminding Nyssa of the time she captured Quinn, then a fugitive on the run from the Empire. Nyssa certainly could never forget the punch Quinn threw, catching her right on the nose. The memory brought a smile to her lips.

Quinn stiffened in her arms. She lunged at Aryis, a primal growl escaping her throat.

"Quinn, no!" Nyssa hissed, pulling her back as Athen stepped between the women.

"Why is that traitor here? Why would you bring her here?" Quinn sobbed. Nyssa wrapped an arm around her.

"How do you think we found you?"

"She did this to us," Quinn whimpered, the pain and helplessness in her voice cutting Nyssa to the quick. She had started to work through her feelings for Aryis, dealing with her resentment, but Quinn's raw anguish churned up the anger lodged deep inside.

"We'll deal with her later," she said, locking eyes with Aryis. It sounded like a threat. And Nyssa had to admit, it felt like one. Whatever progress they had made, it all seemed to dissipate as sadness settled on Aryis's face. "Everyone, let's get tethered back up. Athen at the front, then Quinn, me, and Aryis."

"What's going on?" Quinn asked.

"Shadowstepping," Aryis replied.

"Wha—"

The door creaked open. A burly man stood in the doorway, eyes wide. He started to reach for the dagger at his hip, but Quinn, in a blur of motion, crashed into him. She covered his mouth, forcing him against the wall.

After a breathless second, she stepped back and let him crumple to the ground. She turned toward them, a bloody dagger in her hand.

Talon.

Quinn had taken it off of Aryis in the blink of an eye, so fast even Nyssa missed it. She wiped it on the man's sleeve before handing it back to a wide-eyed Aryis.

"Are you okay?" Nyssa asked.

Quinn held up her left hand. Her ring and little finger were red, swollen, and crooked. "I was beat when I wasn't perfectly compliant. He broke a couple of my fingers when I wouldn't give him my toldoku."

Nyssa seethed while she gently took Quinn's hand, examining the broken fingers. As much as she would like to find Suvi and kill her for what she had put them both through, they needed to get out of there. The adrenaline of finding Quinn was beginning to wear off, leaving Nyssa weak. She ran her thumb along the woven leather toldoku before letting go.

"Link up," Nyssa said. Once they tethered to each other, she put her hand on Quinn's shoulder in front of her. "Quinn, keep moving forward. Don't look down. Don't look behind you. What we're doing is dangerous, but follow the rules and you'll be fine."

"I don't understand," Quinn said.

"You will in a moment."

Quinn put her hand over Nyssa's and squeezed. "You came back for me."

Nyssa hummed out a soft laugh. "We have unfinished business, you and I." She glanced back at Aryis and nodded.

With a twist of the Hummingbird, the air in front of Athen began to shimmer and darken.

"What...what the fuck is that?" Quinn whispered.

Nyssa's mouth went dry. "The Realm of Shadows."

A strangled breath left Quinn. After waiting for the portal to fully open, the four of them stepped into darkness.

Once inside the Realm of Shadows, Aryis activated the beacon on the Hummingbird and it flickered to life. She swallowed, hoping to pass through the realm as quick as they could. Everything about this place tugged at her fear and she knew, without a doubt, that they were being watched by something...*other*.

Athen led their small party, wading through walls and doors, ignoring the barriers of the outside world. Quinn gasped the first time they moved through an object. Athen came to a stop in a large room. Men and women milled about, their ghostly forms shifting past them, no idea they were being watched from another realm.

"They can't see you, Athen," Aryis said.

"I know, it's just..." His voice rippled away and back, carried by echoes.

"What's wrong?" Nyssa asked.

"Turn the light off for a moment."

Aryis switched the Hummingbird's lantern off and waited.

"What's that?" Athen asked, his voice rising in pitch.

She focused her eyes forward. Her mouth fell open.

In the distant darkness of the Realm of Shadows, a large, dusky mass headed toward them. Rows upon rows of milky eyes of all sizes stalked them from the middle of the black mass, rolling toward them like a slow wave, rising and falling, chittering, the sound echoing through the endless expanse.

"We have to open a portal and get out of here!" Athen said.

"We can't. Not here," Aryis replied. "We'll be overwhelmed by guards."

"What do we do?" he asked. "That thing is getting closer."

Aryis closed her eyes and brought up the mansion's map in her mind's eye. If they couldn't go out through the front of the house, turning around and going out the back was their only option. And out back was a cliff with a hundred-foot drop.

The cliff...

Aryis switched the Hummingbird's light back on. "Turn right and go to the back gardens."

"Aryis, there's nowhere to go but down off that cliff," Athen replied.

"There's a free-fall enchantment off the side of it."

"You're sure?"

"I memorized the whole map, not just the mansion. I'm sure."

"Do what she says," Nyssa ordered.

Aryis found herself suddenly moving, yanked forward by her tether. If they could get to the gardens and open up a portal, get out of this damn place and down to the beach, they might be safe.

A low rumble vibrated through her, making her chest ache. She jumped when something whispered her name, forcing her to do the one thing she wasn't supposed to do—look back.

The dark mass quivered and rolled toward them, speeding up, closing the distance.

"Athen, hurry!" Aryis yelled.

She snapped forward, concentrating on the back of Nyssa's head. If she could just keep her eyes ahead of her, perhaps the creature in pursuit of them would fall back.

A shiver ran down the length of her spine when she felt something brush her heels. She stifled a scream. If she cried out, Athen would stop to help, as would Nyssa. She would doom them, of that she was certain.

The four of them passed through the house and into the back garden. Everything was cast in pallid gray—tall bushes, fruit trees, and endless beds of flowers stretched across the back of the property, the cliff face not yet in view. It was too far away for the Hummingbird's lantern to illuminate.

Aryis glanced back again, her forehead slick with sweat, needing to see how close that...*thing*...had gotten. The black, rolling mass moved both impossibly slow, yet was gaining on them with alarming speed.

Gods, she hated this damned realm.

They needed to get *out*. Her heart jumped into her throat when something tugged at her fingers. She snatched her hands up to her chest, looking down. Black smoky tendrils receded from her view.

Were those eyeballs?

"Athen, please hurry," she hissed.

Their group rushed forward, trudging through the space occupied by a tall hedgerow, coming out the other side, suddenly facing nothing but a drop down to a narrow beach—and beyond that, the sea. A short fence lined the top of the cliff to keep anyone from accidentally tumbling to their deaths.

"This is it," Aryis said, hopeful. "This is where we get out. I'm opening the portal."

With trembling hands, she pulled the Hummingbird down and twisted its body. The portal door began to shimmer into view in front of Athen.

The seconds ticked by far too slowly for Aryis. Perspiration dripped from her forehead onto her hands as she gripped the Hummingbird tight.

Relief flooded through her when the portal finished forming and Athen began moving. She hurried forward, then she stopped with a jerk, halting Nyssa's progress.

She couldn't lift her foot.

"Aryis, what's wrong?" Nyssa asked over her shoulder.

Aryis's feet were rooted to the spot. She looked down. Coils of dark smoke snaked around her legs and crawled up her body. Sickly yellow eyes stared up at her, rows upon rows of them, blinking. Chitters, like teeth clicking together incessantly, echoed in the dark, close and far away and everywhere all at once.

Aryis fought back a scream.

"I can't move," she whispered. Nyssa's head whipped to the side.

Oh gods, she heard me.

"Get Quinn through the portal," Nyssa said before turning back to Aryis.

The black portal swirled behind Nyssa and Athen and Quinn were suddenly gone.

Aryis realized with horror that Nyssa had untethered herself from the other two. "What are you doing?" she yelled.

"I'm getting you out of here, idiot!" Nyssa shouted. She grabbed Aryis's hand and pulled.

Something cold and sharp inched up Aryis's back and crawled over her ribs, further rooting her in place. Icy fingers touched the back of her neck, and she screamed, unable to stop the terror from escaping her lips.

Nyssa pulled harder. Aryis's shoulder was on fire from the strain.

"Nyssa, stop," she pleaded, "you have to get out."

"Not without you!"

Nyssa let go and jerked on the tether line. Aryis barely felt the pull. Something whispered into her ear as the darkness encircled her shoulders. It would soon encase her arms too. She had to act.

"Nyssa, the portal is closing."

Nyssa's bright-blue eyes filled with panic. "I'm not leaving you here!"

"I'm sorry, Nyssa. For everything," Aryis whispered, removing Talon from its sheath. She drew its deadly sharp blade across the thin rope, severing their tether, then shoved Nyssa as hard as she could. Nyssa flew backward out of the portal a second before it closed, her voice echoing through the Realm of Shadows.

Darkness descended over Aryis's eyes and her body went cold. She sighed into the shadows with resignation, sorry for everything she had done to hurt Nyssa and the others and hoping she had done just enough in the end to save them.

Her world stilled, save for the whisper of a low rumbling voice.

You'll do nicely.

Gravel crunched under Nyssa's feet and the sea air filled her lungs. She stared up at Athen. "What did she do?" she whispered.

He looked around, confused. "Where's Aryis?"

Nyssa pulled on the severed rope at her waist. "She couldn't move. She—" She looked down at the rope in her hand. "She cut the tether."

Athen grabbed hold of her, his fingers digging into her arms. "No. Where is she?"

"I'm sorry, she..." Nyssa bowed her head. She couldn't look him in his face. "Something took her."

"We have to go back in!" His voice broke.

"We can't. We don't have the Hummingbird!"

Athen let her go and stumbled backward, looking about ready to crumble. She brought a fist up to her forehead, hitting herself out of frustration. Aryis was trapped in the Realm of Shadows, and her only thought was to sever their tether so she could escape.

"Nyssa, stop," Quinn said, gently wrapping a hand around her wrist.

Nyssa sagged, panting. Her knees wavered, and she grasped at Quinn. "We can't leave her."

Loud voices came from the direction of the house. Guards pushed through hedges and wound around trees, coming after them.

"Shit, they found us! We've got to go," Quinn hissed, running up to the cliff's edge. She pointed to a gap in the chain fence and ran to it, holding her hand out. "Here! The enchantment is here, I can feel it. Come on!"

Nyssa stumbled forward and grabbed on to Athen. "I'm sorry, Athen, I tried to get her back." Her legs were like dry twigs beneath her, ready to snap, her strength gone. She dropped to a knee. "We'll get her back, I promise."

Athen didn't hesitate to pick her up in his arms. "We have to go," he whispered.

Quinn stepped off the cliff into the flow of the free-fall enchantment.

Athen approached the edge. Nyssa closed her eyes and tucked her head against his chest. She briefly felt herself falling, trusting that Athen would keep her safe.

COMPLICATIONS

Nyssa woke up, gently rocking back and forth, the scent of hors-es and sea salt in the air, the sun blazing overhead. Her mind churned, and it took her a moment to realize that her head was in Quinn's lap, with the woman's hand woven into her hair. Quinn's head lolled with the movement of the wagon.

Nyssa smiled and closed her eyes again, enjoying, for a scant moment, the warmth of Quinn's body. Every small buck of the wagon jarred her bones, deepening their ache. And no matter how warm Quinn was, the cold clung to Nyssa as if her spine was made of ice, a reminder of her encroaching death.

She groaned and sat up, waking Quinn. "What happened?" Nyssa asked, blinking the sun out of her eyes. They were in the back of a wooden wagon on top of blankets and what felt like hay underneath. She shifted around and rested against the side of the wagon, shoulder to shoulder with Quinn. Athen smiled back at her from his perch in the box seat.

"We used the free-fall enchantment to get away," Quinn said. "You turned a rather sickly shade of green and lost your breakfast when you got to the bottom. We stole a boat, then this rickety wagon and a couple horses. So, we're thieves in addition to fugitives."

"How are you feeling?" Athen asked.

"Better," Nyssa replied. "How long have I been out?"

"Since yesterday."

The events from the previous day came back into sharp focus. Aryis...they had lost Aryis. "Athen...I'm so sorry. I tried to get Aryis out."

"We'll get her back," he replied. His voice was tinged with sadness, but she knew he was staying strong for her—it's what he did in a crisis. She had to get Aryis out of the damn Realm of Shadows...but how? She groaned, trying to ward off the cold and the pain.

Nyssa turned to Quinn. It was still hard to believe they had rescued her from right under Suvi Rell's nose.

"Let's get this off of you." Nyssa reached up and ran her fingers along the void collar still on Quinn's neck.

Quinn let out a sigh. "I'm so used to this damn thing I forgot I was wearing it. But we don't have the key."

"Shit, I was just concerned with getting us as far from Sarisan as possible, I forgot too. Will brute strength work?" Athen asked.

"See, I'm not the only brute here." Nyssa grinned at Quinn, who returned a smile—that smile could sustain Nyssa forever.

If only her body would comply.

Athen stopped the horses and hopped to the back of the wagon, the vehicle rocking under his weight. He crouched next to Quinn and peered at the void collar, gently examining the lock.

"Ah, this is just a hex lock on the latch. Unpickable," he remarked, "but not uncrushable." The lock shattered as Athen squeezed it between his fingers, the metal no match for his strength.

"Great job, big man," Nyssa said and reached over to press the latch on the collar. It clicked and released, the collar springing open.

Quinn cried out and everything went to shit.

Tendrils of lightning and darkness flowed out of Quinn's hands and sunk into Nyssa's chest. Her muscles tensed uncontrollably and she fell onto her back, deep spasms of sharp pain wracking her body.

Quinn scrambled out of the wagon with a pained shout, and writhed on the ground. Blue lightning laced with swirling darkness arced up and back into her body.

Thunder boomed in the sky.

"Put it back on!" Quinn screamed. "Please!"

Nyssa's eyes snapped down to the collar next to her. She snatched it up and tried to vault off of the wagon, but her foot caught on the sidewall and she tumbled out.

Everything inside her rattled when she crashed into the dirt.

Pushing past the pain, she crawled toward Quinn.

Athen jumped off the wagon and tried to help, but lightning arced and hit him as he approached. He yelped and scrambled back.

Nyssa dragged herself to Quinn, lightning and darkness sinking into her body in a constant flow of magick. She gritted her teeth and pushed forward, Quinn's cries driving her despite the unspeakable pain of the uncontrolled power.

Nyssa dug her fingers into Quinn's cloak and pulled, bringing the collar up quickly around Quinn's neck and snapping the latch closed.

The magick immediately dissipated, and they both collapsed.

Nyssa grunted with each breath. Her whole body shook, icy pain roaring through her bones and muscles.

Quinn's face hovered over her. "Nyssa?"

A large hand patted Quinn's shoulder, and she disappeared, replaced by Athen. Nyssa felt his arms sliding underneath her, lifting her up.

"Be careful with her!" Quinn said from a million miles away as Nyssa closed her eyes.

The fire crackled while Quinn watched over Nyssa, who had been out for hours after the incident with the void collar. Quinn and Athen had settled into an uncomfortable silence—learning about him through Nyssa's stories was different than spending time with the man. Quinn wanted to trust him, but she had always been short on her faith in others.

Except for Nyssa.

Athen didn't talk much, his mood sullen. Losing Aryis in the Realm of Shadows seemed to have broken his heart. While Quinn held nothing but hate for what Aryis had done to her and Nyssa, she knew from Nyssa's stories that Athen's heart was bigger than his stature. He wore his sadness openly.

She drew in a deep breath and let out a little whimper. The twinge of pain in her chest had grown and become constant, its sudden, sharp presence concerning. Her energy lagged as well, Athen's dinner doing little more than warming her.

Quinn poked at the fire with a stick. "Nyssa's dying," she said. It was the first time she'd acknowledged it out loud, though the minute she laid eyes on Nyssa again, she knew. The dark circles, the sunken cheeks, how pale she was...

Athen stirred out of his faraway stare. "Yeah, she is." His expression quivered, as if on the verge of tears, before he cleared his throat. His reaction forced the air from her lungs.

"I was hoping what I did worked."

He scowled. "What do you mean? You destroyed her magick."

"No, it's more complicated than that." Quinn rubbed her forehead, angry at herself for believing she could subvert the rules of magick. Why did she think taking Nyssa's magick wouldn't kill her? Transfer it or destroy it, what did it matter? She had lied to herself in an attempt to kindle a spark of hope to keep going instead of wasting away as Suvi's prisoner. "We need to get her back to Fontaine and Elias. They might know how to help her." It was the only idea she had.

"She's been degrading quicker since we got to Thu'Dain. I don't think the Realm of Shadows helped either," Athen said, his throat bobbing.

"Degrading is such a bad word for it," Nyssa mumbled, startling Quinn.

"You're awake!" Athen replied.

Nyssa sat up with his help. "What smells so good?"

"I made dinner," he said, filling a bowl with stew from the small pot over the fire and handing it to her.

Nyssa smiled and cradled the bowl in her hands. "Quinn, what the hell happened with your void collar?"

"I screwed up." Quinn searched for a way to explain herself. "I...I didn't negate your magick. I took it and pulled it inside of myself, thinking that if I didn't destroy it, you wouldn't die, and I could somehow give it back to you."

Nyssa scowled, confusion written on her face. "How did you even do that?"

"I just did it...I didn't think. Something inside of me shifted in that moment and made the decision for me. But I'm—" Quinn's voice broke.

Nyssa's eyes narrowed. "Quinn? What's the matter?"

"I think your magick is killing me."

Nyssa's stomach dropped. "What?"

"When you took the void collar off, it felt like my body was on fire, like something didn't belong and was struggling to fight its way out. The pain...was excruciating. I don't think we're meant to have another person's magick inside of us."

Nyssa bowed her head. She had come all this way...risked everything for Quinn. This couldn't be right.

Quinn couldn't die.

"The void collar holds it at bay, but I...I know something is wrong inside of me." Quinn put a hand to her chest. "It started small, just a twinge of discomfort. But now, the pain is constant. And it's getting worse."

Nyssa wanted to scream until her voice was gone. Her own magick was killing Quinn. She could barely endure the meaningless cruelty of it all.

She slowly rose to her feet, thankful for a bit of renewed energy from the rest and the hot stew. "I need a moment to think. I'm going to get more water," she said, picking up the teakettle and walking into the trees next to their campsite.

She reached a thin stream after a minute and sat down on a large gray rock, letting the kettle drop and rattle on the ground. She sucked in deep breaths, her chest aching. Her thoughts flew in a million different directions. Someone had to know how to fix Quinn. Aryis, she was smarter than them all. Aryis could—

Aryis. I fucking left Aryis behind. Left her to the monsters...

Nyssa choked back a sob and buried her face in her hands. Aryis was lost to her. Probably dead, because Nyssa couldn't save her.

"Are you okay?" Quinn's voice pierced the darkness.

"You followed me?" Nyssa asked, quick to wipe her tears.

"I'm worried about you."

Nyssa sighed. "I need to figure out how to save you. You weren't supposed to die, I was."

"Is it selfish to not want either of us to die?" Quinn smiled in the moonlight as she approached. Nyssa fought the urge to stand up and just kiss her.

She loved Quinn too much to burden her with a dying woman's desire.

"We'll return to the Whisper and see if Fontaine or Elias have an idea of how to help you. There has to be something they can do," Nyssa said.

Quinn stepped forward. "Something *we* can do. We're in this together, right?"

"You don't understand." Nyssa held her hand out.

Quinn grabbed it and gasped. "You're so cold."

Nyssa reluctantly pulled her hand back. "I'm not going to make it back."

Quinn's eyes pooled with tears. "I did this to you. I'm so, so sorry, Nyssa. You're dying because of me."

Nyssa fought the desire to go to Quinn, to shake her, hold her, comfort her. "This is not your fault. Don't ever think that I blame you."

Quinn took a deep breath, her face wearing the pain she felt inside.

"I need you to tell me you'll keep fighting to figure out how to save yourself when I'm gone," Nyssa said, picking up the teakettle and filling it in the stream, the cold water shocking a little life into her.

"I don't want to think about that. We're going to get you back to the Whisper. Fontaine has to know how to help you."

Nyssa grunted. Fontaine had already exhausted all her knowledge. And Aryis had found nothing either. But Quinn didn't need to know that.

Nyssa and Quinn fell silent, the trickle of the stream filling the void.

"Our *unfinished business*, as you called it," Quinn finally said, her voice low, "perhaps we should talk, Nyssa."

The air was charged, thick with the dangerous possibility of words that could tumble out. The kiss they had shared hung between them, unacknowledged. The kiss that preceded the horror of Suvi's cruelty. Before their fate was set in motion. Nyssa closed her eyes and tried to pull the moment back to her—when it was just the two of them, arguing, misunderstanding each other, and dancing around their feelings.

Now, their kiss seemed like a distant, fleeting memory. One best left to linger in the past. Nyssa pushed off the rock. "It can wait until we get to the Whisper. Let's get back to Athen." She exhaled, tearing her gaze away from Quinn's brilliant green eyes; away from her look of disappointment.

She was running from Quinn yet again, fleeing from a conversation she didn't know how to have.

As they walked toward their camp, Nyssa turned her thoughts on getting back to Le'Caal. Fontaine and Elias would help Quinn, or they would know someone who could. It was the one hope that kept Nyssa upright, putting one foot in front of the other, persisting when all she wanted to do was lie down and rest. To close her eyes and give way to sleep.

To let the darkness in.

TAGALONG

Medias sank into her seat. Curious eyes had followed her when she boarded the train at the station just outside of Ocean's Rest and quickly retreated to her private cabin, a necessity for a Justiciar.

Not that anyone in their right mind would room with a Justiciar for a week-long trip through the coastal towns, terminating in Le'Caal. A week was optimistic—running into delays was a frequent issue. The trains needed constant maintenance and the batteries charged with power, an inelegant but necessary job for some hapless enchanter assigned to weaving recharge enchantment after recharge enchantment to keep the trains running on time.

Medias closed her eyes for a moment and allowed herself to relax. It was insane for her to leave Ocean's Rest to chase after an incomplete vision of a dock and a boat on the off chance it might lead her to Nyssa or Quinn. Her decision would be viewed as sedition and ensured she'd face death if ever caught. But her choice was irrevocable.

She unzipped the front of her jacket and sighed, reaching up to remove her mask, eager to splash some water on her face and settle in for the afternoon.

A click of the door to her cabin startled her out of her repose. She shot up, fumbling for her mask. She barely got it back on before the door opened and Reece stepped inside.

A strange burst of unsettling excitement ran through Medias before it flipped to anger. "What are you doing here, empath?"

Reece threw her bag down on the bunk opposite Medias. "I figure you're following that vision you had and are on your way to help Nyssa, so I'm coming with you."

Medias ground her teeth. Reece possessed galling amounts of audacity. "You need to leave, now. My vision didn't include you."

Reece sighed and sat down. "I'm changing fate. If Nyssa and Quinn can do it...if you can do it...then I am going to do it too. But to be clear, I think your fate bullshit is just that: bullshit. But if there's a chance to help Nyssa or Quinn, I'm coming."

Fighting off a groan, Medias grumbled, "You are an excruciating creature."

"Yes, I have my charms." Reece sat back with a smirk and eyed Medias. "Careful, I can see part of your neck and it's *scandalous*."

Medias glanced down and quickly zipped up her jacket. "How did you even know where to find me?"

"House Fennick has eyes and ears everywhere in Ocean's Rest. A Justiciar buying a train ticket isn't very sneaky. And once I got on the train, I simply opened my magick up and sensed where the dull, emotionless void was. And here you are."

Medias hated that Reece's words stung. "We cannot share a cabin. Justiciars require privacy."

Reece stood and pulled on a small latch on the wall between the cabin's windows. A gossamer curtain floated down from the ceiling and darkened, completely blocking out Reece's side of the room. After a moment, the curtain furled back into the ceiling, revealing a smirking empath.

"Pleased with yourself?"

"Indeed I am." Reece sat back down. "You will have your privacy. What is our destination?"

"Avarest."

"*Tsk*." Reece inhaled a big breath and exhaled dramatically. "You should know that very little happens in Ocean's Rest without my knowledge. Your ticket is for Le'Caal. Don't lie to me again."

A small puff of air escaped Medias. In her time with Reece, the empath had been forward but knew when to back off. Whatever subtle push and pull that existed between them had seemingly been thrown to the wind.

Reece was now willing to *shove*.

She leaned forward, her expression changing, becoming serious. "Nyssa is my friend. You, believe it or not, Justiciar, are also my friend. I want to help."

Medias's stomach did a little flip at being called a friend. "I have no idea what's in store for us, Reece. I cannot guarantee your safety."

"As if you ever could, Justiciar," Reece replied, waving off her concern. "You spend an inordinate amount of time trying to protect people from your visions, but at some point, you're going to have to trust someone. Trust *me*."

There seemed to be no dissuading Reece from tagging along. And if Medias was honest with herself, leaving Ocean's Rest—and Reece—had filled her with regret.

"I do trust you, Reece."

Reece gave her a look that Medias couldn't quite decipher and pulled open her travel bag. She fished a book out of it. "I brought reading material. I figured you packed light."

"You figured correctly."

Reece tossed the book across the cabin, and Medias caught it. "A romantic adventure for your pleasure."

Medias frowned and laid the book down next to her. "Reece, I think it's important you understand that I haven't seen Nyssa in any of my visions of late. I...I don't know if she's still alive."

"Yet, here you are, on a train headed to Le'Caal, abandoning your post in Ocean's Rest. I'd say you have faith that somehow, you're helping her."

Medias knitted her fingers together. "Faith? Hmm...perhaps."

"And if it's not Nyssa we're to help, then maybe it's Quinn."

"They are equally important to me," Medias admitted.

Reece grunted with a smile. "A wonderful thing to hear. Then our interests are aligned."

"It would seem so."

An unsettled scowl intruded upon Reece's features. Medias had grown used to her expressions, and this one usually preceded a difficult question.

"What is it, empath?"

"You leaving Ocean's Rest...that's going to be noticed by the Empire, right?"

There were consequences to a Justiciar leaving her post without sending word to Cardin, and Reece seemed to be dancing around them.

"I've made my choice."

"One that's dangerous for you."

"An understatement." Something within Medias stirred when she saw the look on Reece's face. It was the same look on her father's face the day she left for Ambershine to train as a Justiciar adept—concern and sadness.

Medias hated it.

"I meant it when I said Athen and I can help you disappear," Reece said.

"My fate isn't important."

"The fuck it's not."

Reece's anger was unexpected. Medias leaned back and closed her eyes. "I will deal with one difficulty at a time. For now, the concern is our Cursed God friends."

Friends. It slipped out of her mouth so easily, without thought or hesitation. Medias kept her eyes closed. She could guess at Reece's reaction—that sly smile that she'd display whenever Medias let a bit of her humanity slip into sight.

"Fine," Reece replied. "But you and I will talk about how to keep you alive once this is over."

"Once this is over, then." Medias settled back in her seat and tried to still her mind. But something bothered her. It shouldn't. Logically, she shouldn't care. She opened her eyes and considered Reece. *Dammit.* "Do I really feel like a dull void to you?"

"Ah, I said that to annoy you. You're not just an empty space." Reece's face softened. "It's odd...I can't read your specific emotions, but I can read your *presence*. You have a warm, fuzzy glow, like a summer peach. It's...rather nice, actually."

Medias's mouth twitched up in a smile. It shouldn't matter to her that her presence wasn't just a black void to Reece. But it *did*. "How comforting to know I'm comparable to fruit."

Reece gave her a dangerous smile. "You even have a little dimple, like the top of a peach."

Medias scoffed and self-consciously touched her chin dimple. "It's a family trait."

"Uh-huh."

Being unable to read Medias's emotions didn't seem to stop Reece from knowing exactly how to fluster her.

"I need to meditate, empath."

"Sure."

Medias closed her eyes, relaxed her shoulders, and exhaled, retreating deep inside of herself, even as she felt Reece's dark eyes on her.

INTO THE WOODS

As Athen, Nyssa, and Quinn sat in their rickety wagon, staring at the road into the Umbra Woods, Quinn felt a strange pull to the dark forest that stretched out before them.

She watched Nyssa, her nerves on edge. "Are you sure about this?"

"Aryis and I made it through without...much issue," Nyssa said.

"Then we'll get through too," Athen replied.

"We have to get back to the Whisper for Quinn," Nyssa mumbled, settling down in the back of the wagon. Quinn exchanged a glance with Athen. Nyssa was getting worse, and Quinn sensed it—the glow of Nyssa's presence was growing fainter. Colder. The world was slowly crumbling away underneath Quinn's feet and she wanted to rage against the helpless ache in her chest.

That night, Athen lit a fire and prepared dinner as they set up camp on the side of the road. The horses happily munched on grass, completely unfazed by the Umbra Woods.

Nyssa sat on her bedroll and struggled to take her sweater off. She was covered in a sheen of sweat despite winter beginning its descent.

"I've been ice cold for months, and now I have a fever." Nyssa sighed. "I don't recommend dying."

Quinn moved next to Nyssa and helped pull the sweater over her head. She gasped when she saw a Kraken tattooed on Nyssa's upper back, visible under her thin camisole straps. She instantly recognized the artwork as her own and brushed her fingers over the ink, the creature's bright-blue eyes blazing in the light of the campfire.

"Nyssa…is this…" She couldn't believe it—she had drawn the Kraken shortly after leaving Nyssa in Ocean's Rest, sketching it out on the way back to Arcton Citadel. She'd worked by firelight before she escaped her escort. Now her art was inked onto Nyssa's back.

"Ebe's work," Nyssa rasped. "I made her copy your drawing exactly. Do you like it?"

"Nyssa…" Quinn lost the battle against the lump forming in her throat. There were no words to express how beautiful it was, or how she felt seeing a part of her on Nyssa's body.

Nyssa lay back on her bedroll and exhaled. The air rattled in her lungs as she breathed.

Quinn fought back tears. Nyssa wouldn't live to see the Whisper again, that much was obvious.

"I have to tell you something," Nyssa said, her eyes grave. "What Suvi told us back in Sarisan, everything was true. About you. About my parents. And what Lilliana did."

At the time, as much as Quinn wanted to believe Suvi was spinning a tale, she knew in her gut that it was the truth.

"I'm so sorry, Quinn," Nyssa said.

"For what?"

"My parents stole you for money. What kind of people do that? And they handed you over to Lilliana and Ceril. He was there, Quinn."

Quinn swallowed. "Lilliana told you this?"

Nyssa shook her head. "No, I saw it all from Lilliana's memories. Fontaine used magick to form a link between us. I saw my mother and father for the first time. I saw you as a baby. And myself. We were together on the Demon's Wail. Ceril and Lilliana took us away from the ship, leaving it to the Justiciars and I…I heard my parents die."

Quinn reached for Nyssa's hand. It was so cold. "I'm so sorry, Nyssa. But don't apologize for something you had no control over. You are not your parents."

"No, I'm not, but what they did was wrong. They kidnapped you." Nyssa's eyes filled with tears.

"Nyssa, if they didn't take me, Suvi would have raised me. Do you think that fate would have been any better than enduring Ceril?"

Nyssa swallowed, blinking slowly. "I should never have agreed to go after you when I was ordered to bring you back to the Empire. None of this would have happened if we left you alone and let you be free."

Quinn shook her head. "I think we'd end up here no matter what you did. *Forever entwined*, remember? You and I are always going to be connected. You saw it for yourself—the two of us together as babies. Our story started long before my fist introduced itself to your face."

"Asshole," Nyssa whispered and started laughing.

Quinn couldn't help but join her. Her laughter quickly turned to coughing, her lungs stinging. She put her hand to her mouth and pulled it back.

Dark red blood.

Shit.

"Quinn?"

Quinn raised her eyes to meet Nyssa's gaze. She turned her hand to reveal the ichor.

"We are the worst gods ever." Nyssa lamented softly. "Can't even die right. I thought I'd fall in battle, maybe tumble over dramatically with thunder crashing in the background. Instead, I'm wasting away in the middle of some shitty haunted forest."

Quinn laughed again and wiped her mouth with the back of her hand. Breathing was becoming a labor. Each inhale was like a blade stabbing her chest.

She put her hand up to the void collar at her neck. Would she die with the damned thing on? She swallowed and looked back down at Nyssa's sunken face. Her eyes still blazed with life, blue as the damned sea she was named after.

Quinn glanced over at Athen. He was busy with dinner and kept to himself, perhaps sensing the women needed a moment. Quinn craved several moments.

Endless moments.

"Hey," she said, grabbing Nyssa's hand. Quinn's heart felt like a dark lump in her chest, dreading what the next few days would bring. Nyssa wasn't going to get better.

Quinn needed her to understand how she felt. She plunged forward before she had second thoughts. "I spent more time living in the time spent with you than in my whole life at Arcton Citadel. In the twenty-five years there, I never felt joy. I didn't laugh. I never felt safe. I was consumed by anger and hopelessness. They made me small at Arcton. Then you set me free, Nyssa. You gave me a world I never thought I'd see. I owe any happiness I've ever experienced to you."

Tears fell from Quinn's eyes. She'd admitted more than she had planned, but it was all true. She couldn't tear herself away from Nyssa's gaze. Those blue eyes were shiny with tears, but Nyssa wore a smile that Quinn wanted to sink into forever.

Exhaling, Nyssa said, "I'm so sorry. Returning you to the Empire is my biggest regret. Even after I knew what Ceril did to you, I brought you back. So much for my fucking code of honor..."

Quinn squeezed Nyssa's hand. "I've long forgiven you for that. We've both done things we regret." She dropped her gaze. "You know, when you got back to the Whisper after our fight, I didn't know what to do. Fontaine gave me some advice. She said I needed to be honest with you and not so guarded all the time. I tried to listen to her, but I screwed it all up. I got angry and shut you out, and I hate myself for doing that to you." A nervous energy made Quinn drum her fingers on her thighs as she sat cross-legged next to Nyssa.

Nyssa exhaled and closed her eyes. "Quinn, I didn't leave the ship because I hated you. I'm afraid of hurting others...of hurting you. But I'm mostly scared of you."

Quinn glanced at Nyssa. "You're afraid of me? Why?"

"I'm scared of what I'd do for you. Scared of what I'd do to be with you," Nyssa mumbled, her voice soft and slurred.

Quinn took a shallow breath. Her heart pounded in her ears.

"And I'm terrified you don't feel the same way," Nyssa whispered.

Quinn sat still for a minute, trying to work out what to say, but Nyssa had fallen asleep, her breathing shallow and laced with a wet wheeze.

Quinn squeezed her eyes shut, angry with herself for not being more forthcoming. For thinking that their differences would somehow resolve themselves with time. Why didn't she admit *all* of her feelings?

She looked up and found Athen watching her. The expression on his face belied what Quinn knew in her heart—Nyssa had only days left to live—and it nearly broke her. She covered her mouth to stifle a sob.

Athen got up and brought a bowl of soup to her, giving her shoulder a squeeze.

How was he still able to function? His lover was lost to the Realm of Shadows and his best friend was dying.

Quinn held the bowl in her hands and stared into it, willing herself to be strong. She ate in silence while keeping watch over Nyssa.

Later that night, her eyes grew heavy as she listened to Nyssa breathe, and she fell into a dream. It was the one she had dreamt hundreds of times before, drifting in an icy ocean deep below the waves. A presence was there, and she knew it was Nyssa. The deep thrumming of the sea enveloped Quinn, folding its rhythm into her heartbeat.

Athen wracked his brain for a solution to an impossible problem. Nyssa had gotten worse, drifting in and out of consciousness only two days into the Umbra Woods. They were too deep to turn around, but not yet close enough to the other side either. They were trapped in the middle of the haunted woods and Nyssa was sick.

Not just sick. Dying.

The thought made his stomach ache. He couldn't lose his best friend, not after losing Aryis.

It was too much.

Athen gently laid Nyssa down on her bedroll, and Quinn pulled a blanket over her. Nyssa cycled through the sweats and chills from her fever, mumbling deliriously, her words making little sense.

She smiled weakly at Athen. "Eron said we're going to practice with real swords today, big boy. I'll take it easy on you." Her eyes shut, and she murmured under her breath.

"She's talking about the day I gave her that," he said, lightly caressing Nyssa's face, running his thumb down the scar on her cheek. Tears dropped from his good eye, blurring his vision. "She never got it healed."

Quinn looked at him. "Did she tell you why?"

Athen shook his head. He let Nyssa have her secrets.

Secrets she'd die with.

His heart ached. Helplessness wasn't a feeling he was accustomed to, but so much had happened beyond his control that hurt those he loved: the attack at the Conservatory that drove Aryis away; now her being lost to him in the Realm of Shadows; and Nyssa soon to be lost to him as well.

Rising to his feet, he turned from Nyssa, the fallow look on her face unbearable. Athen walked to the edge of the trees, his chest tight. He didn't know how to *fix* this. He needed to save Nyssa and get Aryis back. But he couldn't come up with one fucking idea.

He snarled, balled up a fist, and drove it into the tree in front of him. A mournful *crack* accompanied flying splinters of wood. He lowered down to his haunches, placing his palm against the tree.

"I'm sorry," he choked out, hanging his head. "I'm sorry."

A hand came to rest on his shoulder. Quinn peered down at him and put on a brave face, remarkable considering what she had gone through. Though...there were times Quinn let the bravado drop and she looked lost. Utterly *lost*.

The trees rustled behind him and Quinn's gaze shot over his shoulder, her eyes going wide. Athen shot to his feet and whirled around.

Three figures stood at the edge of the woods, pulsing with bright-green light. They were human in shape but appeared to be made entirely out of fireflies. Each body flickered and glowed, the fireflies illuminating rhythmically against the dark backdrop of the forest.

Athen peered closer. The trees were different—they were dark and glowed with a deep-purplish light. The air almost seemed to gleam and ripple with energy.

Quinn moved from his side and started walking toward the figures.

"Quinn! Wait!" Athen hissed.

"I can feel them," she said, turning around to look at him. "And I can...hear them. They want us to bring Nyssa and follow."

He shook his head. "Are you insane? We don't even know what they are!"

Quinn's eyes pleaded with him. "I need your help, Athen. They want Nyssa. Please. I can't carry her on my own."

Athen's thoughts raced. Nyssa trusted Quinn, and the women had risked their lives for one another—more than once. And if his gut was right, the feelings ran deep between the two. If Quinn thought this was the right decision, he couldn't very well argue—he was out of ideas.

He got up, crouched beside Nyssa, and slid his hands underneath her, lifting her limp body into his arms. Quinn covered her with a blanket, pausing to squeeze Athen's arm.

"Thank you," she said.

"I'm trusting you. And...whatever those are."

"I know."

Athen cast another glance at the three figures. "Let's go."

Quinn bent down and picked up Winter's Bite, slinging it over her shoulder. She glanced at the glowing figures and nodded.

They turned and walked into the forest.

Quinn followed with Athen beside her—Nyssa nestled in his arms—stepping into the endless darkness between the trees.

A SMALL LITTLE THING, A SPARK

Hours into their journey deep into the Umbra Woods, pangs of apprehension grew in Quinn's gut. They were wasting the remaining life Nyssa had left. Small moans and imperceptible utterances left Nyssa's lips as they traveled, and Quinn's ears pricked up at every single one, setting her heart racing.

Her own body began to drag and ache, the pain in her chest becoming more pronounced, like a dark spot of rot slowly sending tendrils of poison through her. She tried hard to keep up with Athen as they followed the three glowing figures moving effortlessly ahead of them through the woods. The terrain was tricky to navigate at times, and she tripped often over unseen roots. Athen did his best to help her.

Quinn estimated it was well after midnight by the time the three figures brought their group to a moonlit clearing. A massive lake extended out before them. Far off, in the middle of the water, rose three columns of golden light stretching into the sky, glowing brightly in the night.

The sight took Quinn's breath away—they were spectacular. Their presence vibrated deep within her.

She wanted to go to them.

Needed to.

"Do you feel that?" she asked, putting a hand to her chest.

Athen shook his head.

"I do," a weak voice said.

Nyssa stirred in Athen's arms, her head resting against his chest. Quinn went to her, brushing Nyssa's hair out of her face. Her forehead was damp with sweat.

"Where are we?" Nyssa asked.

"Somewhere in the Umbra Woods. Those three brought us here," Quinn replied, pointing to the glowing figures made of fireflies.

Nyssa blinked. "Oh, now that's weird."

"How are you feeling?"

"I'm not dead...I don't think. Is this a fever dream?"

"A temporary reprieve from your malady," a man's voice said.

Quinn's hand flew to the hilt of Winter's Bite.

The man approached them out of a grove of trees close to the water's edge. "No need to draw that weapon."

"Who are you?" Quinn asked.

"The one who sent those messengers." The stranger was Koja, like Elias. His golden eyes shimmered in the darkness, and his blue skin had a satin sheen to it. Wavy white hair framed his face, and he smiled warmly at Quinn.

Something in her gut told her he was harmless.

He looked at Nyssa in Athen's arms. "Nyssa Blacksea, you're close to death. I know you can feel it," the man said. He shifted his gaze to Quinn. "And you, Quinn, will soon follow."

"Who are you?" Athen asked.

"Apologies. We tend to forget societal niceties here in the Realm of Night. I'm Cyphon, the Sentinel of Koras, the god of this realm. I believe you've already met him, Nyssa?"

Nyssa nodded.

"Excuse me?" Athen asked. "Why didn't you mention this?"

"Sorry, big man. I'm still not convinced it wasn't a dream."

"Oh, I assure you, it was no dream," Cyphon replied. "We don't have much time. Athen Fennick, can you carry Nyssa out to the middle of the lake?" He pointed toward the three columns of light. Below sat a small round platform, shiny and black.

Athen looked down at Quinn. "I don't know about this...."

She looked out at the lake and the glowing pillars. She couldn't deny their draw. "I think we need to."

He steeled his jaw before nodding. "You want me to swim?" he asked Cyphon.

"That won't be necessary. Come, Quinn, you as well. You are essential. *Forever entwined.*"

Cyphon strode down to the water's edge and stepped onto the lake, walking on the water rather than into it. Quinn shared a glance with Athen. He raised his eyebrows at her, and she shrugged. There was no turning back. Not now.

Quinn went first, to make sure they would be able to walk on the lake as Cyphon had, and to her surprise, the water supported her. The sensation was strange, like walking on a suspension bridge. The surface quivered underneath her feet, but it didn't unbalance her. She turned and Athen had followed, stepping gingerly atop the water, Nyssa securely tucked into his chest.

The pillars of light grew brighter as they drew closer, and the vibration in Quinn's chest became a constant hum, as if an unseen presence had dived deep into her, resonating with her magick. Not even the void collar could dampen the odd sensation. The warm buzz pulsed from her chest outward, making her fingers and toes tingle. The crooked fingers on her left hand throbbed with a dull pain.

When the group got to the platform in the middle of the lake, they stepped onto its shiny surface and walked underneath the middle column of light.

Cyphon glanced up at the pillars, then back at Quinn and Nyssa. "If I may?" He approached Athen and reached out, placing a hand on Nyssa's chest. Nyssa's bright-blue eyes watched, but she didn't object. A large smile broke out on Cyphon's face. "Ah yes, there it is. Koras was right."

"Right about what?" Nyssa mumbled.

"It's a small little thing, but just enough. A spark of magick still resides within you, Nyssa Blacksea."

BE A FUCKING GOD

Nyssa swallowed, her throat impossibly dry. *A spark of magick is still inside me?* "How—how is that possible?"

"Quinn pulled your magick out of you, didn't she? Not an exact art, by any means, and it seems she missed a piece," Cyphon noted. "You can sense Quinn when she's close, can you not?"

She could but she thought it was her mind deceiving her, a cruel trick of wishful thinking. She put her hand to her chest and looked at Quinn.

"I felt it again when we found you at Suvi's estate. I-I didn't think it was real." Nyssa's eyes filled with tears. "It was you. I felt *you*."

"See? A spark of magick was left deep inside of you," Cyphon said.

Quinn smiled, her hand coming to rest on Nyssa's leg. "What do we do?"

Cyphon glanced up, his face illuminated by golden light. "These are the Pillars of Mercy, a Primalith Shard and a sacred place hidden by the Realm of Night. They're teeming with ancient magick left over from the beginning of time. You have no doubt felt it?"

Quinn looked at Nyssa. "My whole body is vibrating. You?"

Nyssa nodded. It was hard to believe what she was feeling. "I thought it was my fever."

"You are feeling the power of this place. It calls to you and you call back. These pillars amplify ancient magick and will help you find yourself within Quinn. You can manipulate magick, reshape it, shift it. Use the small spark you have within to seek out your magick in Quinn and extract it." Cyphon reached forward and stroked her hair. "I believe it will save you both."

Athen and Quinn stood rapt. For the first time in months, Nyssa felt hope, though blunt and muted. "How do we do it?"

Cyphon grew serious. "Your magick is twisted up in Quinn's magick. You can't just find it and pull it out. You have to untangle it, with great care and patience. Together. It is going to require concentration. Even then, I don't know if you'll be successful."

"*Forever entwined.*" Nyssa tried to smile. "The irony."

"Indeed." Cyphon glanced at Quinn. "That collar will have to come off."

Quinn shook her head forcefully. "I can't control what happens when the collar comes off. I'll hurt Nyssa."

Nyssa reached over and placed her trembling hand on Quinn's shoulder. "We're dying, so we try anything. It's worth it. You're worth it." She nodded at Cyphon. "How do we do this?"

"I can't tell you exactly, this is my first time dealing with such matters. Koras believes you are the key, Nyssa. You can manipulate magick. You need to separate your power from Quinn's and do it carefully, or you'll shatter both of your souls and, well...I'd advise against it."

Death would be the result...Cyphon didn't have to say. It was all but a certainty if Nyssa wasn't extremely cautious. A dull wave of trepidation cascaded through her. "That's comforting," she mumbled.

"You will need strength for this, Nyssa," Cyphon said. He held his hand up in the air and turned back to the shore. The three glowing figures began to lose their shape, forming a loose clump of illuminated dots that moved toward them in unison. "Stand Nyssa up, if you will, Athen Fennick."

Athen put her down and wrapped an arm around her waist to support her. She doubted she could stand on her own without his help.

"Thank you, Athen," she whispered, resting her head against his arm. "I hope this works."

The fireflies reached the platform and floated in the air in front of Nyssa.

"Open your mouth," Cyphon said.

She hesitated.

"Trust me."

Nyssa did as he instructed. The fireflies floated toward her and dove into her mouth. She panicked, but instead of filling her mouth, their energy flooded into her, no longer corporeal creatures. They exploded in little bursts of heat that radiated warmth throughout her. As the fireflies continued to enter her, she felt lighter, her pain falling away until she could barely sense her own body.

"What's happening to me?"

Cyphon smiled. "The fireflies' lives are now yours, for as long as they will last. We must hurry before the gift of their energy wanes. Sit down."

Nyssa obeyed Cyphon, and Athen helped her sit. She ran her hands across the surface of the black platform, the stone cool to the touch. She lolled her head back to stare up at the Pillars of Mercy. How many mortal eyes had seen the beauty of these glowing pillars of light? Her body thrummed with their power.

When Nyssa brought her head back down, Quinn was sitting in front of her.

"Take each other's hand. You cannot, for any reason, let go until the process is complete. Breaking contact will corrupt your link and kill both of you. Athen, please take off your belt. We'll use that to bind their hands together," Cyphon said.

Athen knelt down and pulled his belt out of his pant loops. "Grab each other by the wrist," he said, winding the leather around their wrists and securing it tight. He checked to make sure they couldn't slip out of the binding.

Nyssa shifted her gaze to Quinn. She might never stare into those eyes again if this was unsuccessful. This was all happening too fast. What if she fucked up? She bit the inside of her cheek to stave off tears.

"Ready for this?" Quinn asked.

Nyssa swallowed, her mouth impossibly dry. "Not in the least."

Nyssa's body began to shake uncontrollably, from the cold or her fear, she wasn't sure. Likely both. "I don't know if I can do this," she said, looking to Athen. "I don't even know what I'm supposed to do!"

He steeled his face. "You took a beating every day at the Order when you were a pup and got back up swinging every single time. Keep swinging until you can't swing anymore."

Nyssa exhaled and looked at Quinn, who narrowed her eyes. "Nyssa, you're a god. Be a fucking god," she said.

Cyphon stepped forward. "Athen, it is time for you to leave. You serve no further purpose in this endeavor."

Athen stood, stretching to his full height, towering over Cyphon. "I'm not leaving this platform. You or Koras or your glowing bugs have a problem with that? Tough. I'm not leaving Quinn or Nyssa."

Cyphon laughed. "I forgot how stubborn mortals can be. If you're not leaving, you will need to watch from a safe distance."

He moved to the edge of the round, wide platform, waving Athen to follow. Athen joined him and folded his arms over his chest, his eye on Nyssa. He gave her a nod. She did her best to draw on his confidence and courage, needing it now more than ever.

Nyssa looked back to Quinn, who reached up to the collar around her neck, her fingers on the latch. All she had to do was press the release and the collar would spring open. No turning back.

"You ready?" Quinn asked.

Nyssa's throat was bone dry. If they failed—if she failed—they were both dead. A cold dread crept up her spine, turning to hot panic as it reached the back of her neck. Her breathing became short and fast.

"Nyssa," Quinn said softly. "Nyssa, look at me."

Nyssa focused on Quinn and her green eyes. Those deep-green eyes.

"You need to concentrate. Remember everything Fontaine taught us. Hell, remember everything you taught me about Ithais-Toru. Find your balance. Then fight. Fight for *us*."

Quinn held Nyssa in her gaze, providing her with a calmness she could sink into. In that moment, Nyssa felt infinite possibilities before her, threads of fate weaving and unraveling endlessly, life and death entwined. And the soft glow of Quinn at her side.

She took a deep breath and exhaled. "Let's see what comes next."

Quinn pressed her thumb against the spring lock on the void collar. It fell away from her neck, and she cried out as blue lightning exploded across her body and shadow coiled around her like a snake. The magick flowed over to Nyssa, millions of tiny lightning strikes and shards of darkness sinking into her, relentless and excruciating.

The old wound in her shoulder from the blood wraith began to throb, searing heat pulsating through the poison mark that radiated across her skin. Something else shifted and moved within her. She realized it was Quinn's presence...and her pain. The bond they shared blurred the lines between them.

Nyssa closed her eyes and reached down into herself, trying to find the small spark of magick that still existed; the one tiny shard Quinn didn't extract. It was hard to concentrate, her mind kept getting knocked off-kilter by the unrelenting torrent of pain that seized her. Shadow coiled around her in tightening whorls, sending icy chills down to her marrow.

Exhaling, she redoubled her efforts, Fontaine's voice in her head, sharp and clear: find the calm in the chaos. She expanded her senses and blocked out the dark undercurrent of Quinn's magick to find her own soul and the Ancient Magick within. A soft, glowing warm white orb, its edges dim, came into focus. Nyssa dove deeper, narrowing her concentration.

The spark of her magick wasn't there.

Were Koras and Cyphon wrong about there still being a bit of her magick alive within her? Or worse—what if it was there and she couldn't find it? The acrid taste of bile and copper flooded her mouth, and a hot panic flushed through her body, her mind spinning out of control.

"It's gone...I can't..."

A chill calmness enveloped Nyssa as Quinn's voice washed over her. *Steady. Find your magick.*

Nyssa swallowed blood and saliva, pushing the pain away. She turned inward again, trying to find a small glowing star amid the never-ending darkness, trying to use all the skills and knowledge Fontaine imparted on her.

Quinn's voice anchored her again. *Find it. Together.*

Death hung like cobwebs in every corner of Nyssa's body, pressed into her, but she pushed forward. Then she felt Quinn—inside of her, swimming through the darkness and lightning, pulling Nyssa along. As Quinn's presence grew, Nyssa's pain abated. Another presence slipped on top of Nyssa and Quinn. Somehow, she knew it must be Koras, helping calm her...helping them both.

Nyssa shut out the pain and ignored the rush of blood in her ears, focusing only on the space she inhabited. The world quieted around her, the only sound a distant heartbeat.

Finally, she found it—the smallest shard of dim blue light in the center of her body, hidden but real. She closed in on the spark and wrapped her mind, body, and soul around it, retaking what she had thought was forever lost. The small flicker flowed through her, weak but alive. Now she had to use it to get the rest of her magick.

Nyssa pulled back, outside of her body, outside of the confines of form and time, somehow feeling incorporeal and expansive, as if she were everywhere. She pushed forward, finding a mass of glowing magick, white and blue strands of energy mixed, tangled up like brambles. Nyssa's magick entwined with Quinn's—a confusing mess.

Chaos.

Closing her mind off to all distractions and pushing the pain away for as long as she could, Nyssa centered herself and moved toward the jumbled mass. She waded into it, closing in on a thread of blue energy. The fragment of her magick trembled and twitched toward her, then dove into her body, setting off a cascade of pain.

Quinn screamed in agony, the sound echoing throughout Nyssa's existence.

Nyssa reached out to Quinn. *I'm so sorry.*

Keep going.

Nyssa's resolve wavered for a moment, shaken by Quinn's pain. *Pain or death*, Nyssa reminded herself. *Or pain then death*, her fear corrected.

She took a deep breath, exhaling into the night, and shoved her intrusive fear into a dark corner in her mind, locking it away. With another breath came a realization: for the first time since her magick was taken from her, she felt a spark. Beyond the pain, a tiny kernel of warmth sprouted in her chest from her reclaimed magick.

And with that warmth came hope.

Nyssa focused again and found another fragment of herself, this time tightly entwined in Quinn's magick—a complicated mess she had to unravel, untwist, pull apart carefully.

She tugged at it. The magick slipped from Quinn and back into Nyssa.

Quinn cried out, her pain sending shock waves through Nyssa. Pushing deeper, Nyssa tried to wrap around Quinn and protect her, to take the pain on herself.

Quinn's voice echoed in Nyssa's mind, shaky but resolute. *Keep...going.*

Nyssa obeyed.

Another tangled mess of magick, another extraction. Each transfer of power came with more pain. As she tore parts of herself away from Quinn, agony rippled through both women, each nerve ending bombarded with cold shocks of magick.

The pain became too much and Nyssa couldn't hold back anymore.

A scream ripped out of her, sharp and mournful.

I want this to be over.

She knew she could shatter the glowing center of their magicks and destroy them both, end the pain forever, instantly. It was an unspeakable desire, driven by desperation, and she pushed it away.

Quinn slipped over Nyssa, her presence flowing through Nyssa's body, shimmering through every fiber of her very being. *Keep going. Please.*

Nyssa steeled herself as another shard of blue magick moved toward her. Another complicated mess of energy.

The women worked together, untangling their magick. They continued in concert for what could have been hours or days or weeks, time had been rendered meaningless.

Quinn kept pushing, keeping them focused as they pinpointed each piece of Nyssa's magick, carefully executing a dance of precision and synergy. They were moving as if sparring, their bodies and minds silently familiar with each other. It was an intimate connection that had built over decades as they were unknowingly drawn toward one another.

Finally, the last fragment of magick was pulled back into Nyssa, and she extricated herself from the tangle of Quinn, her presence shrinking and folding in on itself, becoming small again. She collapsed and fell through endless space. Another body fell with her.

Nyssa struggled to open her eyes. When she did, she found Quinn across from her trying to rouse.

Fingers worked at the strap that bound their hands together and Athen's low, calm voice broke through her haze. "Pretty nasty nosebleeds, you two. But you're alive. You're fucking *alive*."

She glanced down—her shirt was covered with blood. Cyphon was crouched next to Quinn, helping her sit up, and the bottom of her face was a mask of red. Athen smoothed Nyssa's hair as she tried to make her hands work.

Quinn groaned and started to convulse. Shadow magick sprang out of her, twisting around her body.

"H-help her," Nyssa pleaded.

Cyphon stroked Quinn's face. "Sleep."

She instantly relaxed, her magick dissipating, and Cyphon laid her down.

He moved next to Nyssa. "You reclaimed your magick, Nyssa Blacksea, and saved yourself. And Quinn."

Nyssa opened her mouth to respond, but her whole body tensed up, her magick suddenly rippling across her skin. Strange—it felt *so* good, but her control over it was nonexistent.

Panic began to take hold.

A hand brushed Nyssa's face, and the world grew small and dark, sleep taking her.

THE BIG MAN AND FRECKLES

Quinn leaned forward and examined the steak and potato pie Athen slid in front of her. It smelled amazing, the aromas of venison, potatoes, and root vegetables mixing with fresh green herbs she didn't know the names of. A deep-brown gravy practically burst out of the pastry when she dug her fork into the soft, flaky crust. She would have groaned after her first bite if she wasn't self-conscious around Athen. But she was grateful for the food he brought to her small cabin.

"So?" Athen asked, hovering by her side, a kitchen towel draped over his shoulder.

"It's delicious, Athen. Thank you for this treat."

Athen had surprised her this day, coming around with lunch. Usually, Cyphon stopped by a couple times a day to deliver food and check up on her. Athen had taken to dragging her out for languid walks along the shore of the lake, insisting she needed fresh air. She didn't say much on those walks, and he seemed content to just keep her company.

He sat in his chair and smiled, then reached forward to pull her blanket up around her shoulders.

She froze mid-bite.

"Oh, I'm sorry," he stammered. "It's instinct."

"You're used to looking after Nyssa like this?"

His cheeks reddened. "Yes. I didn't mean to be forward."

"Indeed."

Quinn didn't quite know how to act around the man, so she turned to an easy topic. "How is Nyssa?" she asked, tucking back into her meat pie.

Cyphon had split the women apart, letting them rest and recuperate away from one another to give their magick time to settle down. Her uncontrolled magickal flare-ups had ceased, but her body was still on the mend. Cyphon set Quinn up in a cozy cabin, and Nyssa in another on the opposite side of him, separated by hundreds of yards on the outskirts of the lake where the Pillars of Mercy hovered. The Realm of Night had receded, no longer enveloping them, but the Primalith Shard still tickled the periphery of her senses when she relaxed and let her magick wander and poke about the world.

Athen smiled. "Nyssa's coming along slower than you, but you're both healing. You're getting your color back."

"Ah yes, just pale again rather than deathly pale."

Athen burst into laughter, choking on his food. Quinn leaned forward and slapped him on the back.

"You're funny," he said, clearing his throat. "You've been holding back."

"When we first met, I wasn't exactly cordial."

"Yeah, you were a bit feral. But I don't blame you. I wouldn't have been nice to us either."

Feral. Quinn laughed. "You know, you don't have to take me for walks or bring me food. If you'd rather spend time with Nyssa—"

Athen held up his hand. "She made me promise to look after you when she was, you know, gone. But, I figure I'll look after you regardless. Besides, when she asks about you, I need a good answer."

The thought of Nyssa asking about her made her blush. "I feel like I already know you from the stories Nyssa shared when we were away."

"Oh gods, I can only imagine what she's told you."

"Only the good stories."

"Did she tell you the one about us getting drunk in Vane and getting into a fist fight...with each other?"

Quinn laughed. "No, I think she left that one out. What happened?" she asked, and took another bite of her steak and potato pie.

With a smirk, Athen relaxed in his chair. It creaked under him as he moved, telling a tale of a misheard dare, dozens of broken liquor bottles, and a large chunk of gold that smoothed over the damage done to the bar they were summarily banned from.

Athen lit up as he told the story, becoming animated, even imitating—poorly—Nyssa's voice as he relayed their argument. His playacting of their fight was even more animated, and he almost knocked over a mug of cider. There was something intensely endearing about his recollection of his teenage years with Nyssa, his boisterous retelling softened by his humor. While Nyssa seemed to be the one to instigate trouble, Athen never seemed to shy away from it.

It suddenly hit Quinn how hard being apart must have been for both of them, the depth of their friendship evident in Athen's broad smile and enthusiasm in telling Quinn what Nyssa used to be like when younger.

"Ah, you really love her, don't you?" Quinn murmured when he finished his tale.

Athen just smiled. "Nyssa is my best friend. She's not always easy—I think you know that by now—but she doesn't do anything in half measures. If she loves you, you're going to feel it. And she'll do anything for you."

"Yeah." At times, it made Quinn ache knowing what Nyssa did for her back in Ocean's Rest, facing down Ceril and a half dozen Justiciars—she truly gave up everything to save her.

"Nyssa is why I'm here. She cares about you, so I want to get to know you better. I know that might be difficult, given my relationships with my mother and Aryis."

Quinn put down her fork. "I don't blame you for their actions."

Athen's face grew dark. "I know you hate Aryis for what she did. But she doesn't deserve to be stuck in the Realm of Shadows. I can't help but think the worst. What if she's dead? I have to get back to her..."

Putting aside her feelings for the woman, Quinn hesitated before taking Athen's hand. She never would have been so forward in the past, but perhaps Nyssa had rubbed off on her. "You don't deserve this pain. You still love her?"

Sighing, Athen replied, "It's that obvious?"

"I don't know a lot about love or friendship, but I see the hurt on your face."

"I'm going to do everything I can to get her home. But after that, perhaps we go our separate ways. I don't know if I can trust her after what she did."

Quinn shrugged and opted for honesty. "I couldn't if I were you."

A heavy sigh left the big man, his sadness plain to see. "I love her more than I can bear to think about sometimes. I reckon you understand that a little."

Quinn opened her mouth and stammered, suddenly bereft of proper words.

Athen chuckled and held up his hand. "I'm only half blind, Quinn. You have feelings for Nyssa."

Quinn cringed. "I'm not well versed in this sort of thing, Athen. Do you...do you have any advice?" Certainly he would think her an utter idiot that she—a grown adult—was asking for advice about how to talk to Nyssa.

He stood up and stretched, then peered down at her with his one golden eye, placing a hand on her shoulder. "Figure it out."

Quinn huffed. "*Figure it out*? Is that the best advice you've got? Nyssa has been your best friend for over fifteen years. What would you tell her?"

Athen smirked. "Figure it out...*idiot*."

With that, he left, closing the cabin door behind him, leaving Quinn speechless and no closer to an answer.

Nyssa's best friend was a damned smart ass.

A SPOT OF TEA

Nyssa sipped her tea, exhaling a warm breath into the cold midday air. The pine trees beyond her porch swayed lazily in the winter wind, small puffs of snow falling off their branches. The chill, crisp air made Nyssa nestle deeper into her blanket.

Sighing, she closed her eyes. She loved the cold—it made her feel alert and alive.

Alive. And it felt *good.*

Nyssa laughed.

She wondered how Quinn was getting on. Cyphon had kept them apart for almost a week and a half, much too long for Nyssa's taste, but she refrained from questioning the man. He was a god's Sentinel after all—not that she understood what the job entailed—and she was his guest. As Nyssa healed and her magick settled back into her body, her impatience to see Quinn became distracting.

As if summoned, a warm glow grew in her chest, strong and comforting. She slowly opened her eyes to find Quinn walking toward her cabin, footsteps softly crunching in the previous night's snow. Nyssa couldn't stop the smile that crossed her lips. She stood and walked to the edge of the porch.

"Did you sneak past Cyphon to come here?"

Quinn grinned, and Nyssa's breath caught in her chest. Those vibrant green eyes were a sight that she had deeply craved.

"He let me come. He said we should be safe around one another now," Quinn said, offering a smile that made Nyssa breathe deeper.

Safe around each other—as if that were remotely true.

Nyssa swallowed. "How are you feeling?" she asked.

"Good, all things considered. You're looking well. Filling out a bit again."

"Yeah, not dying seems to suit me."

Quinn responded with a short chuckle. "May I come up?"

Nyssa moved aside and let Quinn up the stairs, the scent of juniper and winter orchids tickling Nyssa's nose.

Why does she have to smell so good?

Nyssa's eyes were drawn to Quinn's lips—they were redder than usual. "Did you eat all the winter berries off the bushes on your way over here?"

Color rose on Quinn's cheeks. "They shouldn't be so delicious if they didn't want to be eaten."

Nyssa forced herself to turn away—to stop staring at Quinn's lips—and gestured toward the cabin door. "Let me make you some tea."

Nyssa led Quinn inside, then made herself busy in the small kitchen, filling up her kettle while Quinn took off her coat and looked around. Cyphon must have scrounged up clothes for her—leather pants, a thick cotton sweater, and a pair of boots that looked like they had seen a couple years of wear.

Nyssa's eyes followed Quinn as she wandered about the cabin. The small home was cozy, its large, comfortable bed sat opposite the kitchen, a nicked-up table and well-worn chairs between them, where she would sit and read over her meals. A bathtub sat in the corner behind a screen that Nyssa took advantage of every night, luxuriating in a long soak with soothing bath oils that made her skin smell of mint and lemon and soothed her muscles.

A tiny bathroom lay beyond the tub, its mirror scratched and darkened from age. Nyssa stood in front of it often, watching the dark circles under her eyes recede and her sunken cheeks fill out again as the days passed. It was a relief to no longer avoid mirrors for fear of what would stare back at her.

She pulled two mugs down from a kitchen shelf and grabbed the tea tin. Quinn moved to the fireplace that crackled near the front door, a covered stewpot with the day's meal simmering away thanks to Cyphon. Winter's Bite lay on the mantle, and Quinn ran her hand over its hard leather scabbard. Her fingers gently glided over the sword's hilt, lighting upon the toldoku strands woven into the handle.

She seemed lost in thought. Nyssa was thankful for the extended silence, her mind racing to find something not completely clumsy to say.

In the weeks before their capture, it had become increasingly hard to talk to Quinn. Nyssa hadn't known how to navigate the tension between them. Leaving her behind on the Whisper, though only for a week, had complicated everything. As a result, Quinn put up her walls, high and unyielding. They'd reached a polite but frustrating stalemate with each other. Captivity had melted some of the ice between them, but it didn't resolve their issues. They got along out of necessity, ignoring the tension that had built up.

Until their argument...and the kiss.

That damn kiss.

Nyssa had thought about it too many times to count.

"I'd like to talk about our unfinished business," Quinn said, turning to lock eyes with Nyssa.

Nyssa shook her head and chuckled. "Straight to the point." She leaned back against the counter, tapping her finger on the wood, glad to finally be having this conversation. She needed to know how Quinn felt, even though it scared her to no end.

Quinn walked around the couch and closed the space between them, standing at the edge of the kitchen, mere feet away. She appeared calm, but there was an undercurrent of nervous energy that radiated off of her and hung in the air between them, thick with possibility.

Quinn crossed her arms. "I want to talk about what happened in Sarisan. When we argued."

"And I kissed you."

Quinn's stoic expression dissolved, replaced by a glare. Diving right into the subject of their kiss was dangerous.

And Nyssa didn't care. She smiled, emboldened. "And as I recall, you kissed me back."

Quinn's lips parted with an exasperated gasp.

Nyssa shifted her weight and sighed, the smile lingering on her face as Quinn searched for something to say. "I've thrown you off-kilter, haven't I?"

"No, I...it's just..." Quinn's eyebrows knitted up.

The sound of Nyssa's tapping finger filled the silence left in the wake of her seemingly derailed thought.

Nyssa gathered herself and exhaled. There was no turning back from this long-overdue conversation.

"When I left you on the Whisper, I told myself I needed time to be alone, to think, but the truth is I just couldn't be near you at that moment. Not in the way I wanted. My feelings for you are...complicated."

Quinn's face gave away nothing.

Nyssa ran her hands through her hair, and took a breath. "I'm in love with you, Quinn. And that scares the hell out of me." The words came rushing out, a giant exhale of intense, jumbled feelings.

Several painfully long seconds ticked away. Quinn blinked but offered no response, her face unchanging save for a tightened jawline.

A chill of regret flooded through Nyssa's body. "Fuck."

Spinning around to the rough wooden counter, she closed her eyes and exhaled, kicking herself. The worst outcome was mercilessly unfolding.

Fuck. Fuck. FUCK. "Just...just forget I said anything," she murmured.

"Nyssa."

Nyssa fumbled with the tea tin, trying to open it, her hands suddenly useless. Throwing it against the wall wouldn't accomplish anything, but damn if she didn't want to scream and bash the thing into an unrecognizable tangle of metal.

"Nyssa," Quinn repeated, her tone low and insistent. She grasped Nyssa's arm and drew her back around, plucking the tea tin out of her hand and placing it on the counter. Quinn stepped close and pressed up against Nyssa, driving all rational thought out of her mind.

"What are you—"

Quinn shut her up with a kiss. It took a second for the shock to wash over Nyssa; for her brain to restart and realize that she should kiss Quinn back. Embracing the moment, she slid her hand behind Quinn's neck, up into her dark hair. At first, the kiss was slow and earnest, almost cautious. But when Nyssa pulled her closer, Quinn smiled and parted her lips, deepening the kiss. She tasted like winter berries and her body radiated heat through her clothes, flooding Nyssa with desire, turning the kiss raw and passionate.

A soft, remorseful moan left Nyssa's lips when Quinn stepped away. She greedily wanted more even as she tried to remember to breathe. "I was afraid you were going to quietly slip out the door and let me crawl into a corner to just curl up and die."

A joyful laugh escaped Quinn. It sounded light. Free.

Quinn's fingers grazed Nyssa's hands. She opened her mouth, hesitating, a pensive look on her face. A familiar look Nyssa recognized—she was searching for the right words. "I've kept a safe distance from you to protect myself. And because I don't know how exactly to do…this. But, Nyssa, I meant it when I said I owe any happiness in my life to you. You *are* my happiness."

A wave of heat moved through Nyssa's body, coming to rest in the tops of her ears. She leaned forward and brushed her mouth against Quinn's lips, teasing, then easing into a kiss that grew deep and exploratory.

Nyssa didn't know what to expect, but Quinn seemed sure of herself and, moreover, sure of Nyssa. It was a trust Nyssa knew wasn't granted lightly.

Quinn's hands moved to Nyssa's waist, slowly untucking her shirt.

Nyssa pulled out of the kiss, trying to catch her breath. "Quinn, are you sure?"

"Yes. I want this. I want you," Quinn said, her breath quick and her eyes hungry. "I love you."

A soft, happy grunt escaped Nyssa's chest as a silly grin spread across her face. The words, those simple words, made her head swim.

Quinn's eyes sparkled.

Nyssa feigned a kiss, grazing her lips across Quinn's before she bent down and kissed the hollow of Quinn's throat. Quinn's breath turned raspy as Nyssa worked her way up to an earlobe and stopped.

"Do you know how long I've wanted to do this?" she whispered. Quinn's chest rose and fell against her, and a low rumble of contentment thrummed against Nyssa.

Desire, wild and fierce, pulsed throughout her body.

Nyssa took a moment, trying to calm her thoughts and command herself to take it slow. "Is that a no for tea, then?"

Quinn laughed, reaching up to touch Nyssa's face, fingers tracing her scar down her cheek. "I didn't come here for tea."

"Oh, so you came here to seduce me? My idiotic flirting worked?" Nyssa asked, raising an eyebrow, giving Quinn her best teasing smile while trying to ignore her nerves.

"I happen to love your idiotic flirting. And I don't know how to seduce anyone."

"Oh, I think you're learning rather quickly."

Despite the compliment, Quinn appeared nervous. "Be patient with me?"

"I'll take this as slow as you need me to. And if you want to stop, we stop."

"I know. I trust you." Quinn slipped her hand into Nyssa's. Desire crossed over Quinn's face, raw and unflinching, utterly wrecking Nyssa, making it almost impossible to think.

Nyssa squeezed her hand and tugged her along toward the bed.

She exhaled a deep breath, her heart pounding. Surely Quinn could hear it. The heat of her yearning became a steady burn, but a nervous energy rippled through her in kind, exciting and disconcerting. All she cared about was fulfilling Quinn's desires...and providing pleasure.

At the foot of the bed, Nyssa kissed Quinn again, slipping her hands beneath Quinn's sweater to pull her closer, her skin warm and soft. Yielding.

As her fingers ran across Quinn's lower back, thick scars met her fingertips. She stopped.

"Is this okay?" Nyssa breathed.

Quinn smiled at her. "Yes."

"You sure?"

"The scars are a part of me."

Nyssa stroked Quinn's cheek and smiled at the way she pressed her face against her hand. Loving. Trusting.

She swallowed hard and whispered, "I have to be honest. I'm nervous."

"You're the bravest person I know and yet *I* make you nervous?" Quinn asked, a grin tugging at her lips.

Nyssa drew in a breath. "You completely disarm me."

A grunt of pleasure rumbled out of Quinn, and she reached forward to begin working at the buttons on Nyssa's shirt, taking her by surprise.

"I always seem to get the jump on you, Blacksea," Quinn teased with a smirk.

Nyssa huffed out an amused laugh. *The audacity...*

Quinn's fingers were light and warm, like a feather gliding across Nyssa's skin, pushing her shirt off her shoulders. It fell to the ground with a hush, leaving her half naked.

Vulnerable.

Quinn brushed her fingers over Nyssa's collarbone and down her arm, following the marks of the poison scar. Nyssa's lips parted with an involuntary gasp as Quinn's hands slid down to her breasts, lingering. Her touch was light, her fingertips dancing across skin.

It was as if Nyssa were underwater again, sinking quickly, completely at the woman's mercy.

Reaching down to pull Quinn's sweater over her head, Nyssa slowed down, wanting to tease, to draw out the anticipation. She trailed her fingers up Quinn's torso.

Quinn squirmed under her touch and giggled, quickly clearing her throat as if to erase the uncharacteristic twitter of laughter.

"You're ticklish?" A smirk settled on Nyssa's face as she suppressed a self-serving chuckle.

Ah! A weakness to explore. And exploit.

"I most certainly am not."

"Yes you are," Nyssa rasped, realizing that no one had ever touched Quinn for her to know she was ticklish. She wanted to savor the moment, to create an indelible memory.

She slowly snaked the sweater up, brushing her hands up against the skin underneath. Quinn swallowed hard as Nyssa grazed her breasts, indulging in their softness and warmth, and her chest rose and fell with each shaky breath.

The sweater finally came off, and Nyssa pressed her body up against Quinn for a kiss.

The skin to skin contact was intoxicating.

"You have freckles on your shoulders," Nyssa mused.

"Certainly you saw them when we were swimming?"

"Yes, but I didn't get to do this." Nyssa bent her head and peppered kisses on those shoulders. "They're insanely cute," she murmured, enjoying the hitch in Quinn's breathing when her lips touched skin.

When she lowered Quinn down on the bed, Nyssa was practically trembling. She closed her eyes, relishing their closeness and the warmth of their bodies finally coming together. Buzzing below the surface, their soul connection sang, deep and resonant.

Nyssa settled over Quinn and kissed her, slowly moving down to her throat, its pulse thumping under her lips. Quinn responded with a soft growl, drawing a sly smile from Nyssa as her hand drifted down Quinn's torso and lazily undid the buttons on her pants.

When Quinn pressed her body up into hers, Nyssa took a deep breath, the scent of juniper and winter orchids faintly clinging to her. She reluctantly pulled away and slid off the bed, instantly missing the contact.

Kneeling beside the bed, she began undoing the laces of Quinn's boots.

Quinn propped herself up on her elbows and raised an eyebrow. "I can take off my own boots."

"Hush, woman." Nyssa removed a boot and lazily tossed it over her shoulder with a grin. She made quick work of the other boot and socks before hopping around and pulling her own off.

Quinn shook her head, laughing.

Nyssa leaned on the bed and kissed her, then slowly worked the woman's pants and underclothes off. They joined the boots on the floor.

Nyssa had to stop and admire her. Often guarded and cautious, in that moment, Quinn possessed a bold fearlessness that filled Nyssa with admiration.

She exhaled softly. Quinn was stunning.

Sitting up, Quinn moved to the side of the bed and started to unbuckle Nyssa's belt with trembling fingers and a whispered apology.

Nyssa closed her hands over Quinn's. "It's alright, take it slow. I'm not going anywhere."

Quinn's face melted into a relieved smile, and she exhaled a nervous breath before redoubling her efforts.

Nyssa finally slipped out of her pants and underwear, straightening to find Quinn running her eyes over her body. The sensation of Quinn gazing at her with desire for the first time made Nyssa's breath catch. Her scars, muscles, wide hips—any and all features and imperfections she had come to love over time—on full display. The look in Quinn's eyes, her quickened breathing, told Nyssa all she needed to know.

She was *wanted*.

Quinn reached forward to trace the scar on Nyssa's leg. That night in the mill still hung sharply in Nyssa's memory, Quinn stabbing her, thinking Nyssa a threat.

"My leg aches before a rain," Nyssa whispered.

"Sorry?" Quinn said as she smirked and bit her lip. Excitement pulsed through Nyssa, settling between her legs.

"Are you, though?" she teased.

"A little sorry." Quinn raised an eyebrow. "I didn't think you were going to kill me, but I also couldn't take the chance."

"Smart girl." Nyssa bent over for a kiss and Quinn moved back, pulling Nyssa down to her. When she gently bit the bottom of Quinn's lip, the woman groaned and moved her hips up into her, deepening Nyssa's desire.

Even after over a year of wanting and waiting, they were unhurried, languidly exploring each other, skin tightening or giving way under each touch.

Nyssa relished every sound and movement Quinn made, finding them intoxicating. She would murmur into Quinn's ear, gauging her reactions. Nothing was more arousing than hearing her breath hitch and quicken.

The nervous tension in Quinn uncoiled as they continued to roam across one another's bodies. She became louder and more assertive, losing herself in the space between them.

Carefully exploring Quinn's reactions to her fingers, lips, and tongue, Nyssa memorized the way she would move or moan with each experiment. A flick of the tongue in the hollow of Quinn's throat made her breathing deep and raspy, but lips on her breasts, teasing a nipple, made her writhe underneath Nyssa with pleasure.

Nyssa pulled back to watch her face when she finally moved her hand down between them, truly touching Quinn for the first time. Fingers dug into Nyssa's skin as Quinn arched her back, her throat bobbing with each moan. Nyssa took her time until her name was a desperate, throaty whisper on Quinn's lips when she came.

Nyssa smiled and didn't relent, paying attention to how electric Quinn's skin felt to her touch. She painted Quinn's body with kisses as she moved down her torso. Reaching up, Nyssa caressed the palm of Quinn's hand, lacing their fingers together before she moved ever lower.

Kissing the inside of Quinn's thighs, Nyssa lifted her eyes to find Quinn breathlessly watching her. It felt like an act of possession, Quinn completely hers to worship. Nyssa licked her bottom lip, enjoying the anticipation and the flicker of want in Quinn's eyes.

Nyssa dipped her head, wondering how Quinn would respond to her tongue.

She got her answer when Quinn buried a hand in her hair and let out a strangled moan. Taking her time, Nyssa teased and lingered, until she was sure that Quinn was barely tethered to her body anymore before taking her over the edge again.

Nyssa slowly trailed light, lingering kisses up Quinn's body as she recovered from her orgasm, settling over her. Quinn ran her hands through Nyssa's hair and laughed, her whole body shaking, with a smile that dazzled like the brightest stars. Nyssa kissed her again, deep and slow.

Quinn pulled out of the kiss and splayed a hand on Nyssa's chest. Her eyes sparked with hunger.

She rolled Nyssa onto her back and pressed a leg between Nyssa's thighs, and Nyssa let out a low groan. Her breathing quickened at Quinn's boldness, the heat between them making her skin buzz. Nyssa went to kiss her, but Quinn pulled back with a smirk, bending to graze Nyssa's lips before moving away again, and moving down to her neck.

Nyssa moaned. A hot, electric tingle moved through her neck and to the tops of her ears—her neck was her damn weakness. A *glorious* weakness.

Quinn's teasing was frustrating and delighting in equal measure. *Payback*, Nyssa acknowledged with a rueful smile.

Nyssa went to kiss Quinn again and was pushed down onto the bed for her efforts, a sly grin on Quinn's face. Moving closer, Quinn murmured into Nyssa's ear, her voice low and thick, asking for permission. Asking to *taste*.

A strangled *please* rasped out of Nyssa's throat, and Quinn trailed her lips down Nyssa's body, slow and purposeful, until she settled between her legs. Nyssa twisted her hands in the bedsheets, her coherent thoughts shattering. A string of happy curses left Nyssa's mouth with a gasp.

Nyssa wrapped a blanket around herself and plodded to the kitchen, intent on finally making tea. She put the kettle on the stove and settled into her thoughts as it heated.

Sex had always been little else than a fun distraction for her, yet with Quinn, she wanted to dive in and explore every feeling and sensation, finding that she craved intimacy, not just the physical act of sex.

The last couple hours had been different from anything she had ever experienced. And she wanted more...she wanted to take from Quinn and give herself in equal measure.

Arms wrapped around her from behind, bringing a easy smile to her lips.

"I'm finally making that tea I promised," Nyssa said over her shoulder. Quinn swept Nyssa's hair to the side, lightly tracing the lines of the Kraken on her upper back. Gentle kisses and a fluttering tongue followed shortly after, springing goose bumps on Nyssa's skin.

"How long will the tea take?" Quinn murmured in her ear, the vibration of her voice arousing.

"Not too long—"

Quinn's fingers trailed down her stomach. Nyssa swallowed and braced against the kitchen table as Quinn's hand moved lower.

And lower.

"Quinn, I swear, you are..." Nyssa lolled her head back and exhaled a moan when Quinn's hand settled between her legs.

"I'm what?" Quinn purred, her breath hot on the back of Nyssa's neck.

Nyssa abandoned her words, shaking her head. A low, contented hum emanated from Quinn's chest, rumbling against Nyssa. She relaxed back into Quinn, letting the woman do whatever she wanted.

The tea could wait.

A DISTRACTING DESIRE

Quinn climbed back into bed, pulling a blanket up around her shoulders, smirking as she watched Nyssa shake her head at the tea strainer, dump the tea back into the tin, then measure it out again, mumbling about having lost count.

Coming up to the cabin that day, Quinn almost turned back several times, her confidence waning, but in the end screwed up the courage to see Nyssa. There were so many things she'd wanted to say, though unsure of how to proceed. Unsure of what it even meant to be in love. Or if she deserved it.

All of her doubts and fears were put to rest when Nyssa confessed her love.

In bed, Nyssa was attentive in a way that made Quinn's heart race, watching her reactions to everything, ensuring she was enjoying herself. Nyssa teased and smiled, giving selflessly, gentle and powerful, her control over Quinn's body almost transcendent.

Quinn chewed on her bottom lip, wondering if it was possible to stay in the cabin forever. A sense of giddiness overtook her, a distracting desire to explore sex over and over again with Nyssa, making it hard to think of anything else.

She hardly recognized herself like this—taking what she wanted and not being afraid or ashamed. She had come to trust Nyssa more than anyone and that trust melted away her fear and doubt. There was a dichotomy to Nyssa, tender and assertive, with a willingness to allow Quinn to be the same.

When Nyssa returned to the bed, she held out a mug of tea to Quinn.

"Thank you," Quinn said as Nyssa deftly laid across the bed, not spilling a single drop of tea. "The scar on your side, it's new. Where did that come from?"

"Oh that?" Nyssa reached down and touched it gingerly. "I got captured by some bounty hunters. They strung me up and started asking me where you were. Then they got insistent when I wouldn't tell them."

"Nyssa," Quinn breathed. "I'm so sorry."

Nyssa blew on her tea. "Aryis got me out of that scrape. And for her trouble, I threatened her life."

"Not without reason. You shouldn't feel guilty for how you felt about her." Quinn's own feelings toward Aryis were dark and unforgiving, but she kept them to herself.

"You told me that I'm not cruel. I had a hard time remembering that for a while," Nyssa admitted.

Quinn smiled. "Yes, but you did remember. And you have given Aryis far more grace than I would have."

"I don't believe that," Nyssa said. "You can be a hard-ass, but your heart is bigger than you give yourself credit for."

Heat rose in Quinn's cheeks. Still hard to take a compliment, it seemed.

Nyssa sipped on her tea and considered her. "You know, if we weren't complete idiots, we could have been together long before this."

"We had our reasons," Quinn replied. She thought back to her conversation with Fontaine and how astutely the woman had broken down Quinn's fears—what had she ever desired and felt she deserved? Arcton Citadel had burrowed itself into her in devastating, destructive ways, stripping her of her confidence and self-worth. And she would have to slowly dig that infernal place out of her and cast it aside.

Nyssa stared into her mug. "You're right. We both had issues to move past. But just think of how much fun we could have had on Monk's Cove."

Quinn groaned and flopped against a pillow. "True! If I had known—"

"How good I am in bed?" Nyssa gave her a maddening wink.

The woman's confidence was not without merit. A rather large amount of merit. But Quinn rolled her eyes and laughed anyway, not quite ready to feed Nyssa's ego. "Not that I have a basis for comparison, but I'd say you're passable."

"Passable? You probably lost count of how many times I made you—"

"Nyssa!" More heat rose in her cheeks.

An amused smirk spread across Nyssa's face. "You know, you're not so bad yourself."

"Fontaine had some...interesting books in her collection, a bit of a crash course on many different aspects of sex of all varieties. Though I may have been drawn to the ones with women together, for, um..."

"Research purposes?" Nyssa laughed, shaking her head. "I knew it was you reading them! I may have also read one or two."

"Just one or two?"

Nyssa gave her a wink and that cocky grin she had grown used to seeing every day. In the face of that cockiness, Quinn's bravado quickly melted and a wave of uncertainty settled over her. She hated it, but her life had no physical affection in it before now. How could she know if Nyssa truly enjoyed being with her?

"But was I...adequate?"

Nyssa smiled. "Are you aiming for another toldoku for achievement?"

"Nyssa, I'm serious. I'm not...experienced."

Nyssa sat up and leaned forward to kiss Quinn, her lips gentle.

"Adequate is not even close. You were astonishing," she whispered. Nyssa's eyes seared into Quinn, causing her stomach to tighten. How easy it was to get utterly turned on by just a look from those deep-blue eyes.

Quinn leaned forward and tucked a bit of Nyssa's hair behind her ear. Being so close to her, touching her, it felt natural, the barriers between them stripped away.

Nyssa lay back down, not taking her eyes off Quinn. "Oh, and that bit in the kitchen? I heartily approve. You continue to surprise me, Freckles."

The tension in Quinn eased. She felt outmatched, being twenty-six and so dreadfully inexperienced in many things in life. She was convinced she would grow old and die a prisoner of the guild, alone and untouched. The adepts and Masters all shrank away from her. But from the moment they met, Nyssa never pulled away. Never once treated her as a monster whose touch could hurt. Or kill. Not even after what Suvi made her do.

"When I was imprisoned in Sarisan, I thought about you every day," Quinn said. "And I thought about that kiss. A lot. And then, as time went on, I was so scared I'd never get the chance to tell you how I feel. Or kiss you again."

Nyssa exhaled, growing serious. "I would have razed that fucking city to the ground to get you back. I just wanted you safe...with me."

Nyssa's anger had always been so alluring and attractive. It was powerful and fierce. Dangerous. The few times Nyssa turned it on Quinn, the force of it excited her and frightened her in equal measure. It made no sense how much it turned her on, an attraction she was afraid to admit, even now.

Quinn shook her head, her thoughts tumbling, drifting toward a subject that had been unspoken between them for over a year.

Time to come clean.

"I've lied to you for a while now and I want to amend that," Quinn began. "Back on Hannah's Whisper, when that blood wraith attacked, I dove into the Black Sea after you because I couldn't bear the thought of not waking up and having another chance to talk to you, to get to know you. Even though you frustrated the fuck out of me and I wanted to punch you half the time, I still wanted you there. I think I was a little taken with you, even back then."

Nyssa listened intently, her expression a mix of happiness and amusement. "I am kinda irresistible."

Quinn let out a heavy sigh. But dammit, Nyssa *was* rather irresistible. "Now I'm curious. When did you start having feelings for me?" Quinn asked.

Nyssa's eyes searched the ceiling as she thought. "Honestly, the minute I saw you cleaned up at The Lash. I felt as though I recognized you, but from where, I couldn't say. I now understand it's the god bond between us. But as far as wanting to see you naked and do untoward things to you? I suppose that really started when you wore that dress to Lilliana's dinner at Ocean's Keep. That night I felt a jolt of attraction that scared the hell out of me."

With a laugh, Quinn nodded. "I remember the look on your face. I was puzzled by it. No one had looked at me like that before."

Leaning forward, Nyssa slipped her hand behind Quinn's neck and pulled her in for a deep, lingering kiss. "I can't imagine not looking at you like that. Wanting you," Nyssa whispered, her eyes hooded. The contact, the buzz of her words, made Quinn feel warm. Wanted.

Safe.

Quinn pulled away, lying back with a sigh. "I love you."

The smile that settled over Nyssa's features was one Quinn rarely saw—contentment. In this moment, they weren't fugitives or women with scars that never could completely heal. By filling the space between them, they became one entity that moved with purpose and desire. And love.

Nyssa swatted Quinn's leg. "We need to eat," she said, getting out of bed and taking Quinn's tea mug from her. "In this house, we have rules: you must wear pants at the dining table."

Quinn got up and grumbled as she fished her clothes off the floor, hoping that Nyssa would remove them from her later.

As they sat over bowls of hot stew and hunks of crusty bread, Nyssa leaned back into her chair.

"We need to talk about what we do moving forward."

Quinn stood and picked up their bowls to get another helping of stew from the pot over the fire. She considered the question for a minute before answering, making sure it's what she still wanted.

"My plans haven't changed. We need to get Suvi. I think she's our only way to freedom, Nyssa, and I want to be free. *Truly* free."

She set Nyssa's bowl in front of her, and Nyssa caught her arm, pulling her down for a quick kiss. Quinn smiled. She could get used to these moments.

Nyssa tapped the side of her bowl as she watched Quinn eat. Quinn sensed there was more than capturing Suvi on Nyssa's mind.

And she knew she wasn't going to like it.

"You want to find a way to get Aryis back, don't you?"

Nyssa smiled and picked up her spoon. "Am I that obvious?"

"I expect no less from you and your honor code, but Aryis caused our suffering. We almost died because of her."

A frown settled upon Nyssa's face. "She pulled me out of my drunken self-pity and came up with a plan to rescue *you*. I would have died piss drunk with a knife in my back or would have been captured and delivered to the Empress for her to take my head. I wouldn't have gotten you back without her."

"And you wouldn't have needed to rescue me without her betrayal, Nyssa," Quinn pointed out sternly. "She hurt you. Deeply. And I hate her for it."

"I wanted to hate her for so long. And...I did. But she made sure I got out of the Realm of Shadows, otherwise I would have been trapped too. She saved me, and then you and I were able to save each other. I just want to get her back and...see if maybe there's a world where she and I can work our way back to friendship. You know that this is all tearing Athen apart. He puts on a brave face, but he needs to get Aryis back too. And I won't let him down, not after what he's done for me."

The anger blossoming within Quinn felt out of place after the wonderful day she had experienced. She calmed herself. She didn't have to share Nyssa's feelings for Aryis, but she could help her, knowing Nyssa would stubbornly plow ahead anyway. "I don't want to fight about her. Let's concentrate on making a plan."

"Fair enough," Nyssa replied with a frown. "Let's get back to the Whisper. Regroup and strategize. We'll come up with a plan to get both Aryis and Suvi."

Quinn nodded, content for the moment. "By the way, Athen visited me yesterday."

"Oh?" Nyssa leaned forward with an amused expression.

"It's strange getting to know your best friend after all the stories you've told me. He's a good man. And astute. He sensed there was something between us and I stupidly asked for his advice regarding you."

Nyssa narrowed her eyes, a playful eyebrow perking up. "And what did he say?"

"He was *completely* useless. He said, *figure it out*," Quinn grumbled. "Not exactly a detailed map to your heart."

Nyssa tilted her head forward and laughed, her auburn hair tumbling around her face. "That asshole! That's the same advice I gave him about Aryis. I knew that would come back to haunt me."

"I'm surprised you and Athen aren't a thing."

Nyssa cringed. "Ugh, we kissed once. Once."

"You didn't share that with me!"

The pained look on Nyssa's face made Quinn break out in laughter.

"I love your laugh, you know," Nyssa mused.

Laughing around Nyssa was easy. Quinn could let her walls down and let the tension in her body, coiled up for years, dissipate.

"What say we take a bath?" Nyssa asked, cocking an eyebrow and giving Quinn a wicked smile.

"Is that look meant to seduce me?"

"Is it working?"

Quinn glanced at the apple pie sitting in the kitchen, bursting with apples and cinnamon. Nyssa never turned down dessert.

Ever.

"What about the pie?"

Nyssa huffed out a laugh and stood up, pulling Quinn out of her chair. "I would rather get you naked and wet. We'll have pie later."

Heat flushed through Quinn's body. "Then get me naked and wet."

KORAS THE RECKONER

That night, as Quinn curled up in bed, Nyssa pulled her close and mumbled, "I love you, Freckles," into her hair as they drifted off to sleep.

Quinn woke deep into the night, sluggish and slow to open her eyes. A dream had pulled her under—walking in a luminescent forest, a stream twinkling nearby, an unending darkness dimly lit with stars above her, an icy shadow enveloping her body.

She rose to her feet and glanced back to the bed. Nyssa was curled up in the blankets, beautiful in the pale moonlight that peeked through the windows. The fire had reduced to embers, the air in the cabin chilly.

A familiar presence tugged at Quinn, and she quietly slipped into her pants and sweater, leaving the cabin and Nyssa behind, walking into the forest. Quinn barely noticed the cold of winter on her bare feet.

Minutes of walking brought her to a stream glistening in the moonlight, its lazy flow lulling Quinn. The forest glowed with a purplish darkness that felt...safe. Green dots floated between the trees, drifting like dreams.

She closed her eyes and took a deep breath, the chill night air crisp with snow, pine, and winter orchids.

When she opened her eyes, a stag stood across the water. Quinn knew him instantly—Koras the Reckoner, the Ancient God of the Realm of

Night. He slowly crossed the water, stopping when he reached her. His massive body towered over her and darkness coiled around him like a snake.

Quinn stretched her hand forward, tentative, and Koras nuzzled his forehead against her palm. His touch sent a jolt of energy through her, flinging her senses wide open. The Realm of Night dove into her, filling her with the shadow of night, its stars, the fireflies made of pure ancient magick. The Pillars of Mercy sang its song until her whole body felt untethered from the earth.

Darkness spiraled around her and danced across her skin, its chill making her gasp. It wasn't just darkness, it was the night itself, protective and comforting. Part of her was ashamed that she once believed her power was evil and destructive, no better than the forbidden magick Ceril practiced. It took saving Nyssa to understand she could do both terrible and amazing things with her abilities.

Her chest started to vibrate, and another heartbeat thumped on top of her own, out of sync with hers at first. Slowly, the heartbeats aligned, becoming one.

"Quinn?"

Nyssa. She approached in the dark, her eyes alight with a soft blue glow. Bright golden fireflies darted around her. She came to a stop a few feet from Koras and gave him a deep bow—a sign of respect.

"Isn't he magnificent?" Quinn whispered.

"He is," Nyssa replied with a smile. "When I met him before, I felt my magick in him. And you. I felt you."

Quinn took Nyssa's hand. An energy moved through them, her touch electric, making her gasp. She pulled Nyssa closer. "Kiss me."

Nyssa leaned forward and obliged. Quinn closed her eyes, sighing into Nyssa's warm lips. Deep, distant voices filled her head, some singing, some humming, all in a strange, incredible harmony. Her heart beat harder in her chest, thumping like a bass drum. The line between her and Nyssa blurred as their magick entwined, the edges of her existence softening and stretching beyond the space she occupied in the world. Every part of her body buzzed.

Nyssa's hands encircled the back of Quinn's neck, her bare skin tingling with energy as they kissed. The voices in Quinn's head grew louder, their song of creation and old magick thrumming in through her body. The moment mirrored her dreams of late, of delving deep into the darkness, then rising to meet something massive and inevitable.

Hold out your hand, Quinn said. Her words came without sound, just as they had below the Pillars of Mercy.

Nyssa did as asked, and Quinn hovered her hand over Nyssa's, shadow spilling out. Sensing the power buzzing between them, Quinn teased Nyssa's magick out. Blue lightning and dark tendrils flowed over their hands, twisting and arcing. Beautiful and dangerous.

This is our power.

Nyssa cocked her head, her eyes focused on the magick coiling around their hands. *How are you doing this?*

I think it's the Realm of Night...it blurs the lines between us. Between our thoughts and magick.

Let me try...

A rush of energy moved through Quinn, making her gasp, as Nyssa flowed her power into her. The connection she had with Nyssa was growing stronger over time. And there was something otherworldly about it—beyond the Realm of Night and Koras.

A faint rumble pulsed against Quinn's senses, breaking through the other voices, making her fingers vibrate, almost as if Nyssa's power was coursing through her. Another entity pulled at them—more specifically, at Nyssa. Something possessing immense power, both deep inside of Nyssa and distant at the same time.

Nyssa scowled and turned her head.

Koras spoke, his voice rumbling through Quinn. *She calls to you, Nyssa Blacksea.*

Who? Nyssa replied, her blue eyes burning with a deep-sapphire light.

Narileh the Protector. You died in her arms as Quinn reached out and saved you. You were both reborn in the Realm of the Deep.

The Realm of the Deep?

Under the waves of the Black Sea.

Threads of golden energy encircled Nyssa, winding around her left hand. She raised her arm. A glistening band surrounded her middle finger—a ghost of the ring she once wore, the Kraken engraving pulsing with a deep-blue glow.

My sigil...Narileh. Nyssa looked at Koras. *Can we meet her?*

Perhaps one day. If you can get past her Sentinel.

One god at a time, Nyssa, Quinn said, a smile creeping onto her face as the power of Koras's magick flowed through them. *Koras, thank you for saving us.*

You saved each other. I merely gave you a small push.

Nonetheless, thank you.

Nyssa squeezed Quinn's hand, her face growing serious. She turned to the Ancient God. *Koras, my friend is trapped in the Realm of Shadows... Is she...* Nyssa's face fell.

As much as Quinn hated Aryis, her heart broke for Nyssa.

She is still alive, Nyssa Blacksea.

Nyssa's grip on Quinn's hand grew tighter.

I need to get to her, Nyssa insisted.

I know. But you must be careful. My brother awaits.

Your brother?

Tajal the Curious.

Quinn swallowed, remembering the deep sense of dread that crept over every inch of her body from the second she stepped inside the Realm of Shadows.

Will he hurt Aryis? Nyssa asked.

The longer he has her, the more lost she'll become, until her mind no longer is bound to your world. Tajal is...complicated. Your pain will tempt him.

What if Tajal didn't want to let Aryis leave? How far would Nyssa go to rescue their betrayer?

Tajal hurting Nyssa was a possibility Quinn couldn't face.

How do I save my friend? Nyssa asked. *How do I get back into the Realm of Shadows and find her?*

Koras's four white eyes blazed. *You have everything you need.*

Quinn shook her head. That wasn't a proper answer. *Wait, we need more inform—*

Koras's voice rang loud and steady in her head. *Go, daughters, the world calls you back.*

Darkness swirled around Quinn and Nyssa, sweeping them up. Quinn found herself falling, weightless. Koras's presence vibrated through her whole body, louder and more intense with every passing second.

Then, suddenly, silence.

She opened her eyes and found herself staring up at the stars, her back pressed against the cold earth. Her breath hung in the air above her face. Sitting up, she laughed, her eyes wide. The Realm of Night had released its hold on the two of them, but what a wonderful experience, unlike any she had felt before.

"Did that really just happen?" she breathed.

Nyssa stirred beside her and held her hand up. The glowing band around her finger was gone.

"Koras is my sigil, isn't he?" Quinn asked.

"Yeah, I think he is," Nyssa said with a soft laugh. "He's a noble symbol for you."

Quinn lit up at the thought. It seemed like such a small thing. Most sigils were woven into family histories, but as an orphan, she had no knowledge of her background and what symbol her family might have chosen as their talisman, if any. Athen had chosen for Nyssa—and his choice of a Kraken was dead-on.

Quinn made a silent pact with herself to live up to Koras's trust in them. In her. She didn't quite understand why they were favored by the Ancient God, but she was immensely grateful.

"Koras didn't tell us how to get Aryis out of the Realm of Shadows," Quinn said.

"Nope. He pulled an Athen on us."

Quinn rolled her eyes. "Figure it out?"

"Figure it out," Nyssa sighed.

SPARRING

Nyssa kicked Quinn in the stomach, sending her reeling. Quinn stumbled back, grunting. She pushed her raven-colored hair out of her face with a frown.

"I'm so sluggish," she grumbled.

Nyssa bounced on her toes, still trying to wake up after their late-night visit with Koras. It still didn't seem real. "You'll get back in shape. We both will. We have to be ready for whatever Suvi throws at us."

She exhaled and watched her breath fog in front of her. Her toes were freezing, but she had insisted on bare feet and arms, tossing her jacket on the cabin steps, braving the winter cold as she once did at the Emerald Order when she was younger. The Masters would make the adepts practice barefoot until they could no longer take the cold. One by one they would run inside to warm up.

Nyssa was always the last one left. It was a matter of pride to never give up before anyone else. Quinn called her crazy, asking her to at least wear boots, but it had been so long since Nyssa trained and she wanted to strip back to basics.

"Come on, let's go again," she said, willing her muscles to calm their shivering. She smirked and sent a spark of lightning toward Quinn, hitting her in the earlobe. Quinn jumped and laughed, as Nyssa had hoped she would.

Nyssa closed her eyes and focused, growing still, locating Quinn by sensing her magickal essence. She waited with a smile until the magick shifted, moving toward her. She sidestepped, avoiding a punch, then opened her eyes and lightly smacked Quinn on the back of her head with her palm.

Quinn rounded on her, anger and frustration bubbling behind her scowl, a mood Nyssa knew too well. Quinn came at her again with a flurry of punches that Nyssa managed to block before she ducked into a fist that slammed into her jaw. Stars burst in front of her eyes and she stumbled back.

Not allowing her time to recover, Quinn slammed a palm into Nyssa's chest. Nyssa left her feet and landed hard on her back, the air rushing out of her lungs. Quinn quickly moved over her, threatening another strike as Nyssa gulped for breath.

"Yield!" Quinn commanded.

"I yield," Nyssa choked out.

Quinn's face melted into concern. "Are you okay?"

"Sluggish my ass," Nyssa said while Quinn pulled her to her feet.

"You're still recovering."

Nyssa frowned. "My magick has settled back in, but my body is...taking its time getting reacquainted with being healthy." She was a step slow, out of sync and creaky, her body early in its journey to feeling *right* again. "You seem to be faring better."

Quinn brushed a stray strand of hair from Nyssa's face, sending a flush of heat through her veins.

"I was dying much slower than you due to the void collar. I can't believe I have that abomination to thank for delaying my demise," Quinn said. "Plus, I'm a capable fighter, thanks to you."

"You're a capable fighter because you have talent."

"Oh, well, that's entirely true."

"Impressive!" Athen smiled as he walked down the path to Nyssa's cabin.

Quinn turned bright red. "I didn't know we were being watched."

"Nyssa's been teaching you Ithais-Toru?" Athen asked.

"Yes. And I'm rather good, I'm told."

He snorted. "I see Nyssa has influenced your humility."

"Not entirely. I've always been a bit of an arrogant ass, according to Nyssa." Quinn smiled up at him.

"So, anything new with you two?" Athen asked, rocking back on his heels, the grin on his face positively wicked.

Nyssa shot him a look, and he awkwardly winked, as if he had something stuck in his remaining eye and was trying to blink it out.

"We figured it out," Quinn said, her tone dripping with sarcasm.

Athen took a step toward her before stopping. He raised an eyebrow. "Can I hug you?" Quinn rarely let anyone touch her—he was learning her ways, gentle yet persistent, as he had once been with Nyssa.

Quinn scowled before seemingly losing the fight against the smile that rose on her lips. "Fine."

Athen wrapped her up in a big bear hug, lifting her off the ground. "I give good advice, right?"

"You give shit advice," Quinn mumbled, trying to hug Athen back.

Nyssa cleared the lump in her throat and willed her eyes to stay dry. To see them so friendly with one another—her two great loves coming together—meant more to her than she could express.

Athen put Quinn down and wrapped an arm around Nyssa. "You two are looking a sight better than when we first got here."

Nyssa nodded, leaning into him before she turned serious. "We have to talk. About Aryis."

Quinn and Nyssa filled Athen in on what they had learned from Koras—his face lit up when they told him Aryis was still alive. "But, the longer she is in the Realm of Shadows, the worse off she'll be."

"Fuck," he whispered. "Look, I could use your help to mount a rescue, but I'm not going to beg. I'll go it alone if I have to."

So many complicated feelings were twisted up in Aryis Devitt, but Nyssa knew one thing for certain—Athen would not relent until Aryis was safe.

"You're not going back into the Realm of Shadows."

His face darkened. "Nyssa, you can't stop me—"

"I'm going back in myself. Alone." Nyssa glanced at Quinn, whose face was inscrutable. "I've found the barrier between realms before, I think I can do it again."

"I can help you," Athen insisted.

"No. I'm not risking your life."

He glanced over at Quinn, who shook her head. "Don't argue with Nyssa. You and I both know better, you won't get your way."

Athen's face settled into a scowl. "Fine."

Nyssa let out a big sigh. "It'll be tough, though. Finding the Realm of Shadows, finding Aryis...I don't know exactly how to do that yet."

"We go back to where we lost her?" Athen suggested.

Nyssa nodded. It was their best option. Their only option, really. "Agreed. But getting to her...that's what I can't—"

Quinn let out a sharp gasp. "Fuck. We're idiots."

"What?" Nyssa asked.

"Koras *did* clue us in on how to get Aryis back, Nyssa. Your ring. I saw her wearing it when you all rescued me." She walked over to the steps and picked up Nyssa's jacket. "You can sense your magick on this jacket, your boots...Winter's Bite. Remember when Fontaine told us our magick sort of rubs off onto our possessions? You'll be able to sense your ring if you focus."

"Shit, you're right," Nyssa said. "But I can't sense something that far away. We'll need to get back to Suvi's estate and get me as close as possible to where we lost her." She fixed Athen in her gaze. "I'm going to get her back, big man, I promise. We'll leave tomorrow to return to Le'Caal and the Whisper."

Athen nodded.

Nyssa turned to Quinn, and braced her head in her hands. "I know you don't like this, but I have to—"

"Stop." Quinn grabbed Nyssa's wrists. "I hate Aryis because of what she did to us, but I wouldn't condemn her to be a prisoner in the Realm of Shadows. I'll help you. But this is our chance to accomplish what we originally set out to do. If we go back for Aryis, we grab Suvi too."

Nyssa wanted to kiss Quinn so badly, but knew it would make her self-conscious with Athen staring at them. "That's...going to be complicated, but you're right, that'll be our chance to get Suvi. You're amazing, you know that?"

"So many compliments today. Watch out, I might get a big head," Quinn whispered.

A second passed before Athen cleared his throat. "Could one of you explain what you mean by grabbing Suvi?"

Nyssa grimaced and scratched her head. "Um, so, we've had this idea for over a year now. Aryis kind of threw everything off-kilter, but we're going to kidnap Suvi Rell and trade her to Empress Kalla for our freedom."

Athen's one good eye roamed between the two women, and Nyssa braced for his reaction. After several awkward seconds, he said, "That's completely insane. I'm in!"

Of course he was. From training at the Order together, to bar fights in Vane, and now kidnapping a goddamn queen, Athen would always be by Nyssa's side when she needed him. "I love you, big man. I couldn't have made it this far without you."

"Well, that's damn true." He smiled, trying once again to wink at Quinn.

"You need to work on that," Quinn remarked.

Nyssa stood at the lake's edge, peering out at the black platform in the middle of the water. She couldn't see the Pillars of Mercy, but she could feel their magnetic pull.

"I'm not sure this is a good idea," Quinn said.

Nyssa glanced over her shoulder. "C'mon, I know you're curious too."

"Curious to see if you'll walk on water, yes."

Nyssa stuck her tongue out and hovered her foot over the lake before taking a step. She barely caught herself from plunging headfirst into the icy water when her foot sank into the water.

Laughter burst out of Quinn. Nyssa threw up her hands.

"What the hell? You guys walked on the water!"

"Because we were in the Realm of Night, Nyssa Blacksea," a voice scolded. Cyphon walked toward them, joining Quinn. Nyssa grumbled and stepped back out of the lake with wet, cold feet. A shiver ran through her, as did a twinge of regret. Her clean, dry socks were already packed up.

"You're able to see and do things in the Realms that you can't do in this plane," he continued.

"Like when we can hear each others' thoughts?" she asked.

"Yes. You two are bonded, your souls entwined, but it takes an Ancient God to link your minds." Cyphon gestured to the lake. "What did you intend to do out on that platform?"

"I just wanted to see the Pillars again before we leave. I can feel them, but I don't see them."

"They are only visible in the Realm of Night."

"What are they?" Quinn asked.

Cyphon smiled at her. "Primalith Shards like the Pillars are a focal point of ancient magick, remnants of a long-dead past. Most were dormant until twenty-seven years ago, when they lit up again."

Nyssa walked toward Quinn and Cyphon, her feet squishing in her boots with each soggy step. "When we were born, you mean?"

"Ancient power ebbs and flows. It sinks into a long slumber, then reawakens when it is time. And it is time for ancient magick to rise again. You two were born, the Pillars of Mercy reignited, and other burgeoning signs of old magick are all around us."

"Like the tress and sea singing?" Quinn asked.

"Yes, among other things," Cyphon replied.

"Just a question, but...do you have to be naked to hear the singing?"

"What an odd query. No, of course not."

"I knew it!" Quinn said.

Nyssa shook with laughter. Cyphon seemed confused.

"Why did Koras bring us here?" Nyssa asked.

Cyphon looked out over the water. "Koras felt you dying when you first met him, Nyssa. And before that, he heard your soul cry out as Quinn took your magick from you. He felt the shift in Quinn, taking something that didn't belong to her. But she saved you both by doing so, little did she know at the time." He turned and smiled at Quinn.

"I don't understand how I did it, though. I can't manipulate magick like Nyssa can, so how was I able to draw her magick inside of me?" Quinn asked.

"Your magicks are connected. I suspect you reacted instinctively, protecting Nyssa and her magick by preserving it within yourself. You're able to do things with Nyssa that you can't do with anyone else."

Nyssa laughed again, and Quinn shot her a look, narrowing her eyes. Nyssa replied with a cocky smirk and a wink.

Cyphon continued. "Koras wasn't even sure if you'd be able to take your magick back, Nyssa. That you two survived is a miracle. Koras is pleased with how you've grown into your power. You will be needed in the times to come."

"Why does that worry me?" Nyssa asked.

Cyphon's face grew serious. "There are others like you. But they do not have your hearts. You must be ready to fight when called."

The news of other Cursed Gods—likely dangerous ones—made her wary, though a pulse of nervous excitement rippled through her. The thought that they weren't the only Cursed Gods in the world was intriguing. But also a problem for another time. She didn't want to contend with anything else at the moment. Not with Aryis to rescue and a queen to kidnap. "Cyphon, we have our own headaches to deal with right now."

"Then deal with your headaches but be at the ready."

Nyssa crossed her arms and sighed. "What if we deal with our problems, then disappear to live our lives in peace?"

"Then I would say Koras and Narileh misjudged you. And I have found that they are rarely wrong," Cyphon said. "Come. Athen is packing up. It is time to say goodbye."

Cyphon accompanied Nyssa and Quinn to their wagon, which waited in a clearing not far from the lake. Two figures made of fireflies stood waiting.

"They brought your wagon and horses here and looked after them these last weeks," Cyphon explained, gesturing to the glowing figures. "There's a trail to the north that will lead you to the Empire's lands."

"Is that how you resupply this little hideaway?" Nyssa asked.

Cyphon's face remained deadpan. "You have deduced my greatest secret."

She chuckled. "Thank you, Cyphon. For everything." Nyssa walked over to the animals. The big white horse nuzzled her face, tickling her with its nose. She nuzzled back, the scent of hay filling her nostrils, while Quinn kept her distance.

Athen slung two large bags filled with food into the back of the wagon for their trip to Le'Caal—supplies from Cyphon.

Cyphon approached Nyssa and held his hand out. The tea tin from her cabin materialized in his palm. She cleared her throat upon seeing it, trying to keep her mind off the wonderful, sexy memories surrounding it.

"A gift for the Cursed Gods," he said, holding the tin out to Nyssa.

She coughed and nodded, trying her best to look austere. "Thank you."

"It's not a regular tea tin. It refills itself."

Nyssa stared at him. "Wait, you weren't refilling it when you visited?"

Cyphon laughed. "No, Nyssa, it is a relic containing ancient magick, the perfect gift for Cursed Gods."

"Wh-where does the tea come from?" Quinn asked.

Cyphon shrugged.

Nyssa frowned at him. It didn't feel like a trivial question that deserved a shrug in response. "Not to appear ungrateful, but is the tea...safe?"

"You've been drinking it for a while. And Quinn has too of late, I've noticed," Cyphon replied, raising an eyebrow. Quinn, predictably, turned red. "Are either of you dead?"

"No, but—"

"Then it's safe," he replied, placing a hand on her shoulder. "Nyssa Blacksea, is a self-filling tea tin the strangest thing you've experienced in your short life?"

Nyssa peered down at the tin in her hands, its metal exterior delicately etched with bamboo trees, a small starling perched in their midst. It even had a small dent in the side. Ancient magick in an unlikely vessel. She smiled. "Thank you for this gift."

Athen climbed onto the wagon, taking the reins. Nyssa made for the back, chucking off her wet boots and stripping out of her socks, but Quinn lingered with Cyphon. Nyssa kept an eye on them as she draped her socks over the side of the wagon to dry, tucking under a blanket to keep warm.

"Will you be...lonely when we're gone?" Quinn asked.

Cyphon's eyebrows perked up and he seemed surprised by the question. "No, my love. There's far more in the Emerrath Forest and the Realm of Night than you've seen. True, my family is long dead, but I have a new family now, strange though they be."

"Emerrath Forest?"

"Ah yes, the name of these woods from a time long forgotten."

"Emerrath," Quinn repeated softly, smiling to herself.

"You ready?" Nyssa asked. Quinn nodded, and Nyssa offered a hand to help her up into the wagon.

The two glowing figures joined Cyphon by the side of the road as they left. Nyssa waved, and the three of them waved back.

"I hope we get to return here one day," Quinn said. Nyssa smiled and tossed her a blanket. They settled in the back of the wagon. Nyssa lay down and watched the snow-laden branches of trees pass overhead as she drifted off to sleep, Quinn's fingers laced in her hair.

REUNIONS

An unpleasant buzz of magick irritated Nyssa's skin as it slowed her ascent up Hannah's Whisper's gangplank. The damn protective veil.

Fucking Fontaine.

The veil turned thick and prickly, entangling her in its magick—a sure deterrent for any intruder.

But Nyssa wasn't just any intruder.

The surface of the veil parted as she let her power flow, tearing a hole in the magick to allow entry. Fontaine would likely grouse about her enchantment being ruined and the mere thought of it brought a smile to Nyssa's lips. Gods, she'd missed that woman.

She stepped on the deck of the Whisper, trailed by Quinn and Athen. Predictably, low droning alarms sounded, Fontaine's sentry magick alerting the crew to trespassers. Nyssa was certain they looked every part the dangerous bunch in dark, hooded cloaks.

"Don't take one more step or we'll cut you down where you stand!" a familiar voice bellowed. Elias barreled down the side of the ship, hands igniting with fire, ready to fight. Fontaine, following on his heels, pushed past him. "Fontaine, careful!" he yelled. She slowed to a stop in front of the threesome.

Nyssa pulled the hood of her winter cloak back, and Quinn did the same. "Did you really think your little veil would keep two gods off your ship, woman?"

Fontaine gasped. A second later, she crashed into Quinn, hugging her tight, pulling Nyssa into the embrace. Nyssa grunted—she never realized that Old Folk were so strong.

"Well, I'll be damned," Elias said, bursting into a smile.

Fontaine let the women go, and Nyssa rushed to give Elias a hug. He pulled her off her feet. "How are you still alive?" he asked, incredulous. He put her down and grabbed hold of Quinn, sweeping her up into a hug. "You are a sight for sore eyes, love."

Word spread quickly among the crew, bringing them up from below deck. Mina and Max clapped the women on the back. Buck grumbled at them, though a rare smile gave him away. Even Yuha gave them an approving nod.

Tears sprang to Nyssa's eyes. Quinn wiped at her face, quick to hide her emotions.

Elias shook Athen's hand and clapped him on the shoulder. "Athen Fennick, good to see you again!"

"Where is Aryis?" Fontaine asked.

Nyssa paused. Despite everything, Aryis's absence made her heart ache. "That's complicated."

Elias rocked back on his heels and shook his head. "How the fuck are you alive? Not that I'm complaining, but we all...I'm sorry, but we expected the worst."

Nyssa smiled. "You want us to tell you our story without getting some food and alcohol in us first?"

"What was I thinking?" Elias said, throwing his hands up in the air. "Max, Buck, haul up drinks and scrounge up some food. Ship meeting at the mainmast in five minutes. Fontaine, repair the veil, if you will."

Fontaine shot Nyssa a look but began weaving a spell to refortify the ship's defensive barrier.

Nyssa gave her a quick peck on the cheek. Fontaine grumbled anyway, though her smile blazed bright.

When everyone was settled at the mainmast with a drink in hand, the crew sat rapt as Nyssa told the story of her journey. Parts of the tale were difficult to recount, her emotions still so close to the surface. The ordeal had taken its toll in many ways.

Nyssa impressed upon the crew how Aryis had sacrificed herself to save her from the Realm of Shadows. "I failed her. And despite everything she did, I miss her." She shook herself and cleared the lump in her throat.

Nyssa left out the more intimate details of the story, not mentioning her budding relationship with Quinn. Questions followed, mostly from Fontaine. She was deeply curious about the Realm of Night and Koras. She bounced up onto her feet and paced, her face lighting up as she extracted every ounce of information she could.

After a lot of drinking and talking, the crew dispersed. Athen and Quinn took their bags to their staterooms while Nyssa stayed behind.

"What are your plans now?" Elias asked.

"Quinn and I will talk to you about it tomorrow. It's getting late," Nyssa said with a yawn. Fresh eyes and minds in the morning would serve them better.

"Of course," Fontaine said. "But there's something you need to know...Suvi wants Quinn back. She's now offering a million and a half gold marks for her. Kalla has matched the bounty."

"Nothing for me? That's rude," Nyssa grumbled.

"The assumption is you're dead. Use that to your advantage," Elias said.

Fontaine waved her hand at them. "Go rest. It is truly wonderful to have you both back and safe, but you look like you could use some sleep."

She wasn't wrong. Nyssa descended the stairs to the lower deck, happy to see the worn-wood walls along the familiar hallway that led to the front of the ship and her room.

She slipped into her stateroom. Quinn was resting on her bunk, hands laced behind her head. "Everything's pretty much as we left it."

Nyssa took a deep breath. "It feels like home," she hummed.

She pulled off her cloak and shrugged out of her leather jacket, walking to the small mirror on the wall. Her face had filled out, the dark circles under her eyes completely gone. Her body was still not back to normal yet, but that would take time and work. Nyssa grinned at her reflection and bowed her head, sighing out a relieved laugh.

"You should know that Suvi and Kalla have *both* placed a million and a half gold marks on your head."

Quinn shrugged. "It's almost flattering at this point."

"I'm tempted to turn you in myself. Think of all the chocolates and pastries I could buy with that much gold."

"And maybe get that jacket cleaned?" Quinn suggested, her face flushed with color from the drinks on the deck.

"How are you feeling?"

Quinn smirked. "Warm. And happy."

"Happy," Nyssa mused. "Did you ever think that would be true again after Suvi captured us?"

Quinn sat up and swung her legs off the bunk. She ran her fingers over the toldoku tied around her wrist, staring at it in thought. When she looked back up, her face was serious. "I used to lie in my cell and try to remember being here, listening to you breathe. I tried to remember what it felt like just being in the same space as you, feeling your presence in my very core." Quinn put her hand to her chest. "Happy isn't even an adequate enough word to describe what I am right now."

Nyssa took a deep cleansing breath. "I used to lie in bed and wonder what was going on in that head of yours."

The serious look on Quinn's face morphed into a smile, making Nyssa's heart lighter.

"I also used to lie in bed and think about how much I wanted you," Quinn admitted, leaning back and giving Nyssa a smile.

Nyssa pressed a hand to her chest. "Why, Quinn, you had salacious thoughts about me? I am *aghast*."

Quinn laughed and stood, crossing the short distance between them. "I'm intensely happy in this moment, but I'll be happier when we're in bed."

"You're insatiable."

Quinn smirked and pressed Nyssa against the small table, her hands slipping under Nyssa's sweater, encircling her waist.

The warmth of Quinn's body quickened her pulse. "Come here," Nyssa said, grabbing Quinn to kiss her roughly, tasting the rum on her lips.

Quinn met her with equal enthusiasm before pulling away. "You know, it's the first day of winter."

"Is it?"

"Happy birthday, Nyssa Blacksea."

Nyssa groaned. "I told you, I don't make a fuss about my birthday."

"Well, I care about you, so I do. Happy birthday." Quinn's eyes twinkled in the low light of the room, her fingers already working at Nyssa's belt. "Now take your clothes off so I can give you your present. A couple times."

A laugh caught in Nyssa's throat. She loved how fearless and eager Quinn was when they were alone. "Yes, ma'am."

A banging on the stateroom door startled Nyssa awake. She rolled the wrong way and fell out of bed, the hard, cold wood floor shocking her naked body.

"Get dressed. You're needed on deck!" Yuha's voice boomed through the door.

Quinn peered over the side of the bed, blinking sleepily. "Are you okay?"

"Mmm, we need a bigger bed. Fuck," Nyssa groaned.

Quinn and Nyssa dressed hurriedly, rummaging through each other's clothing on the floor.

"My sword?" Quinn asked, hopping on one foot as she yanked on her pants.

"Footlocker," Nyssa replied, pulling her own sword over her head. She rushed to the door, her feet bare. Quinn retrieved her sword out of her locker and slung it onto her back. Nyssa was proud to see her thinking like a warrior, reaching for her weapon.

They were both a disheveled mess as they hurried up to the deck. Elias and Fontaine stood with two figures. Yuha strode past Nyssa and planted a fist in one of the strangers' stomachs, bringing them to their knees.

"That's for Crae's Alehouse!" Yuha growled.

"What the fuck is going on?" Nyssa asked.

A white mask peeked out from under the stranger's cloak.

Nyssa cocked her head. "Medias?"

"We found these two on the dock, giving the Whisper a stare. I thought they were brigands looking to make a score," Elias said. "Nope. Just two idiot friends of yours, Blacksea."

"Who's the other idi—"

The second figure flew at Nyssa, tackling her to the ground, arms wrapped around her, squeezing tight.

"You're alive? You're alive!" Nyssa recognized that voice as the familiar scent of lavender tickled her nose. Reece pulled back and grabbed Nyssa's face. "You're alive," she whispered.

Groaning, Nyssa smiled up at her friend. "Fuck, Reece, I think you crushed a rib or two."

Fontaine waved her hands dismissively at the crew. "False alarm, these two are allies. Yes, even the repellent Justiciar," she said, shooting a pointed look at Medias.

Reece stood and helped Nyssa to her feet before throwing her arms around her again. When Reece pulled away, her eyes found Quinn and a strange, happy expression settled on her face.

"You two glow like the sun. I didn't think I'd ever feel this again," Reece said, laughing. "It's...amazing." She narrowed her eyes at Quinn, laughing harder and leaning in, her voice low. "Wow. You feel quite...interesting. Nyssa, what did you do to her?"

"Reece!" Nyssa chided. She didn't want Quinn to kill them all right then and there.

Reece *tsked* at Nyssa and put her hands on Quinn's shoulders. Quinn looked like she wanted to bolt, her face completely red. "I told Nyssa once she had a great capacity for love and she scoffed. But I was right, wasn't I, Blacksea?" Reece asked, tossing a look at Nyssa over her shoulder.

"Gloating, Reece?" Nyssa asked, smiling. But the empath was right. As usual.

"I don't know if I want to die or kill you," Quinn muttered. Her eyes found Nyssa. "Don't say a word."

Nyssa threw an arm around Reece. "It truly warms my heart to see you again. But what are you two doing here?"

Medias got to her feet with a groan, eyeing Yuha, who glared back. "I had a vision. I came. The empath followed like a lost puppy. I'm fine, by the way, your concern is touching."

"I assumed you could take a punch." Reece smirked at the Justiciar before turning back to Nyssa. "We almost missed you. We would have been here two weeks ago, but the damn train broke halfway here and instead of waiting half a day for another, this one decided that traveling by horse was the only option." Reece pursed her lips. "My ass is permanently numb."

Nyssa laughed. "And Medias didn't tell you we're alive?"

"Rather presumptuous to think all my visions include you, Blacksea. I only saw myself on this dock in front of this boat. Alone. The empath insisted on coming along." Medias tried to sound exasperated, but Nyssa caught the barely evident grin on her face.

Medias...likes Reece?

Movement behind Nyssa startled her. Athen rushed past and picked up Reece, giving her a spin.

"Careful, Eyeball!" Reece yelped.

"You're not supposed to call me that in front of others!" Athen chided, laughing.

Medias turned to Nyssa. "I assume from my vision that I'm here to help, so what are you planning, Blacksea? I'm not particularly fond of ships, by the way. The ocean is unruly and disconcerting."

"Kinda like me?" Nyssa asked with a half smile. Medias frowned. Nyssa glanced around at her friends and dove straight in. "I need to get back into the Realm of Shadows to rescue Aryis. Oh, and Quinn and I plan on kidnapping Suvi Rell."

"You're going to kidnap a queen? Why am I not surprised?" Medias asked with a slight lilt to her voice. Nyssa chuckled, guessing that's what passed as excitement for the Justiciar.

"This is your plan?" Reece asked, her tone skeptical. "It's...insane!"

"Perhaps a little insane." Nyssa clapped her hands. "Let's get breakfast. Then we'll talk, yeah?"

ANOTHER INSANE PLAN

After breakfast, Quinn sat quietly and listened to Nyssa explain what they wanted to do as their group of friends gathered near the mainmast, armed with large quantities of coffee to keep them warm. Kidnapping one queen and rescuing another was quite the insane plan...and dangerous.

"You already know I'm in," Athen said.

"Us too," Reece added, raising an eyebrow at Medias. The Justiciar nodded.

"So, we have the five of us. Between Athen, Quinn, and I, that's a lot of firepower." Nyssa turned to Medias. "What exactly is it you do other than see the future? I've never seen you use magick."

"Oh, you have." Medias smirked and raised her hand. Bright light burst in front of Nyssa's face, and she startled, stumbled, and fell to the deck.

"Dammit," Nyssa groaned. "That was you at Crae's Alehouse when Quinn and I were captured!"

"It was indeed. I'm somewhat of a legend there now," Medias said, causing Athen to groan. "I can explode light inside your body as well, and it is rather unpleasant. I'm also trained in knife combat." She patted her daggers, one worn on each hip.

Nyssa wiped at her eyes and took Medias's outstretched hand. The Justiciar pulled her up. "Powerful stuff. Your mysteries unfold like a flower, Medias."

"A scary, weird, deadly serious flower," Quinn added.

To her surprise, the small gathering, aside from the Justiciar, laughed at her offhand joke. Nyssa gave her a bright smile.

Elias and Fontaine wandered up. "When do you want to shove off, Blacksea?" Elias asked. "It'll take a couple days to sail to Sarisan."

Nyssa glanced at Quinn, then back to Elias. "You don't sail into Thu'Dainian waters."

"I don't. But for friends, I do."

Nyssa shook her head. "Elias, no. I can't ask you to do that."

"I'm volunteering," he said. "And I should have offered to take you in the first place to rescue Quinn. For that, I'm sorry."

Nyssa smiled. "Quinn and I can't ever repay you for what you've done for us."

"The deck could use a good mopping—"

"So about kidnapping a queen," Fontaine interrupted. "Elias and I have been doing some thinking. The easiest way to get into the Rell estate is the same way you got out. The cliff at the back of the house. We can take our small boats to the beach under the cover of night."

"How do we get up that cliff?" Nyssa asked.

"You said there's a free-fall enchantment?"

"Yes."

Fontaine smiled. "You can reverse the flow. It should be fairly easy as it's the only component of the enchantment you have to alter."

Nyssa chewed her bottom lip. "Are you sure?"

Quinn spoke up. "You can do it." She didn't want doubt to sink its teeth into Nyssa. Too much would be at stake, and Nyssa needed confidence.

"What about Suvi? How do we know she'll be at the estate? Or won't run as soon as we show up?" Athen asked.

With a sigh, Nyssa put her hands on her hips. "That's the key question."

Fontaine raised her arms above her head and stretched. "Suvi is a creature of habit and, aside from her yearly trip to a vineyard or two, a homebody. We go at night, she'll be there."

"Painting," Quinn said. All eyes turned to her. "Turns out, she likes to paint. The one time I escaped, I may have gotten some of her blood on one of her pieces of art."

Athen barked out a laugh. "I like your style, Quinn."

She grinned. "A short-lived victory before she bloodied me up in return."

The man's tenor grew darker. "I'm sorry that happened to you."

"Thank you, Athen."

He gave her a nod, then looked to Elias. "This isn't just about getting Suvi. This is a rescue mission as well. We're getting Aryis out of the Realm of Shadows. This is nonnegotiable. I won't abandon her."

Elias didn't look surprised. "We expected this. I took a vote in the mess to see if my crew was willing to be a part of a plan that would include rescuing Aryis. It wasn't unanimous, but they're in."

"Thank you. I need to help her..." Athen bowed his head. Reece moved her seat next to him and rubbed his back, a quiet comfort. Quinn wished she had someone like Reece or Athen when she was growing up in Ceril's shadow.

"How will you get into the Realm of Shadows and find Aryis?"

"I've found the boundary between realms before," Nyssa said. "Aryis has my ring. I'll be able to sense it and tear a hole in the realm to get to her. It'll be like tearing open Fontaine's veil. I hope."

Instead of a frown, Fontaine beamed. "You actually listened to me and remembered that your magick imprints on your personal items. I'm strangely proud."

Nyssa crossed her arms. "I'm a great student. Naturally I remembered."

Fontaine appeared dubious. "Quinn figured it out, didn't she?"

"Of course," Quinn remarked, laughing.

"It's settled, then," Elias said. "I'll send our crew into Le'Caal for supplies, and we'll shove off tomorrow. We'll take a wide berth into

Thu'Dainian waters. I want to avoid all ships if possible, even while running invisible."

The small group dispersed once plans were set. Quinn stayed on deck and lingered at the starboard rail, looking out to the sea. She wondered if Narileh waited out there for them, for Nyssa, as Koras had waited for her in the Emerrath Forest.

Fontaine joined her at the rail and nudged Quinn with her shoulder. "Seeing you and Nyssa alive warms my heart in ways that even I have difficulty properly expressing."

Quinn hesitated for a moment, then hugged Fontaine, who let out a surprised gasp before hugging her back. "Your friendship and guidance have meant more to me than I can say. And your advice...I took it."

Fontaine pulled back and took Quinn's head in her hands. "Yes, I can sense a very different dynamic between you and Nyssa. I was right, of course."

"Maddeningly right," Quinn grumbled.

With a pat of Quinn's cheeks, Fontaine spun away from her. "I never grow tired of being right," she crooned.

Down near the bow, Reece and Medias stood in conversation. When Reece glanced over and started toward her, Quinn cursed under her breath. She had no idea what to say to the woman who came to a stop a few feet away.

"I thought I'd talk to you in private while I have a chance," Reece said.

"Uh, sure." Quinn was fairly sure she knew where the conversation was headed, and it was likely going to be awkward. And Reece would be able to sense every little embarrassing emotion.

Reece smiled, her dark eyes pinning Quinn in place. "Nyssa and I have a past. Plainly put, a sexual history."

Quinn swallowed and nodded.

Awkward indeed.

"This is uncomfortable for you, so let me get to the point. That past is in the past. She and I are close, but I'm not a romantic threat."

"I know," Quinn said, confident that Nyssa would never give her a reason to doubt her fealty.

Reece smiled. "Good. I wanted it out in the open so you and I can move forward. Perhaps even become friends?"

What little Nyssa had told her of Reece indicated that the woman could be frustratingly insistent, but underneath it all was a deep well of kindness.

"I would like that." Truth was, seeing Nyssa so happy to be amongst her friends made Quinn desire a small sliver of such joy. And having another friend wouldn't hurt.

"Good. To new beginnings, then." Reece smiled and walked off, passing by Nyssa as she headed below deck. Nyssa joined Quinn and leaned back against the rail.

"What was that about?"

"Just...Reece reassuring me that I don't have to worry about her. In regards to you, that is. She hopes we can become friends."

"I imagine that was a painfully awkward conversation for you." Nyssa bit her lip and grinned.

"Thankfully a short one, but...I think I like her." There was a sincerity to Reece that was wonderfully straight-forward, a trait Quinn appreciated. "I can see why you two were together."

"She shamelessly flirted with me."

Quinn rolled her eyes. "We both know you're the shameless flirt."

A deep, rumbling laugh left Nyssa. "Ah, true. But I swear, she pursed me." She nodded her head toward Medias, who stood near the bow by herself. "I wonder what thoughts run through her little Justiciar head."

"Whatever they are, they're likely very stern."

"I want to have a chat with her." Nyssa whistled at the Justiciar and waved her over.

"You inelegantly beckoned?" Medias asked when she arrived.

Nyssa clucked her tongue. "I'm curious if you've had any visions about what comes next? Maybe something you were afraid to say in front of the others?"

"You want to know if I see success or failure in this venture to kidnap Suvi?"

"Well...yes."

Medias sighed. "My visions have shown me nothing beyond this moment."

"You'd tell us, right?"

"Do you want me to tell you about all my visions that include you, Nyssa? Or you, Quinn?"

Nyssa raised an eyebrow and shrugged. "Is that such a bad idea?"

"Yes," Medias answered. "My visions aren't open for your inspection or interpretation. I share what I wish to share. Some of it is applicable to our pursuits. Some of it is not."

"So, no other visions?" Quinn asked.

"Other than a few irrelevant ones, no."

Quinn's curiosity got the better of her. "Irrelevant?"

Medias scowled, obviously annoyed. She leaned in, her red eyes trained on Quinn. "You really should let a woman make a pot of tea, Quinn," she replied. A wily grin spread across her face before she turned and left.

Quinn's mind ground to a halt, a strangled wheeze escaping her as she tried to exhale.

Nyssa howled with laughter.

WHAT GOES UP

Fontaine wove a spell of invisibility around the two small boats Nyssa and the others took to the beach of Suvi Rell's estate. Elias and Fontaine had insisted on coming, but Nyssa staunchly refused the help of the rest of the crew, though many had volunteered. Her heart swelled from their loyalty, but she couldn't risk their lives.

The group had stocked up on weapons from the ship's hold, Medias patiently fitting a sword and dagger to Reece. Athen preferred his fists. Fontaine only took a small dagger, citing her magick was her weapon. Nyssa didn't think it prudent to argue with the woman.

Quinn carried a void collar and a lock in a sack tied to her back. Getting close to Suvi without her using her magick on any of them would be a challenge, but if Quinn blanketed the estate with her shadow, she could get to her undetected through the dark.

Quinn reluctantly agreed that only Nyssa should enter into the Realm of Shadows while the rest of them lay low, waiting for Nyssa to return before they moved into the house to search for Suvi. Athen and Elias strategized with the rest of the group, anticipating Suvi's elite guard being an obstacle they'd have to fight. Suvi favored fire mages for her guard, but with Fontaine and Quinn's protective barriers, Nyssa was confident they would make quick work of them.

The beach was empty when they reached the shore under the cover of darkness. The seven of them hopped out of the boats and ran to the cliff. When Nyssa reached out with her magick to detect the free-fall enchantment, its colors burst to life, bright and beautiful, full of glowing structural greens and purples, with a vibrant orange column in the center that flowed like a slow-moving waterfall.

Nyssa turned to Fontaine. "I see it all, including the flowing part."

"Good, good," Fontaine said. "That's the only part you need to touch. Concentrate on reversing it. Don't worry about altering the speed or the position. Just direction. Just one variable to account for."

Nyssa nodded and turned back to the enchantment, inching forward until she touched it. The powerful torrent of magick made her arm buzz. She calmed herself and focused, attempting to isolate just the orange flow of energy—difficult, considering the magick spanned over a hundred feet up the cliff face.

Just switch the flow...from down to up. Easy. I pulled my magick apart from Quinn's and lived, this a child can do. I hope.

"Do you need help?"

Nyssa opened one eye to find Athen sidled up next to her. "I've got this."

"Do you? Because you don't seem to be doing much."

"Are you trying to piss me off?"

Needling her had been one of Athen's favorite pastimes at the Emerald Order, and it didn't take her long to realize it was his form of pushing her past her mental blocks. She hated it. But it worked and she fell for his 'inspiration' every damn time.

Nyssa refocused and stuck her hand back into the magick, its power vibrating over her skin. Ignoring the other components of the spell, she only concentrated on the orange, diving deeper until the glowing threads became all she saw.

Lightning rippled off of her hands and into the free-fall enchantment. She wrapped her magick around its center and sank it in hard. Suddenly, the barrier between her magick and the enchantment fell away and she was in complete control. A satisfied smile graced her lips. There was no denying how powerful she felt.

"Hey, Fontaine, watch this."

With a mere thought, Nyssa flipped the direction of the free fall. The orange flow came to a slow halt before winding back up again, reversing direction.

Fontaine squeezed her shoulder. "Good job, though a bit of a gloat."

Nyssa turned to Athen with a smirk. "Ready for you, Eyeball."

"See, I knew you could do it." He rubbed his hands together and stepped into the enchantment. Orange energy sparked around him, but he didn't budge. Nyssa braced herself for his smart mouth, but his body jerked once before he was propelled upward. He ascended up the cliff and disappeared into the darkness near the top.

The group waited, then heard his signal—a low whistle. He'd made it up safely.

One by one, the rest of them stepped into the enchantment, with Nyssa bringing up the rear. She exhaled a deep breath before taking a tenuous step forward. A soft yelp left her mouth when the enchantment yanked her up, and she balled her hands into tight fists, tensing as the magick pulsed around her.

When she reached the top, the odd sensation of being suspended in the air hit her before she flailed and fell to the ground. Athen offered her a hand up, but she popped to her feet on her own, trying to regain some small modicum of grace. Her stomach rebelled a second later, and she lunged at a bush to lose her dinner.

"I could have predicted that," Athen quipped.

She took a couple deep breaths, then straightened up. "I'm okay."

"Nyssa, flip the free-fall direction again so it's ready for a quick escape," Elias directed.

Nyssa nodded. The effort was almost trivial now that she understood how to navigate and manipulate that particular enchantment. "Done."

The group moved forward and crouched behind a row of hedges. Nyssa scanned the back garden, looking for any magick that might trip them up, but found none. Light orbs hung above the garden, dimly illuminating the expanse of grass interrupted by rows of flower beds and gravel paths leading up to the house.

Near the mansion, a wide, shimmering pool of water glinted in the moonlight and low brick walls dotted the exterior—tall enough to give them cover should they need it. Far beyond, the lights in the house were on, a large bank of windows shining from within.

"Where did we come out of the portal?" Nyssa asked, her recollection of events after Quinn's rescue were a bit sketchy.

"Over here," Quinn said, crouch-running along the hedge. The rest followed. She pointed to a small paved area surrounded by flowers and a few low stone benches.

"Shit, that's out in the open."

"You ready?" Quinn asked, her gaze steady. Confident.

Nyssa wished she felt the same way. Her nerves hummed. It wasn't confidence she felt, but fear. She glanced back at everyone behind her. "I don't think I'll have much time before they see me. I may not be out of the Realm of Shadows before you run into trouble."

"We'll worry about that, you get Aryis," Athen said, giving her a nod.

Everyone was putting a great deal of faith in her ability to tear a hole into another realm. Quinn's fingers brushed the back of her hand. "Go find Aryis. Get her back."

Nyssa swallowed and stood up, then dashed over to the small paved clearing, blue lightning sparking on her skin. She had very little time before someone would see her.

Closing her eyes, she stilled her mind and reached out, searching for Aryis. She lost her concentration more than once. It was one thing to sit on the dock on Monk's Cove and lazily open up her senses to the world. Doing it under pressure was a whole other order of complexity.

"Slow your thoughts and shut everything out," Quinn whispered beside her.

Nyssa redoubled her efforts, putting her trust in the others to keep her safe if they were discovered. The world opened up to her, and ambient magick swirled everywhere, various shapes and colors assaulting her eyes and vibrating against her skin. She needed to go beyond their world, to find the edge of the realms again.

A small glow caught Nyssa's attention, impossibly distant and right next to her at the same time, a maddening juxtaposition that felt wrong. But Nyssa immediately knew what it was: her ring.

She deepened her focus and zeroed in on it, trying to pinpoint its location. It felt mere feet away before it stretched out and seemed legions from where she stood.

Raised voices shattered her focus—she lost her grip on the ring.

"We've been spotted," Quinn said.

"I need more time."

Quinn put her hand on Nyssa's shoulder. "Athen and the others will give it to you."

Athen nodded, his gaze firming up. Nyssa had seen that look before—he was itching for a fight.

Quinn leaned in. "I'll help you focus."

Guards poured out of the glass doors of the house, rushing toward them. Athen and Elias ran past Quinn and Nyssa, followed by the others, their weapons out. Athen crashed into a group of guards, fists swinging, sending bodies flying. Flares of magick surrounded Elias and Fontaine. Pops of brilliant white light exploded in the air near the guards—Medias displaying her power.

"Nyssa, close your eyes. Find her again," Quinn rumbled into her ear. "Focus."

Nyssa exhaled and closed her eyes, reaching out again. Magick shimmered next to her, then flowed through her body—Quinn was mixing their powers, helping reinforce and guide Nyssa's efforts.

After a few anxious moments, she found the small glowing ring. Its location shifted wildly, but the more she focused, the less it moved, until it felt like it was right in front of her, vibrating as though it was poised to jump away from her again.

"I got you," Nyssa whispered.

Quinn pressed closer. "Go get Aryis."

Nyssa anchored herself on the ring and pushed toward it with her magick, running into the barrier between her reality and the Realm of Shadows. The boundary pushed back, trying to repel her like it did on Monk's Cove.

She opened her eyes. Lightning flowed out of her—not just from her hands, but her whole body—into a crease in the air. Darkness shifted and swirled around it, wrapping around her lightning. But it wasn't Quinn's magick...

The Realm of Shadows was doing its best to keep her out.

Gritting her teeth, Nyssa kept digging her magick into the barrier, getting a good grip. Whatever was fighting her back sent a stinging wave of cold through her, making her gasp. She shook her head, groaning and pushing the pain aside, not letting it tip her focus. Certain she had sunk her magick in deep, she cast caution aside and tore open the fabric between worlds, stepping through into the darkness beyond.

THE QUEEN AND THE GOD

Quinn felt Nyssa slip away from her as she watched her step through the glimmering dark rift in reality. A chill passed through her when the fissure closed.

"Please come back safe," she whispered. She hated that Nyssa was in the Realm of Shadows. Hated that she had gone back for Aryis, who didn't deserve Nyssa's grace and courage.

Quinn pulled herself away from her thoughts. Twenty feet ahead of her, Reece and Medias were occupied with a large guard. Athen and the others were separated from them, taking on a small contingent of house security. Quinn ran toward Reece, who had a sword in hand, doing her best against the guard that towered over her. She summoned bolts of darkness and let them fly, hitting him square in the chest. He stumbled backward, barely affected.

"Shit," Quinn murmured. Out of the corner of her eye, Medias ran at the man. When she was close, magick flashed from her fingertips and the man lurched and stumbled, grabbing at his head. He shook off the effects of her magick, pulling up to his full height. Medias attacked with her magick again, and the man fell to a knee, shaking his head.

Quinn was amazed he wasn't on his ass.

"He's hard to bring down, like Athen!" Reece yelled.

When Quinn reached them a few seconds later, the guard was already back up on his feet. Medias got too close, and he caught her with a backhand, sending her skidding along the ground. The man turned back to Reece and sliced down at her with his sword.

Quinn crashed into her, and they tumbled to the ground, barely avoiding the sword as it carved through the air and struck the stone-paved walkway.

The sword shattered from the force of the blow.

The guard shouted profanities and grabbed at the women, hauling Quinn up by the back of her jacket. He wrapped a meaty hand around her throat, and she grabbed his wrist, reaching out with her magick. Thick ribbons of shadow dove into his body and she clamped down on his life essence, snuffing it out.

Both of them toppled to the ground. Quinn gasped for air, the wind knocked out of her. Hands grabbed her, and she surrounded herself with darkness, ready to strike.

"It's Reece!"

The woman steadied Quinn as she stood up, the guard dead at their feet. He had gotten too close to seriously hurting Reece and Medias, and Quinn had been far too cautious, hoping to simply subdue him. She couldn't make that mistake again.

"You okay?" she asked.

Reece nodded as Medias stumbled over. Reece let go of Quinn and went to the Justiciar, pushing her hair back to reveal a nasty cut on her head. Blood stained her white mask.

Medias grabbed Reece's wrist and moved her hand away. "I'm fine."

"You're hurt," Reece groused.

"I'm fine."

Quinn spotted Athen, Elias and Fontaine clashing with a group of guards, magick buzzing all around them. She pulled at Medias and Reece. "Athen needs our help."

They ran to the trio. Athen's fist connected with a guard and sent him flying. Elias hit another with a torrent of fire. Fontaine stood behind the two men, out of harm's way, spellweaving. One last guard raised his sword, but Quinn hit him with a bolt of dark matter, piercing his chest with a sharp whoosh of air. He crumpled to the ground. Bodies of guards littered the ground, some dead, some injured.

"No sign of Suvi yet. Are you all okay?" Athen asked, giving the women a once-over.

"We're fine," Quinn said.

"And Nyssa?"

"In the Realm of Shadows."

"Okay, we need to stay together. We can defend best against Suvi's elite guard with wards, so keep Fontaine safe."

Fontaine's hands began moving, a soft murmur of a spell woven from her lips. Shouting from the house pulled Quinn's attention. A throng of guards spilled out from the expanse of glass doors, rushing toward them.

"At the ready," Athen said, balling up his fists.

Silence rushed to meet Nyssa as she stepped into the Realm of Shadows. Before, when she was inside this cursed place, she was dying and without her magick. Now, the magick of the ancient realm surrounded her, making her skin prick up. Darkness enveloped her, though she could see the vast desolate landscape as if the shadows of the realm had their own low, eerie glow.

She turned around and came face-to-face with Aryis. Relief flooded through her, but that relief quickly turned to dread when she saw black tendrils woven all around Aryis. She was ensnared in them, their black veins spider-webbed across her face.

"Aryis!" Nyssa rushed forward.

Aryis's eyes were closed, but her mouth was moving. Just barely.

"Wake up, woman!"

Nyssa's voice reverberated and echoed, moving through her and re-bounding back. She hadn't missed being under the strange effects in the realm. She gently touched Aryis's face. The black veins pulsed. "Please wake up. It's Nyssa."

Aryis's eyes slowly opened, blinking. "Nyssa?"

She sounded a million miles away.

"It's me, Little Hawk. I'm going to get you out of here."

Sorrow overtook Aryis's features, not the smile Nyssa expected to see. The haunted look in her eyes twisted Nyssa's stomach.

"You have to go back. Please go back. Warn them."

Nyssa shook her head, bewildered. "What are you talking about?"

Tears rolled down Aryis's cheeks. "I'm going to betray you. Don't let our ships close to Hannah's Whisper. Tell Elias to run."

"Aryis, that was months ago!"

"Nyssa, run..."

Nyssa examined the dark streaks holding on to Aryis, carefully touching the black tendril wrapped around her arm. A shocking cold met her fingertips, and she snatched her hand back, her whole body aching with a deep, unrelenting chill.

"What is this thing?" she mumbled.

"I'd prefer you didn't call me a *thing*. It's rather rude," a low, rumbling voice boomed.

Chaos broke out all around Quinn as the guards streamed toward them, coming from all angles. Magick emanated from the house.

A lot of it.

A giant ball of fire shot forth from the guards, aimed directly at her. She put her hands up, darkness streaming forth, forming a cloud of shadow in front of her. The fireball hit the cloud and disappeared, its magick squelched by her power, leaving behind a rush of heat that made Quinn flinch.

Fontaine maintained her ward, the effort of keeping up her defenses written across her face. Flames licked around Elias's hands, and he threw orbs of fire as quickly as he could summon them. Athen plowed into a group of guards, smashing his fists against their weapons and bodies.

A flash of light behind her made Quinn whirl around. A guard tumbled to the ground, and Reece rushed forward to kick him in the face.

"Watching your back is tiresome work," Medias said, grimacing through bloody teeth. Quinn nodded at her, glad to have the Justiciar by her side. Bright magick flashed from Medias's fingertips, bursting around their attackers.

Quinn looked back at the house. More magick moved toward them, each small glowing ball of light a person. She checked the pack she wore slung over her shoulder and felt the curve of the void collar within.

"Let's get Suvi." Quinn hefted her sword, striding forward. Medias yelled at her to stay put, but Quinn waded into three guards, her blade at the ready.

Two of them struck at her at once. Quinn sidestepped one attack and parried the other, her sword and arm vibrating from the blow. Without thinking, she spun around and sliced through the torso of the third guard.

A sharp pain swiped across her upper back, drawing out a hiss, and she whirled to face her attacker, her sword spinning with her, biting into flesh—her instinct saving her from another blow. The guard reeled back. Quinn didn't hesitate to lunge forward, the tip of her blade sinking into his belly.

The guard fell to the ground, and Quinn turned to locate the last guard. Silver flashed in the moonlight and the butt of a sword caught her temple with a dull *thunk* of metal against bone. Her world exploded into stars and she crumpled to the ground.

She grunted from the pain and rolled onto her back. A man loomed over her, his blade aimed at her neck. Before she could move, his body jerked, and he fell hard next to her, his eyes wide and still. A dagger protruded from his throat.

Medias's masked face appeared above Quinn, and within a second, she was pulled to her feet.

"You okay?" Medias asked.

"Thank you. Again." Quinn shook her head to clear it of stars. She had gotten lucky, otherwise her guts would have been spilled into one of Suvi's flower beds.

Swallowing, she steadied herself against Medias, her attention turning back to the house. To the magick flowing from it. Suvi had to be there, and Quinn needed to stop her. More guards filled ran out of the mansion, ready to fight and defend their queen.

Quinn steeled herself.

The black mass that surrounded Aryis expanded and uncoiled, tendrils flaring out. Rows upon rows of eyes sprang open and stared at Nyssa.

She stumbled back and quickly drew Winter's Bite.

"Cute sword," a voice said, echoing endlessly in her ears.

Shadowy strands wound around Nyssa. Winter's Bite sliced through one of the coils, severing the spiraling arm. To her horror, ribbons of darkness sprouted from the open wound, new tendrils springing forth and multiplying. They dove into Nyssa's chest, sending a jagged, icy jolt of pain through her.

She wound her magick around the tendrils and released a massive wave of energy, exploding the dark matter into mere wisps of shadow. She shot forward and found purchase on the mass surrounding Aryis—ignoring the blinking eyeball her hand landed on—and sent a bolt of lightning into the thing holding Aryis captive.

The creature lashed out, bashing her in the chest with such force she flew backward and slammed to the ground.

"Nyssa Blacksea, I could flick you out of this realm with the twitch of an eyelash. Do not antagonize me. I have *tenure* here."

Nyssa gasped for breath. "Tajal, that you?"

A small, dark mass separated from the creature surrounding Aryis and coalesced a few feet from Nyssa, whirling into the form of a man. Her mouth hung open at the monster, not sure if she could trust her eyes.

The human-like figure wore a black tuxedo and top hat above a tangled, roiling mess of tentacles and eyeballs that held the shape of a head.

The thing bowed to Nyssa and doffed its hat.

"Greetings, godling, I am Tajal the Curious."

The creature in front of her, despite its fancy suit and rough form of a man, was horrific, its numerous eyeballs floating in a sea of shiny black tentacles, their pupils milky yellow, like the guts of crushed caterpillars.

Nyssa swallowed back her fear. "I came for my friend."

Tajal floated closer and offered her a hand. Nyssa sent a spark of lightning at him. He flinched back, and Nyssa got to her feet.

"You lack proper manners, Blacksea! Who raised you to be such a ruffian?"

Behind Tajal, Aryis stirred. "Nyssa? Why are you here? Please go back and warn everyone. I will betray you. I will hurt you. Suvi will take everything from you. Please, run."

"Why is she like this? What did you do to her?" Nyssa asked.

Eyes blinked at Nyssa and something resembling a mouth smiled in the mass of tentacles. "Aryis Devitt did this to herself. Her joy, her anger, her love, her pain—she's feeling it all, over and over again. She caused you pain and now she relives it endlessly. You were right, her heart was bound to shatter into pieces one day. Who knew she'd do it to herself?"

Nyssa gritted her teeth. Tajal was referring to a private moment shared between her and Aryis. An excruciatingly painful moment for them both.

"Release her. Please."

Tajal stepped back and cocked what passed as a head at her. "And why should I?"

Nyssa swallowed. Why indeed? Aryis had hurt her in ways she never fathomed possible. But Nyssa wasn't ready to throw her away.

"You're called Tajal the Curious, right? Not Tajal the Destroyer or Tajal the Irredeemable Asshole. That leads me to believe you can be reasoned with."

Tajal blinked at Nyssa and smiled wide. Rows of jagged fangs lay in his mouth. "Nyssa Blacksea, do you know how long it's been since I dined on someone's pleasure and pain? Then you bring this one to me and, oh, what a delightful feast she has been. Seems I got her at the right time. Her life before she met you was so…mundane. Flavorless. But you, you introduced love. And pain. Succulent, luscious pain."

Nyssa shook her head. "I didn't introduce pain into her life."

"Didn't you?"

"I…" Nyssa stopped. There was no denying she had made all of her friends' lives more complicated. Being in her orbit was dangerous. Athen and Aryis had already suffered so much. What about Reece and Medias? If Ceril caught them…they would both be killed. And Elias and the crew of the Whisper had lost so much.

All because of her.

"I'm trying to understand your mortal emotions. Take pain, for instance. I hypothesize that the more you love, the more you suffer. Love is the pathway to pain. What do you think?" Tajal asked, training all his eyes on Nyssa.

"I—I think you're right."

"Then why do you mortals seek it out if it creates so much pain?"

Nyssa's only thought was of her friends. And of Quinn. "It's worth the fucking risk."

Tajal blinked at her and his horrific smile receded. Nyssa got the impression the Ancient God was taken aback.

He waved an eye-balled hand at her. "I can see why Aryis likes you. You're not proper or pretentious. You cut to the quick."

Nyssa exhaled and returned her sword to her sheath. It was apparent that a blade wasn't the way to fight Tajal—if fighting was even the way to free Aryis.

"What do you want for her?" Nyssa asked.

"Ah, bargaining? This is fun."

"Tajal, please. Let's just get to what you want. Believe it or not, you're not my main priority tonight."

"Ah yes, your intrepid little plan to wrest a queen away from her throne. What a feat that would be! I wish you luck."

Nyssa pursed her lips, her patience draining, quickly replaced by anger. "Tajal!"

The Ancient God rose up, seemingly taking umbrage at her tone, and frowned. "Honestly, Aryis has gotten a bit gamey. But you...you're still untapped. Just a quick nibble, get down to the marrow. Pleasure or pain, what should I take?"

Nyssa held out her hand, not even thinking. "Pain."

"Nyssa Blacksea, you are truly a gentlewoman, but you, like Aryis, need to learn how to bargain better."

Tajal laughed, the rumble of the sound enveloping Nyssa. Twisting black tendrils and eyes sprang out of his body and wound around her wrist, torso, legs...by the time she realized how trapped she was, it was too late. A tendril snaked up her arm.

Nyssa panicked, blue lightning rippling all around her.

"Strike out with your magick and the deal is off," Tajal's voice boomed throughout the Realm of Shadows. "You may be a god, but I am ancient. Do not assume I will be merciful."

Terror rose in her gut, but she couldn't risk angering Tajal and losing Aryis. They could both die at the hands of the Ancient God. The tendrils wound around Nyssa constricted, squeezing the air out of her lungs. Dark, spindly strands coiled up and around her neck, forcing her head back. She gritted her teeth and tried to move, tried to breathe deep, but Tajal enclosed himself around her.

His voice filled her head.

Just a taste, Nyssa...

Quinn darted between the large sculptures dotting the garden near the house, figures of men and women and animals carved out of stone. She stepped out from behind a massive lion and reached forward with both hands. Darkness coiled forth, laying waste to the guards that set themselves against her. Though more rushed to replace them, including fire mages, she didn't care. These men and women were mere foot soldiers, not who she wanted.

Finally, Quinn spotted Suvi standing by the doors of her mansion barking orders.

It seemed the Queen wasn't able to stay away, a warrior at heart as Fontaine had said. Suvi caught sight of Quinn, and her mages threw up wards to protect her.

Quinn balled up her fists and attacked with more tendrils of shadow, surrounding Suvi's guards and sinking it deep into them, putting them on the ground, some alive but more likely dead.

Fire flashed in the corner of her eye, and she formed a defensive wall of shadow without thinking, deadening the flaming ball. She just needed to get closer to Suvi and put her down like the others, gain enough ground to get a collar around—

Crushing pain and icy fear slammed into Quinn. She stumbled back, clutching at her chest.

Nyssa! Something's wrong. Oh gods...

"Quinn, are you hurt?" Medias yelled, yanking her back behind a statue for cover.

"It's Nyssa," Quinn groaned. Nyssa's presence had faded when she stepped into the Realm of Shadows, but now Quinn sensed her again, and something was dreadfully wrong.

Her stomach dropped as wave after wave of agonizing fear hit her.

Nyssa's fear.

"Fight, Nyssa," she whispered. There was no way to reach her now—so she pushed through Nyssa's fear, swallowing down her own rising panic.

Quinn straightened up and shook Medias off of her. "We need to get Suvi! Athen, push forward! Suvi's up by the house. We'll cut through her defense to get to her, and I'll get the collar on her."

Athen rallied and continued to attack the guards around them, using the statues as cover as he pushed forward. Fireballs from Suvi's fire mages struck the statues, embers raining down, lighting the ground underneath. Fontaine kept weaving her wards, trying to move with Athen and Elias to keep them safe. Athen, for his part, was laying waste to guards left and right, his strength and invulnerability making him an impressive foe.

Numerous bodies lay scattered in Suvi's massive garden, a seemingly endless stream of men and women at her disposal.

Quinn drew her sword, saving her magick for Suvi. "Please come back to us, Nyssa," she whispered.

She stepped back into the fight, Medias on her flank. A guard rushed at her and she tried to compensate. Steel bit into Quinn's torso, a barely deflected sword strike finding flesh. She pushed past the pain and struck out with her magick, driving it through the woman who had gotten far too close to spilling her guts on the ground.

A fireball flashed past her and hit Athen. He shrugged it off, but Quinn could tell by the hard expression on his face that it had hurt. He barreled forward and sent the attacking mage flying across the garden, smashing into the house. Next to Athen, Fontaine kept fighting, but blood trickled down her cheek, her face lit up by the barrage of fireballs that slammed into her wards. Elias stuck by her side.

The longer this battle went on, the harder it would be to win. Suvi had far more manpower, with more likely on the way.

I need to end this.

Quinn looked past the guards in front of her and spotted Suvi just inside the house. A tall older man stood at her side, his sword at the ready. Quinn sheathed her sword and struck out in all directions with darkness, winding it around their attackers and shredding everything in sight. Guards fell before her, and she advanced. Suvi spotted Quinn and pointed, giving orders to the men around her.

"Quinn, wait!" Medias yelled behind her, but she wasn't about to stop. The collar had to go around Suvi's neck. Quinn sensed a flare of magick—mages rallying their power, preparing to strike. She stopped and concentrated, sending out a wide arc of shadow toward Suvi and her guards, with the intention to cause as much pain as possible. They couldn't fight if they were writhing on the ground. The effort made her suck in a breath, sapping much of her energy.

Before her, men and women cried out. Those that remained on their feet scattered away, their faces and shouts betraying their fear.

Quinn focused again and sent out another wave of magick, hitting more guards. She kept advancing despite Athen and Medias calling her name.

She rallied for one more wave of shadow as she closed in on the house.

Quinn curled her hands into fists and zeroed in on Suvi. If she could hit her from afar with a spike of negating magick, maybe she could shock her for a short—

The wall of windows at the back of the mansion exploded. A massive gust of wind hurled deadly fragments of glass through the air. Quinn barely got her arm up to protect her eyes as shards sliced into her. She staggered backward, disoriented, her ears ringing.

Suvi's voice rose above the din. "Matthys, hit her again!"

Quinn gritted her teeth and started to call darkness forward again, trying to push away her pain. She needed to concentrate to turn the area around her into night and entrap her enemies in darkness. It would exhaust her, but she couldn't lose Suvi now.

Shadow flowed off of her before a gust of wind lifted her off her feet and sent her flying backward. She slammed against a statue and tumbled to the ground, glass crunching and cutting into her flesh.

Her magick died on her fingertips.

An oppressive presence slipped over Quinn's mind, enveloping her. Pain built behind her eyes. She tried to grasp the presence with her magick and destroy it, but it evaded her, sinking its claws in deep.

"No," she whispered.

Nyssa tried to center herself and prepare for Tajal's assault, but there was no way to remain calm once he began pulling forth her pain. He didn't take one moment of agony or heartache—he tugged on them all, making her relive every single one. Memories flashed in Nyssa's head, cutting through her, cruel and deep, until they began to layer on top of one another.

Dagger twisting.
So scared.
Poison flowing.
So scarred.
Sinking into the Black Sea
Lungs filling with water.
Blood pooling around Eron.
Broken and bleeding in the snow.
Sword arcing to kill. Kill. Kill.
Juliana's empty eyes.
Pain spilling out like blood and glass.
Friend turned betrayer.
Kneeling before a queen.
Magick torn; taken.
Falling and failing and failing and falling,
falling,
falling
deep into the dark, icy sea...

The pain of those memories multiplied and folded in on itself, over and over, before exploding, shaking her to her core. Relentless waves of agony crashed into her body, and her heart pounded, threatening to break.

Tajal's voice echoed in her head, omnipresent. *Your pain is different. Luscious.*

Dizzy and disoriented, unmoored from anything she could hold on to, Nyssa lost control, unable to keep her magick contained. It sprang forth like hot glass slicing across her skin, tearing another scream out of her. Her magick itself was now agony.

I warned you, godling, Tajal snarled.

"I...can't...stop it."

Nyssa's memories kept looping over and over and over, sliding and crashing into one another, until one became more prominent than the others—her fight with Quinn after they had run into the Emerald Order adepts. Arguing with Quinn had torn Nyssa apart, their resentment becoming daggers they relentlessly stabbed into one another.

Nyssa replayed her memories, helplessly watching as she spit venom at Quinn. *"You had nothing to lose, but I lost my family!"* She had eviscerated Quinn, reeling from her own pain, lashing out like a wounded animal.

"You're my family, Quinn," Nyssa whispered, wanting the pain to stop. Needing it to. "You're my family. You're my family. You're my family—"

The memory changed, morphing into what she had wished happened. Nyssa watched her own face go from rage to affection. "You're my family, Quinn."

An angry voice boomed in her head, squeezing into the corners of her mind. *What are you doing?*

Nyssa ignored Tajal and tried to alter the memory again, to say what needed to be said in the moment. She broke out into a sweat, the effort was like digging herself out of her own grave. *"I should never have taken you back to the Empire. I hate myself for it."*

Tajal tightened his grip and waves of pain cascaded through her body like massive shards of ice cracking and shifting. *Nyssa, do not deviate from the memory! This is not what happened and you damn well know it.*

She dug in and pushed further. Not only was she changing in her memory, Quinn's anger receded, her face open. Receptive. Nyssa stretched forward, trying to touch Quinn, who remained just out of reach. *"I'm scared of you because I love you."*

"I love you. Love...you..." Nyssa whispered.

An exasperated sigh echoed across the Realm of Shadows, vibrating through her body. She fell to the ground, her pain abruptly gone. Her whole body trembled.

"Your pain was so lush and delicious, but you had to go and change things," Tajal said, looming over Nyssa. He had grown larger, now at least ten feet tall. "You're not meant to change memories. They're set. Immutable."

Nyssa struggled to push herself onto her elbows. "They're my memories. That's what I wish I had said at the time but I...I was a coward." Admitting it left her vulnerable and raw. But she needed to say it aloud.

Tajal flopped on the ground in front of Nyssa, collapsing and spreading apart, eyes rolling in all directions, several rolling into her legs as he lost his form.

Then, just as quickly, he regained it, eyeballs and dark matter coalescing until he sat cross-legged in front of Nyssa.

Eyeballs blinked at Nyssa. "You regret. Chances not taken. Love unspoken."

Nyssa let out a short breath, wrapping her arms around herself. "Yes."

"Interesting. Occasionally, I feel something strange and I try to capture it so I can unravel it and understand what it is...but then the feeling becomes a butterfly and flutters away. I can't dissect it and get to its core. Not like I can with your pain. Or hers," Tajal said, eyeballs rolling back to look at Aryis. "Love is even more confusing...elusive..."

He seemed...sad. Was he in pain too?

"I...don't understand," Nyssa said.

"Neither do I." Tajal rose up to his full height, his limbs moving and rearranging themselves until he stood above her. "I will give Aryis back to you, but I want something of yours."

Nyssa stared up at him. Of course there would be a price. "What?"

"I found something else in that head of yours that I rather enjoy. The memory of your parents. The only one you possess. Not even yours, really, but stolen from someone else. I want it."

Nyssa's breath escaped her.

It was a complicated memory, wrapped in pain, longing, regret...and it was the only time Nyssa had laid her eyes on the faces of her mother and father, heard their voices, saw their love for her as they begged Lilliana to save her life...

But Nyssa wouldn't fail her friend.

"Fine. Take it," she said.

"Nyssa, no," Aryis whimpered.

Nyssa struggled to her feet and growled at Tajal, "Fucking take it."

The Ancient God smiled, and threads of his body wrapped around her. She braced for pain, but this wasn't like before. This time, his touch was feathery. Gentle. He stepped forward and brushed her forehead. A chill washed through her and was then gone.

Nyssa frowned. The memory of her parents—their faces and voices—sat beyond her reach, in the periphery of her memories, inaccessible.

Save for one thing: the pendant of a demon's head was all she could recall.

Her mother's pendant.

"I left you with a scrap," Tajal said before moving aside and looking back at Aryis. The dark tendrils around her began to loosen and uncoil. When she was free of his grasp, he pushed her forward. Her legs gave out and she fell.

Nyssa scrambled over to her. "Aryis! Are you okay?"

Aryis's voice was a desperate whisper. "You have to go back. I'm going to...going to...I..."

Anger and concern bubbled up, and Nyssa whipped around to face Tajal. "Why is she like this?"

"She's scattered. A bit here, a bit there, back and forth. Things will settle for her with time. Ha! With time! Would you consider that word play? Or irony?"

Nyssa stood and pulled Aryis to her feet, putting an arm around her waist to hold her up. Aryis's head lolled against her shoulder.

"If she doesn't recover, I'll come back here and kill you for doing this to her," Nyssa said.

Tajal cocked his head. It continued to rotate until it was upside down, all the while fixing Nyssa in his gaze. He held his arms wide, and they began to expand and flow in all directions, like dark water. The Ancient God grew in size, filling Nyssa's field of view. The sight was terrifying, but she held her head up and focused on one eyeball as endless eyeballs popped up.

"Do not threaten me, Nyssa Blacksea. They call you a Cursed God, but you are nothing more than an infant. I am timeless. *Endless*."

At the end of her tether, Nyssa gathered her courage and straightened up to her full height. "And I couldn't give a good goddamn fuck. I'm tired, Tajal. Now, let us leave."

Tajal's measureless eyeballs blinked at her in one slow movement. He stilled. "You are a prickly woman. Go on, get."

Tajal blinked again, and Nyssa and Aryis were kicked out of the Realm of Shadows, tumbling to the cold earth of the Rell estate.

SHADOW AND STORM

Nyssa lay on the ground, clutching an unconscious Aryis, thankful to still be alive and free from the Realm of Shadows.

But something was wrong.

Quinn was wrong.

Nyssa pulled Aryis behind a hedgerow, tucking her away from the battle still raging. "Rest here, Little Hawk," Nyssa said, hoping she would be safe somewhat hidden from view.

She spotted Athen and the others and broke into a run toward them, her heart hammering in her chest. A large group of guards had them pinned down behind a line of massive stone garden statues, stopping them from advancing on the house. She called her magick forth, striking guards with bolts of lightning. Nyssa reached Athen and dropped beside him, clasping his arm.

"You're a welcome sight!" Athen said.

"Aryis is safe!" she said.

A pained smile crossed his face and he grunted.

"Is everyone okay?"

"Quinn went after Suvi. It's not good Nyssa," Medias said.

Reece crouched next to her. "Quinn feels so strange...something's wrong."

"I know," Nyssa replied.

A loud crack made Nyssa jump. The statue they were hiding behind shattered, shards of stone raining down on them.

"Fall back!" Nyssa yelled.

Athen nodded and gestured toward a low brick wall that edged a pool of flora and lily pads. "Follow that to the opposite side, there's more cover over there."

Fontaine wove a spell and tossed out a shimmering shield of light, a quick protective barrier to aid their retreat. Athen got everyone moving, crouching low and staying behind the wall. He beckoned Nyssa to follow, but she shook her head, then stood and turned. If she could pull attention to herself, the others could get to safety and regroup.

Bodies lay everywhere in the garden—some moving, some not. The acrid scent of blood and smoke filled her nostrils, pulling forth a memory as her stomach lurched. It reminded her of the night of Winter's Fire, when wraiths had spilled the blood of innocent people.

"Nyssa!" Athen yelled.

The air around her darkened, growing thick with cold and shadow.

"Quinn," Nyssa whispered. She stilled and concentrated, attempting to get her bearings to extend her senses out. A small white glowing orb, surrounded by swirling dark purple energy, drew her attention.

There you are.

Quinn's soul drew her forward. She plowed through the darkness and ran straight into Quinn, her eyes pure black. Suvi was in control. Shadow oozed off of her and swirled in the air around them. Quinn lunged, but Nyssa spun out of her path and caught her with a punch in the mouth. She spilled to the ground, screaming with rage.

"Why aren't you dead?" Quinn hissed. "You should be dead! Quinn took your magick!"

Hearing Suvi's words come from Quinn's mouth made Nyssa's stomach churn. "Stay down, Quinn, I don't want to hurt you!"

Nyssa summoned more magick, letting blue lightning encompass her and illuminate the darkness. She whirled around, looking for Suvi, trying to find her essence. A figure appeared in the darkness and Nyssa gathered her power, ready to attack.

A wave of pain ripped through Nyssa, and she staggered forward, falling to one knee. Glass sliced into her leg, and she let loose a string of profanities. She had taken her eyes off Quinn, desperate to find Suvi, and paid for the distraction.

An arm wrenched around Nyssa's throat, cutting off her air. "Why aren't you dead?" Quinn yelled into her ear. "Why do you have your magick again?"

Quinn grasped Nyssa's chin, and a familiar, sickening pulling sensation made her panic. Nyssa had fought too hard, been through too much, to have her magick stripped from her again. She grabbed Quinn's wrist and zapped her. Quinn screamed and clamped down harder on her neck. "I'll kill you both," she hissed.

Nyssa sent another bolt of lightning through Quinn, this one far more powerful, and they flew apart. Nyssa crashed to the ground. Shards of glass crunched underneath her, poking into her back and neck. She sucked in a sharp breath at the sudden slicing pain. Lightning crackled through her, her nerve endings on fire. Forcing herself to sit up, she found Quinn across from her, dazed, black eyes blinking at Nyssa, pain etched on her face.

Nyssa had to end this before one of them died. She shot forward and crashed into Quinn, wrapping her hands around her throat. Quinn's black eyes widened.

Nyssa closed her eyes and drove her power deep into Quinn. Suvi's magick was twisted up inside her, tendrils of glowing red magick coiling around her essence.

Nyssa swallowed back her fear and began prying the white and red energy apart.

Quinn's throat constricted under Nyssa's hands, an agonizing scream piercing her ears.

"I'm sorry," Nyssa whispered.

Another scream echoed in Nyssa's ears. Suvi's. Thunder growled in the sky, but Nyssa kept ripping at Suvi's magick, tearing it away from Quinn's soul. Her eyes snapped open as Quinn desperately clawed at Nyssa's throat, curling one hand around her neck and clamping down hard. Nyssa struggled to maintain her focus.

"I'm taking her back!" Nyssa yelled.

A violent wave of darkness exploded from Quinn, hitting Nyssa like a train. She flew back, and glass ground underneath her when she landed, biting into flesh.

Quinn struggled to get to her feet.

Another tendril of darkness burst out of Quinn's hands and hit Nyssa. She cried out, the twang of copper in her mouth. Boots crunched against glass as Quinn approached with a wicked smile.

"You should have never come back here, Blacksea." Quinn swung her leg back. Nyssa barely moved her arm in time to block the full impact of the kick to her head.

Nyssa's world turned white, her mind and body slipping away, drifting on the edge of consciousness. A thundering *boom* pulled her closer to awareness. Then another, followed by a flash of lightning.

Stabbing pain snapped her back to full awareness. Quinn stood on her left palm, grinding Nyssa's hand into the glass shattered all over the stone terrace. Nyssa opened her eyes and sucked in air, coughing violently as smoke clung to her lungs.

"You'll have to kill this body, Blacksea. I won't stop," Quinn said, leering down at her with a savage smile.

"I'm not going to kill you, Freckles," Nyssa breathed. "I love you, even though you're kinda being an asshole right now."

The expression on Quinn's face changed, flickering with confusion. Suvi probably didn't expect that one.

"C'mon, Suvi, use one god to kill another. Maybe you'll get it right this time," Nyssa taunted with a grin.

Quinn knelt next to Nyssa and pressed a palm down on her chest, putting her full weight into it. Nyssa locked her hand over Quinn's and smiled. Another look of confusion crossed the woman's face before she let loose a torrent of darkness that ripped through Nyssa, as if her chest was being shredded by a thousand blades. A mixture of bile and blood rattled in Nyssa's throat as she screamed.

"I can feel Quinn trying to fight me. She's terrified I'm going to kill you," Suvi said through Quinn. "And when I do, it'll break her, knowing I used her body, her magick, to end you."

A dull, burning anger seeped into Nyssa's bones. Her fear and doubt had held her back for so long. She had kept pushing her feelings for Quinn down before ultimately pushing her away. Now Suvi was going to end what barely had time to blossom between them.

Nyssa sent a jolt of lightning through her hand into Quinn.

Quinn smiled. "I barely felt that. You don't have the strength to go as far as I will to stop this."

Nyssa tried to inflict another jolt, but there was no force behind it. Above her, the sky flashed, blue lightning fighting with the darkness of night.

"Nyssa, we can end this amicably. Look at all the people you've hurt. And as ever, the people you are closest to are the ones who pay the price. Surrender yourself to me and I'll let your friends live. And you and Quinn can live out your lives here. Captive, but alive."

"You'd collar us. We'd be your prisoners forever."

Black eyes stared down at her. "Would you not show your friends mercy, show them your grace and allow them to live? They'll all die here tonight by Quinn's hand. Is that what you want? To kill them and destroy her?"

Bile rose in the back of Nyssa's throat. She didn't have the strength to fight Suvi and Quinn. She had miscalculated—she thought their power would be enough. It wasn't, not in the face of a ruthless queen who would kill without a thought.

Athen shouted, his voice strangled with tension. And pain. So rare to hear from him; and intensely frightening.

Nyssa turned her head. Quinn's darkness had spread, ensnaring Athen and the others, trapping them. Suvi could do anything she wanted to them with Quinn's power—squeeze the life out of them, drive slivers of shadow into them, shred them to pieces.

Nyssa held fast to Quinn's hand and screamed Athen's name. Quinn bucked back and flung a fist into her face, snapping her nose. Nyssa called out for Athen again, hot blood misting above her face, expelled by her breath.

No response.

"What is your choice, Blacksea?" Suvi asked, softening Quinn's voice.

Nyssa searched Quinn's face for an answer. She desperately wanted Athen and the others safe but surrendering to Suvi meant putting Quinn back in a collar.

And deep down, Nyssa knew Quinn wouldn't last back in captivity.

Fear threatened to drag her under—the fear of dying, the fear of her friends losing their lives because of her, the fear of losing Quinn forever to despair.

Thunder boomed overhead, and Nyssa exhaled, gazing at the weak flashes of blue lightning fading in the sky. Fontaine had insisted that Nyssa dive into her magick and embrace the primal chaos of it in order to go beyond her limits, to unleash her unrestrained power. But every time Nyssa lost control, people got hurt.

Quinn's darkness coiled around her body, holding her down. It wrapped around her throat and tightened, like a rope of glass shards around her neck. The darkness crawled across Nyssa's mouth, prying it open, gagging her. Quinn stared down at her, her face twisted by Suvi's hate and desperation.

Suvi was going to rip her apart. And with Nyssa dead, Quinn would again be her prisoner.

The ghosts of Nyssa's doubts—her fear of losing control and hurting people, of not being worthy of the power she wielded—clung to her like cobwebs. Those ghosts were about to cost Nyssa her life and the life of the woman who never doubted her for an instant. She couldn't surrender Quinn to Suvi.

There was no other choice but to let go.

To risk everything.

She gritted her teeth, embracing her power and its danger. "Be a fucking god," she whispered.

Nyssa let her magick go, unfurling it into the sky above her, unleashing her rage into the storm. Currents of energy danced across her skin, wild and chaotic. Blue lightning threaded through the clouds above. She curled her fingers around Quinn's hand, and their magick sparked off of one another, shards of bright-blue light shimmering across the threads of purplish shadow. Thunder thrummed in Nyssa's chest.

She closed her eyes.

The storm raged and Nyssa gave herself to it, her body no longer contained to the flesh-and-bone vessel tethering her to the physical world. She unwound herself across the sky—the electricity dancing through the clouds pounded along her nerves, beating in time with her heart.

Nyssa stretched herself out and collided with something desperately familiar. A small, warm sliver of Quinn, untainted by Suvi's presence. Nyssa wrapped her magick around that sliver, hiding that small part of Quinn from Suvi.

"I have you, Quinn," she whispered.

Quinn didn't reply save for a slow, low pulse that Nyssa knew was her. There was pain, a tension clinging to Quinn's presence—whatever small part of herself she had separated from Suvi's influence was suffering.

Darkness rippled in all directions, the air growing colder and colder, Suvi gathering Quinn's power for a final strike.

Nyssa swallowed back doubt. She would have one chance at calling forth enough energy to do what she needed.

A massive ball of energy formed in the sky.

Nyssa's lips parted. "Help me."

Quinn's grip tightened on Nyssa's hand.

The ball of energy coiled like a spring, pausing for an endless moment before uncoiling into a bolt of lightning. Nyssa twisted herself around it, and another presence wrapped around her—Quinn, giving her the small, untainted part of herself.

Instinct took over, Fontaine's voice echoing in Nyssa's head: "Trust yourself". Nyssa let the edges of her existence completely blur, her magick, her body, Quinn, the storm, the power, all becoming one. All becoming her will, primal and unbound.

The hair on Nyssa's arms rose. Lightning tore out of the sky and plummeted toward them—a strike poised to kill them all if it was off its mark. But she had to stop Suvi, to get her out of Quinn's head.

A deafening crack of thunder assaulted Nyssa's ears, and her vision went white as a torrent of lightning struck the ground. The stone terrace buckled and bucked, tossing Nyssa and Quinn into the air. When Nyssa landed, her skull cracked on the gravel and glass beneath her. Quinn collapsed on top of her. Nyssa's breath caught in her chest, her body numb.

For several moments, she blinked up at the sky, at the blue streaks of light threaded with darkness illuminating the roiling clouds. Smoke wafted over her, bringing the smell of burnt wood and flesh.

Am I dead?

Quinn stirred on top of her, and Nyssa found herself staring up at green eyes. Brilliant green eyes.

"There you are, Freckles," she whispered.

Nyssa groaned as Quinn shifted her weight and rolled off of her.

"Are we dead?" Quinn mumbled, her fingers grasping Nyssa's hand.

Nyssa squeezed back, turning her head to take Quinn in, relief flooding through her when Quinn smiled back, though her face was criss-crossed with shallow cuts, bloody and dirty from the smoke. But she was alive.

Beautifully *alive.*

"Everything hurts," Quinn moaned, fighting to sit up with a grimace. Bits of glass stuck to her, blood flowing from numerous injuries. She reached over and helped Nyssa up. "You brought down the sky's fury."

Nyssa smiled, then winced, her nose aching. Broken yet again. "You helped me, gorgeous."

"Nyssa, I'm so sorry. I almost killed you."

"Hey, that wasn't you. That was Suvi." Nyssa squeezed her hand again.

Quinn set her jaw and nodded, wrapping her hands around the back of Nyssa's neck, and drew her forward, resting her forehead against Nyssa's. "I love you," she whispered.

The mournful sound of a woman sobbing pulled Nyssa out of her daze.

"Suvi," Quinn snarled. She grunted and got to her feet, grabbing Nyssa's wrist and hauling her up. Quinn's eyes darted around, and she started forward, tugging at Nyssa to follow. Nyssa barely felt her legs beneath her, scared she'd just stumble and fall, but somehow she managed to trail Quinn.

After a few steps, they came upon Suvi. She clutched the body of a man, his skin cracked and blackened. Nyssa's stomach lurched at the sight.

"He saved me. He pushed me out of the way and saved me," Suvi murmured, her eyes drifting up to Nyssa, her expression cold and hateful. "You killed my brother, monster. I'll make you beg for death."

Suvi's eyes began to turn black, and Nyssa felt her presence slip over her. Quinn lunged forward and smashed a fist into Suvi's nose. Suvi's magick immediately fell away, and Nyssa grabbed a handful of Suvi's hair, yanking her up with what little strength she had left.

"You going to kill me now?" Suvi slurred, her eyes slow to focus. Blood streamed out of her nose.

"You're far more valuable alive," Quinn said. She took a void collar out of the pack at her side.

"No!" Suvi growled.

Quinn affixed the collar around Suvi's neck, locking it shut.

Nyssa yanked Suvi backward and gripped her throat tight below the collar, squeezing. Suvi gurgled, fighting against Nyssa's grasp. "You imprisoned Quinn. Hurt her. Used her against me. I should kill you," Nyssa growled, her mouth next to Suvi's ear.

"I did say I could make you do unthinkable things," Suvi rasped.

"For her, yes," Nyssa whispered, tightening her grip. Suvi struggled against her.

"Nyssa," Quinn said, her tone cautious.

All Nyssa had to do was squeeze harder until Suvi stopped breathing. She could end her right there without batting an eye.

Quinn slowly shook her head. "I know how you feel, but we need her."

Nyssa met Quinn's gaze. Their freedom was in her hands. Quinn's freedom. How long had Quinn lived in captivity or on the run? Trading Suvi to Kalla would finally set them both free. Nyssa tamped down her anger and shoved Suvi away. The woman sank to her knees.

"I'm quite sick of listening to the Queen's mouth." Quinn rummaged through her bag, finding rope to bind Suvi's wrists and a gag to silence her.

Nyssa glanced down at her trembling hands. She balled them up into fists to calm herself.

"Are you guys okay?" Athen asked, approaching cautiously, trailed by the others. "Everyone back inside their own heads?"

"Yeah, big man," Nyssa said. "You hurt?"

"A bit singed, but I'll live."

Quinn shook her head, her face collapsing. "I'm so sorry, Athen."

Athen put an arm around her. "Hey, it's okay. I know Suvi was in your head. We're fine."

"I...I hate that she made me hurt you," Quinn rasped, her eyes scanning the group.

"We're alive. A little black and blue, but we're alive," Fontaine said. "There's a reason we're not dead, Quinn. You held Suvi back with what little control you had."

Quinn scowled. "But how?"

Fontaine smiled and smoothed back Quinn's hair. "Your force of will is more powerful than you realize. Magick alone isn't power."

A look of relief cascaded across Quinn's face, and she leaned into Fontaine, allowing the woman to wrap an arm around her.

Next to them, Reece supported Medias, helping her stand. Medias looked worse for wear, a gash in her shoulder and at her hairline, her white mask splashed with blood. Elias and Fontaine looked tired but unhurt, save for a few cuts and scrapes.

Nyssa put her hand gently on Medias's arm. "You're hurt."

"Medias took it upon herself to go on the offensive as we retreated and got a little banged up." Reece gently moved an errant, blood-soaked strand of hair away from the Justiciar's face.

"I swore to protect you all, empath," Medias said.

"That you did," Nyssa replied. Medias's red eyes met hers, and Nyssa nodded. The Justiciar had done far more than Nyssa had ever asked. "Thank you, Medias."

Fontaine smiled. "I'm so proud of you two. As your mentor, I shall take a small modicum of credit for your victory."

Nyssa's heart grew lighter. Making Fontaine happy had become an unexpected delight. She turned toward Suvi's estate. More of it had caught fire, the smoke billowing into the night sky. In the distance, klaxons sounded the alarm in the city of Sarisan. By now, the citizens of the capital had seen the fire.

And they would watch the symbol of Rell power burn in the night.

"We have to get out of here," Nyssa said. She pulled Suvi to her feet. The woman's face was streaked with smoke and tears. In one moment, she had lost her brother and her freedom. If Suvi were anyone else, Nyssa would feel pity for her, but Suvi had caused her and the people she loved tremendous pain. Nyssa didn't give a shit about her feelings.

They limped their way back to where Nyssa had left Aryis. She slowly stood up as the group approached her.

When Aryis saw Quinn, she rushed forward, grabbing her. "Quinn, we can stop this. You have to tell Nyssa I'm going to betray you all. She won't believe me."

Quinn gave Nyssa a puzzled look. "What's wrong with her?"

"She's just confused," Nyssa said. She pulled Aryis away from Quinn and took her head in her hands.

"Hey, look at me. We're fine. We're all fine."

"I can stop me from hurting you if you'd just listen..." Aryis whispered, her eyes losing their focus.

Nyssa swallowed hard. She hated seeing Aryis so lost.

Athen stepped forward. "Aryis."

"No, no, no, no, no." Aryis reached her fingers toward his eye patch before she drew back, as if scared to touch him. "You need to go back and stop this from happening."

"Come here." Athen wrapped Aryis in a hug, which she struggled against at first before melting into his arms, softly sobbing. "I have you. You're safe."

Quinn put a hand on Nyssa's shoulder. "We have to go."

Athen led them to the safe-fall location. He scooped Aryis up into his arms and pressed a kiss to her temple before stepping into the enchantment. The others followed him, leaving Suvi, Nyssa, and Quinn on the cliff.

"I will kill you both for this," Suvi hissed.

Quinn stepped up to her. "How many innocent people has your family killed over the centuries?" She yanked Suvi's arm and spun her toward the burning estate, pointing to the destruction. The flames had grown higher. "We've ended your dynasty. No one need ever fear the name Rell again."

"You think that's true as long as I'm alive?" Suvi asked.

There was a certainty in Suvi's voice that Nyssa couldn't ignore. The woman, even imprisoned, had a confidence that seemed unshakable.

It didn't matter, though. Suvi would soon be the Empress's problem if things went as planned. Nyssa brought Suvi to the cliff face and gave her a shove. The downward flow of the safe-fall enchantment pulled her away from them and she floated down.

Quinn stood next to Nyssa and leaned against her.

"I'm so tired," she whispered. "And I have glass in places I shouldn't have glass."

Nyssa chuckled and wrapped an arm around Quinn's shoulders, kissing the side of her head. She exhaled a breath she felt she'd been holding since they first came ashore. "We kidnapped a goddamned queen."

She stepped away from Quinn and smiled at her, stroking her face. Her whole body ached and demanded the sleep of a contented woman with Quinn wrapped up in her arms.

"Go on," Nyssa said.

Quinn stepped into the safe-fall enchantment and disappeared.

Nyssa turned back to glance at the blazing Rell estate one last time before stepping off the cliff.

A MEMORY OF TOMORROW

Nyssa yawned and stretched, quickly regretting it with a grimace. Every last fiber in her body ached. Slowly, she swung her legs off the bed and leaned forward, resting her elbows on her knees and her head in her hands. At least she didn't have a headache—a small mercy.

She was certain she had slept a full day, if not longer. The exhaustion of using every last bit of her magick ran deeper than even her hardest days training at the Order. She looked at her hands and swallowed, cautiously calling her magick forth. It sparked and danced across her fingertips. A relieved smile settled on her lips.

A hand crept up Nyssa's bare back.

"You cannot seriously be awake right now," Quinn drawled. "I can feel your magick. Is everything alright?"

Nyssa glanced back at Quinn. "I just...I wanted to make sure my power was still there. Is that strange?"

Quinn opened her eyes. "No, I understand. This ancient magick has sunk its teeth deep into us now. I keep forgetting how odd it must be for you to possess magick after so many years without it. And this power...it feels so different from what I had before."

Nyssa smiled at Quinn, checking over the bandages dotting her body. Buck had the whole crew on standby when they returned to the ship, and he oversaw the worst injuries, stitching people up between swigs of rum and grumbling orders at his temporary underling medics. More than a few healing disks were used on the deeper wounds, including a nasty cut on Quinn's back.

A smile crossed Nyssa's lips, remembering the ornery old man doting over his charges. "Clean that wound out! Bandage that tighter!" Buck was a damn good medic, proud of his work, but most of all it was obvious that he cared deeply for everyone on the ship. He even mixed a tincture to help Aryis sleep. Only Medias had tried to push Buck away, insisting she was fine, but gave in and let him use a disk on her shoulder when Reece got serious and browbeat her. To the Justiciar's credit, and Nyssa's amazement, she didn't make a sound as the healing disk did its work.

With all the supplies used, not to mention a great deal of rum consumed, Athen promised to resupply the Whisper when they got back to the Empire.

The Empire—Nyssa had tried to keep everything simple, tackle each step of their plan bit by bit. Soon, they would be back in Imperial waters and would approach Kalla with an offer she couldn't refuse—Suvi Rell. Then they'd figure out what to do about Ceril Anelos. Nyssa hadn't forgotten about him and his role in her parents' deaths, or what he did to Quinn. He needed to answer for his crimes.

But the Empire, Kalla, and Ceril were a problem for the next day. Now, she needed a moment—just one moment—to enjoy their victory.

She lolled her head back and sighed. "I smell like a campfire."

"Go take a bath," Quinn mumbled.

Nyssa reached over and stroked her cheek. She was met with a smile and a happy rumble from the back of Quinn's throat.

After throwing on a robe and gathering some clothes to change into, Nyssa shuffled down to one of the bathrooms and drew a bath, shaking a generous amount of medicated salts into the tub. She climbed in, hissing as the salt bit at every last nick and cut on her body. The bath turned soothing after a few minutes, and she tipped her head back, savoring the warmth enveloping her aching muscles.

Bathing was slow going. Her left hand was mostly useless after Suvi used Quinn to grind it against shattered glass. She favored the hand, doing her best to not stress her stitches. Buck would yell at her if he had to redo his work.

Part of her would rather face Tajal again than a surly Buck.

She worked soap through her hair a few times until she was certain she had washed the scent of smoke out. She drained her bath and ran another, intent on getting Quinn out of bed and cleaned up. They could sleep the rest of the day, but she wanted to freshen up her clothes, sheets, and bandages to wash the smoke, dirt, and blood from their time in Sarisan away.

Nyssa dressed and went back to her room, pulling a grumbling Quinn out of bed and pushing her down the hall and into the bathroom. She helped her undress and removed her bandages. The stitches across Quinn's back were the worst of her injuries, and she swore profusely when she sank into the tub and its bath salts.

The act of caring for Quinn made Nyssa strangely tranquil. She slowly worked soap into Quinn's hair with one hand, massaging her scalp. A moan rumbled in Quinn's chest, and the back of Nyssa's neck grew hot over that guttural sound of contentment.

When clean, Quinn climbed out of the tub and sat on its edge in a towel, letting Nyssa re-dress her wounds. Nyssa knelt in front of her, fingers gently applying gauze and bandages over her cuts and scrapes.

Quinn caught Nyssa's hand as she worked.

"Everything okay?"

Quinn locked Nyssa in her gaze. "There are going to be times when my brain screams at me that I don't deserve you. That I don't deserve this life or any sort of happiness. Please pull me back from that dark place when it happens."

Nyssa leaned forward and took Quinn's face in her hands. "Always," she said, kissing her, slow and gentle. "Always."

Quinn closed her eyes and exhaled. "There's parts of myself that I haven't shown you...parts that scare me. I could hurt you."

"Loving you is worth every risk I could possibly take. I'm not going to run away, no matter what."

"Promise?" Quinn looked like a child asking for a sliver of kindness, to never be abandoned again.

Nyssa smiled. "I promise. You trusted me and let me in. Your love is a gift, and I'm not going to squander it. It's you and me now. Always."

"Thank you," Quinn said, letting out a long sigh, her face lightening up as if finally shrugging off a long-endured burden.

Nyssa sat back, continuing to bandage Quinn's wounds. She knew they would both have to unravel the years of self-doubt and fear that the guilds had imparted on them. And she could do that for Quinn.

Anything for her.

After Nyssa was content with her bandaging, she helped Quinn get dressed in a set of cotton pants and an undershirt, rolling up the pant legs so they didn't drag on the floor.

"Sit down," Quinn ordered. "You need your hand re-wrapped properly."

Nyssa sat on the edge of the tub and watched Quinn take care of her. The look of concentration mixed with concern on Quinn's face made Nyssa smile as her hand was tenderly redressed.

"Do you want some food or to go back to bed?" Nyssa asked when Quinn finished. Her stomach grumbled its own reply.

"Griddle cakes with honey?" Quinn asked. Her tongue darted out to lick her lips, and Nyssa's gaze tracked the movement.

"Griddle cakes it is," she agreed, silently cursing her wandering mind.

The pair was met with a hearty greeting from the crew when they entered the mess, and Buck rushed over with two plates of food, including the griddle cakes he was in the habit of making for breakfast.

He carefully examined Quinn's bandages and snorted at Nyssa when she told him she redressed Quinn's wounds. "It's an—mmm—acceptable job, Stitches."

A few minutes later, Medias shuffled in, followed closely by Reece. Medias looked worse for wear, but Reece seemed to be keeping an eye on her, a fact that wasn't lost on Nyssa.

"Nice to see you two up and about," Reece said, plucking a piece of bacon off Quinn's plate.

"Hey," Quinn softly grumbled. She had come to be a voracious eater and likely wasn't above starting a fistfight over bacon. She looked relieved when Buck came over with two plates for Reece and Medias.

"How is Aryis?" Nyssa asked.

Medias grunted. "Tajal mixed up her brain a bit, but she's slowly coming around. Her sense of time is realigning to reality."

"And Athen?"

"Watching over her like a one-eyed hawk," Reece said.

Nyssa chuckled, heartened to hear the news. "Aryis is resilient. She'll find her way."

The expression on Quinn's face darkened. Nyssa tapped her finger on Quinn's forearm. "Hey, give her a chance, that's all I ask. Remember how an obstinate—but intensely charming—Emerald Order adept gave you a chance despite you being a massive pain in the ass?"

Quinn smirked and exhaled forcefully. "And look how that turned out. You've gotten me into one mess after another."

Nyssa arched an indignant eyebrow, scoffing, "How dare you."

Quinn stuck out her tongue.

Nyssa broke out in laughter, wincing. "Stop! Laughing hurts."

"Serves you right," Quinn mumbled into her cup of coffee.

Nyssa flared up and pinged Quinn with a small spark of lightning, making her yelp with laughter.

"Hey! No magick in my mess!" Buck barked from the kitchen.

"You two are children," Medias grumbled as she fought off a smile.

Nyssa made her way up to the deck, still sore and stiff, even after days of rest. She didn't mind the aches and pain—it reminded her she was still alive. And there was no way she was going to miss the first night of Winter's Fire. Two years ago was her first run-in with Quinn, and how different things were now. Wonderfully different, if rather unpredictable.

Reece, Quinn, and Medias were on deck, sitting on crates, chatting and drinking as the crew ambled about, celebrating the holiday. Athen and Aryis sat nearby. Aryis was still recovering from Tajal's influence, and seeing her getting some fresh air made Nyssa's heart a little lighter. Nyssa paused next to them, giving Aryis's shoulder a squeeze before wandering toward Quinn.

The mood on deck was festive, light orbs strung up to illuminate the boat as the drinks flowed. Yuha pushed a mug of ale into Nyssa's hand and patted her on the head. "Good little godling," she slurred.

Nyssa laughed. "You're drunk."

"A bit."

Mina and Max milled about the deck, handing out Winter's Fire lanterns, and Elias asked everyone to gather and settle down for a toast.

He approached Quinn and put his hand on her shoulder. "First, a bit of business. We have a friend and crewmate who, for most of her life, didn't have a home, a family, or even a name of her own. I hope she feels she has found the first two here, on this ship." The crew stomped their feet, signifying their agreement. "Now, as far as a name, Quinn has chosen a surname for herself. I give you: Quinn Emerrath."

"A noble name!" Athen shouted, raising his mug. Everyone raised their mugs and cheered, bringing a blush to Quinn's cheeks.

"And Quinn Emerrath has asked to give the Winter's Fire toast tonight," Elias added.

Nyssa raised an eyebrow, curious.

Quinn stood and cleared her throat. "This is a favorite poem of mine, one I think is a lovely way to welcome the first night of Winter's Fire." She raised her mug and locked eyes with Nyssa.

> "Hold fast, my love,
> One final time, before I slip under the waves
> Where I will descend and become the Song of the Sea.
> The Song of Winter.
> The Song of the lost Gods.
> Here, I will rest in your embrace
> For an eternity,

Amidst the stars in the deep blue sea."

The Winter's Fire toast stopped Nyssa cold, the words familiar. Intimately so.

It was the poem she had written in Quinn's book underneath the sketch of the Kraken. Hearing those words on Quinn's lips took her breath away.

"Happy Winter's Fire!" Elias said. The crew raised their mugs and cheered. "Get your lanterns ready."

Quinn crossed over to Nyssa. "I hope you're not mad. I found the poem when Aryis returned my book a few days ago, but no one knows it's yours."

"I...I wrote it for you," Nyssa admitted with a whisper, the tops of her ears on fire. No one had ever read her work. No one.

Quinn leaned in, the scent of juniper gently tugging at Nyssa. "I adore it."

Lanterns were passed around and lit. Elias held his up, casting his eyes among the crew. "Speak your wish into the flames and let them go into the night."

Nyssa smiled and whispered her Winter's Fire wish into the lantern's flame, not taking her eyes off of Quinn. "Let her be free." She raised her lantern and let it go, and Quinn did the same.

As they watched the lanterns ascend, Nyssa felt Quinn brush against her. It was becoming a habit, the light touches, and every time Nyssa's heart skipped just a little.

After the lanterns were released, the crew got back to celebrating. Quinn sat with her sketchbook in her lap, busy on a new drawing, working in the light cast by the orbs that swayed back and forth above them. Nyssa laid down at Quinn's feet, groaning as she stretched out on the deck, folding her hands behind her head.

Her eyes roamed the dark sky. Red lanterns dotted the sea of stars that extended in all directions. The sails swayed above her, casting shadows and moonlight across her face. Sea brine tickled her nose, and the soothing thumps and dings from the mast made her smile, sounds of the Whisper she had come to love. She placed her palms face down on the deck to feel the groans and creaks of the wood beneath her, closing her eyes and luxuriating in the moment.

At sea, surrounded by her friends. Safe.

Finally safe.

The hum of Quinn's voice vibrated in her chest, the sound mixing with the fluttering of cloth in the wind.

A spark of recognition lit within Nyssa. This was her dream—the one she'd dreamt since she could remember. The dream she thought was a memory of the past.

But it wasn't. *How?*

She opened her eyes, turning her head to Quinn.

Dark charcoal stained Quinn's fingers and the bandages on her hands, and she smiled to herself while she sketched, humming the song from Nyssa's memory.

Nyssa exhaled sharply, her eyes wide. "It was you," she whispered before scrambling to her feet, hissing as her body objected to the sudden movement.

"Nyssa? You okay?" Reece asked.

Nyssa stood over Quinn, who looked up at her with a puzzled smile, moonlight glinting in her green eyes.

"It was you," Nyssa whispered to Quinn. "It was always you."

Nyssa bent down and kissed Quinn, slipping her fingers behind her neck. She didn't know how long the kiss lasted, losing herself in Quinn, needing to feel her, to make sure she was real.

Whoops and hollers rose from the crew when Nyssa broke the kiss. Buck walked up with a large jug of rum.

"About goddamn—mmm—time," he said, winking at Quinn before he tipped the jug over her cup.

In the dim light, Quinn turned bright red. Nyssa couldn't stop herself from smiling. "I'm sorry, I know you'd rather be discreet, I just...I can't explain it right now, but you..." She shook her head, unable to find the words to explain the impossible. Years of dreaming about a memory of *this* moment.

Quinn grabbed her and pulled her down. "I didn't hate it," she said before kissing Nyssa back. The crew cheered and whistled, louder this time.

Quinn's lips curled up under Nyssa's.

"I'll fight every last one of them for you, if you wish," Nyssa whispered when she pulled back. "Maybe teach them some respect."

"We're pirates, Nyssa. I'd be a little disappointed if they didn't take it out of our hides," Quinn replied with a soft smile.

Nyssa sat at Quinn's feet, leaning against her legs. Listening to the scratch of Quinn's charcoal pencil against paper, Nyssa closed her eyes. After a time, Quinn wove her fingers into Nyssa's hair as she drew, and Nyssa sighed, her skin tingling under Quinn's gentle touch.

EPILOGUE

Arch Justiciar Decia tapped her pen on the paper sitting in front of her, its contents had to believe. Suvi Rell had disappeared from Sarisan two weeks prior, the Rell manor burned to the ground and her brother dead. Reports were slow and scatter-shot with reliable details, but one thing was certain—Thu'Dain was bereft of a leader.

She poured herself a tea and leaned back in her chair. The Rell dynasty had seemingly met its end—or had it? Where was Suvi? The Empress had called an emergency meeting of the Sun Council later that day to discuss how to proceed, given the news. Maybe now the endless wars with Thu'Dain would cease...

A frantic knock at her office door pulled Decia out of her thoughts. "Come."

A pale, lanky guard rushed into the room, out of breath. He stammered out a few confusing words.

Decia held up a hand. "Stop. Gather your thoughts. Then speak."

The guard nodded and exhaled a big breath. "Arch Justiciar, there are visitors at the gates requesting an audience with the Empress."

She sighed. There were always visitors trying to see the Empress. And the guards knew better than to bother her with such mundane requests.

"I fail to see how this concerns—"

"Arch Justiciar, it's Nyssa Blacksea and Quinn Emerrath."

Decia stilled. "Are you sure?"

"Yes, ma'am."

"Have they hurt anyone?"

"They haven't done anything aside from a little display of magick to prove who they are. Their eyes...the magick on their skin..."

"How many people are with them?"

"They only have one person with them. They claim it's...it's Suvi Rell."

"Impossible," Decia whispered, leaning forward. *Impossible.* "Do they have a Justiciar with them?"

"No, Arch Justiciar. It's just the three of them. What should we do?"

Decia pulled at the bottom of her jacket and glanced around, as if she'd find an answer among the books and papers of her stark office. She picked up an orb from her desk.

"Onyx Squad to the Arch Justiciar's office, immediately," she said into the orb before it floated off her palm and whizzed out of the office. She would need the magick of the Elite Guard at her side.

"Go to the Empress and insist upon seeing her, under my orders. Let her know who's at the gates. But do not talk to anyone else, do you understand? The Empress only."

"Yes, ma'am," the guard said, stumbling out of the office, careening off the doorframe as he rushed through. This was likely the most terrifying day of the poor guard's life.

Decia let out a shallow breath.

She opened her desk drawer and pulled out two velvet bags, removing a void collar from each. She wouldn't let the Cursed Gods—if it was truly them—step one foot onto Sun Palace soil without being collared. The risk to the Empress, to the capital itself, was too great. But if they did indeed have Suvi...

What sort of insane women, wanted by the Empire, would march a Rell queen right to their front door? What were they planning? Decia tried to ascertain the angles, to see the danger.

And what of Justiciar Medias? She had disappeared from Ocean's Rest with that empath, abandoning her post. She had to be with Nyssa and Quinn. And if she was...

A cold chill ran through Decia. If Medias was helping the Cursed Gods, she was committing treason. And the punishment for a Justiciar was death.

She bowed her head, swallowing down her fear. "Oh, daughter, what have you done?"

Acknowledgements

Writing a book is no small feat. Inspiration comes from a myriad of sources. For me, it's a weird mix of kung fu movies, Miyazaki's films, Radiohead, powerful women, the sound of falling snow, and the gentle, warm hue the light takes on just as the sun is setting. Aside from inspiration, writing a book well takes far more than just the lone author. A number of people contributed to this book being written, edited, and out in the world.

I want to thank the small army of people who helped me make this book and The Blacksea Odyssey shine: Max Gorlov, L.R. Friedman, Chinah Mercer, Zoe Markham, and Chris Yarbrough.

I'm eternally grateful for my friends, close and far, especially the FBC Crew, Duy, Lucia, Cal, Scott, Dan, Niecy, Merritt, Jo, Aimee, Meagan, Kirsten, Cristina, Brandi, and Dani. The support and encouragement is priceless. Love all of you guys!

And lastly, thanks to the two biggest people in my life:

Joe, a trusted mentor and my biggest supporter. Navigating life with someone who is always rooting for your success is priceless. I love you, big bro!

Lisa, my girlfriend, though we both know that's in insufficient term for what you mean to me. Finding you at this stage in my life was the biggest surprise. I'm so happy I took a chance and went on a date with a nerdy Trekkie who loves hockey. I love you, woman!

What's next for Nyssa?

The third book in the trilogy, ***Unyielding***, is coming October 23, 2024. Preorder at amazon.com.

What were Nyssa and Athen up to before the events in Unworthy? Download my free short story, Whiskey and Wagers, and find out.

Stay updated on the latest *The Blacksea Odyssey* series news by signing up for my newsletter at www.javodvarka.com. The newsletter provides all the latest book and author news, free giveaways, deleted scenes, sneak peeks at my works in progress, and the opportunity to join my ARC (advanced reader copy) team. This trilogy isn't all you'll see of this world or Nyssa Blacksea...more adventures for our heroes (and villains) await.

And finally, a request. Reviews from readers like yourself are the life blood of indie authors, so if you would kindly take a moment and leave a review for this book, I would be eternally grateful.

About the author

J.A. Vodvarka is an adult fantasy author, combining action, humor, romance, and unique world-building to create epic fantasy stories with a ton of heart. The Blacksea Odyssey trilogy features strong, sensitive, kick-butt women in a semi-modern setting.

Her writing is inspired by: a childhood spent watching kung fu movies, Toshiro Mifune's swagger, a splash of Hayao Miyazaki's mysticism, her 5000+ comic book collection, and a love of fun, smart, and complex female characters who appreciate a fine dessert.

Originally from Illinois, J.A. received a degree from UIUC in English and American Literature and Creative Writing. J.A. currently resides in Houston, Texas with a surly French bulldog, Emmitt.

Connect with J.A. Vodvarka on her site: www.javodvarka.com or on social media: linktr.ee/javodvarka

Content warning

This book is darker than *Unworthy* and all my books are intended for an adult audience (18+). *Unbound* contains graphic violence, child peril and death, torture, profanity, gore, mention of physical abuse, and explicit sexual scenes.

Please email me if you have any questions about the content warnings – blacksea@javodvarka.com.

www.ingramcontent.com/pod-product-compliance
Lightning Source LLC
Chambersburg PA
CBHW021409010826
48972CB00014B/963